CLASS OF TWENTY-EIGHT

Best Wishes

Neil Moloney

NEIL MOLONEY

PublishAmerica
Baltimore

ISBN: 1-4241-1076-9
PUBLISHED BY PUBLISHAMERICA, LLLP
www.publishamerica.com
Baltimore

Printed in the United States of America

ACKNOWLEDGMENTS/DEDICATION

I am grateful to Seattle Assistant Chief of Police Clayton E. Bean, retired, and to retired Police Majors Harry L. Schneider and Raymond L. Carroll, and to King County Police Detective Jay E. Moloney and to former Marine and friend Paul E. Jones (now deceased) who served in a Marine combat unit in the South Pacific, for their generous and valuable advice that went into the creation of this book. I am also indebted to Lori Moloney and Traci Hollingsworth for their inexhaustible assistance in correcting my many spelling and grammatical errors for the final draft of the manuscript, and to my wife, Delaine, for her patience and understanding when I was locked away in my office for months at a time trying to develop this story into a fitting tribute to a dedicated group of young men and women who served their country in time of need.

Chapter 1

Except for the muffled moans of the wounded and calming voices of the corpsmen, it was quiet on this bleak and barren hilltop in the Western Pacific. Yet only moments ago, the roar of gunfire, intermingling with the curses and screams of men dying, filled the air. Now, all across this small bit of real estate there was a stillness of sound that locked out everything else.

It was an eerie calm which settled across the top of this small plateau. Occasionally this emptiness was broken by the clink of an empty canteen, or the slide on an M1 as it ratcheted forward, preparing a .30-caliber round for its deadly journey. Still the war went on. In the distance could be heard the crack of artillery or mortar as they exacted their toll upon one side or the other in this raging conflict. For now, however, the battle for this small island would have to continue without the services of the men from Second Battalion, Charlie Company.

With a lull in the fighting, Captain Scott Jackson and his two platoon sergeants, Donald Niles and Rick Conlan, studied the condition of their troops. In a strictly military sense, Charlie Company accomplished their objective. They drove a superior force from this now nearly barren plateau and, for the moment, held the advantage over the enemy—but at what price? Forty-eight members of the company lay among the dead, with more than two score wounded. Some would not live through the night. Several more were prostrate in the 100-degree heat.

Sickened by the carnage about him and trying grimly to hide his despair, Jackson turned his attention to the two sergeants standing nearby. All three men, with their torn and grime-covered dungarees and ten-day growth of beard, had been pushed to the limit today. They, like their troops, looked worn and haggard. They needed a rest, but there was no time. After setting up a temporary perimeter, the captain, beckoning to the two sergeants, moved out of earshot of the troops.

"Are your people ready?" he asked, quietly. His softly worded inquiry, more of a warning than a question, was entirely clear to both sergeants. "If the bastards hit us hard, we're going to be in tough shape."

"We're ready, Capt'n," replied Sergeant Conlan, as if the question were irrelevant. "My people only have about two clips apiece; they know it's bayonet time."

"My guys are ready, Captain," Sergeant Niles replied soberly, clearly recognizing the predicament they were in.

"But we've got to get the wounded out of here as soon as we can," he added quietly. "If the Nips hit us hard and we get pushed off this ridge we're apt to lose 'em all."

"I know, Sergeant," Jackson responded, nodding, the two men noting his grim expression. He knew firsthand that retreating troops had little time to worry about the wounded when they too were trying to stay alive.

"We could send the walking wounded down now, Capt'n. With one or two troops, they'd have a pretty good chance," Sergeant Conlan offered.

"No, we'll wait until the corpsmen finish up; maybe by then we'll have some relief up here. We can send 'em back with the escort party at that time; we can't afford the manpower now. In the meantime let's take a look at what we've got left." Turning to Sergeant Niles, he said, "You'd better look to their equipment. The damn water situation worries me."

"I know, Captain, it will be a problem before this day is over," Niles responded, shaking his head.

"Okay, but let's deal with it. Sergeant Conlan and I will check our outposts; assign some of your people to gather the Japanese hardware."

Sergeant Niles, a member of the "Old Breed," a veteran of earlier campaigns in the South Pacific, kept reminding the troops to conserve their water.

"Ease off on the water, you guys," he growled, adding forbiddingly, "What you've got in those canteens is all you're gonna get." His warning came too late, most of the men had long since consumed what was in their canteens; they were drinking the brackish water from nearby bomb craters.

Niles, like his fellow sergeant, was nearly six feet tall, but unlike his colleague, raw-boned, with the build of an athlete. His loose dungarees, now covered with sweat, concealed his magnificent physical stature. As he moved quickly from squad to squad checking on his men, there was little doubt but that he kept himself in top physical condition. In training he routinely ran two miles every morning carrying an M1 rifle and full pack; few of his colleagues were able to keep up with him.

"You guys know damn well your water is as important as your ammunition. So knock it off! Chew on a rock if you have to."

Looking down into one of the bomb craters, where six of his men had taken cover, he spotted Tommy "Crybaby" Gunther. The man was new to the company, but at twenty-four, older than most of those in his platoon.

"You already finished yours off, didn't you, Gunther?" he said accusingly.

"I'll make it, okay, Sergeant," the man responded meekly, not returning the sergeant's steely gaze.

"You're damn right you will, but you'd better not get anybody killed because you can't follow the rules."

If there was one among them, Private Thomas Gunther played the role of the dim-witted company clown. Unkempt and slovenly in appearance, his boorish mannerisms incessantly angered his sergeant. His kind Niles had seen before. He believed the man to be both a laggard and a coward who lacked any sense of responsibility to his fellow Marines. Niles was sure that the man would eventually get someone killed through his antics. Gunther's colleagues knew him to be a lazy bastard, always relying on someone else to carry his load. When the sergeant moved on, the man, cautiously looking around, muttered, "Screw him, who the hell does he think is, a general?"

"Get the hell out of here, Gunther," one of his companions growled. "I don't want to die in the same damn hole with you."

"Yeah, why don't you grow up?" another man protested. "You keep bucking that sergeant and he'll make sure some Jap puts a bayonet right up your ass."

"Screw you, Mac," Gunther replied. Then throwing his critic a mock salute, he slid down to the bottom of the hollow, where he filled his canteen with the brackish rainwater trapped at the base of the crater.

As Niles moved across the plateau, a weather front began to move in on the island from the west. If it passed over them, it could solve their water problem, at least for today. Just in case it came their way, Marines all across the plateau grabbed their ponchos and laid them out to catch whatever rainwater they could.

Assigning a squad to gather whatever weapons were available, Niles' men collected a large assortment of machine guns, rifles and swords, dumping them into a nearby crater. To these he added a half dozen satchel charges; if overrun in the middle of the night the Marines would deny these weapons to their adversary.

After checking on the perimeter defensive positions, Captain Jackson and Sergeant Conlan took a five-man squad in search of the men from the forward machine gun positions that were overrun earlier in the morning. They found all but one. Two of the dead, apparently surviving the initial attack, their bodies, bound hand and foot and decapitated, were in a nearby crater.

Like his colleague, Sergeant Conlan was a professional soldier, but even with ten years as a Marine, and two invasions under his belt, the sight of the decapitated corpses sickened him.

Conlan was a reluctant manager of men, but the Corps gave him no choice. On Guadalcanal, after an early morning banzai charge by Japanese troops, he was the only one left alive in his squad. His reward was the Silver Star for "Heroism on the Field of Battle" and a promotion to Sergeant. The Corps did him no favor. He did not relish the thought of ordering a group of young kids to hold a defensive position knowing that most of them would not survive the initial onslaught of a determined foe.

Jackson was quick to learn of Conlan's unwillingness to push his men to their ultimate limit, but he respected the man's military perspicuity. The sergeant's knowledge of jungle warfare, learned on Guadalcanal, was invaluable. Much of Charlie Company's successes during these last two weeks were directly attributable to the advice offered by this outspoken, yet unassuming military professional.

"I need your thoughts on what we've got here," Jackson said to Conlan, quietly motioning the man to join him in their hastily constructed command post.

"You know what we've got here," the man replied, sliding down into the CP with a grim twist to his mouth, his words clipped short, staccato like. Although reluctant to lead, he held no aversion about telling the brass what he disliked about the way they ran this war. "We got a skunk by the tail, Capt'n, and he's gonna shoot us in the ass, unless somebody down there on the beach gets us some help up here. We need ammunition, weapons, and water. A couple hundred Marines and a little artillery support would sure as hell help too."

The man's helmet could not mask his grim appearance. Black soot and coral dust, mixed with blood from multiple lesions crisscrossing the right side of his face, gave him the look of a walking corpse. A sniper's bullet came close enough to send a shower of splintering coral into his face and neck, but the projectile meant for his head missed its mark.

"I know, Sergeant," Jackson replied, pursing his lips and nodding in agreement. "But you saw what was going on down there on the beach. A lot of our guys are still stuck there, and they're gonna die right there if we don't keep these bastards off this ridge." Sergeant Conlan did not respond.

There was no agreement on the number of enemy soldiers Charlie Company killed this day, one man counted 382, another over 400. There was, however, no disagreement on the number of Marines killed during this ferocious battle, which lasted less than two hours.

Shortly before dusk, the much-needed supplies and medical assistance arrived at the command post. The accompanying corpsmen helping with the most severely wounded quickly loaded the injured onto stretchers for transport to the Regimental Aid Station. For some it would be their last journey.

Except for the moonlight and the occasional overhead flare, had it not been for the white corral it would have been near pitch-dark on this small mountain. It was after midnight when the entourage of stretcher bearers, ambulatory patients, and their armed escort departed the command post. The walking wounded, teaming up with a comrade, began what turned into a nightmarish journey in the dark.

Moving across the top of the plateau and down the face of the cliff below, both pockmarked with craters, was difficult in broad daylight—in the dark it was a horrific experience for the entire party.

Halfway down the face of the escarpment, a flash of light unexpectedly silhouetted the column against the backdrop of the grayish-white coral hillside. A flare, floating across the ridge, outlined a small group of enemy soldiers moving directly into the path of the advancing column. They opened fire on the wounded Marines and their armed escort. The walking wounded, accompanying corpsmen and stretcher bearers ran for the nearest shell crater. Members of the escort party quickly silenced the enemy's guns, but not without a cost. During this short skirmish one member of the escort party died, four others sustained serious injuries. After attending to the four injured men, the group continued on their dangerous trek. They reached the aid station shortly before dawn.

"Capt'n," Conlan's quiet voice startled Jackson, who had dozed off; looking at his watch, Scott was surprised, it was nearly 4:00 a.m. He had been sleeping for more than an hour; he was cold.

"Thanks, Rick, I should have been awake," he offered quietly, yet thankful for the opportunity for the few minutes' rest his body so badly needed. Sergeant Conlan's response surprised him.

"No, sir," he replied quietly. "You needed the rest. I'd of let you sleep longer but it looks like we've got company coming, sir."

With dawn breaking, the two men watched as a group of Marines made their way across the plateau toward the CP. From the command post, which was set up in a crater near the northern tip of the plateau, Conlan, using the captain's field glasses, watched the approaching troops from the minute they cleared the ridgeline. Turning to Jackson, he smiled.

"Someone down there on the beach must have heard me, Capt'n," he said. "But that ain't a helluva lot of people, sir. I was hoping for a whole damn army," Conlan offered, somewhat derisively, handing the binoculars back to his boss.

When they got closer, Jackson could see that it was the battalion commander, Lieutenant Colonel Robert Pugh, accompanied by several armed escort personnel. In the group were a lieutenant and more than two dozen enlisted men, including two sergeants.

All were heavily armed and each man carried three or four canteens of water. Periodically, whenever a sniper opened up on them, they ducked into one of a dozen craters which dotted the immediate area. Sergeant Conlan's riflemen returned fire, temporarily silencing the hidden gunmen.

"Good morning, Captain," the colonel said as he and the lieutenant slid into the bunker. "I thought I'd come by and see how you were making out."

Bull! Jackson thought. *He is here to relieve me of my command.*

"Good morning, sir," he replied, his greeting perfunctory. He was wary of a Marine colonel who just days ago seemed so brutal and callous when he said to Jackson, "Get off your ass and move forward, you've got to clear that ridge." His first comments today, however, were conciliatory.

"I understand you sent your injured men down to the aid station last night."

"Yes, sir; there was a short firefight, but I believe they all made it, sir," Jackson replied, somewhat apprehensively.

"No, I am sorry, Scott," the colonel responded quietly. "I understand two men died before they got to the beach."

Obviously saddened by what he just heard, Jackson sat quietly, shaking his head. He did not respond. Yet, he was surprised by the colonel's attitude; for the man's reputation had preceded him. He was known throughout the Corps as a commander who cared little about the difficulties or hardships his men may encounter. He was not known to sympathize with those who found themselves in dire straits in the course of a battle. Nevertheless, today he appeared to be truly concerned for the welfare of Scott's men; however, he quickly changed the subject.

"Your supplies seemed to have arrived without difficulty. Do you have everything you need?" he asked, matter-of-factly.

"Yes, sir. If they don't hit us any harder than they did yesterday, I think we can hold. But those people on the next ridge are taking a heavy toll on our men. They're damn good and tough to knock out. I have lost nine men to snipers. They're located near the top of that ridge," he said, pointing at the hillside, handing his binoculars to Colonel Pugh.

"Our air cover quiets them down, but only for a while, Colonel... They duck back into their holes — and then the bastards come right back at us when the smoke clears."

"I want you to move on that ridge this morning, Captain," Colonel Pugh said, after scanning the hillside above. "We've got to put those people out of action. I'll leave you twenty-five of my men and four corpsmen; I know you're short.

"Third Battalion will move on the stragglers from your encounter yesterday. They will come down across the airstrip and mop up that group. Our UDT people have blown the remaining obstructions on the reef and the LSTs have come ashore and off-loaded our heavy equipment. We'll give you artillery and air support, just let Battalion know."

"Thank you, Colonel." Jackson was pleased; his boss was not going to relieve him after all, at least not today.

"Don't thank me, Scott," the colonel answered solemnly. "Your people did a hell of a job up here, we should be thanking you. If you had not taken this hill, every one of us would have been in trouble. The Nips could have pushed us right into the damn ocean." Then placing his hand on Scott's shoulder, he studied the junior officer. "You don't look well, Captain. How badly are you injured?"

"I'm all right, Colonel," Scott replied, quietly. "The corpsmen have done a good job."

Rising, the battalion commander turned to leave, then almost as an afterthought added, "I'll try to get you out of here tomorrow, Scott."

"Not without my people!" Jackson blurted out.

Colonel Pugh appeared startled by his subordinate's response, but he made no further reference to the subject.

"The Navy bombardment shall begin at zero nine hundred. We will follow up with an air strike. If the airfield is operational by noon, we should be able to get some napalm into those caves. Move your men out at ten hundred hours."

When Colonel Pugh, his aide and accompanying security detail headed back to the regimental CP, Jackson waved for Niles and Conlan and the two NCOs who came with the relief party, both buck sergeants, to join him in the command post.

"Gentlemen," he said to the two new men, "split up and work with Sergeants Niles and Conlan. We need to cut down the size of these platoons so we can get a better handle on our people." Both NCOs nodded in agreement without comment.

"Get 'em squared away with ammunition and water, we've got a job ahead of us."

"Yeah, I'll just bet we have, Capt'n," Conlan scoffed, shaking his head. "The Old Man wants us to take that damn ridge, doesn't he?" he said, motioning toward the nearby hillside.

"You're right," Scott lashed out. "That's what you signed on for, Sergeant."

"Fair enough, Capt'n. I had that coming, but the Old Man saw the shape our people are in and what it's cost to get this far, I was just trying to tell you we need more than water and ammunition. And look at you; you're damn near dead on your feet."

"Hold it right there, Sergeant," Scott responded wearily, shaking his head. "I appreciate your concern for my welfare and that of your men, but let's not forget why we're here. Those people on that ridge are still picking our men off down on the beach and those big guns are raising havoc with our supplies, so let's just do the damn job."

"Yes, sir," the man responded without further comment.

Still, Jackson knew Conlan was correct, but right now, he was too tired to think. He was in no mood for a discussion on why they might not be able to capture the adjoining ridge.

Turning to Sergeant Donald Niles, he asked, "You got any problems with what we're about to do, Sergeant?"

"No, sir," Niles replied, shaking his head. "Tell us what you want, Captain; we'll do it."

"How about it, Rick?" Jackson asked, turning back to address Sergeant Conlan.

"For Christ's sake, Capt'n, you didn't have to ask," the man replied quietly. "You know me, I was just sounding off, and I just figured you needed some rest."

"Thanks, Rick. Yes, I knew that," Jackson replied, offering a grim smile.

Turning to Sergeant Niles once again, he said, "Don, I want you to take the lead on this. Move your men in a wide sweep across the hillside. Sergeant Conlan will provide cover fire. When you get to the top, hold your people there. They will be tired and I want Conlan's platoon to take it from there. This should give your men a chance to rest until Rick's platoon gets a foothold on the top. Any problem with this?" he asked. Both men looked at one another, and then shook their head.

The Marines took cover in craters all along the edge of the plateau wrested from the Japanese the day before. From there they watched as the warships' big guns rained destruction upon the jagged chasms and steep sides of the nearby hilltop.

The huge naval shells finding their mark sent showers of rock and shards of steel flying through the air. The giant shells, easily seen passing overhead, before exploding on target, cut down everything in their path. Several times they struck close enough to endanger members of the company; rocks, shrapnel and debris rained down on men who had taken cover nearby.

When the bombardment ended, Navy and Marine fighter bombers quickly appeared. Sweeping in over the ridge, they came dropping their bombs, then returned to strafe enemy positions.

Black and gray smoke again billowed up from the hillside; with the wind carrying it across the battlefield, the entire ridge soon became obscured. Unfortunately with this billowing cloud of smoke and dust masking the target, two pilots mistakenly strafed Jackson's position. Luckily, no one was hurt; however, the men from Charlie Company quickly realized just how easy it would be to become a casualty from mistakes made by their own people.

Shortly before ten hundred hours the last Corsair made its strafing run across Ridge 120; this was the signal—Scott's men set out across the narrow void between the two ridges. Descending the near perpendicular cliff on the Westside of Ridge 120, they quickly made their way across the mangrove swamps between the two hillsides, and then began their ascent.

The assault on Ridge 120 was a rerun of events experienced three days earlier. Marines working in squads attacked a series of caves, one after the other, first with rifle fire, followed by grenade launchers, mortars, and flamethrowers. Men with M1s and Browning Automatic Rifles provided cover fire. Ricocheting bullets, bouncing off the rock walls of these natural fortifications, forced enemy soldiers to retreat deeper into the interior of the caves.

Relying upon the BAR and riflemen for cover, other members of the company tossed grenades or dropped TNT satchel charges from above into the openings in the earth's crust. The men's sweat-stained dungarees, covered with dust and ash, made them nearly invisible against the blackened hillside. It was a tough, dirty task, yet they moved relentlessly forward, crawling from cave to cave.

Five hours into the fray, Sergeant Niles's platoon, not waiting for Sergeant Conlan's men, broke over the top, only to be met by a hail of machine gun fire coming from a concealed revetment. Somehow the enemy pillbox survived repeated bombardments. Niles and another man were cut down almost immediately. Although wounded, the sergeant was still alive. He crawled over to the young Marine and began a valiant effort to pull the injured man into a nearby crater. He was hit again; this time he did not move.

"Here they come, Capt'n," Sergeant Conlan yelled. Both men's attention diverted by their colleagues' violent death, were surprised by the sudden reappearance of enemy troops directly in front of Conlan's platoon. Approximately fifty Japanese defenders emerged from what apparently was an escape hatch from below ground. Rather than risk any others in attacking across the top of this flat ridge, Jackson asked Battalion for another air strike.

"They're out in the open," he yelled into the radio to the Navy/Marine ground/air coordinator. "They're moving south, in platoon strength, toward our position."

Within minutes, the air attack began again; it continued without letup for nearly twenty minutes. As the last plane pulled away, the company moved over the crest of the ridge, out onto open ground. Beginning their perilous journey across the plateau, Jackson's troops came across the mangled remains of hundreds of Japanese soldiers. The American planes and naval gunfire caught many of the enemy troops out in the open; their bodies littered the barren landscape, a landscape now nearly devoid of all living matter.

To no one's surprise, however, moving toward a pile of twisted and burnt-out, yet still smoldering tree stumps in the middle of the plateau, Charlie Company encountered more than a score of Japanese soldiers. They too came scampering out from a hole in the ground. In small, fast-moving groups each led by an NCO or officer, they charged across the plateau, firing their weapons at the Americans.

"Take cover and let 'em have it!" Jackson yelled to his troops, now positioned across the narrow part of the plateau. His people, quickly dropping behind tangled tree stumps and into bomb craters, fired directly into this seemingly endless line of enemy soldiers. Closing with the Marines, the encounter rapidly became another hand-to-hand bayonet-, knife-, and bullet-filled whirlwind of sweating, bleeding, and dying men.

When it was over, of the nearly 200 Marines who started the assault five hours earlier, only 122 were still on their feet. Nearly all of the Japanese soldiers were dead, or lying in grotesque positions in their final death throes. Some of the enemy wounded ended their lives with a grenade clutched firmly against their chest. Others, concealed behind the stump of a tree or coral outcropping, tried to kill any Marine that came within view.

When these hand-to-hand struggles ended, Sergeant Conlan appeared to be in a state of shock. He returned to the edge of the ridge and stood mute, as if in a trance staring at the lifeless body of Sergeant Donald Niles.

Conlan and Niles joined the Marine Corps in nineteen thirty-four; they were eighteen years old at the time. Conlan, the son of a Mississippi sharecropper, and Niles, a high school dropout from New York City, served together with the First Marine Division on Guadalcanal and again on Cape Gloucester.

They were not close friends, but they understood and respected each other's abilities. They were proud to be members of the "Old Breed," these former members of the *Raggedy Ass Brigade* from Guadalcanal—they paid their dues as members of one of the greatest military organizations in the world.

"Sergeant Conlan, get your people under control," Jackson yelled. However, Conlan gave no indication that he even heard his boss, forcing his captain to grab him by the shoulder, physically moving him away from their dead colleague. Pushing the man toward a group of Marines standing as if frozen in time, staring at the body of Sergeant Niles, he yelled again, "Conlan, get those men moving! We've got to be prepared for another attack, then go after those caves."

"Do it now!" he shouted.

Sergeant Conlan, staring directly at his captain, mumbled something unintelligible and slowly walked away. Thankfully, the two sergeants who joined the company from Colonel Pugh's relief party earlier that morning took over Sergeant Niles's duties. Their men began moving ammunition and TNT satchel charges over the edge of the ridge, passing them on to the remaining troops.

With Sergeant Niles no longer available to keep him in line, Private John Gunther took advantage of this unexpected opportunity to pursue his personal interests. He spotted the body of a Japanese officer not more than fifty yards away. Setting his rifle aside, he looked around, and then quickly made his way toward the dead man.

"Come back, you crazy bastard," yelled a Marine from his squad as he saw Gunther leave his cover. The man paid no attention to his colleague; within seconds, he reached the officer's body. Gunther was after the man's sword. Grabbing the leather scabbard protruding out from under the dead man's torso, he turned the body over, freeing the blade. As the scabbard came loose, a grenade rolled out from under the corpse—John Gunther made sure that his mother would receive that gold-star flag from her neighbors; it would soon hang in his honor, in her front window at her home in Texas.

With Sergeant Niles out of the picture, a corporal from Michigan, not waiting for instructions, grabbed a TNT satchel and dashed toward the mouth of a nearby cave. Pulling the primer, he hurled the explosive charge into the opening. Hastily retreating a few yards, he dropped to the ground. After the explosion, he stood waving his arms, yelling, "Come on, you guys; let's get these bastards."

"No! Hold your positions," Jackson cried out. He did not want a repeat of yesterday's mistakes, where his men, caught out in the open, were unprepared for the Japanese response. Their naïveté cost the lives of more than a dozen inexperienced young men such as the boy from Michigan. They had much to learn about the art of warfare from this group of Japanese soldiers who honed their warrior skills in China and later defeated the British and French armies in Southeast Asia.

Cautiously scanning the terrain before them, he called out once again to the sergeants. "Spread out, but hold your men back until we know what we've got here."

While uttering these words, a secondary explosion rocked the entire ridge, drowning out his voice. Suddenly, the white coral around the Marine from Michigan seemed to shimmer in the sun's rays. The earth beneath him mushroomed upward for a moment, and then collapsed.

When the smoke and dust cleared, nothing remained of the cave opening except a giant crater. There was no sign of the Marine from Michigan. He had disappeared into the top of what turned out to be one of the largest fortifications on the entire island.

Days later, when Marine engineers excavated the cave, they found two large-caliber howitzers and the remains of nearly 100 enemy soldiers. However, there was no sign of the boy from Michigan. The two heavy weapons found inside the cave mounted on rail-cars allowed the defenders to roll the guns back and forth, deep within the recesses of this inhospitable cavern. The guns could be brought out, or concealed, as the need arose.

Before the dust settled, Jackson formed the last of his troops into two skirmish lines. Sergeant Conlan led one, with the two sergeants from Colonel Pugh's staff taking the other. Following their captain, they began to move out across this 200-yard-wide plateau. Their mission now was to seek out and kill enemy snipers still concealed in the rubble. In the last twenty-four hours, snipers killed or wounded more than a dozen members of Charlie Company; now it was payback time. Enemy sharpshooters were hidden somewhere in this maze of shell craters and shattered trees and Jackson planned for them to pay a high price for the annihilation of so many of his men. "Find 'em and kill 'em," he said as they moved across this narrow strip of coral. His men, now numbering less than 100, were fully confident that the Corps *owned* "this rock"; after all, they bought and paid for it. However, their confidence was short lived, for within minutes, a hail of small arms fire again greeted the group.

The devastation caused by the repeated shelling of the Navy's big guns and bombs from the Hellcats and Corsairs created a labyrinth of craters, broken stumps and splintered trees. This maze of unnatural terrain gave enemy soldiers an ideal place in which to hide. Notwithstanding that, Marines, now forced to root out this very stubborn, well-entrenched foe, slogged doggedly onward. In moving across the plateau, repeated face-to-face confrontations occurred, precipitating violent hand-to-hand encounters.

The sound of small arms fire and grenades, thrown by troops from both sides, reverberated across the pockmarked plateau. In spite of the difficulties encountered, the company moved with determination across the open ground, but before the day was over they would again pay dearly for this jagged pile of rock in the Western Pacific. Nevertheless, by seventeen hundred hours, they succeeded in securing the entire ridge. In doing so, members of the company, with naval and air support, killed more than 300 Japanese soldiers. Uncounted numbers of others died in the caves below their feet.

Yet the cost was high. Since D-Day, the company suffered over 80% casualties. Of the near 300 men who survived the landings on Orange Beach, less than 50 men were now capable of shouldering a weapon. Some were walking wounded. Captain Jackson himself was exhausted; he was barely able to walk, and the members of Charlie Company who were still on their feet needed rest.

As Jackson and his radioman, Corporal Bobby Chrisman, reached the northern crest of the ridge, they unexpectedly found themselves face to face with two Japanese soldiers.

"Holy Christ!" Chrisman yelled. "Look out, Captain."

For a moment, startled by the appearance of the two Marines, the enemy soldiers remained motionless. Suddenly, one lunged at the radioman with his bayonet. Scott whirled to face the second soldier. He was too late; the man fired his rifle, the bullet striking Jackson in the chest, driving him backwards. As he fell, he began firing, emptying the clip from his .45 into the two enemy soldiers. One of Jackson's bullets struck the first man in the forehead, his lifeless body tumbling down the slope of the hill. Hit in the chest, the second soldier collapsed on top of Jackson.

The encounter was over in seconds. Pushing the dead man away, Scott crawled over to his injured radio operator. Blood was gushing from the man's neck, his throat pierced by the bayonet.

"Hold on, Bobby—we'll get you out!" Jackson exclaimed, knowing there was nothing he could do. The young man grabbed hold of his captain's jacket, his eyes begging for help. Scott was unable to stop the flow of blood; the war was over for Corporal Chrisman.

Trying to regain his feet, Jackson turned just in time to see a Japanese officer, armed with a sword, come at him from the edge of the ridge. Lunging at his adversary, the officer swung the long, bright-colored blade in an arc; unable to defend himself, Jackson stumbled over the body of the dead radioman. He went down hard, and the tip of the long sword, finding its mark, cut him across his back. With the Japanese officer raising the sword once again, to deliver the coup de grace, Rick Conlan moved quickly. Approaching at a dead run, with a loud curse, he fired a dozen quick rounds from a Thompson submachine gun. His bullets tore into the swordsman's face and chest, spinning him around, where he dropped, face down onto the rough coral.

When it was over, the scene was surrealistic. Death and devastation were everywhere. Jackson sat beside the dead soldiers looking at the body of the Japanese officer. He was one of the men seen earlier in the day, leading the assault on the Marines at the north end of the ridge.

As Rick Conlan and members of his squad began to gather around, Scott, looking up at the sergeant, blurted out, "What the hell is happening to our world, Rick?"

There was no time, nor need for the sergeant to answer the question. Jackson collapsed, falling back against the body of his radioman.

"Get a corpsman over here," Conlan yelled, looking at a nearby Marine, frozen, as if in shock from the carnage around them. "Move it, damn it!" he cursed. Then ripping open the front of Jackson's dungarees, he moaned, "Oh God," noting a small bullet hole in the man's lower chest, as frothy red foam began to come from Scott's nose and mouth. Rolling him over, he cut the dungaree jacket away, exposing a long slicing wound, running from Scott's shoulder blade to his webbed gun belt. Had it been deeper it could have disemboweled him.

Captain Jackson regained consciousness two days later. He was on a hospital ship in a ward with twenty other wounded Marines. He tried to move, but found he was bound to the bed with sheets and towels. His cursing attracted the attention of a Navy doctor and nurse attending to others nearby; they quickly responded.

"So, you have decided to rejoin the living, Captain," the doctor offered. "It's nice to have you here in our floating hospital... Welcome aboard," he smiled. "I'm Doctor Ryerson."

Jackson tried to talk; he managed to utter, "I need a drink."

"Certainly," the doctor replied. "However, let's get you a little more comfortable first. We had some pretty rough weather the last couple of days and I didn't want you falling out of your bunk."

Ryerson loosened the two restraints that held his patient's arms and removed the broad sheet that firmly secured the man's body to the bed. The nurse, taking a cup with a protruding straw, gave him a drink of water.

"How'd I get here? Where am I?" he demanded, his voice a guttural whisper.

"You're on a hospital ship," the doctor answered, as he examined his patient's bandaged leg. "You were brought on board three nights ago and we got underway shortly afterward... You're going home."

"What about Charlie Company? What happened to 'em?"

"I think I'll leave the telling of that story up to a friend of yours, Captain. She's on board."

"Who's on board?" he grunted, obviously bewildered by the doctor's answer.

"Lieutenant Kosterman, she works in surgery. When she reports in, I will tell her you're awake. Now let's take a look at what happened to you.

"In this war, Captain, we evacuate our wounded. You'd think someone would've been smart enough to get you out of there," the doctor offered derisively, his voice tinged with bitterness. Apparently, Doctor Ryerson was exasperated with the military for the failure of commanders to evacuate the critically wounded in a timely manner. Yet, from his tone of voice, it was obvious there was more to it than that.

"I'm in the business of saving lives," he growled. "I can't do that when you people come off the line, half dead. You must have been in Bob Pugh's command. I've been patching up his mistakes ever since the war started. He wants that bloody star on his collar and he doesn't give a damn that someone may have to be killed to get it." The doctor paused, now listening to his patient's heartbeat.

"The bullet that entered your chest, Captain, nicked your lung as it passed through your body. You came awfully close to bleeding to death," he observed, without any show of solace or compassion.

"The knife, or sword wound to your back will give you lots of pain, but thanks to your web belt, there's no major damage to your internal organs.

"We found a large bruise on your left hip. There is some internal hemorrhaging; it will cause some discomfort for several weeks, but there is no fracture. Last, but not least, we sutured a wound on your right leg," he added, gently pressing the injured limb. "It'll take awhile before you're fully recovered.

"The good news..." the doctor continued, now halfheartedly, "you should be up and on your feet within two or three weeks. A month or two after that," he said, with an obvious show of cynicism, "you'll be ready to go back into this gristmill."

Doctor Ryerson's unflattering comments, obviously directed toward the military hierarchy, were not lost on the nursing staff.

They had heard it all before from this 200-dollar-a-month surgeon. A Selective Service Board in the city of San Francisco decided the military could use this medical professional's talents, even if he must leave behind a lucrative stateside private practice. Ryerson was not a happy man. He never thought he would ever have to work on a hospital ship in the middle of the Pacific Ocean. Before the war, he hoped to become one of the wealthiest, if not one of the most prominent physicians in the State of California.

"Where're we going?" Scott asked, not comprehending Doctor Ryerson's cacophonous vilification of the military hierarchy, nor fully aware of his surroundings.

"Pearl Harbor, Captain. When we get there we'll most likely send you on to the States, probably to the Naval Hospital in San Diego. We will worry about that later, now get some sleep, Lieutenant Kosterman will wake you when she comes in. I understand she'll have some good news for you."

Jackson, heavily sedated, dropped off to sleep almost immediately. When he awoke, it was to find Doctor Ryerson and a nurse changing the bandages on his leg.

"Where's Kosterman?" he asked as soon as the cobwebs cleared.

"She spent three hours with you after she got off her watch this morning," the nurse responded. "She didn't have the heart to wake you. You have been sleeping for more than fourteen hours, Captain. When Doctor Ryerson finishes changing your bandages, I'll let her know you're awake."

Before the doctor finished his task, his patient drifted off to sleep. Within the hour, Lieutenant Sophia Kosterman entered the ward.

Chapter 2

Nineteen twenty-eight was a good year for most Americans, for those living in the northwestern United States it was an exceptionally good year. The Great War ended favorably for the United States and its allies; the postwar recession that followed hostilities did not take a drastic toll on the American labor force. On the East Side of the Cascade Mountains, farmers were getting unprecedented prices for their crops. Prosperity, so elusive for such a long time for the American farmer, seemed just around the corner.

The northwestern states were experiencing near full employment. The huge shipyards on Puget Sound and along the Columbia River returned to near normal production. Dismantling or reconfiguring the nation's warships for peacetime commerce provided employment for thousands of skilled tradesmen and the returning soldier alike. Americans found a ready market for scrap metal in the Far East; unpredictably, Japanese industry acquired an insatiable appetite for steel. Their leaders apparently became obsessed with the idea of becoming the superpower of the Western Pacific; the Empire of Japan became one of America's most valuable trading partners. This Japanese dream opened the door for many of America's entrepreneurs of the twenties.

On the west side, cargo ships, loaded with scrap iron, grain, or manufactured goods, departed daily from Puget Sound ports bound for Tokyo, or Shanghai. Some carried more than a dozen different makes of automobiles, manufactured in Detroit, with each company vying to capture the Asian market. Timber harvests in the Northwest nearly doubled since the war, and building contractors found it difficult to keep up with the demand for new homes. Urban areas exploded with new growth. Both railroad and maritime industries flourished. Cargo passing through Puget Sound ports rivaled that of New York City.

Every week, more than a dozen ocean liners visited Seattle, and other West Coast cities. Decks, crammed with vacationers, honeymoon couples, or business executives, headed across the Pacific to Hawaii or Asian ports, or down the coast to sunny California.

Before sailing, many of the passengers and crew picked up a newspaper or magazine from one of half dozen kids who peddled the sheets along the waterfront. One of these young entrepreneurs was Scotty Jackson, who sold his first newspaper on the streets of his hometown when he was only twelve years old. One of his first customers was the captain of a Japanese cargo ship. After school, the boy sold the *Seattle Star* throughout Skid Road and along the shores of Elliot Bay, or chased after any magazine or book desired by one of his many customers. By the time he turned sixteen, because of his dependability and personality, he made a name for himself all along the waterfront. The regulars could expect to receive the daily paper by the time they closed shop for the day or sat down for dinner.

"What're the headlines today, Scotty?" one of the cops asked, while sitting astride a beautiful black three-year-old gelding. It was Officer Charles "Chuck" Sackett, one of more than four dozen mounted officers assigned to the waterfront. He was always Mr. Sackett to the newspaper boy.

"Hi, Mr. Sackett," the lad smiled, handing a paper up to the big man with the huge mustache and long hair that hung down over his uniform blouse collar. "I've got three Japanese cargo ships in, Mr. Sackett, and one Russian and two cruise ships."

"Business must be good," the officer responded as he handed a nickel to the boy for the newspaper.

"No, it's great, Mr. Sackett!" the youngster exclaimed with a grin. The mounted officer laughed. "What'd ya sell to the foreign swabbies; they can't read American, can they?"

"Some of them can, particularly the Japanese, but the Russkies want the Sears Roebuck catalogues. I think they just look at the pictures," he smiled. "The cruise ships are loading out now, so I gotta go. See ya, Mr. Sackett," he called out as he hurried off toward Pier Sixty-Six.

Turning to his mounted partner, John Culp, Officer Sackett said with a grin, "That's some kid. He's gonna make it okay."

"Yeah, he's a charmer," Culp responded. "He's got that gift of gab like his old man. You Irishmen are all alike. It must be inherited."

Sackett ignored his partner's remarks; he merely replied, "I don't know how the kid does it, he's playing football at school and he's down here every night until dark. With this strike coming on, I don't like it. Some of these kids are apt to get hurt."

Officer Sackett and the other cops were fully aware that trouble was brewing on the waterfront. It could explode out into the streets at any time. Whenever a ship tied up at one of the three score *finger piers* along the waterfront, striking longshoremen invariably set up a picket line. To keep the peace, the Chief of Police assigned more than fifty mounted officers to patrol the area. In a series of job actions against the ship owners, violent confrontations frequently occurred between the maritime workers and police. The West Coast Longshoremen's Union took full advantage of the busy maritime industry, at every opportunity pressing for higher wages and better working conditions for their membership.

In the political and social arena, the biggest news was the nationwide dispute raging over Prohibition. Law enforcement in every large city in the country faced a critical challenge. Trying to enforce a law where there was little or no support from the public created a dilemma for the police and wreaked havoc within the criminal justice system. Illegal liquor imports and clandestine stills, manufacturing quality liquor, flourished throughout the country, the Northwest was no exception. This underground distribution and sale of alcohol created a completely new class of business entrepreneur: the bootlegger. The sale of liquor soon became a booming business employing thousands, and a get-rich-quick philosophy prevailed throughout the industry. Within months of the Ratification of the Eighteenth Amendment, an undeclared war erupted as bootleggers battled each other over territory.

In spite of these problems, Edward John O'Dea, Catholic Bishop of Seattle, took full advantage of the strengthening economy, albeit helped in part by his frequent and often harshly worded edicts to members of his flock. During his bishopric, he initiated the construction of more than a dozen churches and elementary schools throughout the diocese. One of his greatest accomplishments was building an all-boys high school. The school, named in his honor, opened its doors in 1924, but it had yet to be completed.

The religious community was at odds on the ability of the Church to raise sufficient funds to complete the bishop's ambitious building programs. In January, as continued financing for his many building projects appeared to be in question, the Church placed a hold on construction of the gymnasium, auditorium, and sports stadium at the high school. Even with the growing economy, divisiveness within Bishop O'Dea's flock began to threaten the prospects for sustained financial support. Contributions from parishes outside of the metropolitan area began to dry up. These parishioners were quick to realize that the cost of sending their children off to the city for a religious education was nearly prohibitive.

Bishop O'Dea and the Brothers at the school were well aware of this growing conflict, a dispute fueled in part by ever-increasing labor costs; in spite of these problems, the Bishop took steps to assure the school's continued existence. He purposely kept tuition at a minimum, relying upon both the business community and various fund-raising activities throughout the diocese for financial support. He also counted on his business friends and religious colleagues, at more than a dozen colleges and universities throughout the country, to repay long-overdue favors.

Bishop O'Dea expected a bountiful harvest in the form of scholarships for his graduating class. In his thirty-two years of service to the Church, he earned the respect of the religious community. In addition, hundreds of business and political leaders throughout the Northwest owed him a debt of gratitude. His continuing exhortations to his ever-expanding flock, where he encouraged them to support those who looked favorably upon the needs of the Church, worked in his favor. He expected that his friends would not let him down.

By the end of May, because of mounting publicity, the school expected a large turnout at the school for commencement exercises. To accommodate the expected crowd, they moved the program to the nearby Broadway High School Auditorium. At the graduation ceremonies for the class of '28, from the dais, Dean of Students Brother John Alan had a surprise announcement.

"Parents, guests and my dear students," he offered, solicitously, waving a handful of papers overhead as if to get the crowd's attention. "Bishop O'Dea has requested that I announce the names of those from the graduating class of nineteen twenty-eight who have been awarded college scholarships for their academic and athletic accomplishments here at O'Dea High School."

Parents immediately quieted their children and talkative friends; a hush settled over the auditorium.

"You parents will be happy to know," he exclaimed loudly, exhibiting his tobacco-stained teeth in a broad grin, "that every member of the class of nineteen twenty-eight has been awarded a college scholarship." The crowd, erupting into cheers, drowned out the rest of Brother John's announcement. Bishop John O'Dea's wish came true. There would be no lack of students, or for that matter lack of funds, in the years ahead. The possibility of a college scholarship for a son or daughter was an enticement that even the most parsimonious member of his church could not ignore.

NEIL MOLONEY

Scott Allan Jackson, the son of second-generation Irish-American parents, graduated with the class of '28. He was seventeen years old. The young man and his four closest friends received either an academic or an athletic scholarship to the University of Washington, or to Notre Dame University. Others, equally rewarded, received fully funded scholarships to more than a dozen academic institutions.

Jackson and two of his friends appeared to be half-starved kids down on their luck. The tallest was Mark McGinnes, at six foot six, followed by Jackson and his other friend, Paul Addison, both at six foot two. However, Cornelius "Corky" Shay and Kenji "Peewee" Tanaka, their longtime companions, did not fit that mold. Shay was the son of a wealthy architect; his father made a fortune in the postwar real-estate building boom. Kenji Tanaka's father owned a combination grocery and dry goods store in Japantown that catered to the community's burgeoning Japanese population.

Corky was short in stature, but never short of money. Besides loving to eat, he liked to be in style, always wearing the latest fashions, black corduroy slacks, cardigan sweaters, and a fine leather jacket. Except for the extra 50 pounds he carried around his middle, he was a handsome teenager. However, at five foot seven, he was always just a candy bar, or two, shy of 200 pounds.

Yet for all his extra weight, what he had in common with his friends was that he was a star athlete, earning letters in both baseball and football during his junior and senior years. Few opponents made it through the O'Dea High School football line when Shay was playing; he was a tough and tenacious kid who loved the game. The tougher the opposition, the better he liked it.

Ken or Kenny Tanaka, as most of his classmates called him, was two inches shorter than Shay. Because of his small size, when he was in junior high school, his closest friends tagged him with the nickname Peewee. But the name failed to depict the true physical prowess of this young man while in the sports arena. Kenji worked after school and on weekends in his father's business. His muscular development, acquired in moving produce in and out of his father's warehouses, served him well on the football and baseball field at O'Dea High School. One day, Corky Shay complained to one of his teammates, "Tackling Peewee when he is carrying the ball is like trying to stop a wild bull. He just bowls you over."

Peewee, overhearing his friend's comment, responded with a smile. "You've got to hit your opponent low, Corky, that's why some of those bigger guys get by you."

"Yeah, sure, Peewee," Corky replied with a wry grin, "every time I try that with you, you just jump over me."

Jackson, standing nearby listening to this exchange, entered the conversation, "The only way to handle Peewee when he's got the ball, Corky, is to grab him by the neck and hang on. That's what I do." Scott laughed. Their coach, standing nearby, only smiled; he was obviously pleased with the performance of his star players.

Peewee's father, Yoshio, and mother, Kim Tanaka, came from Japan in 1905, finding employment in the produce gardens in the Valley. By 1920, they had acquired enough capital to open a small grocery store in Japantown that catered to the Asian population. Yoshio Tanaka, unimpressed with what he learned in the public school system in Japan, wanted more for his three children, thus the Church in his newly adopted country would educate Kenji and his two sisters. Yet, the family continued to be faithful to the Buddhist religion, attending weekly services in the local temple.

Peewee and Corky's three school friends, however, were so skinny a good wind might have blown them away. Still, Timothy Walker, the coach at O'Dea, expected these five boys to be the ones from the class of '28 most likely to receive athletic scholarships. The boys did not let their coach down.

Corky Shay, however, would have no need for financial assistance; his father had already arranged with the Holy Cross fathers for his son's enrollment at the University of Notre Dame. However, the Jackson, McGinnes, and Addison families were not in a position to provide financial support for their children. Although Jackson gave some thought to pursuing a college degree, no one in his family ever before finished high school, let alone graduated from a college or university. Right now, he had no interest in pursing a college degree.

The Tanaka family never doubted that their son would attend the university, scholarship or not. Kenji's parents were fully aware of the advantages offered by a college education for their American-born children. They opened savings accounts for each child when the child was born and, once old enough to work, required the children to contribute toward their future educational needs.

The five boys had been together since entering grade school. Once in high school, they became experts in disrupting the Christian Brothers' solemn routine of study, prayer and quiet meditation expected of all students at O'Dea High. The boys prided themselves in being able to outwit most of their fellow students and, on occasion, even their teachers. Frequently their antics became the subject of conversation by those in authority, both on and off the school grounds.

They seldom paid for a streetcar ride. En route to school, one of the boys would board the front of the trolley, then with great fanfare attempt to distract the conductor. The ruse, pretending to be searching pockets, looking for the nickel to pay the fare, usually worked. Meanwhile, the others, grabbing on to the rear stair railing, or climbing through an open window, got a free ride, until chased off by the conductor.

On occasion, their pranks went too far. One day, while Bishop O'Dea was attending the football team's afternoon practice, the boys slipped away, taking with them the 100-foot-long mooring rope used in the school's tug-of-war games.

"Take that end," Scott said excitedly to his friends. "Tie it to the base of that telephone pole. Come on; hurry up, before Coach catches on."

"What are you gonna do, Scotty?" Corky Shay asked, somewhat bewildered; he and Peewee had not been let in on Jackson and Mark McGinnes' scheme, which their two friends had come up with when school let out for the day.

"Yeah, Scott, what's going on?" Paul Addison asked, somewhat skeptical of his friend's instructions.

"Come on, Paul, move it," Mark McGinnes said, grabbing his friend by the arm. "We ain't got much time. Help me tie this off."

"You guys are nuts," Addison added with a grin, as he helped McGinnes and Shay secure their end to the telephone pole. Jackson and Peewee, grabbing the other end, tied it to the back bumper of the bishop's new Studebaker touring car. With the two ends securely fastened, the results were predictable. The laws of physics would complete their task.

By the time the football team headed for the showers, it was dark and Coach Walker accompanied Bishop O'Dea to his car.

"That's a fine-looking team you have there, Tim," the bishop said, complimenting Coach Walker as he climbed into his automobile. "What's our chance of taking the All-City title this year?"

"Very good, Your Excellency. This is undoubtedly the best bunch of kids I've ever coached."

"Good," the priest smiled. "I'm looking forward to the boys representing our school. I'll drop by next week, but I must be on my way."

"We're up against Broadway High on Friday, sir."

"I'll be there, Timothy."

"Good-bye, sir," responded Coach Walker, as the bishop drove away. The coach was delighted that the man took time out of his busy schedule to drop by to watch his team practice. However, his delight was short-lived, for the bishop did not get very far. With the two ends of rope securely fastened, when it snapped taut, it not only tore the bumper off the bishop's car, but the sudden stop threw the man into the steering wheel, breaking his glasses; he ended up with two black eyes.

The following day, the five culprits were standing before Brother John Alan in the principal's office.

"Who put you up to this stunt of yours, Cornelius?" he growled at Corky Shay, unleashing a string of very unchristian language. "I know your father, he would not allow such conduct to be perpetrated by a son of his; so I suppose it was Mr. McGinnes, or Mr. Addison. Am I correct in this assumption?" He did not wait for Corky's response. "No, this stunt has all the earmarks of Mr. Jackson and Mr. Tanaka, is that correct, Kenji?" he growled, throwing a mean look in Scott and Kenji's direction.

"No, sir; I did it on my own." Kenji blurted out, nervously.

"I don't believe you," Brother John snapped. "Let's not get yourself in any deeper than you already are by lying about this."

"I did it, Brother John," Scott stated forcefully, interrupting Brother John's colloquy. "Kenji didn't have anything to do with it."

"I might have know it was you, Mr. Jackson. This is just the kind of deed someone of your background would try to pull off. What made you think you could get away with it?"

"It wasn't Scott, Brother John. I did it," responded Corky Shay, loudly insisting that his friend had no part in what Brother John called this stunt. However, before he could say any more, Mark McGinnes stepped forward. As he approached the educator's desk, Brother John raised his ample frame out of his chair and he was now standing behind it with his favorite yardstick in hand.

"This was my idea, Brother John, and I thought it was a damn good one," Mark responded with a curse. The boy's demeanor and self-confidence appeared to shake Brother John's resolve.

"I didn't expect the bishop to get hurt, and I'll pay for the damage to his car, but you're not going to use that stick on me anymore," his words threatening. "I'll guarantee you that," he added.

It was obvious the man now had second thoughts about using the yardstick as a weapon against any of the five young men.

"I had no intention of hitting any of you," Brother John declared, glaring at the boys standing before him. "As of right now, all of you are expelled from O'Dea High School," he growled. "You are finished here; I will notify your parents of your delinquent behavior and adolescent actions. You people have continually disrupted our studies here, but you are not going to get away with it any longer. You will not return, nor will you graduate with your class. Now get out of my office."

"Holy crap! He really dumped on us, didn't he?" Corky exclaimed as the boys headed for home.

"I didn't think we'd get away clean this time, Cork." Mark McGinnes' laugh was hollow. "But, yeah, I guess you're right, he dumped on us real good."

"Sorry, guys, I guess I didn't think about the consequences," Scott offered, apologetically. "But I didn't think they'd kick us out."

Bishop O'Dea remained in seclusion for more than a week. However, had Corky's and Kenji's fathers not intervened, the boys would have been expelled. Mr. Shay was no lightweight when it came to supporting the Christian Brothers' school; and Yoshio Tanaka was one of the Church's principal benefactors. He supplied most of the fresh produce and wine at the numerous fund-raising dinners and celebrations hosted by Bishop O'Dea in his diocese.

Scott knew he would have to sell a lot of newspapers to pay his share of the costs to repair the Bishop's automobile and to buy the man a new pair of spectacles.

Another stunt had even greater potential for more serious consequences. In early February, Shay's parents traveled to southern California on vacation. John Shay's mother was to look after her grandson while the boy's mother and father were out of town. With his parents gone, Corky and his friends decided to skip school. On Monday morning, they caught a streetcar out to the Bay Marina, where John Shay's seventy-two-foot sailboat was tied up.

The *Sparkman and Stephens Motor Sailor*, with its twin masts, teak decks, staterooms, crew's quarters and fully stocked liquor cabinet, was a top-of-the-line watercraft. John Shay routinely hired two Alaska fishermen as deckhands when he and his family sailed on Puget Sound. They also accompanied the family on their annual trek to Juneau.

Corky Shay made the trip twice with his parents. Both times his father put him to work as an apprentice seaman. On occasion, in the calm waters of Elliott Bay, he let the boy captain the craft. With his parents out of town, Corky figured he would take his friends for a short sail across the Sound; they planned to return by early afternoon so their parents would not be aware that any of them skipped school.

"Damn it's cold out here, Corky!" complained Peewee as the boat cleared the marina. "Maybe this wasn't such a good idea."

"Yeah, Corky!" exclaimed Scott. "You can't even see the city now. It looks like we're running into one helluva snowstorm."

Unfortunately, neither Corky, nor his friends had paid any attention to the weather forecast. Earlier that morning, the Coast Guard posted storm warnings throughout the entire Puget Sound region. The area was about to be engulfed by one of the worst winter storms ever to hit the state.

"Where the hell are we, Corky?" Mark McGinnes asked, trying desperately not to show his fear. "I can't see a damn thing." With salt spray and blowing snow completely obscuring everything around them, he was obviously worried.

"Yeah, Corky," Paul Addison added, "I don't like this. Let's go back," he said, looking at Kenji and Jackson for support.

"Oh, come on, we're all right," Shay offered, his tone of voice not reassuring at all to his classmates. It was obvious he was not expecting this storm when they left the marina.

"I think Paul's right, Corky," Mark McGinnes offered, shaking his head as he tried to steady himself as the bow of the boat lurched high out of the water. When it came crashing down, glasses, chairs, cushions, and Mrs. Shay's wall decorations went flying across the cabin.

"We'd better head for home, Corky," Scott added. By now it was obvious to Shay's friends that their high school companion's sailing skills were less than Corky had led them to believe.

"I'd go back, Scott, but I don't know where the hell we are," Shay shouted, over the sound of the storm. "I can't see anything and the compass is acting crazy."

"What's going on, Corky?" Mark McGinnes asked as the sailboat's twelve-cylinder engine suddenly went silent.

"Oh man!" Shay exclaimed, now clearly worried. "Looks like we're out of gas."

"Y'know, Corky, this ain't funny anymore," Kenji said, his voice strained with worry. "Turn this damn thing around and let's go home. We'll get picked off out here by a damn ferry boat or a ship." Corky was trying frantically to restart the motor while the boat pitched and rolled violently. In the raging storm that followed, the north wind carried them blindly into the middle of one of the busiest shipping channels in North America.

That evening, when Grandmother Shay had not heard from her grandson, she called the police. It was still snowing, but the wind let up.

The desk officer tried his best to reassure her. "Now, now, Mrs. Shay, the streetcars are running two to three hours late and some have shut down for the night. But don't worry," he said. "Your grandson's probably out sledding with his friends."

Shortly before midnight, Mrs. Shay received a call from Scott's mother, Barbara Jackson; she too was looking for her son. The woman had already talked to the Addison and McGinnes families, neither of their boys came home from school. Mrs. Jackson, expecting that Kenji was with his four friends, asked if anyone had heard from the Tanaka family. Mrs. Shay told her, "No," but she would call Mr. Tanaka right away.

It was still snowing the next morning. The entire Puget Sound region, now blanketed with more than a foot of snow, with three-foot drifts in places, came to a standstill. Temperatures throughout the area dropped below 20 degrees. Mrs. Shay and the parents of the other boys were frantic. They checked the school and learned that all five boys failed to show up for class Monday morning. City police agreed to look for them, but they did not know where to start.

Mrs. Shay sent a telegram off to her son and daughter-in-law in California to notify them Corky and his friends were missing. The

Shays replied they would catch the next available train out of Los Angeles for home. Adult members of the other families were not much help. During the night, they contacted the boys' classmates, but no one knew where they could have gone. As darkness approached on the second day, the snow let up, but there was still no word of the missing students.

The following morning, with the entire Puget Sound area bathed in brilliant sunlight, temperatures climbed into the mid thirties. Throughout the city, homeowners were out with their shovels digging out, while scores of children, sled or toboggan in hand, began the trek up their favorite hill.

Shortly before noon, two mounted patrol officers arrived at the Shay residence. It was Officer Charles Sackett and his partner, John Culp. Mrs. Shay was preparing coffee and rolls for the parents of her grandson's friends when the officers knocked. Although obviously distressed, she invited the two men to join them.

John Culp, clearly to the annoyance of his partner, asked Mrs. Shay a question without any thought as to the close ties the missing boys might be to their families.

"You don't suppose they ran away from home, do you? They do this before?" he asked callously, his comment more of an accusation than question.

"No!" Mrs. Addison responded sharply, clearly agitated by the officer's insinuation. "These are good boys—they would not do that."

"Oh my, no," responded Mrs. Tanaka, clearly upset by the officer's insensitive comment. "Kenji would not run away from home."

"I'm sure you're right, Mrs. Tanaka," Officer Sackett responded, intervening into this strained conversation. "I know your sons, they're good boys. They have to be close by; we just need to put our heads together and figure out where they are. They probably tried to call you, but lines are down all over the city... We'll find them, don't worry."

Officer Culp assumed, as the boys did not attend school on Monday, they were probably runaways. Yet, without letting on to family members, Officer Sackett was uneasy with the particulars surrounding this incident. With the severe weather conditions these past two days, there was no telling where they may be.

Later that morning, the manager of the Bay Marina called the local police precinct to report a stolen boat. The missing boat and the disappearance of the boys were quickly connected. Precinct officers notified the Coast Guard. Later that afternoon, the captain of an outbound freighter advised the Coast Guard that a sailboat was apparently in distress on the west side of Puget Sound. He reported he spotted the craft, high on the rocks, on the north shore of Blake Island. It appeared to have sustained heavy damage.

By six o'clock the next morning, the boys were back home. Three hours into their excursion, when caught in the fury of the storm, they unfurled the headsail, only to become the victim of the ferocious wind. From their jumping-off point at the marina, the craft, carried ten miles downwind, slammed onto the rocks on the north shore of the deserted island. Other than being scared, cold, wet, and hungry, the young men suffered no ill effects from their outing.

Upon graduation, Scott and his friends did not have time to worry about college—there were more pressing issues. After commencement exercises, the five young men got together at Corky Shay's home to finalize their plans for the summer.

"What're we gonna tell our folks?" Shay asked quietly as he went over to shut the basement door so their conversation would not by heard by his parents.

"Tell 'em the truth, Corky," Jackson replied, with a shrug and wave of his hand. "It's only for the summer and we're all going together. Hell, you'll be back in plenty of time to go to school."

"I can't go, Scott," Peewee said, apologetically. "I know when we talked about it last month I thought it would be a great idea, but my old man would kill me. Besides, I have a full-time job for the summer in Dad's store. It doesn't pay very much and I'm not crazy about it, but with the scholarship and support from my folks, I can still work there while I'm at the university. I'm sorry, but I can't go."

"Yeah, I think we all knew that you probably couldn't go, Peewee," Scott responded, with a wave of his hand. "But Mark and Paul and I don't have a damn thing. We expected it would give us the opportunity see the Midwest and earn a little money, maybe buy a car when we get back."

"I don't know," Mark McGinnes said, entering into the conversation. "My mother will have a fit and I know what my dad will say. 'I came from the Dakotas and there ain't a damn thing there except snakes, mosquitoes, and dust storms.'" He laughed.

"What about you, Scotty? Your mother's going to be sick." Kenji Tanaka inquired, clearly concerned for his friend's future. "Everybody knows she's worked like hell to get you and Beth through high school."

"She'll be all right. I'll tell her the same thing these guys are gonna say, 'We'll be home by the first of September, that will be in plenty of time,' but I'm not so sure I'm going back to school."

"What! What the hell are you talking about?" Kenji exclaimed, looking at his friend in disbelief.

"Yeah, for Christ's sake, Scotty," Corky responded aloud, not believing what he just heard. "You're not serious, are you? With your grades, you can go to any damn school in the country."

"I know, but look at how we live. We're dirt poor and with my old man so crippled, he can't get a decent job. I know he expects me to get out and go to work; it would be a lot easier on my mom if I did."

Scott's friends were incredulous. He was their best friend, a scholar, athlete, and the uncrowned leader of their group. With two university scholarships waiting in the wings, his friends could not believe it possible that he would not go on to school. This should not happen. Baffled by their friend's response, they did not know what else to say.

Scott put the issue aside for this evening when he suggested they go out and see if they could rustle up some bootlegged whiskey and celebrate, and possibly find some girls.

"What about your sister's girlfriends?" Mark McGinnes asked with a grin, throwing a look at Kenji and Paul Addison.

"Hell, they're just kids," Scott responded. "What we need are women; we need to broaden our horizons," he laughed.

"I don't know, Scotty," Paul Addison responded with a wry grin. "I saw you making out with that Donahue gal the other night at the Orpheum—she's a good looker."

"Cut the bull, you guys," Scott responded with feigned innocence and then, changing the subject, added, "Let's go over to Rademaker's; he's got some pretty good booze—two bucks a pint."

"He ain't gonna sell it to us," Peewee scoffed. "No bootlegger in his right mind is going to peddle that stuff to a bunch of kids."

"You guys will have to stay outside. I get it all the time for my old man," Scott offered, with a show of audaciousness, although not fully confident that he could produce what he promised. He was not sure he would be able to persuade Rademaker to sell him a pint this late in the evening; the bootlegger knew by this time of night Scott's father would be at work at the Ballard Sawmill.

Chapter 3

The night before leaving for the Dakotas, Scott's father broached the subject of his son's education.

"What about the university, Scott, are you going to attend school this fall?" he asked, solicitously.

Surprised by the question, Scott looked at his mother, before responding. He always assumed his father wanted him to enter the workforce as soon as possible to help support the family.

"I thought you wanted me to go to work, Dad."

"I did. I could have got you on at the Mill, but you have a future now, go after it. You can work part-time and still get an education; you're gonna need it."

"What if I wait a year? I'd like to get away from the books for a while."

"Won't you lose your scholarships?" his mother asked. She was listening to the conversation while clearing the dinner table.

"I don't think so, Mom," he responded.

"You'd better check, son," his father cautioned him. "I think that's a one-time shot; you take it when it's offered, otherwise I think it's gone."

"I'll check, but I want to take this trip with the rest of the guys — we'll be back in plenty of time for the fall semester."

What he did not tell his parents was that he wanted some time away from the daily routine of schoolwork. He thought it best if he did not mention the fact that he was sick and tired of the religious discipline, delivered almost daily by the Christian Brothers at Bishop John O'Dea High School.

"Give me some time, Dad," he pleaded, promising he would go on to college, after he had a chance to see the world. The four young men planned to work the summer in the wheat fields of the Dakotas, where Scott hoped to earn enough money to purchase a used car. To him, a car was more important than school.

A week after graduation, much to the displeasure of their parents, the four classmates caught a Northern Pacific freight heading for Chicago. Kenji Tanaka saw them off as they climbed into an empty boxcar on the eastbound freight train.

"I'll see you guys in September," he yelled out to them as they waved good-bye.

"While we're gone, take care of our women, Peewee," Corky hollered back. He laughed.

En route to North Dakota, the immediate goal of the four boys was to explore the Rocky Mountains and the Midwest, at the expense of the railroad. Eventually they would find work in the wheat fields of North Dakota. If everything went according to plan, by the end of summer, Scott would have the money he needed to buy that car.

Arriving in Fargo in July 1928, the four young men learned a tough financial lesson. High wages for unskilled workers was a myth. They quickly discovered that field hands seldom received more than a dollar a day, plus room and board for pitching grain bundles into a threshing machine. Two dollars was the going rate for driving a team of horses. Work began at dawn and ended at dusk. By the end of harvest, Scott saved only thirty-six dollars, certainly not enough to buy a car. His three friends did not fare much better.

That fall, as planned, Corky Shay, Paul Addison and Mark McGinnes returned home to enter college. Although his three friends suspected that Scott was not going with them, it was not until they were ready to board the train that the issue came up.

"You're coming with us, aren't you, Scott?" Corky Shay asked. "Your folks will be expecting you."

"No, I've already written to Mom. I told her I was going to stay on here another year. I'll see you guys next fall. Okay?" he said smiling, while giving Shay a bear hug.

"How come, Scott? You'll get a free ride at the university," Paul Addison stated matter-of-factly. "Why not take advantage of it?"

"No, you guys go ahead, I'll catch up to you next year," he grinned, shaking hands with McGinnes and Addison. "So long, guys," he added quietly as his three friends boarded the train for home.

Paul Addison and Mark McGinnes, along with Kenji Tanaka, would take full advantage of their scholarships at the University of Washington. Corky's future was secure; when he got home, his parents would ship him off to the University of Notre Dame. As the train pulled away from the platform, Scott had to smile; all three of his friends bought coach class tickets, no-one was *riding the rods* this time.

"You ever milk a cow, kid?" the middle-aged man asked as he introduced himself to Scott at the Fargo rail station warehouse. "My name is John Harter, what's yours?"

"Scott Jackson, Mr. Harter. No, sir, I ain't ever milked a cow," he answered straightforwardly.

The rancher smiled at this response. "Do you know what a roustabout is?" he asked.

"Yes, sir," Scott responded politely.

"Well, I pay twenty dollars a month and keep, but you're gonna have to learn how to milk a cow, ride a horse, drive a truck and shovel manure. Are you up to that?"

"Yes, sir."

"My place is forty miles south of here; we'll head out as soon as the wagon is loaded."

With harvest over, Scott went to work on John Harter's cattle ranch near Fargo. Although he had never ridden a horse, nor milked a cow, he was about to learn how to do both.

Hard work, however, was never a guarantee he would earn the money he needed to buy the car he wanted. He worked six days a week from daylight to dark, for the twenty dollars a month, as promised by the rancher.

However, on Sunday, he was off, and each weekend, with a horse to ride, he explored a different part of this huge ranch. He hated the bitter cold in the wintertime. Still, he loved the openness of the Midwestern countryside and was often amazed at the spectacular distances one could see over the low rolling hills. John Harter taught him to hunt game and frequently he returned to the cookhouse with a goose, wild turkey, or the occasional antelope.

At first, Scott was not sure he made a wise choice. *Perhaps*, he thought, *I should have gone home with my friends*. Yet there was nothing there for him. He was sure his family would not miss him. With him gone, it would be one less mouth to feed. There was no girlfriend at home. During this past year in the Dakotas, he became acquainted with more young women at the Saturday night barn dances than he ever met in his hometown—so much for learning about the opposite sex in a school managed by the Church.

In the fall of 1929, Scott climbed aboard a westbound freight and made himself comfortable in an open boxcar. He was going home. The train was due to leave Fargo the next morning. Shortly after midnight, awakened by a solid kick aimed at his back, he yelled a curse at the perpetrator, when a second man grabbed him by the hair and began dragging him toward the open door of the rail car. As he struggled to get up, the man that kicked him grabbed his legs and the two men literally threw him from the boxcar out onto the ground. Quickly regaining his feet, he was about to challenge the two when the first man, jumping down from the open car, barked, "You're under arrest, punk."

Scott was about to take a swing at the man but froze in place upon hearing those words; he knew better than to attack a cop, even a railroad cop. The two men were dressed in dirty gray business suits, with vests, striped shirts, string ties, and wide-brimmed Stetson hats. Both wore cowboy boots and leather gloves.

The larger of the two carried a baton; the other man gripped a small, heavy weapon, covered with leather, with an attached thong. This was something that Scott had not seen before. He had heard about it, however, from other field hands. Some suffered the misfortune of being on the receiving end of such a weapon wielded by a yard bull. Farm hands told him it could lay a man out without leaving so much as a scratch on his body.

"Let's see some identification, kid," the older man demanded. Jackson, breathing heavily, with hands trembling took out his wallet and showed them his high school Student Identification Card and track and football letter certificates. Then, taking a letter from his jacket pocket that he received from his mother, he unfolded it and handed it to the older of the two railroad men. The younger man laughed at this, suddenly grabbing the wallet from Scott's hands.

"What else have you got in there, Sonny Boy?" he snarled as he began to search through the wallet. Finding three one-dollar bills, he asked, "Where's the rest of your money? In your boots? Get 'em off!" he demanded.

Bending down to untie his boots, Scott uttered a curse, "You bastards, professional policemen don't rob people… You're just a couple of crooks."

Out of the corner of his eye, he saw the smaller of the two, as the man swung the sap toward his head. He tried to dodge the blow but the flat side of the weapon caught him just below his right eye; before he crumpled unconscious onto the ground he heard the man laugh.

Thrown into a cage on the back of a model-T Ford truck, he regained consciousness shortly before being booked into the Fargo City Jail on a charge of vagrancy. The following day, Scott went before a local magistrate, which resulted in a conviction in a hearing that lasted less than a minute. The judge gave him an option, a 100-dollar fine, or ten days in the local lockup.

There were more than a dozen others caught up in these same circumstances. Yet Scott fared better than most. Although the right side of his face was black and blue and an eye swollen shut, he still had his summer's wages. Before boarding the freight car, he concealed eight crumpled twenty-dollar bills in the lining of his coat. The two railroad dicks missed his stash.

He worked off his sentence by digging ditches for the City Water Department. It was hard work, yet the ten days passed quickly. Within hours of his release, he was again on his way home on another westbound train; if everything went according to plan he would be home in time for Christmas.

Arriving in Seattle in December of 1929, he found little change within his family, yet evidence of the October stock market collapse was everywhere. Stores were empty and the streets crowded with the unemployed. Men, some with their families, traveled throughout the city by wagon, or vintage truck, openly selling a lifetime's accumulation of personal goods.

Scott's father was more fortunate than most. Although disabled in the Great War, he continued his employment as a security guard at the local sawmill. However, the man earned barely enough to support his wife, Barbara, and daughter, Elizabeth. "Beth," at eighteen, was in her final year at Holy Names Academy, a Catholic high school for girls.

Scott's mother took in laundry and cleaned homes on Queen Anne Hill, an upscale residential area near the center of town. The woman, a devout Catholic, insisted that her children receive a religious education. To pay their tuition, she worked as janitress on the weekend in the two schools her children attended.

The older man was not pleased that his teenage son was back in town, without funds and without a job. After three days, Scott said his good-byes to his mother and sister and left his parents' home. He joined thousands of other unemployed tradesmen, hobos, and drifters who roamed the streets of the city sleeping in abandoned buildings, tar paper shacks, or empty boxcars near Union Station. Now and then, he found shelter at one of the Skid Road missions and occasionally at a job site.

One evening in January, he stopped by Tanaka's store to see his old high school friend, Kenji. He found the young man in the back of the store off loading a produce truck. Peewee greeted him with a smile and huge bear hug.

"Scott, where the heck have you been? I've been looking all over town for you," he said. "I called everybody I could think of. Beth told me you were sleeping at one of the missions—what's going on?"

"I'm doing okay, Kenji; don't worry about me. What about you; are you going to school?"

"Yeah, I'm a sophomore; I'm in the Civil Engineering School at the university. Everything is just fine."

"Are your folks okay?"

"They're fine. Dad put a little money away before the stock market went belly up and he still has a good business—people have to eat. I work on the weekends; I hit the books pretty heavy during the week. But things are going good for me; what about you, are you okay?"

"I'm fine, Kenji," Scott responded quietly. "I just haven't had much luck finding a job."

"I know—it's pretty bad; Dad laid everyone off. He and Mom and my sisters manage the store. What about your family?"

"They're okay—they all have a job; so they're better off than a lot of others."

"Good. Hey, let's go get a beer and talk. I'll take the truck." The two men got into the now empty produce truck and Kenji drove to a waterfront bar.

"You look healthy, Scotty. You look like you put some meat on your bones. North Dakota must have been good to you. Was it?"

"Yes, it was in a way, but there's no work there; but I think it's worse here, Kenji."

"Yes, I've seen it. There must be thirty or forty thousand people downtown looking for work."

The two former schoolmates chatted back and forth for more than four hours, with Kenji filling Scott in on the antics and travels of their high school friends.

"Corky is still at Notre Dame, and Addison and McGinnes are second-year students at the university. I see them on occasion if we happen to have classes in the same building," Kenji said.

Although Peewee made no mention of it, once the three friends entered the university's social arena, Kenji's Japanese ancestry became an automatic bar to many of the events attended by the predominantly white student body.

Reflecting back on their high school days, he smiled, adding, "Those were great times, Scott. I could not have had a better bunch of friends than you guys. Even my closest Japanese friends were envious of the rapport and camaraderie that existed between the five of us. Looking back on it, we did some damn foolish things though," he laughed. "Your rope trick with Bishop O'Dea's car tops anything that has ever been done to a priest, Buddhist or Catholic. Now, even my dad thinks it was funny, but at the time he beat the heck out of me."

Scott recalled the pure excitement and joy he experienced whenever the five young men succeeded in getting the upper hand on Brother John Alan with one of their juvenile pranks.

Both men laughed at Kenji's retelling of the rope trick, with Scott adding, "I didn't know you got whupped," he said, trying to still his laughter, "but I guess we all had it coming. And Corky's old man could have killed us all for what we did to his boat."

Changing the subject, Kenji asked, "Are you going to go on to school, Scott? What about the scholarship, is that gone?"

"No, I'm still not interested in school, Kenji. I'll find my niche someday, but right now I just need a job."

"What about fishing? Many of my friends have their own boats, and some make a good living, particularly those working in Alaska. Would you be interested?"

"I suppose I could try it. I'm at the point where I'll try almost anything."

"Okay," Kenji replied. "You're staying at my place tonight and tomorrow I'll talk to some of the guys at the Terminal."

One week later, Scott obtained a berth as a deckhand on board an Alaska-bound trawler. Robert Sato, a friend of the Tanaka family, was the captain; the other three members of the crew were also Japanese Americans. Working in the Gulf of Alaska fishing, Scott was surprised at the amount of money he earned during his first voyage. By the end of the season, he cleared over a 1,000 dollars.

Routinely, upon returning from Alaska, the boat tied up in Bellingham Bay, where the fishermen worked the waterfront selling fresh fish and crab. Both Chinook salmon and Alaska spider crab were in high demand. Buyers paid fifty cents for a large crab and up to a dollar for a whole salmon.

Their next stop was in the city of Everett, where they again set up their *Fresh Fish* sign. They sold nearly half their catch there before bypassing Seattle to stop in Tacoma.

Upon reaching homeport, the remaining supply of fish and crab went to a local cannery, farmer's market, or to the many fishmongers that frequented the waterfront. These men and women bought the last of their catch for distribution throughout the suburban areas and on to farming communities on the east side of the state. Some of the fish peddlers continued inland to Idaho and Montana. In 1930, miners in Idaho and Montana would pay up to two dollars for a large spider crab.

The following year, Northwest fishermen encountered problems trying to sell their catch. The city faced its most severe crisis since the Great War, where labor unions now battled each other and local businessmen for control of the maritime workforce. The longshoremen's strike had tied up the entire waterfront.

Entering the harbor, they found dockworkers picketing on nearly every pier. When they attempted to tie up below the fish market to offload their catch, the strikers threatened the crew. Outnumbered, and with a load of fish and crab that needed fresh ice, the captain decided to return to Fisherman's Terminal. Later, the men gave away most of the catch, dumping overboard what remained. Unfortunately, their earnings for the entire year were gone.

After that, Scott roamed the waterfront for days looking for work, without success. Disheartened, he returned to the boat, packed his belongings, and caught a streetcar for home.

Arriving at his parents' residence in the early afternoon, he was surprised to find the entire family at home. His father was listening to the news on the radio their son purchased for them the year before. His mother and sister Beth were in the kitchen—they were happy to see him, home again, safe and sound. In recent years, the violent storms in the Gulf of Alaska claimed the lives of a dozen young men from the Northwest. The Jackson family was thankful that their son was not among them.

"Look at you!" Scott exclaimed affectionately, embracing Elizabeth as she cuddled up to him. "You've grown up. You're beautiful."

"Hi, big brother," she replied, smiling, comfortable in his muscular arms as they hugged each other.

"You're gonna stay home now, aren't you, Scotty? Dad says you've sown your wild oats," she grinned, throwing a glance at her father. "So why not stay around? Everybody has been asking about you; even Amy. You ought to call her."

"You mean Freckles?" he laughed. "Last time I saw her she was just a kid."

Beth, now looking at her mother, responded seriously, "She's no kid now; you ought to see her." Mother Jackson smiled—she was pleased that her two children were home; they were a family once more.

Elizabeth Jackson, now nineteen years old, was a beautiful girl. She, too, was tall, nearly five foot ten, with long, curly black hair and flashing blue eyes. Her faded and worn homemade gingham dress did not detract from her appearance. While he was gone, his baby sister had developed into a fully grown young woman. She worked as a clerk for the City Water Department. Earlier in the day, her boss sent her home. The city administration expected local longshoremen were about to march on city hall. With the father working in a sawmill and a son who started out peddling the sheets on the waterfront when he was twelve years old, the Jackson family was fully cognizant of the impact a maritime industry strike could have upon their lives.

Many of those familiar with the history of the dockworkers believed the city administration precipitated this particular job action. Union leaders alleged that the police assaulted their members without provocation, when the longshoremen lawfully exercised their constitutional right to demonstrate. The local press ran one exposé after another supporting the union's charges; banner headlines accused the boys in blue of using excessive force.

Unfortunately, the administration, often at the behest of maritime officials, was not above using the police to thwart the unions' efforts to organize. In reprisal, members of the left-leaning West Coast Longshoremen's Union threatened to shut the city down.

That afternoon, fifty mounted police officers supported by over 200 foot patrolmen flooded the waterfront. Presumably, they were there to maintain the peace. However, it soon became apparent that the officers were there to move the strikers off the docks and out of the streets, by force if necessary.

After a minor clash on Pier Fifty-Four, Jerry Mulligan, the chief of police, chose to sweep the waterfront of anyone participating in the labor protest. Before the day was over, mounted officers began swinging their riot batons at anyone seen carrying a picket sign.

Despite the city's problems, Beth was delighted to have the day off; she looked forward to spending the entire day with her brother. That evening, she and Scott, along with her boyfriend, visited a waterfront bar across the street from the West Coast Coal Terminal.

From the front windows of the bar, they watched as the police moved against more than 200 striking dockworkers who blocked the entrance to the Black River Coal Company's loading dock. Several of the strikers fled into the bar to escape the charge of the mounted officers. Not all of them made it before feeling the sting of a riot baton. Patching up injured dockworkers was a well-practiced skill for the bartender; he was kept busy this evening.

Later that night, after Beth and her friend left for home, Scott, who was drinking heavily all day, got into a fight in the bar. The bartender called the police; when they arrived, the officers arrested Jackson for assault. The two striking dockworkers, who challenged the fisherman, needed emergency hospital treatment. On the way to the police precinct, one of the officers recognized their intoxicated passenger; he played football against Scott in high school.

"Your name's Jackson, isn't it?" the younger officer asked, shining his flashlight into the face of their prisoner.

"Yeah, so what?" Scott responded, disdainfully, wiping sweat and blood from his eyes with the back of his hand.

Ignoring their prisoner's ill-mannered reply, the cop responded, "You were one of the Gladiators from the class of twenty-eight, weren't you? I played ball against you guys. You guys were pretty damn good...but we beat your ass," he laughed.

Rather than booking him, the officers took the young man home. When they brought him to the front door, his sister, startled by Jackson's appearance, gasped, "My God, what happened?" Although her brother won the fight, the barroom brawl had taken its toll. With his shirt torn, his face bruised and bloodied, she could not believe what she saw.

"Patch him up, miss, and put him to bed," the older of the two cops advised, adding, "If he comes back out on the street tonight, he'll go to jail."

She assured the officers her brother would not be back on the street.

"Send your brother down to city hall when he's sober," the younger cop said, smiling. "We could use someone who can fight like he does."

Unexpectedly, the maritime labor unrest of the thirties provided job opportunities within the police service for several young men in the community.

Chapter 4

A week after his encounter with the two dockworkers, Scott stood in line at the Civil Service Department seeking employment with the city police force. In high school he was an excellent student; the entrance examination was not a problem for him. Two days later, after taking the oath of office from the City Comptroller, he, along with twenty other recruits, went to George Goldstein's uniform store. Here they purchased the necessary accouterments of a police officer.

"You'll look magnificent in this, Officer Jackson," Herman Goldstein assured his customer, as he measured and fit Scott's uniform blouse. "Of course you are rather thin, if you gain a little meat on those bones of yours, come back—we'll have the tailor make some adjustments."

Looking in the shop mirror, Scott thought he looked more like an overstuffed orca than an underweight cop. For the moment, however, he was not concerned with his appearance.

"How much is this outfit gonna cost?" he asked.

"Only five-dollars a month," the shopkeeper smiled, skillfully avoiding Scott's question. "Your credit will always be good here, so don't worry." Yet, the man was unable to hide the haughtiness of a business entrepreneur with an open-ended commitment from the city to equip all newly hired police officers.

"We'll take good care of you fellows," he promised, as he placed the uniform into a large bag and handed it off to his customer. "You come back now," he said with a smile, knowing these men had no place else to go for their uniform needs.

Carrying his new uniform in the large duffle bag, Jackson caught a streetcar to return to Police Headquarters. Reporting to the property clerk that same day, he picked up his badge, baton, twelve rounds of ammunition, and a .38-caliber Colt revolver. The following night, January 10, 1932, he reported for duty on the third watch. His supervisor teamed him up with an experienced patrol officer on a beat in Chinatown.

Patrol officer Jackson soon discovered that police work was not what he expected, nor was he prepared to handle the obligations the public imposed upon the men wearing the blue uniform. The fact that he neither understood nor trusted the police bothered him; he could not forget his brush with the law in North Dakota. Still, while so many of his friends were unemployed, he knew he was fortunate to have a job.

Within two weeks of donning the uniform he was once again back at his old high school alma mater, but this time there were no school books to master, no teacher to appease. Much to the annoyance of his former mentor and dean, Brother John Alan, his duties merely required him to keep the peace at a basketball game.

Brother John had not changed much. He was fifty-four years old now, but a little heavier than when Scott last saw the man. The black suit with its Roman collar could not hide the rotund body of this educator. His gray hair served to highlight the red flush of his face and double chin. Cheap red wine and a lack of physical exercise left their mark on the man's body.

Upon seeing Officer Jackson in his police uniform, the teacher was less than cordial toward his former pupil. In the presence of more than a score of gawking students, he lashed out.

"What in the devil are you doing in that uniform, Scott?" he snapped. "I thought you might wear prison garb some day, but I didn't expect to see you in a police uniform." The teaching

Brothers at O'Dea High School expected great things from this triple varsity athlete who maintained a near straight "A" scholastic record during his high school career.

Every parent understood the goal of the Christian Brothers who ran O'Dea High School with an iron fist; even though their sons may not have. In the short history of this educational institution, graduating seniors were expected to go on to college. Once they attained the higher degree, the school administration assumed that each would become a successful business executive or political leader within the community. "Those of you that don't measure up," as Brother John stated so succinctly, "will probably end up behind bars."

Three of Brother John's earlier students, one a former city police lieutenant, were presently serving time at McNeil Island Federal Penitentiary. Customs agents caught them running illegal liquor into the country from Canada.

Scott's frequent encounters in high school with Brother John left their mark. He had no fond memories of this smart-mouthed would-be priest, a derisive appellation bestowed upon the man by his students. In Jackson's mind, he was a poor example of a professional teacher. He was quick to lay a yardstick across a student's back if a boy came up short on a school assignment.

"Hello, Brother John," Scott responded, finding it difficult to be civil. "I would think you of all people would recognize that policemen provide a pretty valuable service to the community."

"Don't give me that, Scott," he snorted. "If you'd of put your mind to it you could have made something of yourself."

Jackson shot back, "What? You'd have me become a teacher so I could whack kids too, kids who can't defend themselves?"

Brother John's face turned beet red.

"Good day to you, Mr. Jackson," he snapped, then abruptly turned and walked away. It was apparent to Brother John that the Christian Brothers at O'Dea High School would have to look to someone else from the class of '28 for distinguished alumnus accolades.

Scott was soon to learn there were some unanticipated necessities that went with enforcing the law. Since leaving high school, he was free to come and go as he pleased. Now, however, less than three months into his new job, he found his freedom severely restricted. He worked a ten-hour shift, six nights a week, in a part of the city unknown to him. Yet, he grew up in this city. In high school, he and his friends explored all the mysterious places that the city fathers would just as soon have kept hidden. The managers of more than one speakeasy, burlesque theater, or whorehouse in Chinatown found it necessary to throw the boys out of their establishments. However, as a young man, Scott was not accustomed to visiting Skid Road hotels and the back alleys of his hometown in the middle of the night. Yet, now these haunts were as much a part of his beat as the fashionable avenues of the city.

Under the best of circumstances, a visit to one of these seedy businesses often involved an encounter with the sordid side of humanity. Arresting an alcoholic to protect him from himself, or a mentally disturbed person who ran amuck with a knife or gun, became routine. Helping the county coroner's staff carry a corpse down the back stairs of a flophouse in the middle of the night was never pleasant. At worst, when the victim had been dead for days, or weeks, the task became loathsome. When that occurred, Jackson and his partners routinely returned to the precinct for a shower, change of clothing and a strong drink.

There were many cold, wet nights ahead for this rookie. In spite of that, only once did he complain.

"What are we doing out here, Pete?" he asked his partner. "We're cold, and wet; at least the poor bastards we put in jail are warm and getting their two meals a day." He received little consolation in his colleague's response.

"You signed on, Scotty; you can always turn in your gear," Officer Homer "Pete" Petersen replied, unsympathetic to his partner's complaining. "But you'd better look around; you're getting a hundred bucks a month, while most of the folks you and I deal with don't have a damn nickel to their name."

As the weeks went by, Scott's attitude toward the police began to change; he became more comfortable and even encouraged by the unselfish response of his colleagues toward the thousands of hungry and homeless persons they encountered on the streets of his hometown. The officer's thoughtful and compassionate response to the needs of so many good people, unemployed, or down on their luck, was routine for this rooky policeman.

However, with the stock market crash of '29, police officers joined the rest of the American labor force in the search for the resources to feed their families. When available, they took odd jobs laying brick, repaired automobiles, or worked in carpentry shops, or at manual laborers' jobs. Several owned electrical, plumbing, or cabinet shops, operating out of a basement or backyard garage.

One officer, Ernest Woods, went right from his patrol car, six days a week, to labor as an iron worker at the Olympic Foundry. By 1932, the foundry laid off most of its employees but kept Officer Woods on as a security guard. The Foundry was one of the most successful businesses in the city, yet it too soon succumbed to the ravages of the Great Depression.

To his surprise, Scott's education and work experience before joining the force was somewhat different from his fellow officers. Very few of the older men graduated from high school. Many served with the Army during the Great War; others worked in local plants as skilled tradesmen before joining the department. Unlike Scott, most of these men were married with families and they found it very difficult to make ends meet financially.

As time went on, Scott also began to feel more positive about most of his police superiors in their endeavor to make the city a safer place in which to live. Yet, he could not forget the hostile environment he encountered from two representatives of the law enforcement profession while in the Dakotas. Those appalling events now clearly influenced his day-to-day police decisions. Whenever forced to take into custody someone for a minor transgression of society's rules, his partner often marveled at Jackson's patience. Scott would do whatever he could to get the transgressor into a Skid Road Mission or Salvation Army facility for assistance rather than booking the person at City Prison.

During the Depression, this was a continuing challenge for a beat officer. Large signs posted at city hall and in other public buildings, and in and around the entryway to restaurants and business firms, clearly informed everyone that "vagrants" were not welcome. Nor were the unemployed who sold apples, wood carvings, or knickknacks on the street corners to survive embraced by the city. Jackson's sergeant was quick to notice any encroachment by these persons into the realm of the successful businessman. It was the beat officer's task to see that street vendors did not set up shop in competition with nearby merchants. Early on, Scott was brought to task on this issue.

"Damn you, Jackson!" his sergeant cursed, "Get that riffraff out of here. What d'you think the city hired you to do? It sure as hell wasn't to stand around picking your nose. You get this damn beat cleaned up and keep it that way, or I'll have your ass up before the man."

"Yes, sir," Scott replied, dismayed by his superior's tone of voice and deprecating remarks. "But most of these guys aren't a problem, Sergeant," he added quietly. "They're just looking for—"

"Don't you tell me what they're doing," his sergeant growled, cutting him off sharply. "I can see that with my own eyes. They're pissing in the alleys and throwing their crap all over the streets. Now you get off your ass and move them out of here, or you're off the beat."

His boss was Sergeant Frank Manley, a tall, lean, red-faced Irish cop, with more than twenty years' service. Always impeccably dressed in what was obviously a professionally tailored uniform, his spit-shined brogans, polished daily by the bootblack on the corner, set him apart from other cops on the beat. Nevertheless, Jackson's first impression of the man was not unlike that of his fellow officers, they thought he was "an arrogant son of a bitch, overimpressed with his own importance."

One night while on patrol, Jackson's partner Pete Petersen saw movement inside a local jewelry store. "Look sharp, kid," he said, grabbing Jackson by the coat sleeve. "We've got somebody inside," he whispered, reaching for his weapon. The interior of the store was dark, but there appeared to be someone, possibly a lookout, standing near the front window. Although nearly obscured by darkness, Scott caught a glimpse of a shiny object on the darkened figure. When the intruder moved, the object reflected light from the dim glow of a streetlamp across from the store.

"I see him, Pete," Scott replied quietly as the two men hurried toward the store.

"Watch it, Scotty," Petersen cautioned. "There may be more than one inside."

The two officers quickly separated, initiating a procedure both men had participated in many times over the past two years. Jackson took up a position in the dark, just outside the front entrance, and Petersen, with gun drawn, hurried toward the alley.

The plan required the officer who entered the darkened alley to announce his presence in a loud voice. With any luck, the thieves usually attempted escape through the front door of the business. Thus the unsuspecting culprits generally came out onto a lighted street, into the hands of a waiting officer. It did not always happen that way, for there was no telling what a thief would do once trapped inside his victim's premises.

Within seconds of Petersen entering the alley, Jackson heard three quick gunshots. He looked into the store, but could not see any movement. Racing to the rear of the building, he called out, "Pete, where are you?" There was no response.

He cautiously entered the darkened corridor; when quite suddenly from the far end of the alley, he saw the flash from two or three weapons being fired in his direction. Jackson froze, he did not realize that he was targeted until it was too late; this was his first encounter with an armed assailant who was now trying to kill him. Suddenly, something hit him in the face near his left eye and he went down on his knees. The firing continued and he could hear the whine of bullets ricocheting off the brick wall above his head. While still on his knees, he returned fire. Yet, he could not see anyone, only the bright flashes from the assailants' weapons in the distance.

Jackson survived this violent encounter; unfortunately, Pete Petersen was not so lucky. The older officer, shot three times in the back, died before an ambulance arrived. The bullet that struck Scott fractured his cheekbone and tore away flesh. Extensive skin grafts over the next several months were necessary to repair the damage.

In May, Jackson received a call from Kenji Tanaka inviting him to attend his graduation exercises at the university. Peewee graduated summa cum laude, with a degree in civil engineering, and received multiple job offers. He accepted employment with the State Department of Transportation in bridge design and highway construction. After the ceremony, the Tanaka family invited Kenji's former O'Dea High School friends who attended the graduation to a party at their store in Japantown. Scott, Paul Addison, Mark McGinnes, and Corky Shay attended the traditional Japanese celebration, honoring Mr. and Mrs. Tanaka's firstborn child. Mrs. Tanaka and her daughters served what Kenji described was a traditional Japanese/American dish, steak and lobster, along with heaping bowls of white rice and a special dish, nigiri zushi (rice balls and fish). The family also provided abundant amounts of sake, the traditional Japanese rice wine, and American Scotch whiskey.

With the festivities continuing into the early morning hours, the district beat officers dropped by to investigate. Mrs. Tanaka insisted that they stay to eat, telling Scott to invite all of his friends from the precinct.

"This looks more like a policeman's ball than a graduation celebration," Scott commented to Kenji. "Peewee, these guys will eat your parents out of house and home."

"Don't worry about it, Scott," Kenji laughed. "My folks are happy to see policemen; in this business they have to deal with some pretty nasty customers. Mom doesn't remember much about Japan. She was only a teenager when they left, but neither Dad nor Mom has too many good memories about the Japanese police."

"Will they ever go back?" Scott inquired, curious about the background of his friend's family.

"They'd like to. They came from Osaka, and my grandparents still live there. If my job turns out okay, I might take them back. I would like to see Japan. As you can guess, growing up in this part of town, we've heard a lot about it, and all of us can speak Japanese."

"That would be a great trip, Kenji. I hope you can go."

"It would be nice, there's a cruise ship out of San Francisco to the Orient; it sails once or twice a month. I'll have to check it out."

Jackson remained on the Chinatown beat for nearly five years. Since Kenji's graduation, he had seen little of his old high school friends. Kenji moved out of the city and the others were preoccupied with their own careers. Promoted to sergeant in 1937, Scott later moved on to the detective division, where he received a second promotion in 1939, this time to the rank of lieutenant. In February, he assumed command of the Homicide Squad's night watch.

"Our kids did great this year, Coach, congratulations."

"Not bad, Father Joe," Scott smiled as the two men shook hands after dinner in the hall at Saint Anthony Church.

"Eleven out of twelve games, Scotty, I'd say that's darn good. Our kids earned this honor," Father Joe Roberts, the parish priest, responded, as the two men returned to the dining room where the West Side Italian Club members were busy clearing tables. Saint Anthony's eighth grade basketball team, the Spartans, coached by Jackson, took the All City Championship; tonight, the Italian Club honored the team and their coach at the club's annual banquet.

After the children and their parents headed off for home, more than a dozen friends of the Coach and Father Joe gathered around one of the tables for a drink. In the conversations that followed, the discussions quickly turned to the war in Europe. An intense argument soon ensued over this raging conflict, with one of the men commenting, "We ought to let that bunch over there kill each other off."

Rick Blanchard, a member of the Italian Club's Board of Officers, trying to mollify some of the more injudicious participants in this spirited discussion, took the middle ground. "I don't think that'll happen. The war will soon be over; both sides are nearly exhausted," he offered. "Without help, Russia can't possibly recover and Germany won't survive another winter. They'll have to quit." He sounded rather convincing.

"I'm not so sure you're right, Rick," Father Joe responded with a grimace, shaking his head; showing a concern for a war which he believed could easily spin out of control. "Roosevelt may have the country into the war by forty-two, or forty-three at the latest. I think it all depends upon how England and Russia fare. I don't think Great Britain can hold out much longer, even if the US continues to provide assistance." This was something these men did not want to hear—many of their sons were of draft age.

To Jackson, the war in Europe was the least of his problems. From his perspective, this past year was a disaster. His love life, as he told his friend Detective Lieutenant Bobby Hart, was a complete shambles. He had been studying for promotion and the long hours did no go over well with his girlfriend, Amy Donahue. The two had dated one another for more than two years; when he proposed, she accepted, they planned to be married in May. However, on more than one occasion he broke a date with her at the last minute. After a fifty- to sixty-hour workweek, combined with his coaching responsibilities, there was little time for the social amenities demanded of his fiancée. When he did not show for a dinner party with Amy and her parents, she broke off their engagement. Now it did not appear that she was interested in rekindling their love affair. For months, he tried to win her back, but she was not of a mind to forgive him for the way he treated her and her family.

Although Amy continued to be cordial and appeared to enjoy their occasional evening together, it was apparent that she had other interests—they did not include her former lover. Scott admitted this worried him. He did not want to lose her; he had just lost his partner, Detective Oscar Johnson, to retirement. He and Johnson worked together for more than five years; now he felt quite alone. Johnson's departure bothered him more than he liked to admit. He believed the city lost whom he considered to be the most knowledgeable and competent investigator the Northwest ever produced. However, the senior detective was not only his mentor; he became a close friend. Now, with Amy Donahue gone, this was a troublesome time for this lonely young police officer.

Shortly after Detective Johnson retired, the chief of police ordered the chief of detectives to reopen the Masterson case. Masterson, a police captain, commanded the Columbia City Police Precinct before leaving the department under a cloud of suspicion. Several of his colleagues believed that he killed his family before he left the force.

In 1939, Masterson's wife and two daughters disappeared from the family home in West Seattle. Reportedly, the man put his family onboard a train bound for San Diego, where they were to visit Mrs. Masterson's sister and her family. Yet, the police could never show that the family ever boarded the train for California, let alone arrived at their destination. There were few leads to follow and the two detectives found no trace of the missing family, or evidence sufficient to charge anyone with a crime relating to their disappearance.

Nevertheless, based upon the physical evidence found in the family home and interviews with dozens of witnesses, Lieutenant Jackson and Detective Johnson suspected that Masterson killed his wife and their children. Shortly after their disappearance, the man resigned his commission and moved to California, allegedly to look for his wife and daughters. He since moved on to Mexico, where he was no longer available to answer questions about their disappearance. Still the Chief of Police wanted the case settled with a suspect in jail before he retired.

Jackson knew the chances of solving the case were about one in a million. He was in fact looking for a miracle, knowing such things seldom happened in the real world. However, no matter how bizarre the case, he knew the public often expected the police to unravel the most enigmatic of schemes that a criminal mind might conjure up. The officer smiled when he thought how even here at Saint Anthony's they expected minor miracles. When classes began in September, the school principal, Sister Superior Margaret Ann, asked him to solve what she maintained was a serious criminal offense. Apparently, it became almost a weekly occurrence at the school.

During his lunch break one day, Jackson drove over to discuss the "crime" with Sister Margaret Ann. By the time he arrived, most of the school's 500 youngsters, finished with lunch, scurried off to the playground. However, several of the older children knew the Coach, and their curiosity got the best of them. They quickly gathered outside the principal's office, only to be shooed away by one of the nuns.

"Good afternoon, Mr. Jackson," Sister Margaret Ann greeted her visitor, "I see you have several fans among our student body."

"Good afternoon, Sister," he smiled, greeting her cordially. "They're a great bunch of kids, aren't they?"

"Yes, some of them are," she acknowledged, apparently reluctant to grant such appellation to the entire student body. She flashed a disagreeable glance at the young boys who, lingering nearby, were trying to learn what business their coach may have with the school principal.

"I'm glad to see you today, Lieutenant," she said, addressing him formally. "Our latest crime occurred just hours ago. It has forced the closure of two of our classrooms."

"I'm sorry to hear that, Sister," Scott offered sympathetically.

"I think you'll understand, Lieutenant, just how serious this crime is if you will accompany me to the boys' lavatory."

He agreed and the woman led the way from her office, accompanied by six other nuns, who fell in behind them as they made there way to the boys' lavatory. Once inside the toilet facility, it did not take long for this experienced detective to unravel Sister Margaret Ann's crime problem. Stopping by the lavatory shortly before classes convened, a group of older boys routinely pulled a water pipe loose from an overhead water closet. About every fifteen minutes, the tank filled and flushed automatically. With the pipe disconnected, the water flowed not into the urinal, but out onto the floor, across the hall and into the classrooms. Consequences were quite predictable; the boys forced the closure of the classroom for an hour, sometimes two, until the janitors cleaned up the mess.

"I reasoned that if we could just put a little 'detective powder' on the plumbing, we would be able to get to the bottom of this," the woman offered. "I read about this, Lieutenant, in a *True Detective* magazine. It can only be seen under ultraviolet light," she said, as if eager to let this police officer know she was not entirely ignorant of the criminal investigator's craft.

While she was describing the gravity of the crime, Scott was watching the other nuns as they stood nearby. Dressed in their black and white habits, they reminded him of penguins at the zoo—looking him over closely, nodding in agreement with every word spoken by their superior. He wondered, if he were not a police officer, would they have been here in the boys' lavatory with him? Probably not. They were obviously protecting Sister Margaret from some dire fate that may befall her should she go unaccompanied to the boys' toilet with a strange man, particularly a police officer.

He was amused, however; it was not every day that a detective came to investigate such a daring misdeed as was occurring here. He smiled; finally, here was a crime that even he could solve.

Before the week was over, the nuns at Saint Anthony were convinced of his expertise. Scott asked Officer George Anderson to drop by the school. Officer Anderson operated a small plumbing business out of his garage. Within a couple hours, the man completed the necessary repairs—policemen could handle minor miracles, after all.

Scott woke up early, fixed himself a cup of strong black coffee, and began to shave. He had a splitting headache which he attributed to too many glasses of wine, along with Father Joe's Scotch at the Italian Club dinner. Today of all days, he needed his wits about him. Once again, he was going to ask Amy Donahue to marry him, but he needed to get the cobwebs out of his head and butterflies out of his stomach. He was to pick her up at four o'clock. The two of them were to take in a movie and then go on to dinner.

Joe Donahue, a successful civil attorney, pampered his only daughter, Amy, from the day she was born. Money was not a problem. The girl attended the best of schools and enjoyed the luxuries available to those with ample resources. This included frequent Caribbean cruises, trips to Hawaii or Palm Springs, and the opportunity to hobnob with the Hollywood set at Sun Valley. Yet, she wanted more.

The lavish displays of wealth exhibited by some of her friends did not impress Miss. Donahue. She found many in her age group, raised under similar circumstances, to be quite shallow people. They seemed to have no desire, ambition, or aspiration in life other than to take over "Daddy's" business, or inherit the family fortune. Amy was not interested in either of these two prospects.

Accepted into law school at the university, she used her father's influential position as a member of the University Board of Regents to gain entrance into the Naval Recruit Officers Training Course.

When Joe Donahue heard about this, he exploded. "Amy, what the hell are you thinking of?" he screamed. "Women should not be a member of a military organization, that's a man's job."

"You're wrong, Daddy. Look at what's happening today in Russia and China; women are serving right alongside men in both the Army and the Navy. Why should we be different?"

"This is outrageous!" he growled. "The Navy is no place for a woman. They will put you on a ship somewhere in the middle of the damn ocean. You don't belong there."

"Daddy, I'm going to be a lawyer, I'm sure the Navy will find a use for my services someplace besides aboard ship," she replied, attempting to calm her father's fears for the well-being of his only daughter.

Joe Donahue lost all around; when Amy graduated from high school, he planned for his daughter to attend the Ivy League school of her choice, but when she refused to leave her hometown, he relented. Still, he vehemently opposed her enlistment in the NROTC—yet Amy prevailed. Whatever the future held for her, she alone would be the mistress of her own destiny. Graduating from law school in 1941, near the top of her class, she received a commission as an ensign in the United States Naval Reserve; Joe Donahue was proud of his baby daughter.

For a moment, Scott thought he misunderstood what he heard on the radio. Then the announcer repeated himself, "The Japanese have attacked Pearl Harbor."

They're all nuts, he thought, *who in his right mind would attack a place where the Navy maintains such a huge naval presence?* Yet there was no misunderstanding the seriousness of the broadcast. He turned the dial on the radio; every station that came on was broadcasting bulletins about the attack. Every four or five minutes they would report details of the attack, repeatedly broadcasting the same information.

Shortly after lunch, Scott's mother called to see if he heard the news. She was, as always, worried about her only son. He tried to reassure her that the attack was probably not as serious as the broadcasts indicated. Nevertheless, the woman was concerned that her boy may follow his father's example. In 1917, Scott's father left his young family to fend for themselves; he enlisted in the US Army. His departure changed their lives forever. Scott's mother ended the conversation with the admonition, "Don't you do anything foolish, Scotty."

Within the hour, Amy Donahue called to cancel their date; ordered by the Navy to report for duty, she was on her way to the

Sand Point Naval Air Station. "I'm sorry, Scott," she said. "I can't go to the movies, and dinner's out of the question."

"That's crazy, Amy," he protested, clearly annoyed by this turn of events. "Pearl Harbor is three thousand miles away. They can take care of themselves. What the devil is the Navy thinking of?" he asked scornfully.

"I don't have time to argue with you, Scott, I've got to go."

"No, don't do that," he exclaimed, but she never heard his response.

Later, his next-door neighbor Dan Kaufman came over and Jackson broke out a bottle of Scotch. The two of them spent the remainder of the day listening to follow-up broadcasts about the attack.

After losing his wife and only child in a traffic accident, Kaufman, at forty-four, never remarried. In 1918, he, as a young man, served in France with the American Expeditionary Force.

"I'd go again," he said, "but at my age, I don't think they would take me."

Jackson was curious. "Why the heck would you do that?" he asked, surprised by Kaufman's statement. "Surely two or three years in the Army would be enough for one lifetime."

"No, Scott," he replied, shaking his head. "My outfit never saw action; I was a mechanic in an ordinance company. That's what I do today. I never did find out how I would react to someone shooting at me."

"Who, in his right mind needs that, Dan?" Scott asked, perplexed by his friend's comment. "You can read about that, nobody wins in those situations."

"You know all about that, Scott," Kaufman replied, obviously confounded by his friend's comment. "People have tried to kill you and you responded very appropriately, but I'll never know if I possess the same courage. Maybe I would turn and run. Some of our people did that in France. Who knows?" he said reflectively as he poured himself another drink.

"No, Dan, you wouldn't turn and run," Scott replied, persuasively. "I know you probably better than you know yourself. Men like you just don't do that. You'd do the right thing."

Yet Jackson was not so sure it would be that easy. It was one thing to try to defend yourself as a police officer, but it was quite another, he thought, when the object of war was to kill as many of your enemies as you could before they killed you.

He could not sleep that night. He knew he had drunk too much and that was part of the problem. However, that old feeling about a police officer's worth and his standing in society kept coming back to haunt him.

He remembered that when he first went to work on the police department, he did not particularly like cops. He found others who felt the same way. Many believed they were the dregs of society, hired by the rich to keep the poor, the black, the Indians and Chinamen in their place. Just where that place was, he never found out.

Once again, plagued by the thought that he was not even capable of accomplishing the simple tasks required of a police officer, he did not know where to turn. This was something he had not experienced since he first came to work on the force. Could it be, he wondered, that he wasn't qualified to do the job that he'd been hired to do? Yet, by the time Detective Johnson retired, his superiors considered Scott to be a superb investigator; after all, the police department provided him the best teacher the department had to offer. Still, since his mentor's departure from the force, Jackson's squad had yet to solve a major case and the Masterson investigation haunted him.

Thinking about that case, he muttered, "Oh God! Maybe I wasn't cut out to be a policeman." Detective Johnson and his former boss, Chief Inspector Donald Swenson, were the most professional police officers he'd ever known. He knew he could never attain the investigative skills of Johnson, or the police expertise of the chief inspector.

On Monday, December 8, he did not go to work, choosing instead to stay close to home listening to the radio. He was hoping to hear from Amy Donahue; she did not call. Later that morning, sitting alone in his living room, he listened to President Roosevelt's address to the Congress of the United States. He thought it the most impassioned speech he ever heard. When the President said, "I ask that the Congress declare that a State of War exists between the United States of America and the Empire of Japan..." it sounded like a call to arms. More precisely, to Scott, it sounded like a personal invitation from the President of the United States of America to join what undoubtedly would be the great crusade of his lifetime. This was an invitation he could not ignore. Before the President ended his address to Congress and to the nation, Police Lieutenant Scott Jackson made up his mind—he would join the military service.

Arriving at the United States Navy and Marine Corps recruiting office at two o'clock in the afternoon, he found that there were over 300 others with similar intentions. They were crowded into the lobby and inner offices of the building, awaiting their turn to enlist.

Much to his surprise, in this crowd of young men he counted more than fifty police officers. Most were patrol officers. He recognized several from the precinct but did not know those from the outlying stations. There were more than a dozen detectives, and a few sergeants already standing in line; he knew these men. Nearly all were younger than he was, but several were over forty years old. He wondered if the military would take the older officers.

At the far end of the lobby, he recognized a group of former O'Dea High School students. Among them, Paul Addison and Mark McGinnes, two members of the old Gladiator group from the class of '28. Since graduation, on occasion, Scott would receive a note from his high school friends, but this was the first time he had seen any of them in more than a year.

Police officers are a close-knit group; they travel in different circles, so the story goes. Yet the reality of it is that police officers lose track of their close friends, simply because of the hours the cop works. Saturday, Sunday or a holiday are just another workday for most harness bulls.

"Hello, Paul, Mark, I figured I might see you guys here," he offered with a smile as the three men exchanged handshakes.

"Hi, Scotty! You got the bug too?" Mark McGinnes exclaimed as he grabbed Jackson in a bear hug. "I thought you'd go Army."

"I did too, Scott," responded Paul Addison. "Your Dad was Army, wasn't he?"

"Yeah, but the Marines have a prettier uniform," Jackson responded with a grin.

"Don't give us that, Scott," McGinnes replied, "knowing you, you've got it all figured out. You guys will be in the middle of it with the Japs before the Army gets their act together."

"No, Dad was very proud of the Army, I just thought I'd do something different."

While at the university, both Addison and McGinnes enrolled in the NROTC program and, upon completion of their four-year commitment to the Navy, remained in the Reserves. Both men were pilots. If they passed their medical examination today, they too would report immediately for duty; they would join Amy Donahue at Sand Point Naval Air Station.

Jackson now found that he had little in common with his former friends. Paul Addison became a rich man operating a commercial real-estate business. He took full advantage of those caught up in the Depression; many of the unemployed found it necessary to sell their homes in order to feed their families. Addison handled dozens of these sales.

Mark McGinnes, starting out as a junior partner in Joe Donahue's law firm, was now a prominent civil attorney. Corky Shay, another member of the old Gladiator group, following his father's example became an architect, with his own thriving business. None of Scott's friends disappointed the Brothers at O'Dea. Nor was Scott a disappointment to his former colleagues.

Through the press, they kept track of their erstwhile classmate. Since joining the force, Jackson was the subject of a dozen headline stories, including the shootings in Chinatown in 1933. In 1936, he was involved in another gun battle, this time with two bank robbers who had taken hostages. Cornering the two culprits in an abandoned building, a team of detectives led by Jackson killed both men. In 1939, he was the lead investigator in the kidnapping of a child, which led to the arrest of the suspects who had killed their young victim.

Press coverage was extensive this past year. Scott made the front pages of all three newspapers because of his work in the Masterson investigation. It was not favorable. The media questioned the integrity of the police brass, and the expertise of the lead investigator in the case. Scott, however, had his supporters. His staunchest fans were his childhood friends from O'Dea High School. In "Letters to the Editor," his friends challenged the news media in these most recent attacks upon their former colleague.

Before moving off to their respective examination rooms, the three men engaged in small talk. Reminiscing for a few moments, Scott found that neither man had lost his sense of humor. He laughed when reminded of the shenanigans they had pulled off at O'Dea High School. Along with Corky Shay and Peewee Tanaka, the school had not since seen the likes of these former students.

"In case you hadn't heard, Corky joined the Army," Paul Addison added as he and McGinnes moved off with a group of naval reserve officers into the medical examination room. "He's to report in at Fort Ord, California."

"No, I hadn't heard. Wherever he goes, Corky will do just fine," he responded. "What have you heard about Peewee?"

"Nothing," Paul Addison said, shaking his head. "You knew he took his folks on a trip to Japan, didn't you?"

"Yes, but I haven't talked to anyone in the family," Scott replied. "I figured he would be back by now."

"No. I think there is a problem there. I talked to his sister a month ago; she said Immigration held up their return. She hired an attorney to find out what was going on."

"My God!" Scott exclaimed, "How will they get back now?"

"They won't, Scott; not now." Mark McGinnes responded, shaking his head. McGinnes spoke with some authority on the subject, having represented several immigrants in Federal Court in recent years. "They'd better pray for a short war. We have to go, Scotty. Good luck to you."

"Same to you, Mark, take care of yourself."

"Good-bye, Scotty," Paul Addison said, shaking Scott's hand. "Brother John would be proud of us," he offered with a grin as he followed Mark McGinnes. "It looks like the class of twenty-eight will be well represented in the United States military service."

Just as a group of twenty or thirty would-be enlisted men were lining up for their medical exams, Scott spotted a young boy he knew quite well. It was his former partner's son, James Michael "Mickey" Johnson. He was only sixteen years old. The boy was in the tenth grade at West Seattle High School. It was obvious the youngster had seen his father's former partner; he quickly turned away, trying to avoid Jackson. Stepping out of line, Scott tapped the young man on the shoulder.

"Hello, Mickey," he said, offering a friendly smile.

"Hello, Mr. Jackson." The boy looked stricken, clearly upset that he was discovered here by his father's best friend. "You won't tell Dad, will you?" he blurted out, loud enough for those standing nearby to hear.

"No, Mickey, I won't, but, before the Marines will take you, you'll have to tell him. He will have to sign for you. At your age you can't get in without your Dad's okay."

"I had my birth certificate changed," he replied, appearing quite proud of this accomplishment.

"Don't use that, Mickey." Jackson responded, "Tell your dad. He'll sign, but I'm sure he'll want you to finish high school first."

The intense interest shown by those close enough to hear this somewhat animated conversation amused Scott. It was rather obvious to this cop that several others standing in line here today did not meet the required seventeen-year age minimum.

Chapter 5

It was mid morning when Jackson got off the train at Union Station in San Diego. He was one of more than 300 men and boys arriving from the Northwest who enlisted in the United States Marine Corps that second week of December, 1941. As promised, a Marine Corps representative was on hand to greet their newest members.

The recruits, some dressed in suits, others in jeans or corduroy pants and jackets, with a sprinkling of blue coveralls, ranged in age from sixteen to thirty years. Many of them carried a small suitcase, but more than one had stuffed everything they owned into a blanket roll carried over their shoulder. During the early days of the Great Depression, Scott remembered seeing hundreds of similarly dressed men riding the rails as they crisscrossed the country looking for work.

The Marine Corps' representative that met their train was dressed in a khaki shirt and green trousers, with matching garrison cap. To these young recruits he looked more like a sumo wrestler than a representative of the United States Marine Corps—he was Sergeant William J. Sutton. He was a short, powerfully built, barrel-chested man. He appeared to be in his late twenties or early thirties. Billy Sutton was only five feet seven inches tall, but when he weighed in at the Marine Corps Wrestling Team's facilities, he tipped the scales at 180 pounds. However, unlike the sumo wrestlers, there was very little fat on this man's body.

When he moved, one could see the flexing of muscle through his skintight, highly starched khaki shirt. Three razor-edged vertical creases, finely sewn into the back of his shirt, stretched to the breaking point. His garrison cap, crown-indented, fore and aft, sat at an angle over his right ear; this, along with the spit-shined shoes, was the trademark of a seagoing Marine. Born on the Yakima Indian Reservation in Central Washington, he liked to tell his fellow Marine drill instructors that his mother was the great-granddaughter of Chief Kamaiakan of the Yakimas. After the Indian uprisings in the Oregon Territories in the 1800s, the US Army relocated his great-grandmother's family onto the sprawling Yakima Indian Reservation in Oregon Territory. The woman's father was a white man; he was a member of the United States Cavalry—his company traveled cross-country from Montana to the Territory to put down the short-lived insurrection.

Sutton's mother and father were both born on the reservation, his father serving with the United States Army Cavalry in the Great War. In 1930, when Billy Sutton was sixteen years old, he joined the Marine Corps. This Yakima Marine was proud of both his Indian heritage and the family's history of military service.

"Line up, you jack-offs!" the sumo wrestler yelled. "Three lines along the platform; move it, now!"

This was the first and only words of greeting the 300-odd Marine recruits would receive from a representative of the United States military this warm December morning in the city of San Diego.

Startled by the man's obviously hostile tone of voice and apparent dissatisfaction with these would-be Marines, several recruits, now gawking at the short man in the green and khaki uniform, did not budge. Some wondered who this little bastard was with the big mouth and three stripes on his shirt sleeve. He did not look like a Marine, at least not like anyone they had ever seen. Except for the men coming from the larger cities, few of the recruits had ever seen a real-live Marine. The recruiting posters in their hometown post office always depicted a tall, handsome white man in dress blues, with white hat and gloves. A picture of a five-foot-seven half-breed Indian Marine sergeant, dressed in khaki and green, never adorned the walls of a federal building.

"Ow! Goddamn it! Son of a bitch, that hurt."

The outburst came from a recruit in response to the sting of the sergeant's swagger stick. He was a tall, lanky kid from Vancouver, not yet old enough to shave. This was Billy Sutton's way of introduction to his charges.

"For now, Slim, I'll pretend that I didn't hear what you said," Sergeant Sutton responded with a grim smile, then added, "but you'd better move your ass before I kick it. Now get in line. I want you up front here where I can keep an eye on you.

"Now hear this, all of you," the sergeant shouted over the hiss of steam emanating from a nearby railroad locomotive. "My name is Sergeant William J. Sutton. I am your sergeant!" he roared, "and your DI," he added. "Those initials stand for drill instructor. And they also mean that I'm your new boss, you shall address me as 'Sergeant, sir'!" he said, emphasizing the *sir.*

"In case you got on the wrong train in Washington or Oregon, let me remind you where the hell you are; you're in the United States Marine Corps now. There is only one way out—that's over my dead body. From this moment on, when I tell you to get up, you get up. When I tell you to get down, run, stop, jump, or stand at attention, you will do all of those things immediately, or sooner. You will not ask why. Now, keep your mouths shut, pick up your bags and follow me to the street." Although Jackson was at the far end of the formation, he had no trouble hearing or, for that matter, understanding the sergeant's instructions.

The column of men quickly wound their way through the railroad station to the street, where they boarded a half dozen city buses. Within the hour, they arrived at the nearby Marine Corps Training Depot. Scott marveled at the ability of this man. Unaided, he moved 300 men through the hustle and bustle of the crowded train depot and out onto the street. Once there, they boarded the waiting buses and were off within minutes for the Marine facility. He thought, *I might learn a great deal from this Indian sergeant.*

Private Jackson arrived at the United States Marine Recruit training depot on the afternoon of December 17, 1941, just ten days after Congress declared war on the Empire of Japan. At the quartermaster's warehouse, he picked up his basic military equipment, all of it left over from the Great War—it reeked of mothballs and Cosmoline. Jackson and those who arrived with him moved into housing at Tent Camp Number Two. Recruits who had come earlier in the week already filled to overcapacity the old wooden barracks and the recently added Tent Camp Number One. Nearby, as Jackson's platoon moved into their accommodations, Tent Camp Number Three began to take shape.

Later that day, as the men moved into formation on the parade ground, Sergeant Sutton and Assistant Drill Master Corporal Michael Lane singled out Jackson and the kid from Vancouver, and another recruit from Oregon; the reason being that they were the three tallest men in the platoon. Scott, at six foot two, was a half-inch taller than one and slightly shorter than the other one. This was of some significance to the Marine Corps, if to no one else. Drill instructors selected the three tallest men in a platoon to lead each of its three columns. The shortest, or the "Feather Merchants," as the smaller men were so inappropriately designated, brought up the rear.

Some described these weeks in boot camp as hell on earth. Although Scott thought he was in excellent physical condition, he quickly discovered he was mistaken. The recruits' day began at zero five hundred hours with a training film or lecture in the base theater, then to the parade ground for an hour of calisthenics, followed by a five-mile run. After breakfast, one to two hours was devoted to classroom exercises. These quiet sessions did not last long enough for most recruits. They dreaded what was to follow— three trips through the obstacle course (four or more for laggards), then an hour of survival training in the swimming pool.

Each afternoon, recruits again participated in calisthenics, then close-order drill, bayonet practice and hand-to-hand combat exercises. At the end of each day, every fiber in Scott's lean, muscular frame ached. On Saturday morning, the end of the second week of boot camp, Sergeant Sutton prepared his platoon for the weekly inspection of the training battalion by the base commander. On this day, Private Jackson, quite by accident, lost his position as the first man in the third column of Platoon № 27.

"Jackson, get in here," the drill instructor called out as the private walked by Sergeant Sutton's tent.

"Yes, sir," Jackson responded, quickly entering the man's tent and coming to attention in front of the platoon sergeant's desk.

"What'd you say, Private?" the drill instructor growled.

Then Scott remembered. "Private Jackson reporting as ordered, Sergeant, sir."

"Okay, Jackson, get over to Supply and pick up our pennant. You know where to go?"

"Yes, sir, Sergeant, sir."

"Then move it."

"Yes, sir, Sergeant, sir," Jackson replied, quickly retreating from the DI's tent.

At Ship's Stores, Scott discovered that the supply sergeant was not about to be interrupted by a new recruit; the man was overseeing the process of issuing uniforms to the latest group of recruits to arrive at the training depot. After waiting anxiously for nearly twenty minutes, he obtained the pennant and rushed back to the parade ground. Once there, he found his platoon was already in place with the battalion, in preparation for the commandant's formal inspection.

He was at a loss as to what he could do. Should he walk or run across the parade ground in front of 2,000 Marines, their officers and noncoms, or should he wait? For what, he was not sure. Corporal Lane helped him decide.

"What the hell are you doing here, Jackson?" Sergeant Sutton's assistant drill instructor growled.

"Not sure, Corporal, sir; I wasn't sure if I should cross in front of the formation, or wait."

"Wait for what? What d'you think is gonna happen to you out there? Get your ass across to the platoon; but before you go, that's not a goddamn hockey stick you're carrying, hold it high, like this."

The corporal showed him how to carry the pennant, and Private Jackson quickly began his lone trek across the parade ground to his platoon. In doing so, it was necessary to march the entire width of the "grinder" under the watchful eye of more than two dozen officers and noncoms.

Halfway across, the battalion commander, using a loudspeaker, the sound reverberating off the walls of nearby barracks, asked, "Mr. Sutton," he paused as if to make sure he had everyone's attention, "is that your platoon's pennant we see in the middle of the parade ground?"

Sergeant Sutton, looking somewhat sheepish, answered, "Yes, sir. That's my man, sir."

"Well, Mr. Sutton," he added derisively, "I suggest you have your lost young man join his platoon, so we may get this parade underway." About that time, Jackson arrived at Platoon 27 carrying the pennant.

"I'm sorry I'm late, Sergeant," he said, apologetically.

"Sergeant, *sir*," Sutton reminded Scott of the proper military etiquette.

"Yes, sir, Sergeant, sir," Scott repeated the expected appellation.

"Do you know the purpose of that pennant, Jackson?"

"I believe so, Sergeant, sir."

"Well, just in case you don't, let me tell you. The military pennant has a long history; it dates back to the days of the Roman Empire.

"When Caesar's legions marched across Europe, their warriors were led by men carrying their clan's colors. The pennant, carried by a guidon, was a gathering point. After the battle, those still standing rallied around the colors. When that happened, commanders could assess the number and the location of the surviving warriors. The responsibility to carry the fight to the enemy then rested upon their shoulders. Are you ready to accept that responsibility, Jackson?"

"Yes, sir, Sergeant, sir."

"Can you march in a straight line without wandering all over the goddamn map?"

"Yes, sir, Sergeant, sir, I can do that."

"Then get your ass out in front on this platoon and lead this bunch of shitheads in a straight line."

"Yes, sir, Sergeant, sir."

Physical activity, calisthenics, running, and bayonet training continued, along with the endless close-order drill on the grinder. This routine, which began almost immediately upon their arrival, never let up. During these long, tedious hours, Private Scott Allan Jackson guided Platoon № 27 in a *straight line*, both on the parade ground and to and from each training exercise.

The length of Jackson's stay in boot camp, originally scheduled for eight weeks, depended entirely upon the Empire of Japan, and upon the needs of the United States Marine Corps. Five weeks into basic training, as ordered, Scott once again reported to Sergeant Sutton at the DI's office, a tent located on the edge of the parade ground.

"You sent for me, Sergeant, sir?"

"Relax, Jackson," Sutton offered quietly, "the sergeant major wants to talk to you. I don't know what he has in mind. Let's go."

Upon entering the sergeant major's office, Jackson snapped to attention before the man's desk; with a note of trepidation in his voice, he addressed the training battalion's top NCO.

"Private Jackson reporting as ordered, Sergeant Major, sir."

Sergeant Major Lyle Cook, a large, rawboned man, sitting behind a well-worn desk in a wicker chair, looked over the top of his glasses at this recruit standing ramrod straight before him. Hanging from a coat rack on the wall behind Cook, his green blouse, with its six stripes and five hash marks, deliberately displayed for all to see, silently announced to all who entered his presence he answered only to the base commandant.

"Jackson, hmmm," he responded gruffly, lurching back in his chair, closely examining Scott from head to toe. Then turning to Sergeant Sutton, with a wry grin he asked, "Is this the best your platoon has to offer, Sergeant?" his acerbic inquiry more of a challenge than a question.

"He'll do the job," Sergeant Sutton replied, with a smile, knowing Lyle Cook's penchant for bluster. "What have you got in mind, Sergeant Major?"

"He's been selected to attend Officer Candidate School; you think he'll be a credit to the Corps?"

"He's an excellent candidate, Sergeant Major," Sutton responded, exhibiting a degree of confidence in a member of his platoon not heard before by Jackson. "After all, he's from my platoon."

"Don't pat yourself on the back yet, Sergeant Sutton," he laughed. "We'll see how your people do next week on the range." Then turning his attention back to Private Jackson, he said, "Get your gear together, Jackson, and be at the main gate at seventeen hundred hours."

"Yes, sir, Sergeant Major. Thank you, sir."

"Don't thank me, Jackson," he growled. "I did not send you there. Now get the hell out of here and get your sea bag packed."

"Yes, sir, Sergeant Major, sir." Scott responded. As he turned to leave the sergeant major's office, Cook called after him, "By the way, Jackson, good luck." He was smiling.

"Thank you, Sergeant Major, sir."

Returning to his tent, Scott packed his sea bag, stripped his bed, neatly folding the two blankets across the bottom of the cot. By the end of the day, he was ready for shipment to Quantico, Virginia.

Before checking out, he dropped in at the DI's tent to see his platoon sergeant. Sutton was proud of the fact that one of his charges would attend OCS. When Scott entered the tent, occupied by a half dozen drill instructors, Billy Sutton announced loudly, "Listen up, you jarheads. This is Scott Jackson. He may be your new CO someday, so treat him kindly."

Upon hearing Sutton's comment, the drill instructors smiled, then each man in turn came over to this newly selected officer candidate, shook Scott's hand, and said, "Good luck, Jackson."

At seventeen hundred hours, Sergeant Sutton saw his protégé off at the main gate. The two exchanged handshakes. "Good-bye, Scott," the "sumo wrestler" offered, his voice warm and friendly. "Good luck to you. You'll need it, I'm afraid this is going to be a long war."

The ride across country on a Southern Pacific passenger train, coach class, was far different from what Scott remembered about traveling by rail to the Dakotas when he was a kid. Nineteen-twenty-eight seemed like such a long time ago. When the train pulled out of San Diego, en route to Washington, DC, every car was loaded with Army, Navy, and Marine personnel. The roster of troops included forty-two officer candidates, destined for OCS at Quantico, Virginia.

Stopping at Phoenix for a crew change and supplies, the passengers descended like locusts upon the railroad station and surrounding businesses. The stopover provided a much-needed respite for these recruits now crammed into too few rail cars. There was no way the railroad could meet the emergency wartime demands unexpectedly placed upon their equipment and crews. With more than 500 men aboard, dining and toilet facilities were woefully inadequate to the needs of the troops. Water and food supplies were quickly exhausted. Across the station platform there was another train, only this one traveled west. It too carried a full complement of military personnel.

Upon arrival at the Marine Training Base at Quantico, Virginia, Scott found this East Coast base and its environs less chaotic than that of San Diego. Yet the sting of their drill instructor's swagger stick across the back of their head or buttocks reminded them they were still in the Marine Corps. At seven a.m., or seven hundred hours the following day (Jackson never got used to the military's way of keeping time), they were back on the parade ground. Their drill instructor was Sergeant Leroy Ketchum. After an hour of close-order drill, he assembled the platoon in a nearby training classroom, where they awaited the arrival of Brigadier General Lawrence J. Packard. Packard was officer in charge of the Marine Corps' Officer Candidate Training Program. When the general arrived, Sergeant Ketchum yelled, "Ten' hut!" bringing the entire class scrambling to their feet, backs ramrod straight.

In his discussions with these men, General Packard appeared to be genuinely concerned for the well-being of each officer candidate. He questioned several about their experiences to date with the Corps. He asked about their families, where they came from, their accommodations, including the problems encountered on the train ride across country. Then the man began to explain the Corps' role thus far in the war.

"Our forces are retreating in every theater where we have engaged the enemy," he said, unapologetically. "But, gentlemen, the war ain't over yet. As a matter of fact, for the US it's just getting started.

"For now," he continued, "Marines will fight America's enemies almost exclusively in the Pacific Theater of Operations. The Corps has neither the troops nor the equipment necessary to challenge a large enemy force. That is a role the Army will undertake and they will do a magnificent job. At this time, there are 65,000 of us wearing this green uniform of ours.

"Our people will plug the holes in the dike, whenever and wherever that may occur. Right now it's in the Western Pacific, on Wake Island, Bataan, and even in Hawaii.

"You men possess work specialties which are critical to the Corps' needs. You will receive your commission at the end of this four-week training program and you can be expected to be at your duty post shortly thereafter."

Until now, many of those in the room were not fully cognizant of what would be expected of them upon graduation from Officer Candidate School. Yet before General Packard finished his talk, they all knew what they were in for.

The general continued, "Hundreds of thousands of enlisted personnel will be depending upon you to guide them through what will be the most challenging time in their young lives. The Corps will expect you to impart your knowledge and skills from your civilian occupation on to these young, inexperienced Marines."

For those sitting in that room on this cold day in January 1942 it became perfectly clear what role they would play as junior military officers in this worldwide conflagration. They were not destined to lead men into battle against America's enemies on land, at sea, or in the air. They would soon be classified by their uniformed brothers-in-arms as "stateside soldiers"; all of them were fully aware of the stigma that went with the territory. Not one of them would be destined to see action in this war.

General Packard continued, "You veteran pilots will, upon graduation, begin training both naval and Marine aviation cadets. In that training, the cadet will be expected to gain the necessary skills to take on the world's most formidable combat aviation group, the Imperial Japanese Air Force."

Half way through his presentation, he again emphasized, "The Corps does not have much time. How much time?" he asked, quietly, and then, answering his own question, he replied, "Only God knows."

In civilian life, a half dozen of the officer candidates managed large transportation facilities, fleets of trucks, tractors, or automobiles. They would teach young men how to service and maintain a whole array of vehicles, from tanks and armored personnel carriers to the new amphibious tracked vehicles soon to be mass-produced on the assembly lines in Detroit.

Addressing Scott's law enforcement colleagues, the general added, "Last but not least, eight of you are experienced police managers. We will expect much from you. It does no good to recruit and train young men, and soon young women, if they are going to wind up in a brig, city jail, or state prison. It will be your job to train and guide the largest number of military police the naval services have ever seen."

He went on to explain that the Navy planned to train over 50,000 military police and naval shore patrol personnel during the next year. This group of men would work with civilian authorities to keep the peace on the streets of the nation's largest cities. Scott and his colleagues would provide training for these newly assigned military police and for thousands of civilian security guards.

"You shall also train this large contingent of military men," he said, "to protect the persons, facilities, and equipment of the United States at more than one hundred shore facilities throughout the country."

Concluding his hour-long welcoming address to this group of officer candidates, General Packard added, "Gentlemen, that's why you're here. The Marine Corps will always be grateful that you volunteered your expertise and services to the Corps and to your country. I sincerely wish you all the best in your endeavors to help win this war. Any questions?" he asked. There were none.

It did not take long for Jackson to realize that neither he nor anyone else in this room would serve in a combat role in this war. Although classified as "essential to the war effort," General Packard was not preparing them to take command of a tank or infantry platoon, or to fly a combat mission with an aviation unit. Their only marketable skill of value to the Marine Corps was the expertise they brought with them from civilian life.

That night, this former city police lieutenant sought out others from his class chosen to attend OCS simply because of their police expertise. He wondered if these men felt as he did. Entering the PX, he ran into Sean O'Neil, a former cop from New York City, and Bob Karr, from Los Angeles. O'Neil was a lieutenant with more than ten years' experience in patrol and investigative assignments, and Karr, another ex-lieutenant, came with eight years' experience behind him training LAPD officers. Jackson had met Karr on the train en route from San Diego; he quickly recognized that these two former cops wanted to talk.

"How about buying you a drink, Scott?" Karr offered.

"You bet," Jackson responded. "Let's see what the beer garden looks like."

"What did you think of General Packard's little speech today, Scott?" Sean O'Neil asked, as the three men made their way to a table.

"Same as you, Sean," Scott responded, shaking his head. "It's a bunch of bullshit. When I enlisted, I thought I would get away from police work. Looks like I was mistaken."

"You think there's any way we can get out of this?" Karr asked. It was obvious he too was upset with General Packard's presentation, worried that he would not see combat. "I didn't enlist in this outfit to train a bunch of damn kids to be policemen."

"I don't know, Bob," Scott replied. "However, I don't think this would be the time to raise the issue. We volunteered, remember? Right now I doubt that General Packard or anyone else in command would be too sympathetic to a request from us for a combat assignment."

"I agree," O'Neil responded. "I think we're stuck. We'll have to ride this out."

It was clear to Jackson, in talking to these former cops, they were no less discouraged than he was. Like him, they joined the Marine Corps to fight the Japanese, yet General Packard made it perfectly clear that they did not have a snowball's chance in hell of doing that. They were going to be cops again, cops assigned to some Godforsaken place, thousands of miles from home—it was as simple as that.

That evening, with Taps signaling lights-out, a discouraged OCS candidate from the Northwest lay in his bunk in the dark, wondering what the future held for him. It was past midnight when he finally fell asleep.

Chapter 6

On 10 March 1942, Second Lieutenant Scott Jackson, just out of OCS, arrived at his new duty station, Marine Corps Barracks, San Diego, California. That afternoon, he reported to the Commander Shore Patrol, Eleventh Naval District for southern California. His new boss was Marine Colonel Josh Enright, a twenty-year career officer.

Except for a tour of duty in the Philippines, Enright was a stateside Marine. Some members of the "Old Corps" considered his administrative position a lightweight assignment. Yet many pursued such duties for it provided an alternative to combat command in securing promotions within the Corps. This was particularly true since the Navy played a role in selecting future leaders to command the organization.

The Marine Corps' administrative officer worked closely with the Navy brass; and the Navy literally controlled the destiny of those seeking promotion to the higher ranks within the Corps. Thus, Marine officers tried to get to know their bosses; yet it went far beyond that. The social life of the stateside officer and his wife played an integral role in bolstering the image of the husband. That was not always possible in such remote places as Guantánamo Bay, Nicaragua, or in the Philippines. It was much more apt to materialize in places such as San Diego, Quantico, or in Washington, DC, particularly during peacetime.

Enright held a bachelor's degree in political science from Virginia Military Institute at Lexington; while in New York, he earned a master's degree from Columbia University. Stateside assignments truly had advantages if one were interested in attaining an advanced degree or furthering one's career through a political connection. The colonel was a product of the system; he took advantage of every opportunity to advance his career. Nevertheless, he was good at what he did; this Marine was no lightweight.

Scott soon found himself in charge of five sergeants and thirty-three enlisted military policemen. They would investigate crimes committed on military facilities. In addition, they were to provide military assistance to local authorities in San Diego and Riverside Counties. It was like being back on the beat, back where he began his career, ten years earlier, as a rookie cop. Although disheartened by the assignment, when he arrived at his duty station, he kept his feelings to himself

From his first day on the job, he felt quite at home on the streets of San Diego. The sights, sounds, and smells of this seaport city continually reminded him of his hometown. Although the total civilian population was somewhat less than that of Seattle, the military presence more than made the difference. For years, San Diego was the home port for the Navy's Eastern Pacific Fleet. Naval and Marine training facilities located within the city provided a continuing flow of manpower for the military, plus a significant if somewhat unpredictable source of revenue for the city treasury.

During the Great Depression, Congress would not be overly generous toward the military, yet the bombing of Pearl Harbor by the Japanese quickly changed all of that. It was soon to have a direct impact upon the economic well-being of this coastal community. By the summer of 1942, the city became the nucleus of the largest concentration of naval forces ever assembled in the western United States. In just months, this quiet little town on the bay became a military colossus. Eight naval facilities located within the district, with more under construction, provided near full employment for the community at large. Two of the main facilities, the Navy and Marine Corps Recruit Training Stations, welcomed hundreds of recruits almost daily.

Across the bay, on North Island, lay one of the largest naval air stations in the country, while just forty miles to the north, the vast reaches of Camp Pendleton dwarfed the surrounding communities. This sprawling base provided advanced training for Marine infantry, amphibious and tank corps operations.

On his first day on the job, Scott took a quick tour of the metropolitan area with San Diego Police Captain Richard Streeter. That was all he needed to understand why his commanders selected former cops with his background and experience to attend Officer Candidate School.

"I understand you were a cop in Seattle, Scott. What'd you do?"

"Much the same as you, Captain."

"Call me Rich, without the sir," he smiled. "We're not quite as formal as you folks in the military."

"Okay, Rich. I spent six or seven years on the beat in Chinatown, then worked Homicide for three years. I stayed on third watch most of my career."

"Third watch," Streeter laughed. "Well, welcome to police work in San Diego, Scott; I don't think I'll ever get off this damn shift. Since the war started, we hired nearly two hundred people and as you can see a lot of them are on this watch. Less than half have graduated from the Academy. I am supposed to see that they get at least a basic understanding of their responsibilities on the street. The best I can do, however, is to team them up with an experienced man."

"How many did you lose when the war started?" Scott asked.

"In December forty-one, nearly a hundred; I don't know how many left since then. What is it about you young police officers? Seems to me that some of you are in an awful hurry to get yourselves killed."

"No, I don't think so, Rich," Scott responded, seriously. "No one thinks about dying for his country when he enlists."

"Maybe you are right, Scott. I suppose I'm lucky; I was too young for the last one and too old for this one."

"It's more likely, Rich, that most of them were a little bored with their job; they probably figured history was being made by the American military and they wanted to be a part of it."

"Is that why you enlisted?" Streeter asked, as the two men stopped for coffee at an all-night diner.

"I guess you could include me in that group; you'll have to admit, these are historic times. It could turn out to be one of the most exciting times in our life."

"I hear you. Maybe if I was younger I might feel that way, but y'know, a lot of these young guys won't be going home."

After the two men ordered their coffee, Captain Streeter changed the subject.

"Your people have been a godsend for the police department, Scott. In the last six months, the city's population has exploded. The Mayor's Office recently estimated that there are approximately eighty thousand military men and women and their dependents on the streets, in the shops, stores, or hotels of the city at any given time. And as you can see, during the nice weather, thousands of them will flock to the city's parks and beaches."

"Well, so far the weather's been perfect," Scott replied, pleased with the pleasant weather he encountered since he first arrived in December 1941. "On an evening like tonight, I suppose there'll be a large crowd out on the beach."

"Yeah, maybe fifteen to twenty thousand; they'll be a problem tonight. Since December 7, we have been damn short of staff; we cannot handle these crowds when they get ugly. We'll be relying heavily upon your people to police your own."

Captain Streeter's duty watch began at 6:00 p.m. and continued into the early morning hours until 4:00 a.m. There were 152 police officers assigned under his command to patrol the downtown section of the city. San Diego officers worked six days a week, ten hours a day. So much for the old story that police work in California was much more attractive than in Scott's hometown. At any given time, due to vacations, illness and regular days off, Streeter would often have fewer than 100 officers available for duty. Most of the officers worked one and two-man patrol vehicles. Others walked beats in the heart of the city and from Union Station to the Harbor.

Located in the tenderloin core of this burgeoning urban area were more than 10,000 businesses that served the needs of the public. Among these, bars, dance halls, tattoo parlors, theaters and pornographic peep show houses. Much to the chagrin of the city fathers, there was more than a smattering of hotels that were nothing more than fronts for prostitution. These continued to be a problem for both civil and military authorities.

At the request of the mayor, Colonel Enright's military police personnel joined forces with San Diego officers. For their use, the city provided an abandoned office complex near city hall. The officers and enlisted men in the Military Police Company assigned to assist Captain Streeter and his men obtained housing at Marine Barracks. Within a week of Jackson's arrival, twenty-five members of his company began learning the layout of the city by accompanying San Diego city cops on routine patrol.

During Scott's first month on the job, his men, working with local police, investigated the death of two enlisted personnel from nearby bases—they died in traffic accidents. The two dead servicemen would not see their nineteenth birthday. Throughout the district, thousands of alcohol-related incidents required both a military and civil police response. Bar and street brawls became a common occurrence, with both combatants and the MPs frequently requiring medical attention. There were other challenges. On a late Friday evening, a near riot erupted outside the Grant Hotel in downtown San Diego. Naval and Marine personnel became involved in a brawl with civilian "Zoot Suiters," touched off when one of the civilians, dressed in his high-waisted baggy attire, made a pass at a young soldier's date. Four of Scott's men, injured in the fray that followed, required emergency medical treatment.

The following morning, shortly after Scott had gotten to sleep, he woke to the blaring noise of a trumpet, played loud and off key.

"Murph, get the hell out of here!" he yelled, as he threw a pillow at the culprit. He knew who it was before he even opened his eyes. Navy Lieutenant Jack Murphy, a would-be musician assigned to the North Island Naval Station, made a habit of annoying his Marine Corps colleagues. Murphy worked liaison with the MPs and San Diego Police, he and Scott becoming friends almost immediately upon meeting each other.

"Get your butt out of the sack, Scotty; I've found us a bungalow apartment. Let's go; no more six o'clock revelry," he said, smiling. "It's on the beach; there are chicks every place you look."

"How much money?"

"Don't worry about it; if we can get another guy, we can split it three ways—probably thirty-five a month."

Scott would not miss the amenities of the BOQ, for he found it near impossible to sleep in the daytime with the continuing arrival and departure of transient officers. That weekend, he and Jack Murphy moved into their rental unit on the beach, not far from Police Headquarters.

Although unhappy with his continuing role as a police officer, albeit a military policeman, Scott's superiors looked upon his assignment as "necessary to the war effort." However, at every opportunity, much to the consternation of his commanding officer, he continued to seek a combat role. Within three months of his arrival in San Diego, he broached the subject of a transfer to a combat unit with Colonel Enright. Upon receipt of Scott's written transfer request, Enright sent for him. Receiving Jackson cordially in his office, Scott sensed the colonel was displeased that this newcomer did not want to be a part of his team.

"Stand at ease, Lieutenant. Relax and let's talk about this transfer request of yours," the man offered politely, yet firmly. "My first thoughts were to reject it out of hand, but let's see if you can persuade me otherwise. Looking at your record," he continued rather dryly, pointing at a file on his desk, "you come highly recommended, but you haven't been here long enough to even train your own people. Suppose you try and convince me that I could justify approving your transfer."

"I volunteered, sir, because I believe I can contribute something worthwhile to the military," Scott responded earnestly. "I have commanded uniformed men in the field, albeit policemen, but my entire career has been spent serving government in field assignments. I firmly believe that I could better serve the needs of the Marine Corps in a combat unit. As to your concern about the training and readiness of MPs assigned under my command, there are two other lieutenants available in the district, O'Toole and Cooke. They are both good men; they could assume that responsibility."

"I don't think so, Lieutenant." Colonel Enright responded coldly, obviously insensitive to his subordinate's aspirations. "Apparently Headquarters also figured otherwise, or they would not have assigned you here in the first place." Then glancing at his watch as if to indicate he was a busy man, he added, "We'll talk about this another time, Lieutenant; I'm going to deny your transfer. You're excused."

On his way out of Enright's office, Scott ran into Lieutenant Calvin Riggs, the colonel's administrative officer. "Why so grim, Scott?" the man inquired, sensing things had not gone well this morning between Jackson and their boss.

"So much for military courtesy, Cal, he might as well have thrown me out the damn door."

"He's a cold-hearted son of a bitch, Scott. You might as well face it; he's not going to let you go. Your outfit makes him look good and he's bucking for that big star."

"I know that, but I am not going to give up, I'll go over his head if I have to."

"Be careful, Scott. He wants to make brigadier and he will use you. If you bring his boss in on this, you'd better do it by the book."

On his way to his office, Scott made up his mind; he would give the Corps 110% in his present assignment, and wait and see. Something might happen. He remembered General Packard's dire comments about the failure thus far of the Allies to stop the

Japanese juggernaut in the Pacific. He reckoned the enemy's successes could work in his favor. The Corps may need his services in a combat unit before this war was over.

Unlike their lieutenant, the military police officers who worked for Scott were in no hurry to leave the US mainland. They considered themselves very, very lucky to have received a stateside assignment.

Notwithstanding Colonel Enright's denial of his request for transfer, Jackson would be the first to admit that the duties of a stateside Marine officer were both challenging and exciting, especially for young, single officers. Monday through Saturday, he worked an evening shift at Police Headquarters. On occasion he would switch nights off with one of his colleagues, or run two furloughs together for extra time off. This allowed him the opportunity to take in the nightlife in Los Angeles with Jack Murphy. Lieutenant Murphy, never one to miss out on a social event, continually reminded him of the opportunities that they, as young, unmarried military officers, were missing out on in Los Angeles.

"Let's go to LA for the weekend, Scott," he suggested with a grin, "we'll take in the sights, maybe meet some gals and party. What d'you say?"

"You know anyone there? What would we do?"

"No, but I ain't gonna let that stop me. We could go to the Hollywood Canteen, look it over, pick up a couple of chicks, and take 'em to dinner, maybe do a little dancing. Whatever meets your fancy, okay?"

"I'm ready," Scott replied, yet he was in no mood for socializing. "I need to get away from the street for a while."

"What's the matter? You and the colonel tangle again?" Murphy smiled. He was aware of Scott's earlier encounter with his boss.

"No. He's just a damn hardhead, but I am going to hit him with another transfer request at the end of the month. I remember what they told us in OCS about following the rules, 'If it's not in the Corps' little black rule book, it can't happen. However, if it's in the book, it shall happen.' Well, it's in the damn book. He has not responded in writing to my request for a transfer, so I'm going to force him to do just that. I'll go over his head if I have to."

"You're pushing your luck, aren't you?" Murphy responded with a questioning look.

"Probably, but this war will be over before you know it and I'll go back home without contributing a damn thing toward our victory."

"I hear you," Jack Murphy responded calmly, attempting to mollify his friend, "but the military is different, Scott. Sometimes you have to give in and just do what you're told."

"I know, Murph, but I'm committed about this. When this is over, I want to be able to tell my kids I did something in this war besides rounding up young servicemen who drank too much booze."

On Saturday morning, the two men caught an early train out of Union Station for Los Angeles. They took in the sights in the big city, including a visit to the Hollywood USO Canteen. In the early evening, they boarded a streetcar bound for the Palladium Ballroom. When they arrived, they found the dance hall crowded with uniformed servicemen and women. Dozens of civilians, mostly young women, highly visible in their colorful dresses, appeared eager to entertain the visiting service personnel. After a couple of dances, the two men moved into the cafeteria, where Jack Murphy spotted a group of Navy nurses.

"Holy Moses, look at that!" he exclaimed. "Hey, those are the gals we saw get on the train in Dago, I've met one of 'em. Come on. They look like they want to party," he said, grabbing Scott by the arm as he headed across the cafeteria. Murphy did not have to say any more; both of them had enough to drink that neither man was inclined to let their inhibitions stand in their way.

"Which one? Who is she?"

"The blonde, she works at the hospital at North Island. The other one, with the long hair...I don't know who she is, but I have seen her somewhere. The other two appear occupied. I'll take the blonde. Let's go."

The two quickly strode over to where the two nurses were sitting, where Murphy unabashedly introduced himself, and his friend. As it turned out, his only contact with the woman before this night was while he stood in line for his routine shots at the base hospital. That did not deter him.

"I'm Jack Murphy, this jarhead is Scott Jackson," the Navy officer exclaimed, with a grin. "Can we buy you ladies a drink, or would you like to dance?" Both women acknowledged Murphy's brash approach with a smile.

"You bet, Lieutenant," quipped the blonde girl, with a grin. "Come join us."

Jackson figured Murphy's bold overture had the advantage of expediency, if not prudence; yet it seemed to work for him. Turning to the young woman with the long hair, he boldly announced, "I'm a lousy dancer, Ensign, but I get better as the night wears on. Would you care to dance?"

"How about a drink first," she replied softly, "and we'll get acquainted. We just got here, I'm Sophia Kosterman."

"Hi, Sophia, I'm Scott Jackson."

"How nice to meet you, Mr. Jackson."

"Scott, please," he replied, with a grin.

She held out her hand. "Okay, Scott it is. Please, sit down. Where're you from, Scott?"

"Seattle, and you?"

"Pittsburgh," she laughed; a soft pleasant laugh. "Just think of that, we live a continent apart, if it wasn't for this bloody war we'd never have met."

Sophia, at twenty-three, worked at Camp Miramar Base Hospital, near San Diego. The facility served the medical needs of the officers and men of this huge Marine aviation center and a nearby naval support facility. Although nearly overwhelmed by her beauty, Scott found her easy to talk to; she was a lovely young girl. She spoke openly about her family, explaining how she happened to join the Navy Nurse Corps.

"Since I was a child I wanted to be a nurse, so when I finished high school I enrolled in the nursing program at the university. I planned to work at St. Luke's Hospital in my hometown, where my mother worked and where I was born. The Japanese attack on Pearl Harbor changed all of that. When I finished school, I enlisted and soon found myself here.

"Now, tell me about you, Scott."

"Heck, there's not much to tell. When I finished high school I bummed around for a couple of years and then joined the police force."

"That must have been exciting; but tell me about your family—brothers, sisters; everything, I want to know more about you."

Before Scott realized it, he talked without letup for nearly an hour, telling her about his hometown, family, and friends. Quite suddenly, he realized that their companions were out on the dance floor, leaving the two of them alone; he was embarrassed. He apologized. Not realizing until that moment how long ago it was that he had the opportunity to enjoy the company of such a beautiful woman.

"I am so sorry, Sophia," he offered. "You didn't come here to listen to me."

"You don't have to apologize to me, Marine," she said, her voice warm and friendly. "I came here to enjoy myself and you'll never know how much I've enjoyed your company this evening, unless, of course, we spend the rest of it together," she smiled.

As she suggested, they stayed with one another for the remainder of the dance program. Throughout the evening, Harry James and his band entertained the large crowd of young men and women. With the band leader's solo rendition of "Carnival" closing out the evening, the musician held the audience transfixed on the dance floor. Scott and Sophia held each other closely, swaying back and forth to the rhythm of the music. When it was over, the entire group of nurses and their "escorts" caught the 2:00 a.m. train for San Diego.

Two days later, Scott and Sophia got back together. He picked her up at the Naval Hospital and they spent most of that afternoon lying in the sun at Mission Beach. The two enjoyed each other's company and in a matter of days they were together again at the officers' rented bungalow. They both worked the late-night shift, so early afternoon rendezvous became routine. Frequently they could be seen sailing on the bay, or lying on the beach in the warm southern California sunshine.

Kosterman, at five-ten, 135 pounds, with long brown hair, flashing blue eyes and a captivating smile, was a stunningly beautiful young woman. Her rich mix of Irish and Polish heritage was exhibited by her every movement. Yet when she joined the Nurse Corps, by her own admission, she was, as she said, "Not much to look at. I wasn't just thin, I was a scrawny kid.

"I had a terrible time, Scott, trying to gain weight; although looking back on those days, I guess I was not unlike many of my classmates. The only decent meal many of us got came when we worked a full shift in a restaurant; several of us worked in the cafeteria while attending the university. But look at me now," she laughed, "since I enlisted, that good old Navy diet and our Saturday morning drills and workouts in the gymnasium have done wonders for my figure."

Scott, awestruck by her beauty, thought that if she were ever a scrawny, thin kid, no one would know it now. Her fully developed figure, with its dark bronze southern California tan, turned more than one eye on the crowded beach at Mission Bay. Moreover, as Scott was soon to discover, wherever she went, at the base hospital, or on the street, both men and women turned to look at this tall, beautiful woman, impeccably dressed in her blue and white nurse's uniform. He soon found himself enjoying the attention the two of them received when he was with her.

However, much to the chagrin of some of her female colleagues, Sophia was also the pride and joy of the Navy Nurse Corps. Her work schedule being interrupted by Public Relations personnel for photographs became routine. Near life-size pictures of this beautiful woman were on display in naval recruiting stations throughout the nation. Their purpose was to entice young women from all over the country to join the United States Navy Nurse Corps.

Scott was not sure he was in love with Sophia Kosterman, but he loved everything physical about her. It was hard not to, for her exceptional beauty and charm fascinated him. The ever-present smile, the dark blue eyes and long hair, which she kept in a sweptback, boyish pompadour, enthralled this Marine from Seattle. When not in uniform, Sophia brushed her hair out so it hung down to her shoulders, completely mesmerizing her friend.

He liked her impish smile and the way she looked at him and teased him when they were in bed together. She was a complete woman. At one time, he honestly believed that no one could have provided him with the sexual pleasure and contentment which he had experienced years before with his former girlfriend, Amy Donahue. Now he was not sure what was happening, but he had not felt this way since he first dated Amy.

However, Scott and Sophia's time together was soon to end. On 21 December 1943, she called him at work, something that she had never done before. He was somewhat apprehensive, until he heard her voice, she sounded so happy.

"Scott," she said excitedly, "I've been transferred. I am going overseas; I'm to be assigned to a hospital ship."

"That's great, honey," he responded. He was happy for her; this was what she wanted, yet he regretted the fact that their time together would soon end. It meant the end of their trips to the beach, the evening dinners, and dancing at the Grant Hotel ballroom.

"Can we get together tonight, Scott? They have granted me a three-week leave; I am going home for Christmas. My train leaves tomorrow at ten o'clock."

"You bet; I'll pick you up. Is three o'clock okay?"

"Sure. During the holiday season, I can be with my family for a few days and then be back here right after the first of the year. We can be together for at least a week before I leave for overseas. Okay?"

"Okay, honey. We'll have dinner at my place; I'll see you at three o'clock."

Sophia's orders required her to report to the air facility at North Island on 10 January 1944 to prepare for embarkation. The directive did not include the date of departure. However, in 1944, plans of even the most determined traveler could not compete with the priorities of the military services. Forced to reschedule her departure from the East Coast, she did not arrive back in San Diego until the morning of 10 January, the very day she was to report to North Island.

Later that evening, the two said their good-byes in the nurses' quarters at the naval facility. There were no tears. This would be her first experience aboard ship and first time ever outside the continental United States. She looked forward to this new adventure. Scott was envious. However, as he drove away from the North Island facility, he was troubled. He had enlisted in the Marine Corps after the attack on Pearl Harbor to see action in this war. Despite that, here he was, two years later, still working as a police officer, while his girlfriend was off to war. "Damn the Marine Corps," he muttered.

The following morning, Lieutenant Kosterman, along with 65 other Navy nurses and nearly 10,000 Marines, boarded troop ships tied up along Harbor Drive. At eight hundred hours, 12 January, her ship took its place in a large convoy of naval vessels off the coast of southern California—their destination: the South Pacific.

That evening, when Scott entered his office near city hall, he closed the door behind him, and then, turning to his typewriter, prepared another transfer request. This time he made a carbon copy for Colonel Enright's immediate superior, Brigadier General Max Schelling. Before leaving his office, he dropped both memorandums into outgoing mail.

Chapter 7

By 1944, more than a half million service personnel filled to near capacity the available military housing in southern California. Therefore, it was no surprise that even with an increase in staff, Jackson's MPs found it near impossible to meet the demands for assistance from local authorities. Although most military camps were huge, permanent housing quarters were scarce. Those who came late to bases in San Diego and Riverside Counties moved into either a Quonset hut or tent. For those families who accompanied a military husband, or father to the West Coast, it became near impossible to find adequate housing.

These thousands of young men and women in the area placed a huge burden upon civil authorities in the delivery of goods and services. Demands for police and fire protection increased tenfold. With the shortages in food, gasoline, and coal outstripping available supplies, local agencies turned to the military for assistance. Although rationed, many consumables were readily available at exorbitant prices on the black market. Cadres of thieves, burglars and stickup artists entrenching themselves in the black market, became a serious challenge for both military and civil authorities.

To combat this increase in criminal activity, in January, Jackson's MPs and Naval Shore Patrol officers combined forces with Naval Intelligence and the Army's Criminal Investigation

Division. Their goal: stop the theft of supplies from military bases and railroad warehouses. Trucks, weapons, food, gasoline and other rationed goods from unguarded warehouses were the targets of those dealing in the black market. On military posts, the chief culprits were service personnel and civilian contract employees. These individuals had ready access to a mountain of military stores.

Many of those taken into custody by the MPs were vicious young criminals in uniform. The policy of hometown jurists deferring a sentence of a convicted criminal, if the culprit voluntarily enlisted in the military, created more than its share of problems. It proved to be beneficial for the civil jurisdiction where the person committed his original offense. Unfortunately, it needlessly burdened the military with criminals who should have been locked up. Some of the more violent used their newly acquired combat skills to wreak havoc on the streets of nearby cities.

On January 15, Sam Gregory, an agent with the FBI office in San Diego, dropped into Jackson's office. Gregory's duties included assisting Scott's people in the recovery of stolen property and criminal record checks of service personnel taken into custody by the MPs.

"Hello, Sam." Scott responded cordially. "What's going on today?"

Gregory, a senior agent with the bureau, was one of the few old-time agents not sacked by J. Edgar Hoover when he took over the FBI leadership in 1924. He was a conscientious law enforcement officer; a former Southern Methodist University football star, a deacon in his church and, for his age, in excellent physical condition; criteria which held him in high regard with Hoover.

"LAPD arrested a gun dealer, Scott," he responded. "They confiscated a half dozen .45 automatics stolen from the armory out at Camp Elliott. During interrogation, the man claimed he got the weapons from a group of thieves who plan to burglarize the same facility next weekend. I've got the location and maps of the warehouse area and I figured maybe you and I could plan a little reception for them," he laughed. "Just remember I'm a one-man squad, so we'll have to rely on your people to take these bastards down."

"Good," Scott replied, smiling. "I'm tired of fighting this military bureaucratic bullshit; let's you and I just go arrest some bad guys and lock 'em up."

"You sound a little cynical, Scott," Gregory responded, shaking his head. "Are you still locking horns with the colonel? Murphy told me of your problems. How come all you young guys want to go someplace where you might get your damn head shot off?"

"No, I know I'm lucky to be here, Sam; but this war isn't going to last much longer and I'd like to get a crack at these guys before it's over."

Gregory, with pursed lips and a wry grin, just shook his head again. He could not understand why nearly every stateside Marine he talked to wanted to do battle with the country's enemies, while those who had seen action in the South Pacific never wanted to go back.

"You may get your wish before you know it, Scott. I'm not nearly as optimistic as you are that this war will end anytime soon." The man was dead serious.

Based upon the information supplied by Gregory, the agent accompanying Jackson and eight military police officers set up a nighttime surveillance of the warehouse. Shortly after midnight on the second night of the stakeout, the officers saw three men climb to the roof of the armory; within minutes, they made their way down into the building. As Scott was about to tell his men to move in, a military truck entered the drive and backed up to a loading dock. The officers waited. A warehouse door soon opened and the thieves inside began loading the truck. Scott ordered his men to move in. The culprits opened fire on the military police. In the shootout that followed, the MPs captured five suspects, killing one. Two of Scott's men required hospitalization for bullet wounds.

Two of the five suspects taken into custody were enlisted men assigned to the base; the dead man was an AWOL soldier, a man with an extensive criminal record for petty offenses.

Even with the arrests and shootings at Camp Elliott, which garnered considerable news coverage in the local press, there was no letup in the MPs' workload. Scott's people, working ten-hour shifts, with the unrelenting need for testimony in both civil and military courts, allowed for little free time. Yet, the combined law enforcement endeavors continued with some spectacular successes. Still, Scott could not find himself to be nearly as enthusiastic with the results of their actions as Colonel Enright was. At a press conference held in General Schelling's office, Enright, without any mention of his lieutenant, publicly commended the Joint Military Police Task Force for their "spectacular successes in breaking up a black market ring." However, as Scott expected, the favorable publicity of the unit's achievements could only exacerbate his situation; Colonel Enright loved the limelight and Scott's people made it all possible.

The afternoon following the press conference, as Scott and Jack Murphy lay in the sun on Mission Beach, Murphy asked about Colonel Enright. Scott did not wish to talk about his boss. "I've got to get the heck away from him, Murph," he said. "I know him well enough to know that sooner or later he and I are going to clash over my transfer request and I would like to avoid that. But I'll be like a neighbor of mine at home. He served with the AEF in Europe in the First World War. In the two years he spent in France, he did nothing but work as a mechanic repairing heavy equipment."

Murphy smiled. "Seems like you and I have had this conversation before. You know the military, Scott. They figure you are a square, so they stuff you into a round hole. Look at me, a schoolteacher, now I am a babysitter. All these young guys that your people lock up, I'm supposed to see that they get back to their ship in one piece." He laughed. "There is no justice, Scott."

"Well, pursuing these crooked bastards wasn't what I had in mind when I joined the service, Murph. I don't have a snowball's chance in hell of seeing combat in this war, unless I can get *old hard-ass* to change his mind."

"From what I know of Enright, Scott, he ain't gonna do that," Murphy responded, shaking his head. "All the press coverage your people are getting for him just inflates his ego. He sees that brigadier general's star at the end of the rainbow."

Scott received his first correspondence from Sophia Kosterman, in mid February. He reread her letter several times. It brought to mind a flood of delightful memories; reminders of a time filled with love and affection. Since she left, he realized that his love for her was so strong and enduring that her absence left a huge void in his life. Until he could hold her close once again, it would remain. He could not believe he let her slip away without asking her to marry him.

Sophia was excited about her new duties aboard ship; he was happy for her, but thankful she was alive and well. Although censored, her correspondence left no doubt that she was in a combat zone in the South Pacific. After reading her letter repeatedly, Scott became more disheartened, he was the one who stayed behind, while the person he loved went off to war. He figured he lost all around. He not only lost Sophia, but he lost his battle with the brass to meet an enemy soldier face to face on a battlefield.

Slipping Sophia's letter into his shirt pocket, he set off for Colonel Enright's office. He decided it was time for a showdown with his battalion commander. He was fully aware that such action might be risky. Yet he believed there was justification for this approach: Colonel Enright had not responded in writing to any of his written requests for transfer as was required by naval regulations. Enright's staff merely called and told him that the colonel summarily rejected his request. No explanation accompanied these notifications.

Today, his commanding officer was not pleased to see this second lieutenant, requesting once again a transfer out of his command.

"The sergeant major tells me you still want out. Is that correct, Lieutenant?" the colonel demanded gruffly.

"Yes, sir," Scott answered politely, standing ramrod straight before the colonel's desk. "I've been here two years, sir. During that time, more than a dozen officers, junior to me, have transferred to combat units. I would like to see action before the war is over."

"Lieutenant," Enright responded coldly, still seated at his desk, looking over the top of his glasses, "the Marine Corps doesn't give a damn what you would like. You were sent to OCS because the Corps was in need of your civilian specialty; we still need that specialty."

"I understand that, sir. But I could serve some useful purpose overseas."

"We don't need you overseas, Lieutenant," he growled. "We need you here. I told General Schelling that, and he agreed. I do not think it would be in your best interest either to bother the general again." The veiled threat was not lost on Jackson. Still, he believed the colonel's continued denial of his transfer justified sending a copy of his request to Schelling's office.

"You've done a good job here, Lieutenant, I can't deny that. But you readily admit you're not a military professional; you want to return to civilian life when this war is over, right?"

"Yes, sir, I do," Jackson responded. "But—"

Enright, rudely cutting him off, suddenly lashed out. "Then why the hell can't you be satisfied with what you're doing? Besides, what do you have to offer? You do not have a military education," he said, with a note of derision in his voice. "You have never commanded a rifle platoon, or even operated a tank. What would you do?" He, demanded, then, not waiting for his subordinate's reply, added disdainfully, "You wouldn't serve any useful purpose in a combat unit."

His scathing remarks angered Jackson. "I am sorry, sir," Scott shot back, "but I don't agree with you. I could learn to command an infantry platoon, or operate a damn tank, if that's what it takes to get out of here."

He knew his tempestuous response to the colonel's condescending diatribe was unwise. In the Marine Corps, it was not customary for second lieutenants to challenge the wisdom of their commanding officer.

Enright, removing his glasses, his face flushed, stepped out from behind his desk. Then, addressing Jackson in a barely audible voice, he replied, "I think this conversation is concluded, Lieutenant. You are excused."

Embittered, Jackson stormed out of Battalion Headquarters, heading off to the officers' club. He needed a drink. Later, en route back to his office, he made up his mind not to accept the colonel's decision. He could not remain with the military police for the duration of this war; still, he had no idea how to get out of his present assignment.

Much to his surprise, three days after this latest encounter with Colonel Enright, Scott received notice of his promotion to the rank of first lieutenant. A directive ordering his immediate transfer accompanied the promotional order. He was to report to his new duty station with the United States Naval Investigative Service (NIS) at the North Island Naval Air Station (NAS).

There would be no congratulatory handshake, or well wishes from his commanding officer. The sergeant major merely called him into Battalion Headquarters and handed him a copy of his orders. It appeared that Colonel Josh Enright found an opportunity to get rid of a "problem." Colonels in line for promotion to a brigadier general's slot could not afford to have a disgruntled subordinate within their command, in this case, a competent officer, determined to get his own way. Such a subordinate could jeopardize an aspiring full colonel's climb up the promotional ladder. With Jackson gone, his unanswered transfer requests would no longer be an issue.

"Congratulations, Lieutenant," the sergeant major said, shaking his head, with a grimace. "I guess expressing your point of view pays off. Sometimes..." He paused. "But, if you'll pardon me for saying so, sir, I wouldn't try it too often in the Corps. You might just need the colonel or even General Schelling in your corner someday."

"I appreciate your advice, Sergeant Major," Jackson replied, with a smile. "Thank you."

Although unexpected, he was grateful for the promotion and new assignment. At least it was a refreshing change of duty. For the first time in two years, he could work a straight Monday through Friday day watch. No longer would he be responsible for handling the typical wayward serviceman on the streets of the city.

With this new responsibility, he assumed command of a staff of twelve noncommissioned investigators. His unit's charge: "Investigate serious assaults, critical injury accident cases and the deaths of military personnel on naval installations." In southern California, traffic accidents continued to be the primary killers of young servicemen and women, both on and off military reservations.

Jackson's men, mostly former city detectives from throughout the country, were all experienced, professional investigators. They were not only good at what they did, but unlike their boss, they enjoyed their stateside assignment.

Within a week of moving over to NAS, Scott received an unexpected visitor at his office. It was Admiral John Wycoff, the former head of the Thirteenth Naval District in Seattle. Based in Southern California, the admiral now commanded the Supply and Logistical Support Group for the entire Pacific Theater of Operations.

Jackson was surprised to see the man he met in 1935 at the US Naval Air Station in Seattle. Their paths crossed because of the antics of a local Naval Reserve officer who worked for Scott at the time. With considerable amusement, he recalled the admiral's response to Police Patrolman John Markovich's behavior in the skies over Seattle, on that warm summer day so many years ago.

On July 4, 1935, Police Sergeant Jackson and his squad of patrol officers were assigned crowd control duties for the annual Independence Day parade. In addition to the many VIPs invited to attend, there would be at least 200,000 visitors on hand for this annual Fourth of July celebration. Additional thousands of boating enthusiasts would show up that afternoon for the tugboat races on Elliott Bay.

It was a warm and beautiful day in the Northwest. By the time the parade participants arrived, the temperature moved into the mid-seventies. The military marching units, high school bands, and floats, bedecked with flowers, ribbons, balloons and their somewhat scantily clad beauty queens began to assemble. Shortly after ten o'clock in the morning, officers streaming out of Police Headquarters headed off to their assignments.

Sergeant Jackson's squad of thirteen men reported to their posts, two to an intersection in the immediate vicinity of the reviewing grandstand. The only man missing was Police Patrolman John Markovich. Markovich, a United States Navy Reserve flight officer, now on military leave from the department, was the holiday duty officer at the nearby naval district's aviation training facility.

The city's mayor and his guests, seated comfortably in temporary grandstands built for the occasion along the avenue, seemed to be thoroughly enjoying the parade. Governor Wallace Emory was there, along with Rear Admiral John Wycoff. There were more than a score of other military, political, and business VIPs attending from throughout the Northwest.

Shortly after the parade got underway, a single-engine military aircraft appeared low over the parade route. With the military bands, and the Army and Navy marching units leading the way, it appeared the low-flying aircraft was a part of the planned celebration. As it drew closer, with the crowd's attention now focused on the aircraft, the plane suddenly went into a steep dive, aimed directly at the reviewing grandstand. The noise, speed, and exceptionally low level of the aircraft caused several very startled guests in the grandstand to vacate their seats.

Leveling off near the top of the nearby high-rise buildings, the plane continued along the parade route for more than a mile, then left the area as quickly as it appeared.

Exhibiting considerable embarrassment by their hurried exit from the grandstand, the mayor and his guests began, with some confusion, to return to their seats. One of the visitors commented that the pilot scared the hell out of him. While others quietly chuckled at their fellow VIP's comment, the aviator's antics did not amuse the mayor's military guests. These men found it near impossible to obtain funds from a close-fisted Congress during the Depression. They did not need their efforts jeopardized by some idiotic military pilot pulling off such a stunt as was exhibited here today.

Sergeant Jackson could not believe what he saw. Yet, it appeared that most of the onlookers believed it to be part of the Fourth of July festivities. They enjoyed it immensely. Later, Scott learned the aircraft was a Navy plane piloted by Police Patrolman John Markovich.

The following day, Scott accompanied Police Inspector Donald Swenson to the naval air facility. Admiral Wycoff invited the two men to have lunch with him at the officers' club. The admiral, familiar with Markovich's police background, believed the Navy owed the city an apology.

"No. No, Admiral," Inspector Swenson responded, he was embarrassed that a police officer, under his command, would jeopardize the reputation of both the Navy and the police department. "We should have fired that young man long ago. He certainly gave us plenty of justification. It would have saved both the Navy and the police considerable embarrassment." Admiral Wycoff thought Inspector Swenson's suggested course of action was a little too harsh. He suggested there was a way to resolve this "little problem" as he called it.

"I could arrange for Lieutenant Markovich to be recalled to active duty, *for further training,*" he offered with a smile. "We would, of course need to ship him out to a training command some distance away, possibly to the Panama Canal. Either there, or to a location where the protestations from the natives are not likely to be heard in Congress."

Scott smiled when he thought about that meeting so many years ago. He remembered that it was almost comical at the time. Especially when Admiral Wycoff added, "The transfer might be in the best interest of both the Navy and the police department."

Today, Admiral Wycoff appeared to be genuinely delighted to see this tall, unpretentious former police officer from Seattle. Jackson was surprised that Wycoff even remembered who he was. The two men laughed as they discussed the circumstances that led to their first meeting at US Naval Air Station, Seattle. When Scott asked about Markovich, Admiral Wycoff responded candidly, "We sent him here to naval air. I suppose he is out there in the Pacific on a carrier somewhere. He's probably doing an excellent job for us." With that, the admiral explained the reason for his visit.

"Shortly after the war started, Scott, I was promoted to Vice Admiral; this meant relocating my family. The War Department moved us from the West Coast to Washington, DC. More recently, with another promotion, I brought the family with me to California. Both moves," he said, "were difficult for our children.

"Our youngest, Timothy Joseph, was twelve years old when we moved to the East Coast. We settled in at Falls Church, Virginia. However, Tim was unhappy there and soon ran away from home. A week later, the police in West Virginia picked him up; we drove over and got him. He did okay for a year or so; however, this past week he took off again. This time he left a note saying that he was going to Seattle to join the US Merchant Marine Service.

"He's big, Scott. Big enough to pass himself off as seventeen, but he is only fourteen years old. My wife and I are worried sick," the admiral added, his voice trailing off, as he paused, looking away from his host. "We haven't heard a word from him since he left and I was wondering if you could help us." Scott could see the man was clearly concerned for the well-being of his youngest son.

"I'm sure we can, sir," Jackson offered, as he took notes on the boy's physical and clothing description. "If you could send me a picture, it would help. However, I will get this information off right away. I am sure you and Mrs. Wycoff are upset over this,

Admiral; however, nearly all of these youngsters turn up within a few days. Undoubtedly, the police will find him. If he is bent on joining the Merchant Marine Service, he should be easy to locate."

"You really think so, Scott. Are you sure?" The man looked worried yet relieved by what Jackson said.

"Yes, sir, our people run across these kids all the time. If he went to Seattle, we'll find him," Scott responded confidently. "I'll call you as soon as I hear anything."

Wycoff expressed his thanks; he appeared to be relieved when Jackson said he was sure the police would locate the boy without any difficulties.

When the man turned to leave, Jackson asked, "How'd you learn I was posted here, sir?"

"I went to Colonel Enright's office; he told me all about your work. He said you did an excellent job for the Navy. Enright thought you might be the best one to turn to. He told me of your desire to get overseas. I can understand that. I would love to go myself, Scott, but I cannot. I suppose I'm too old," the admiral replied, shaking his head. "My boss has been kind to me though, he tells me I'm needed here. Maybe I could do something for you… We'll see."

With these parting words, Scott figured the Wycoff boy could be his ticket to a combat command before this war was over. John Wycoff was in a position to get him out of the military police business. When the admiral left the office, he was sure of one thing, the sooner he found the admiral's son, the sooner First Lieutenant Scott Allan Jackson would be on his way to the South Pacific.

Within the week, he heard back from the police in Washington. Seattle officers picked up the admiral's son on the waterfront. As promised, the young man tried to join the Merchant Marine Service. Beat cops, alerted to be on the lookout for him, detained him, placing the boy in protective custody. Jackson telephoned the good news to Admiral Wycoff at his home. Overcome with emotion, the man handed the telephone off to his wife.

Ten days later, Scott received a call from the admiral's secretary, Alice Gooding.

"Lieutenant, the admiral would like you to come by for coffee tomorrow. Can you be here at ten hundred hours?"

He smiled; she sounded like a drill sergeant. "Yes, of course. I'll be there."

"His schedule is tight, Mr. Jackson," she added brusquely, "you might plan on getting here a few minutes early."

It was obvious the admiral's secretary routinely made sure that junior officers arrived on time and did not keep the admiral waiting. She probably also made sure they did not overstay their welcome. He assured Miss Gooding he would be there, on time.

Entering the admiral's office the next morning, he found Miss Gooding to be a middle-aged, gray-haired woman, wearing horn-rimmed glasses and a whole array of costume jewelry. She was dressed formally in a fashionable suit, white satin blouse, and high-heeled shoes. Except for the overabundant display of jewelry, she was an attractive woman. She carefully examined her boss' visitor. It was obvious from her attitude that she did not think very highly of junior officers.

"Remove your hat, Lieutenant!" she snapped.

"Yes, Ma'am," Scott responded politely, her shrill voice quickly reminding him it was not only drill instructors who expected prompt obedience.

"Take a seat," the woman said, her voice cold and harsh. "The admiral's in conference."

The woman's supercilious behavior did not amuse her visitor; for Scott had known too many competent secretaries, secretaries who treated even the lowly Marine boot as someone *very special*. However, as Scott suspected, Miss Gooding's perceived authority appeared more imagined than real.

John Wycoff, opening the door to his office, was delighted to see Jackson. He quickly ushered several members of his staff out, and then rushed to greet his visitor.

"It's good to see you again, Lieutenant," the admiral said, with a smile, as the two men exchanged handshakes. "Come in, please. We'll start off with a cup of coffee," he added, turning to Miss Gooding. "Would you mind? Please."

Miss Gooding promptly carried out her ministerial duties, pouring each man a cup of strong black coffee, and then left the office, closing the door behind her. With the door shut, the Navy man quickly dropped the formality of rank.

"Scott, I'm so glad you're here. I am very pleased with the work your men did for me and my family." He was in good spirits, clearly delighted that his guest had been of help to him and his wife. "Our son is with my wife's sister and her family, he'll finish the school year in Seattle. We will worry about next year when the time comes. Our family is back on track, for now; thanks to you."

"That's great, Admiral. I'm glad to hear that."

"Now that's behind us, Scott," he said, waving his hands in the air as if to close the door on his personal problems. "Let's talk about you. What do you know about tracked vehicles?"

Without waiting for this junior officer to respond, the admiral launched into an enthusiastic yet one-sided dissertation about the ordinance carried in Marine Corps inventory.

"Scott, we have a new weapon in our arsenal; it's a newly designed amphibious armored personnel carrier. Technically, we call it a Landing Vehicle, Tracked, or LVT, and I would like you to look at these for me. Some of your people call it an *amphtrac* or *amtrac*," he said, spelling out the words, "or simply a *tractor*."

"I'd be glad to, sir," Scott replied, cautiously, not knowing what he was getting into.

"I'm sure you've seen many of the older craft both here and at Camp Pendleton and know their purpose. But take a look at these," he said, handing the junior officer several pictures. "That's one of the latest models. Look, here's another," handing a large photograph to Jackson. "Notice the heavy armor." The admiral went on to describe how the craft could provide excellent firepower for troops in the field. Equipped with .50-caliber machine guns mounted on turrets, it was a formidable-looking armored craft. Some were equipped with both machine guns and a howitzer.

"I want you to look at all our tracked vehicles, including the M4 Sherman tank. However, I want you to concentrate your study on the amphibian-tracked vehicles, Scott. These are, in effect, mobile pillboxes. They can operate on either land or sea. They are capable of providing cover for an invading force almost anywhere as they move against an armed enemy." There was no question the admiral was excited about this latest model of the amphibious landing craft.

"They sound like an all-purpose machine, Admiral."

"Oh, they are much more than that, Scott!" he exclaimed. "We used one or two of the earlier models in the landings at Tarawa and at Kwajalein and Eniwetok. With some success, I might add. But as you undoubtedly heard, our losses on Tarawa were horrendous," then, pursing his lips and shaking his head, he added quietly, "completely unacceptable."

"I understand that, Admiral; there are some pretty ugly stories circulating about our problems there."

"I've heard those. Unfortunately, some of those stories are true. Many of our people died needlessly in that invasion. Some place the blame for this on the poor performance or outright failure of our ordinance, particularly our landing craft. I don't," the man said, raising his hands as a cautionary gesture, again shaking his head. "Those who have made such claims don't know a damn thing about these machines.

"There were several reasons why so many young men died on that island, Scott," he added gravely. "But equipment failure was not the primary cause. The Japanese were well equipped, trained and securely entrenched; we underestimated those people. We won't do that again." He paused, obviously reflecting on the carnage inflicted upon the Marines by the Japanese at Tarawa.

"I'd love to go ashore with the troops on one of these craft, but my boss would never agree to that. I'm afraid at my age I'd just get in the way, yet you could be my eyes and ears out there."

"I would like that, sir," replied Jackson, not fully realizing yet what his role might entail. Nevertheless, when the admiral added, "out there," he knew he had finally gotten his long sought-after transfer.

"Scott, I need to know the limitations of this latest-model LVT. To do that, I need a man right there, on site, not as a combatant, but as an observer. I need someone to scrutinize, study and record, and to photograph these machines in a combat situation. My staff and I have been charged with that task.

"My office must be in a position to vouch for the tactical capability of the LVT. The Chief of Naval Operations needs to know if the craft can perform as planned. When our forces invade Japan, the Navy will need a reliable platform on which to move men and equipment from ship to shore. It's my job to find the most suitable craft to accomplish that task."

The admiral suddenly stopped talking as if to give this young Marine officer an opportunity to think about his proposal. Then he quickly added, "With your sailing experience in the Alaskan fishing fleet and your investigative background, I think you're just the man that could do this job for us. What do you say, Lieutenant?"

For a moment, Jackson was speechless. He wanted to see action in this war. However, as Colonel Josh Enright so forcefully pointed out to him, he was not a trained military man. He was just a police officer, nothing more. He was well aware that he lacked the experience and training needed to qualify him to do what Admiral Wycoff proposed. Still, if he turned the job down, he knew his chances of squaring off with the Japanese in the South Pacific were nil.

"Yes, sir, I'll be glad to do that, sir," he answered enthusiastically, concealing his apprehension. "Though I'll need to brush up on the operation of these vehicles. But I'm sure I can handle the assignment." Yet, never before in his entire lifetime was Scott so unsure of himself.

"Good." The admiral appeared to be delighted with his response. "The staff will get you started right away with the Tank Training Battalion at Camp Pendleton. Then, in a week or two, we'll send you out to the Marine Amphibious Training Base. Landing exercises will begin on the peninsula before the end of the month. After that, we will ship you out to Guadalcanal. The

Marines have a training base there on a little-known island called Pavuvu. I understand it provides us with ideal conditions for carrying out tactical exercises.

"By the way, we're going to promote you to the rank of captain. You'll be surprised how much more attention is paid to a Marine captain than what your single bar commands."

Chapter 8

On 4 April, Captain Jackson reported to Marine Tank Training Battalion, Camp Pendleton, California. Early the next morning, he was in the field.

The Marine Corps carried in inventory both the medium M4 Sherman and the lighter M5 Stuart model military tank. Equipped with a twelve-cylinder engine, the M4 was the tank of choice for the Corps. Although classified as a medium tank, to Jackson it seemed like a monster; it truly was a killing machine. Some came with a 105mm howitzer, others with a flamethrower, along with three machine guns, while a few came equipped with 76mm-long, high-velocity guns for antitank warfare. The Sherman tank was a most formidable weapon.

Scott learned quickly that the mission of the M4 was to destroy the enemy's heavy weapons and kill as many enemy soldiers as one could before the enemy put your tank out of action. He thought the term "out of action" was truly appropriate. If you were in one of these tracked vehicles when it became disabled, it often meant that everyone inside was dead.

He never ceased to wonder at the skill with which the crews maneuvered these giant killing machines. Although to him, the ride in one for an hour was worse than being in the ring for three rounds with his amateur boxing champion and friend, Police Lieutenant Hal Brown. In the blistering 100-degree heat of Camp

Pendleton, the exterior of the tank became too hot to touch. The interior of the machine, with its smell of fuel and cramped quarters, reminded Scott of the fishing boat he sailed on in the Gulf of Alaska.

On his first day out, with the vehicle careening across the desert floor and on into the mountain training grounds of this huge military base, Scott soon found himself getting nauseous. His driver, Oliver "Ollie" Hjermstead, a sergeant from Los Angeles, looked at his passenger and smiled.

"Chew this, Captain," he said, handing his passenger a pack of gum. "The first time around, nearly everyone gets sick in these damn things. Sometimes this helps."

Although he wore earplugs and a helmet, when the tank crew opened fire with the cannon, the first shot nearly lifted him out of his seat. Instantly, smoke and the smell of gunpowder filled the passenger compartment. With the second round, Jackson vomited, losing his morning breakfast.

By noon, the joint air-ground training exercise was over. The entire battalion of nearly fifty tanks and two dozen F4F and F4U Marine Corsair fighter bombers returned to base. The tank crews formed up by company as a fleet of fuel and service trucks arrived to ready the machines for the afternoon program. No one broke out a mess kit or field-ration lunch; instead, each circle of tanks was alive with enlisted men and officers alike with fuel cans, wrenches and grease guns in hand.

Before anyone would eat lunch, equipment needed servicing or repair and testing or removed from the field. When damaged beyond the capabilities of the crews to repair, the machine was loaded onto a transport truck and returned to the ordinance depot. It was not until the entire company was ready to return to the field that the company broke for lunch. The commander, a thirty-one-year-old professional from New York City, Major Bob Evanston, called out, "Chow time. Let's eat."

Captain Jackson was in no shape to take on a can of military rations with its dried meat and rock-hard cookies. He grabbed a cup of hot coffee and a bucket of water and climbed back into the iron monster. Before the afternoon exercises began, he would have to clean the vomit off his clothes and from inside the tank. Later, as he emerged from the hatch, he heard Evanston calling out, "Let's get at it, gentlemen. We've got a helluva lot work ahead of us."

Walking over to Jackson, Evanston was smiling. "Scott, I should have told you at chow this morning; layoff the greasy food. These are rough riding machines, until you get used to 'em."

"Thanks, Bob," he responded with a grimace, his stomach churning. "I won't forget."

At the end of the day, every muscle and joint in his tired body ached. Upon returning to camp, he and two other officers went for a swim in the ocean. By the time they got into the water, the beach was quiet; it was almost dinnertime and most of the officers were on their way back to their tents.

For several minutes, he was alone, floating in the gentle waves offshore. Here he watched a small flock of seagulls soaring high above in the warm offshore breeze. They seemed to rise and fall with the air currents as if attuned to the waves below. Thinking about these last few weeks in San Diego, he had to smile, for it was Admiral Wycoff's fourteen-year-old wayward son who *rescued* him from Colonel Enright's command.

For a moment his thoughts turned to Sophia Kosterman; not having heard from her for over a month, he wondered where she was. One of his colleagues interrupted his musing.

"Let's go eat, Scott," the man on shore called out.

After a quick shower, the men stopped at the officers' club for a drink before dinner.

At eighteen hundred hours, he joined more than fifty other officers for mess call. Growing up in a home where his parents raised most of their own food to provide their children with a wholesome diet, he never ceased to appreciate Marine Corps' cuisine. This evening's meal included steak, vegetables, hot coffee, milk and orange juice.

An hour later, officers involved in the exercise, including their CO, and the executive officer of Marine Fighter Wing, VMF XXII assembled in a nearby Quonset hut. Over the next four hours, this group of very young tank battalion, infantry, and aviation officers dissected and evaluated the day's work. Before turning in for the night, they worked out the next day's combat readiness training exercise. It was near midnight before Jackson got to bed.

The following morning and from then on, while engaged in the exercises at Camp Pendleton, Scott limited his breakfast intake to three cups of strong black coffee. On his third day in the field, as they again headed out over the desert and hills of this vast military base toward the nearby Santa Margarita Mountains, Scott rode in a tank equipped with a howitzer.

The ride across the desert floor was no smoother than the preceding days. When the tank began to climb the rocky slope of a small hill, his stomach again began to churn. Yet the feeling of nausea that followed quickly passed. He soon found himself for the first time truly enjoying the roar of the tank's powerful engine.

The Sherman tank normally carried a crew of five, and today Scott took the assistant driver's position. When they stopped at the crest of a hill where the ground leveled, Sergeant Hjermstead called out to his guest, "Take over, Captain."

Jackson soon found himself in charge of what Detective Oscar Johnson called the greatest killing machine ever conceived by man. In maneuvering the vehicle along a dry riverbed, the dust from the lead tanks soon obscured his view. Hjermstead, sensing Jackson's disorientation, yelled, "Keep your eyes on the pennant on the lead tank. He is your guidon. You'll be okay. He's heading due east. That's where we want to go."

Scott was surprised how easy the tank moved over the rough and rocky terrain; just lightly touching the controls turned the vehicle with ease. He had no trouble in staying with the formation as the company moved on into the mountains. Their objective today was to mount an attack directed at dummy fortifications in a nearby valley.

Once the Corsairs completed their bombing runs, tanks moved into position for the attack. Before moving out, however, Jackson relinquished command of the vehicle. "I'm here to learn,

Sergeant," he said to Hjermstead. "I don't want to make a damn fool of myself in front of two thousand Marines."

"Okay, Captain," the man responded with a grin. "We're gonna hit the target the major talked about this morning. It'll get a little hectic for a few minutes."

The entire company rendezvoused at the summit of the second ridge. Identifying their target in the valley beyond, they attacked en masse, firing live ammunition at a make-believe defender.

When the assault ended, Scott thought about Detective Johnson and of what that first-ever mass tank attack must have been like for his former colleague. Johnson, a veteran of the Great War, seldom talked about what happened to him when he was with the American Expeditionary Force in France. Nevertheless, one day, while the two were at lunch, he told Scott of his experience in the Battle of the Somme River. Johnson was one of several officers from AEF cavalry units assigned liaison duties with the British Army.

"In November of seventeen, Scott," he began quietly, "an entire battalion of British tanks hit the Kaiser's people hard. This was the first mass tank attack in the history of warfare. We were near the city of Cambrai, in Northern France. We overran a heavily fortified German stronghold. However, six days later, the Germans drove us back to our original positions. When General Grant said that war was hell, he really knew what he was talking about, Scott.

"Historians never agreed upon the number of casualties; however, I read later that they estimated that between the two armies, more than ten thousand men were killed. It was a horrible thing to experience, Scotty," he added, shaking his head, his lips pursed. "So many good people died needlessly in that war."

Johnson, the former divinity student, would never forget what he saw on that field of battle near the Somme River that day.

Today, looking at the target, a dozen or more vintage trucks and tanks dumped into a narrow valley, Scott wondered what it would be like to be inside one. He hoped he would never find out. Marine

Corsairs moved in dropping napalm first, and then the shells from the tanks' howitzers literally tore the burning vehicles apart.

As the training continued, each day Scott would be in the field from one to five hours, either riding as an observer or driving a tank himself. He learned to guide the vehicle both in formation and in mock assaults upon an imaginary enemy outpost. Although he enjoyed this part of his training, he knew he needed to spend more time working with the crews. These exercises, however, were proof that the secret to success for the Marine's mechanized units was no different from any other operational unit in the Corps. It depended entirely upon two critical factors: first the capability of their weapon, and second the combat-readiness of the crew.

When field training ended for the day, he worked with the young crew members in getting their machines ready for the next day's exercise. Marines inspected every track and tread. The staging area was literally alive with men tending to their equipment; reloading of ammunition would wait until morning, until just before returning to the field.

Non-commissioned officer tank drivers, with their platoon commanders, participated daily in the after-action critiques. At every session, retraining was the word of the day. Company commanders held officers and NCOs alike accountable for their mistakes. Yet they emphasized coordination and teamwork and were never too critical of their subordinates. Jackson noticed that this approach to training was quite different from what he had experienced earlier in boot camp and at OCS.

He was pleased with how much he learned in this short introductory course in armored warfare. If anyone was ready to meet the hazards of combat, the men graduating from the Corps' Tank Training Battalion certainly were.

Time passed swiftly. At week's end, he was on his way to the Amphibious Training Center. The Center, built on a long, narrow strip of sand and rock, lay across the bay from the city of San Diego. Scott tried to visualize just how the amphibious units would measure up to what he had experienced at Camp Pendleton. He wondered if they would exhibit a comparable state of readiness. Would their crews show the same concern for these machines as the officers and men in the tank battalion did for theirs? And if an amtrac broke down at sea, what could the crew do? How would they repair it?

If he had learned nothing else from the short training sojourn with the tank crews at Pendleton it was the lesson taught by these very professional soldiers—your life may depend upon the condition of your equipment.

He arrived at the Coronado Naval Amphibious Base early Sunday morning. Naval personnel, some with their families, were heading off to chapel for Sunday services. Yet, even at this early hour, the station was bustling with activity, with dungaree-clad troops engaged in the business of preparing for war.

Checking in at the Bachelor Officers' Quarters, he borrowed a Jeep to inspect this large naval warfare complex, now crammed with an assortment of amphibious watercraft. He had seen many of these strange-looking craft on San Diego Bay and at Camp Pendleton, but he lacked firsthand knowledge of any of them. Nevertheless, before he again met with Admiral Wycoff, he would have to know not only the technical names of each type of watercraft, but also how to operate and maintain them.

Dozens of LVTs, parked near the water's edge, nearly obscured the shoreline, with more in nearby storage yards. He estimated there must have been over 1,000 craft of one kind or another scattered across this huge facility. Most were being readied for embarkation; several others held in reserve for training purposes showed some signs of damage.

The charge received from Admiral Wycoff was twofold. First, learn the operational capabilities of the craft. Then, in terms of personnel safety, find out if its continued use outweighed its risks to the service. In other words, what were the strategic and tactical potential of the LVT, both as an offensive military weapon and for transport?

This assignment, he knew, would not be easy to accomplish. Fortunately, he learned something of the LVT at Camp Pendleton; he had an opportunity to study the operational manual of each model he saw here today.

The setting for the Amphibious Tractor Training Battalion School at this naval base was a three-room Quonset hut, just yards from the ocean. The training program, however, was as different as day and night from the hands-on training Scott experienced at Camp Pendleton. He was soon to learn that other than two practice landing exercises, he would spend most of his time in a classroom.

Instructors were US Coast Guard, Navy, and Marine Corps veterans of one or more island invasions in the pacific. They were familiar with both wheeled and tracked vehicles used in landing troops from transport ships offshore. The wheeled craft included the infamous DUCK. Unlike tracked vehicles, the DUKW was indeed, as Admiral Wycoff said, something else. Although its official designation was DUKW, it was little more than a two-and-one-half-ton truck, with a propeller. Absurd as it seemed, the designation DUCK appropriately reflected the craft's performance. He was soon to learn that once it became operational, in rough seas, Marines who rode in it were never quite sure it would stay afloat.

On his fourth day at the Amphibious Training Base, Scott boarded a troopship where he watched as troops, with weapons and full packs, disembarked. They were less than 1000 yards from shore. The offloading process was without incident. During the landing exercise, no one was injured. Yet, training films seen earlier in the week were grim reminders that in combat, this was not always the case. Film footage of landings in the South Pacific and from the Mediterranean Theater clearly revealed the risks involved.

Infantrymen carrying combat packs, a nineteen-pound Browning Automatic Rifle, or an M1, and wearing steel helmets were always at risk during these exercises. Were they to fall, the weight of the man's equipment alone could cost him his life. Others most certainly could die in rough seas if caught between a landing craft and the side of a troopship. Disembarking from a large ship under those conditions added a new dimension to amphibious warfare.

Returning to NAS San Diego after the weeklong amphibious training operation, Scott was uneasy about the whole exercise. He was the novice military man in this training group and he was sure everyone in the training command was fully aware of that. Yet something was missing. It seemed to him that tank crews at Camp Pendleton were without question much better trained and organized.

The men at Pendleton respected their equipment and unselfishly cared for the welfare of accompanying infantry. After all, these men invariably depended upon the tank for their protection. They, in turn, could protect the armored vehicle from enemy infantry. Both infantry and tank crews were fully aware that *their* tank could be the key to a successful thrust into enemy territory.

Scott was not sure that this was the case with amphibious units. It appeared that the crews of LVTs looked upon their machines as little more than a means of transportation. Many of them were soon to find out they would prove to be much more than that.

On 19 June, Jackson, along with 200 other Marine officers, assembled at the barracks for roll call. Boarding buses, they soon joined thousands of enlisted men on their way to the waterfront. 20,000 men and 300 Army and Navy nurses assembled along Harbor Drive waiting to board a half dozen troopships tied up along the quay.

It was a warm, beautiful evening in Southern California as the ships moved away from the docks. By the time they reached the mouth of the harbor, lights began to appear all across the city. In the gathering dusk, escort ships began forming up off the coast. It would be a large convoy.

Leaving the harbor, the ship, now loaded with 2,000 Marines and moving slowly, rolled from side to side on the ocean swells. Those on board had a beautiful view of the city and the mountain range in the background. Yet, as beautiful as it was, watching the California coastline disappear over the horizon was suddenly of no interest to Jackson. The novice would-be soldier soon lost his dinner over the fantail of the ship. He could not believe that he could get so sick in such calm waters. He would not fully recover from his seasickness until he again set foot on solid ground at Pearl Harbor.

Of the contingent of Marines on board the troopship USS *Zachary Taylor* today, nearly 500 of them served with the First Marine Division in the Solomon Islands in 1942. These men saw many of their colleagues die in the battles on Guadalcanal and Cape Gloucester. The rest, like Jackson, had never been overseas. Most were just kids, seventeen to twenty years old, with even a few of lesser years. At thirty-two, Jackson was older than most of the officers on board.

Upon arrival at Pearl Harbor, he was glad to go ashore, even if it was only for a couple of days. He and two shipmates borrowed a car and explored the Island of Oahu. By the time they returned to Waikiki, a scarlet touch of red began to appear in the eastern horizon. It was nearly four o'clock in the morning and all three men were in need of hot, black coffee. After obtaining a small room at a local hotel, shared by all, they spent the rest of the day on the beach.

Scott's stopover at Honolulu was a pleasant break and he loved what he saw of Oahu. Even though the islands were operating under wartime restrictions, with its huge military presence and overhead display of barrage balloons, Oahu was still a beautiful place.

Returning to the ship the next day, they found a large contingent of disgruntled men, enlisted and officer alike. All Marine personnel were restricted to quarters. Several of the "Old Breed," or "Raggedy Ass" Marines, as they liked to call themselves, had not returned to the ship at the end of their liberty. These "missing men," after one tour of duty in the South Pacific, were in no hurry to return to the business of war.

Military police began a search in Honolulu of the local bars, whorehouses, and jails for the AWOL troops. By the end of the day, they located all but one, returning the others to the ship. Many of them now fit their vainglorious image—some battered and bruised, uniforms torn or in disarray, others just suffering from a hangover. They truly were dragging their asses. The ship's brig, not large enough to hold all of them, limited the captain's choices for disciplinary action. The wayward group remained confined to quarters. Although the punishment was negligible, the transgressors experienced some discomfort. The stench from the lower decks was overwhelming. The entire ship's hold reeked from the vomit of hundreds of seasick Marines.

Sailing on to the Solomon Islands on the USS *Zachary Taylor* was, at best, an arduous and difficult adventure. An adventure most found loathsome. Poor food, lack of bathing opportunities and the unpleasant smell from the lower decks were enough to numb the senses. Under normal conditions, a fast-moving steamship could make the run to the Solomon Islands in less than ten days. Yet there was nothing normal about a wartime crossing. Because of suspected enemy subMarine sightings, the convoy adopted a defensive zigzag course, prolonging the agony for all aboard.

Chapter 9

The eerie blast of the boatswain's whistle startled Jackson; although he had heard it a dozen times since departing Pearl Harbor, he was apprehensive. With the ship lying quietly at anchor, the sound reverberated throughout the small compartment he shared with five other officers. He knew it to be the harbinger of the now familiar words, "Now hear this, Officers' call!" Broadcast throughout the troopship, no one could escape its reach.

"All officers report to the quarter deck at zero nine hundred hours."

The ship, with its cargo of Marine replacements, was lying off the Island of Pavuvu in the stifling hot sun of the Solomon Islands. Although Scott did not know it at the time, he was still 2,000 miles from their final destination in the Western Caroline Island group.

Pavuvu, described by Admiral Wycoff as a "fine training facility in the South Pacific," was, in fact, a small rat- and snake-infested atoll, teeming with millions of land crabs. The Marines found it difficult to locate enough dry land to set up their tents. The island was little more than a swamp. Yet it gave the men from the *Taylor* an opportunity for a shower and a place to exercise before continuing the voyage.

The replacements would allow the First, Fifth and Seventh Marine Regiments and the Amphibious Corps' Tractor Battalions to be brought up to full strength. They would soon participate in the largest naval amphibious assault operation undertaken in the Western Pacific.

At nine hundred hours, after most of the enlisted troops went ashore, officers gathered on the quarter deck as ordered. Brigadier General Howard D. McAffee was already there. He greeted the men, shaking hands with many as they arrived on deck.

Jackson, the police professional, but novice military man, stood behind the assembled group. He was about to participate as an observer in what would turn out to be the deadliest island invasion yet undertaken by the American military in the Western Pacific.

McAffee began his career as a seagoing Marine; his primary duty: protect the Navy's top brass aboard America's battleships and heavy cruisers. In the '30s, he served in Canton and Shanghai with the American Legation. Promoted to colonel at the beginning of the war, he earned the Congressional Medal of Honor and his Brigadier General's star on Guadalcanal. At fifty-two, the man was the model spit-and-shine Marine officer.

The upcoming strike in the Western Caroline Islands was of great concern to McAffee. The thought that his troops may be facing another Tarawa was always present. On that bloody atoll, the horrific loss of men overshadowed the American victory. The general discussed this with Admiral Nimitz in a meeting with the commander in chief of the Allied Forces in the Pacific. McAffee believed that bombers and naval gunfire could neutralize the enemy in the Western Caroline Islands. Admiral Nimitz did not agree.

The general would do as directed. However, sending a landing party of infantry to attack a stronghold that military forces could eliminate as a threat, by other means, made no sense at all to this seasoned veteran. His only hope was that the additional naval support planned for this operation would reduce the risk for his ground troops. Still, he was confident that his men could carry out this mission with fewer casualties than the Marines had experienced at Tarawa, if, as promised, the Navy provided the additional firepower.

"Gentlemen," he began, exhibiting a degree of self-confidence not shared by some of his senior staff. These men knew their boss questioned the wisdom of this campaign. "In a few days, we will take part in Operation Stalemate. This map will show you where we're going." He motioned for the removal of a white sheet from a large map fastened to the ship's bulkhead. Pictured was a group of islands most of the officers had never heard of.

"Many of you have participated in one or more of these island invasions, where the enemy has been preparing for such an attack as we are about to undertake. The Japanese have been in the Western Caroline Islands for more than a decade. As you may have guessed, we believe the island's fortifications are quite formidable. Fortunately, in this part of the Pacific they no longer have a viable air force. Here, on the Island of Truk," he said, pointing to a small island east of the Palaus, within the Caroline group, "we have eliminated their air capability.

"However," he paused, holding his hands high, palms out, as if to emphasize caution, "we dare not become complacent. Japanese long-range bombers can still reach us from their bases on Mindanao.

"Our experience at Tarawa," McAffee continued, "and in the Mariana Islands has taught us a tough lesson. Our success on the ground will be decided not only by our firepower, but by a combination of firepower, communications know-how and the professionalism of our men."

He went on to discuss the planned offensive in detail. In closing, he added, "We do not believe that our enemy has the same quality of defenses in place here on Peleliu as those we encountered at Tarawa." He paused, looking out over those gathered around to be assured he had their full attention, then warned, "Gentlemen," his tone of voice, now grim, "we underestimated the Japanese defenses on Tarawa, do not make that same mistake here." Several members of his staff nodded in agreement.

Each platoon and company commander received detailed maps and aerial photographs of the island's fortifications. Scott had studied military operational maps during his short stint at

Quantico. These photographs and maps were easy to grasp. After all, what could be so complicated about an island two miles wide and only six miles in length? Two large swamps and few low ridges were about all that showed on the map; and a half mile offshore, a narrow reef encircled nearly the entire island.

Unfortunately, the map did not show the true nature of this ragged piece of white coral, with its ugly ridges protruding above the tranquil waters of the Pacific. Scott was soon to find that neither the map nor the intelligence officers' descriptions of the island bore any resemblance to what the island was like.

Within a week, the entire Division, with its Aviation Support Group, would set sail from the Solomon Islands. Six hospital ships were to accompany the fleet. The presence of so many hospital ships made it obvious—no one figured this invasion would be a walk in the park.

Scott wondered if Sophia Kosterman could be aboard one of the hospital ships. Even though he wrote and told her of his transfer, he had not heard from her in weeks. He realized, however, that she might not have received his most recent letters.

Along with other Headquarters personnel, he boarded LST № 221. This large landing craft was one of more than fifty assigned to the upcoming invasion.

It would be an overstatement to say that an LST was one of the more appealing ships in the Navy's inventory. It was a forbidding, if not ugly-looking craft with its nearly flat bottom and grotesquely oversize loading ramps. A person may wonder how they could possibly move through the water at any reasonable speed; the answer was, of course, they could not. Consequently, it became necessary for the LSTs to depart with their destroyer escorts on this 2000-mile journey, three days before the main convoy weighed anchor.

Marines with their Sherman tanks, half-tracks, and LVTs were crammed together on the vehicle decks. The now famous floating truck, the DUKW, was also in evidence. Every vehicle was loaded with ammunition and supplies. Drinking water, stored in fifty-five-gallon gasoline drums was loaded onto nearly every landing craft.

There were neither enough cots nor bunks to accommodate the number of troops on board the ship. Most of the men slept in, on, or under their equipment. Scott shared an officer's berth built for four, with ten other men.

On the trip to the Western Caroline Islands Marine and naval personnel on board LSTs received one hot meal a day. To accomplish this, the Navy kept the mess hall open twenty-four hours a day.

The journey was hard for everyone on board. Although the movement of the ship created a slight breeze, the boiling hot sun near the equator made the upper decks too hot to lie or sit on. Most of the troops stayed below during the day and suffered in the stifling heat, coming out onto the deck in the evening into the warm night air. Scott was thankful that at least on this trip, he did not get seasick. Many of his shipmates were not that lucky.

The convoy soon ran into stormy weather. The LSTs pitched and rolled with each ocean wave. The bow of the ship would rise high out of the water on the crest of a wave, then fall, with a tremendously loud thump, the impact reverberating throughout the vessel. It was not long before the interior of the ship took on the stench of the *Zachary Taylor*. Many troops, in their frantic effort to get topside or to a latrine before vomiting, never made it. Passageways, stairwells and the vehicle deck became a slippery/ slimy steel skidpan, covered with partially digested food.

Clearing the storm, the waters of the Pacific once more became tranquil. Near the equator, the dolphins and the antics of the flying fish, that for hours accompanied the LSTs, fascinated the troops. These ethereal creatures of the deep, glistening in the sunlight, glided across the top of the ocean's waves. Watching them, the young men on board LST № 221 could put their thoughts of survival aside, at least for now.

Except for the continuous drone of its giant engines, the interior of the craft was quiet. It was hot and crowded below. If not standing in line for food, it often became necessary to stand in line to use the small latrines. At night, the men lay on the steel deck, or sat propped against a tank tread sleeping, or reading from whatever dim light they could find in the interior of the ship.

Scott admired the young Americans who exhibited such exceptional patience and endurance during this difficult voyage. The usual barracks room antics of the stateside Marine were no longer evident. Most of the men, when they spoke, talked softly; others, not uttering a word throughout the voyage.

Some who were yet to experience the stark reality of battle, with its chaos and confusion, often proposed a "what if?" question. When asked of a colleague who fought the Japanese on Guadalcanal, they seldom received a satisfactory answer.

"Keep your head down. Stick together and stay awake," was the best that could be offered.

In daylight, the men field-stripped and cleaned their weapons, something they would repeat often before they came face to face with the enemy on Peleliu. Some quietly honed bayonets or knives on small sharpening stones, others lay on their ponchos staring at the vehicles they would soon be using in battle. A few wrote letters home to their wives, parents, or girlfriends. Navy censors would see that there was no mention of their destination.

On the morning of 12 September, the men on board awoke to the roar of more than 100 guns. The Navy began firing salvo after salvo at a target not yet visible to the men on board the LST. They could hear the cacophony of noise raised by the accompanying warships' fourteen- and sixteen-inch weapons. By the time the men onboard the LSTs came within sight of their destination, battleships and cruisers became clearly visible on the western horizon. The accompanying noise from the large shells, as they traversed in an arc over the troop carriers, was ominous.

Continuing the bombardment throughout the day, the ships' crews carried out their deadly task on into the night. When dawn broke on 13 September, destroyers moved in and shelled enemy fortifications at close range, the sharp crack of the smaller guns echoing off the coral ridges above. On the fourteenth, for some inexplicable reason, the bombardment of the island shut down. Carrier aircraft, however, periodically continued the attack upon enemy fortifications. During this lull, Jackson and twenty other Marine Corps specialists, communications and combat photographers and two civilian war correspondents assembled on the bridge for last-minute instructions.

At the pre-invasion briefing, Scott selected the unit he would accompany during landing operations. Choosing the First Marine Regiment, he believed this would give him the best opportunity to carry out his mission. He would go ashore in the second of three waves of amtracs carrying infantry personnel. These troops would land on Orange and White Beach. All subsequent waves would embark from troopships lying well beyond the reef.

Once the amtracs delivered their precious cargo, they would return to the reef to board personnel from the larger craft. Even at high tide, the larger landing craft would be unable to traverse the reef. Striking a submerged outcropping of coral rock, or steel girders set in concrete to protect the beach, could be disastrous. Underwater Demolition Teams would have to remove these obstructions before the larger craft could offload the Division's tanks, trucks, bulldozers, and heavy artillery.

On the morning of the fifteenth, as the Marines began to disembark from the LSTs and troopships, shelling of the island began anew. It appeared there was no possibility that enemy shore batteries could still be operational after this fierce bombardment.

However, word soon spread throughout Scott's ship that the Underwater Demolition Teams were taking a beating from small arms fire coming from the beach. The unexpected fate of so many of these young UDT men was a sign of things to come; it cast a shadow over the officers and men about to go ashore. Veterans of earlier island invasions knew this could well be their last day on earth.

Once loaded, amtracs with their complement of men and equipment quickly moved away from the LSTs. They began circling, waiting to form up into assault waves.

Farther off shore, operators of the larger craft followed a similar routine. They would take men from the attack transports to the reef; yet, on this tiny atoll, it appeared the Japanese planned for just such an eventuality. When the craft paused at the reef to offload, enfilading fire from concealed cave entrances began to take a heavy toll of both men and equipment.

Outfitted with both movie and still cameras, Jackson was prepared; once again he rechecked both cameras and his .45 automatic and carbine before landing. Going in with this second wave of infantry would give him the opportunity to observe and photograph the first wave as they went ashore. Once ashore, he planned to photograph the third and subsequent waves of landing craft as they came across the reef and onto the beach.

Marine amphibious units formed up at sea, and the initial landings soon began. For a moment, those on board Jackson's amtrac believed they would not make it. As the craft pulled away from the LST it was nearly swamped. Each time they hit a wake of a fast-moving boat, water surged over the gunwale. Troops on board were drenched and standing in nearly a foot of water. That, however, was the least of their worries.

It soon became obvious the two-day bombardment of the island did little to diminish the Japanese Army's ability to defend this island fortress. When the first wave was still more than a half mile offshore, enemy guns suddenly came to life. The Japanese rolled out artillery and heavy machine guns to the mouth of more than a score of caves and began firing at the approaching landing craft. These guns, not seen before in photo reconnaissance flights, quickly zeroed in on the nearest units.

Waterspouts began to appear in front and behind nearby landing craft; within seconds an amtrac and two amphibious tanks took direct hits. All three craft and their two dozen or more Marines simply disappeared in a cloud of black smoke. An artillery round hit another amtrac and it went dead in the water. Smoke and flame began rising almost immediately from the engine compartment of the now disabled craft. Jackson focused his camera on this as a third LVT pulled alongside the burning unit.

Men began jumping from the damaged craft into the nearby amtrac as the fire spread. Within seconds, the burning vessel exploded in flames, damaging the third LVT, killing or injuring more than a score of would-be rescuers. When a fourth amtrac headed toward the stricken men, an officer in a nearby craft, grabbing a bullhorn, yelled at the coxswain.

"Stand clear! Get that son of a bitch ashore, before you're all killed."

Navy and Marine Corsairs, Hellcats, and Avenger bombers circling overhead moved in to attack the caves, yet the shelling continued with deadly accuracy. The landing parties were soon to learn that the caves from which the guns made their appearance were, as on Tarawa, interconnected by tunnels. Their openings in the earth's crust, now hidden by the blackened vegetation, allowed enemy troops to lie in wait, unseen.

As the second wave began the horrific ride toward the beach, Scott's craft began taking fire from a large-caliber machine gun. One round nearly severed the head of a Marine who did not heed the orders of his sergeant to "Keep your head down." The man was standing less than ten feet from Jackson; he wanted to see what the captain was photographing.

Blood, bone fragments, and brain tissue from the dead man splattered across the face of a nearby Marine. The man cursed and wiped the splatter off with his free hand while holding on to the gunwale. Two others, horrified by the sight of their dead colleague and the blood running down the face of another, their faces chalk white, dropped to their knees. Without saying a word, their sergeant grabbed the two and pulled them upright.

Scott began shooting pictures of two tracked vehicles lying dead in the water, both on fire. When his craft went by the stricken vessels, he could see eight or ten backpacks floating on the surface—there was no sign of those who had worn them.

Approaching the shoreline, bullets continued to find their mark, clattering loudly against the heavy armor-plated side of the amphibious craft. Lurching out of the water onto the beach, the operator headed for a narrow opening in a low-lying corral ridge. Suddenly an explosion rocked the vehicle. They struck a mine. Rocks, sand and shards of coral, thrown into the air, fell back onto the occupants, covering them with debris. One track, completely torn away from the LVT, ended up alongside the craft in a mass of torn metal.

Although unnerved by the blast, no one on board was seriously injured. The NCO who, during the trip ashore, picked up the two Marines who nearly fainted, ordered everyone out.

"Over the portside!" he yelled. "Make a run for the rocks." Securing the camera in his backpack, Jackson rechecked his .45-caliber automatic for the fourth or fifth time since embarking from the LST, and then grabbed his carbine with his free hand. For a moment, he listened to the thud of bullets as they continued to rain down on the steel hull of the LVT. With the NCO and the last enlisted man out, he literally dived over the side of the craft. Landing in the middle of a group of Marines huddled nearby, he nearly knocked the NCO to the ground. Unperturbed, the sergeant said, "Welcome to my island, Captain, is this your first landing?"

"Yes, Sergeant, it is, and I hope it's my last."

"Well, if we keep standing here, Captain, it'll be our last. Let's get the hell out of here."

The men made a dash for the protection of a series of coral rocks extending along the beach for nearly 400 yards. Quickly gaining cover, from their new position they could see 300 or 400 Marines huddled against the coral outcropping of a nearby berm. The men were seeking protection from a hail of small arms and mortar fire. For the moment they were protected, yet each successive mortar round inched closer.

Scott needed no reminder of what his task was: observe, and record the effectiveness of the tracked vehicles as they came ashore, particularly the LVT and the amphibious and M4 Sherman tank. But his primary objective from Admiral Wycoff's charge was, "Find out just how effective the LVT is in transporting troops from ship to shore. And could this craft support a landing party once it arrived on the beach?"

With the battle raging about him, he crisscrossed the length of the landing zone for more than four hours, making notes and taking pictures. A score or more LVTs, disabled by mines or artillery fire, provided some protection for those seeking cover from the withering gunfire from the ridges above. Yet he tried not to remain too long in one location as Japanese gunners continued to target those hidden behind the disabled craft. Death and destruction were everywhere.

Looking out to sea, he could see dozens of landing craft burning, and others, inside the reef, sitting on the ocean floor. Their turret-mounted machine guns on some were all that remained visible above the water's surface.

Although his objective was clear, looking at the bodies of dead Marines floating nearby in the surf, his assignment seemed so pointless. The foam along the shoreline, created by the ebb and flow of the ocean's waves, took on a black and pinkish cast from the oil and the blood that flowed into the shallow water.

To get pictures of the damaged amphibious craft, he crawled out into the water and slithered in behind an LVT while continuing to take photographs of other stalled amtracs. Looking north along the shoreline, two LVTs were undamaged and he wondered why they had not come ashore. Running in a crouched position across the beach for a closer look, he nearly collided with General McAffee.

McAffee, against both the suggestions of his staff and contrary to Corps' policy, came ashore with the third wave. General officers were, for good reason, prohibited from doing just that. They were not to go ashore until a secure command post could be set up from which they could operate. Were they to become a casualty during the initial stage of the invasion, it could spell disaster for the entire invasion. Despite that, the general, from the old school, wanted to be where the action was. He needed to see exactly what his people faced on the beach.

"What are you doing, Captain?" he shouted. "You're going to get yourself shot out here in the open."

"No, sir, General, I've got to find out why those two LVTs are abandoned out there in the water."

"Well, hurry on, and then report to me at my command post. I'm setting up shop right there, below that outcropping of coral." McAffee pointed to a small circular area, where four or five staff personnel and a communication team were busily setting up the command post.

Bullets skipped across the shallow water near Scott as he made a dash from his protective cover toward the two stalled craft. His mind racing, it became nearly impossible to concentrate on his assignment.

"What the hell am I doing here?" he muttered to himself, as a Japanese shell exploded on the beach nearby. Stunned by the violent shock of the exploding shell, he went down in the shallow water. For a time, the sound and fury of the battle ceased to exist, shut out by the human ear's defensive mechanism, as if plummeting from a high mountaintop. He stood, shook his head, trying to clear his senses, but there was no sound, yet he could still see the madness being orchestrated about him. It was not until someone grabbed him by his dungaree jacket and dragged him in behind a damaged LVT that he began to recover from the shock of the explosion.

He heard the man, as if from a distance yelling, "Captain, you've got to take cover. Are you all right?" he asked, looking at the trickle of blood coming from Jackson's nose and ears.

Scott responded by nodding his head, not realizing fully what happened. Yet it was the obvious concern shown by this young Marine that forced him to concentrate. As he wiped the blood away on his jacket sleeve, he realized he still had a job to do. He needed to get out to the watercraft stalled off the beach. Nevertheless, his immediate objective now seemed so futile. Why, he wondered, should he be worrying about two stalled amphibious craft when men were dying all around him? There were dead men everywhere. Bodies, body parts, helmets, backpacks, rifles, and heavy ordinance littered the shoreline, or floated in the surf.

"Holy Christ!" he cursed. "This is insane," he said to the young Marine who had pulled him from the water. Without waiting for a reply, he quickly moved on. In the shallow water, he scurried alongside the first vehicle, looking for some sign of damage or a thrown track. Finding nothing amiss, he emerged from the water, quickly slipping over the gunwale into the passenger compartment.

Inside, he found a dead man still sitting at the controls; he was the only one on board the craft. Exiting the rear of the amtrac, he slipped back into the water and made his way to the second vehicle. Looking for exterior damage, but again finding nothing amiss, he hoisted himself over the side and dropped onto the deck of the craft.

In his haste, he slipped and fell, going down hard. The steel deck, covered with blood, oil, and vomit, made it near impossible to stand. Lying there, he realized the craft's engine was still running. Looking around the interior of the vehicle, he saw the operator's body entangled in the controls; the lower part of the man's face was missing.

Two Marines, in full pack, still holding on to their weapons, lay dead on the deck. Nearby, in a gruesome position, was another crew member. His body was missing a leg. Apparently, a mortar or small artillery shell had landed inside the craft, killing all four men.

Working his way back to the beach, Scott could see that the enemy was still concentrating fire on the LVTs and the larger boats at the reef. Bunched together, several amphibious craft began loading troops from the LCVPs; they quickly became the target.

To his left and just inside the reef there was still no sign of movement of the troops he had seen earlier huddled behind the berm. For the moment, the Japanese defenders were ignoring them, yet it was obvious they could not survive long. If enemy mortars did not kill them, the incoming tide would eventually force them out into the open. Few would survive. For now, however, the Japanese took no notice of them. Yet as he watched, mortar rounds began again to drop close to those who sought cover behind this long, low berm that extended out from the shoreline.

North of the berm, 200 or more Marines lay dead or wounded on the sand; some of them had returned to rescue a companion who failed to make it ashore. The would-be rescuers, caught in the open, suffered the fate of their colleagues. Their lifeless bodies now floated in the shallow surf with their friends. He snapped a dozen quick pictures of this barbaric scene, then turned and quickly made his way to General McAffee's command post.

Surrounded by a small group of men, the general was giving directions to two officers busy coordinating an air strike for frontline troops. The Japanese defenders at this time, on this beach, were at most just 100 yards away. Aircraft came in low over the command post, attacking the enemy positions; the roar of their motors temporarily silencing the clamor of small arms fire.

Seeing Jackson, General McAffee grabbed him by the shoulder, pulling him toward a large map spread out on the sand and held in place by four rocks.

"Captain," General McAffee, shouted, "you've got a new assignment with the First Marines. From now on you'll be reporting to Colonel Pugh, there." McAffee gestured toward Battalion Commander Lieutenant Colonel Robert Pugh, kneeling nearby, studying the map, then shouting instructions to a junior officer.

"Look down the line," the general said. "If we don't get those men off the beach, they're all going to die right there. That's part of Second Battalion and most of Charlie Company; their officers and noncoms are either dead or wounded.

"Admiral Wycoff briefed us on your assignment, but I need a company commander and you're it!" he shouted. "I know you don't have field experience, but you attended the pre-invasion planning sessions and you know what we need. Colonel Pugh cannot break loose; we have a problem down the line, but when he is free, you will report to him. For now, however," pointing toward the men holed up behind the long berm, "takeover down there. Get those men organized, and then move them off the beach."

Directing Jackson's attention to the same map Colonel Pugh was using, McAffee said, with a note of urgency in his voice, "Move toward Ridge 120. We have to take that hill before nightfall or we'll all be in trouble. We must silence those guns on the near side or they will pick us off like ducks in a pond. Any questions? If not, move out."

Scott had many questions, but this was neither the time nor the place to ask them. Grabbing his carbine and leaving the cameras behind, he headed toward the stranded company. He ran in a low crouch through the shallow water, weaving in and out between the large boulders and downed palm trees, twisted and broken in the bombardment. Wrenched from the ground by the exploding shells and hurled like straw in the wind, the trees came crashing down along the shoreline in a massive tangle of debris.

Scott had experienced the carnage a lone individual with a powerful weapon could inflict upon a human being, yet nothing prepared him for what he saw here today. Amid this shamble of broken trees and shattered coral lay the bodies of more than 200 dead Marines. Caught in the open trying to struggle though this maze, they were cut down by enemy fire. Some bodies, literally torn apart, lay in stark contrast to others, who showed no sign of the wounds that ended their young lives. Yet, there was no time to think about this.

He covered the 300 yards from the CP to the berm in minutes, yet it seemed like hours as enemy gunfire kicked up sand and shards of coral all around him. Once he attained the comparative safety of the overhead rocks, he looked down the line. "I want to see NCOs...now!" he yelled. "Where are you?"

One man nearby responded with a southern accent, "Yo, Capt'n, Sergeant Conlan here."

Another sergeant, halfway down the line of immobilized men, raced toward Jackson. When he got within earshot, Scott asked, "Where're the rest of the noncoms and the officers?"

"We're all that's left, Capt'n," Sergeant Conlan replied.

Jackson was shocked. "My God!" he exclaimed quietly, suddenly realizing General McAffee was not exaggerating. What could have happened? There should have been four officers and at least ten more NCOs with this group. Although clearly addressing the two sergeants, he spoke loud enough for those nearby to hear.

"Get your men up now. If you stay here, you will die here. We've got to move inland."

Grabbing Sergeant Conlan by the arm, he shouted, "Take half the company and follow me, we're getting out of here." Turning to the other man, he asked, "What's your name, Sergeant?"

"Niles, sir."

"Sergeant Niles, take the other half. After Conlan's men get beyond these rocks, you bring your platoon over the top. We will provide cover fire. And, Sergeant," looking directly at the man, his voice threatening, "I don't want to come back looking for you people. Is that understood?"

"Yes, sir, Captain," Sergeant Niles responded, grim faced. Yet the man appeared to be relieved—finally, someone was going to take charge and get them off the beach. This was something that he was not prepared to do by himself, but he would follow.

Scott did not know what to think; maybe he should not have threatened the man. Right then, however, it appeared to be the right thing to do. He would worry later about his relationship with these two newly acquired NCOs, and this company of Marines who had yet to contribute to the success of this invasion.

When Sergeant Conlan's platoon was ready, Jackson yelled, "Let's go!"

His mind was whirling. The sights and sounds of the aircraft overhead and the crack of nearby gunfire were only dimly recording in his brain. "God," he muttered, "how the devil did I get into this mess?" Then he remembered Colonel Josh Enright saying only weeks ago in San Diego, "You want too much, Jackson, and just maybe you may not like what you get. What the hell makes you think you could handle combat?"

Now, he was not too sure, maybe the colonel was right. Even so, he was sure of one thing: he was not going to die today, on this godforsaken coral beach.

Chapter 10

Climbing over coral formations was a new experience for these Marines. They were quick to discover the razor-sharp edges of coral cut through their dungarees like a knife, and tore at their boots.

Reaching the top of the berm, Jackson could see through the heavy black smoke that the company would have to move inland nearly 200 yards before finding cover. Crossing this short stretch of coral and sand, they would be out in the open, at the mercy of enemy snipers and mortars.

Looking back, to his surprise, men from all along this rock formation began to follow. The sergeants formed the company into two large platoons of nearly 150 men each and these into squads. With some semblance of order, they began the climb. When they reached the top of the berm, they followed the captain and the two noncoms as the three men raced across the beach to what must have been at one time the edge of the island's forest.

Unexpectedly, the company drew very little small arms fire; the reason soon became evident. The ground was still hot from burning debris and clouds of smoke rising from scorched vegetation helped to obscure their movement. A dirty gray blanket of dust covered the white coral; the air smelled of cordite, burnt flesh, and burning oil.

Scott hoped to gain protection once the two platoons reached the tree line, but the three-day bombardment changed the entire landscape of the island. There was no tree line. There were no trees. A jumble of broken stumps, scorched tree limbs and broken bodies were all that could be seen lying in and around huge shell craters, some so large they could swallow a tank. Still, the company moved in from the beach without losing a single man. Enemy fire from a cave opening wounded two men, yet both made it to the protective cover of a crater. Corpsmen quickly attended to them. Browning Automatic Rifle fire silenced the snipers.

Stepping into the cave where only moments before snipers lay in wait, Jackson saw two dead Japanese soldiers near the remains of a large-caliber gun. Because these two survived the bombardment, he suspected there may be more still inside this rock and coral sanctuary carved out of the cliff. Without light, there was no way to tell.

Clearing the entrance, he yelled at Sergeant Niles to have his men fire rifle grenades into the back recesses of the hollowed-out hillside. Explosions reverberated throughout the interior.

Now he needed time—at least a few minutes—time to think his way through this, and time with his two sergeants. He would have to tell the sergeants what General McAffee expected of Charlie Company. He also needed assurance that these two were competent to handle their platoons. Both sergeants joined Scott at the mouth of the cave. It was wide and deep, providing temporary respite and protection for the three of them along with a radioman who was with the men on the beach.

While talking to the two, he learned what happened to the officers and the other NCOs of Charlie Company. Unfortunately, they were on board the LVTs hit by Japanese shore batteries; most of them never made it ashore. Scott actually photographed these very LVTs as the second wave of landing craft moved in from the reef.

Spreading his map out on the floor of the cave, he and his two newly acquired sergeants tried to locate their position. Unfortunately, there were no landmarks other than the ridge above them. Most of the buildings and fortifications depicted on their map no longer existed. Except for one concrete structure still standing in the distance, the buildings that stood here were now mere piles of rubble, one indistinguishable from the other.

Once focused on their approximate location, he told the two men of General McAffee's directions.

"We are to coordinate our advance with I Company and move on the ridge above. They will cover our left flank. Our objective will be to secure the ridge and take up positions along the crest before nightfall.

"When we move up the hill, we should be in a position to protect the western perimeter of the beachhead. Undoubtedly the Japs will counterattack; but if either company fails to accomplish our task, it could be disastrous for our guys on the beach. The Japs will be quick to take advantage of our weaknesses."

Looking at his watch, he said, "We have approximately six hours of daylight left to get to the crest of this ridge. If we don't secure that before dark, the troops on the beaches below will catch hell."

Before leaving the cave, Scott learned that Conlan and Niles were veterans of Guadalcanal and Cape Gloucester. He suddenly realized he had made a terrible mistake. Starting out on a new assignment by threatening men who had survived two invasions was no way to earn their respect. However, there was no time to worry about that. As he climbed out of the cave, they came under attack from weapons fired from the ridge above. Fortunately, no one was injured.

Returning to their men, the two NCOs began moving their platoons across the base of the ridge, gunfire from above intensified when they came into view. Before they traveled thirty yards, the entire hillside suddenly seemed to erupt in a barrage of small arms fire. It came from a dozen cave openings in the heights above.

Once again, Scott asked Battalion for air support; and within minutes, a squadron of naval aircraft was in the air overhead. With the Marines again holed up in bomb craters and behind coral rock formations along the base of the cliff, the planes targeted the front side of the hill. After the last pilot dropped his bombs, the others returned, this time making a run across the face of the hillside, guns chattering.

With the air strike over and after warily climbing out from under the debris of war that littered this landscape, the men moved once more toward the hillside. Yet, moving no more than a few yards, the company came under another barrage of intense gunfire. It started suddenly and appeared to have come from the same caves. Machine gun fire struck a man moving just to the right of Jackson. His piercing shriek of pain, more than the fusillade of gunfire itself, brought the entire company to a standstill. Startled by his screams with this last violent Japanese attack upon their ranks, several men froze in their tracks. They stood out in the open, targeted once again by a second round of gunfire from above.

"Get down! Get down!" Sergeant Niles screamed.

It was not until Niles yelled that they realized the full impact of what was occurring around them. More than a dozen men, mostly from Niles' platoon, were cut down almost immediately. Three men were killed outright; others, although wounded, were quickly dragged to cover.

Taking refuge in a crater, Jackson again called for air support; a dozen or more aircraft appeared above them within minutes. This time, two squadrons of Navy Hellcats and Marine Corsairs roared across the full length of the hillside, firing their guns until exhausting their supply of ammunition. When the air strike ended, Scott reported his losses to a lieutenant monitoring the radio at the regimental CP.

"We need some help up here, Lieutenant," he added candidly. "I need replacements and stretcher bearers to help evacuate our casualties. I have nineteen wounded."

"Hold on, Captain," the lieutenant responded. "I'll advise the CO."

In a few moments, what he got instead was a derisive response from his battalion commander, Lieutenant Colonel Robert Pugh.

Although Scott had yet to meet the man, while in the States he heard much about this most decorated Marine Corps colonel.

"Captain, this is Colonel Pugh," the man replied sharply. "I haven't got any replacements; you'll have to take care of your own wounded." Jackson thought he detected a note of scorn in the man's voice and then was sure of it when Pugh added, "Now get off your ass; you will have to take that ridge with what you have. Go after those caves yourself. Get above them, and close 'em up. If you don't reach the top before dark, you're a dead man!"

The colonel's admonition and foreboding outlook on his future, angered this novice Marine infantry commander.

"What does that son of a bitch expect?" he muttered, fully aware he was not a military professional. "God help me!" Startled by his own thoughts, he suddenly remembered that line officers, whom he met aboard ship who served under Pugh on the Canal, tagged him with the nickname "The Bloody Bastard." They thought he was a man out to make a name for himself irrespective of the casualties which an enemy may inflict upon his troops.

Scott wondered how he could have been so stupid. It wasn't until that moment that he realized what price he may have to pay because of his persistent, if somewhat naïve resolve to see combat in this war. This was no cops and robbers game. His life and the lives of his men depended upon the decisions he would make here today.

Yet even he, the novice, was sure of one thing: he knew they could not stay where they were. Crawling over to Sergeants Niles and Conlan, located behind a large boulder, he told them of Pugh's directive, leaving out the colorful edict the colonel so freely offered.

"You got any ideas?" he asked.

"Well, Capt'n," Conlan responded, with his Southern Mississippi drawl, "those people up there can see the planes coming long before we do; they've got plenty of time to get back in their holes. Unless that pilot can drop a bomb right into the mouth of the cave, they're right back out there, shoot'n at us."

"We could try bazookas and rifle grenades, Captain," Sergeant Niles offered, with a note of uncertainty in his voice. "The large cave entrances are too far away though and it would be tough to get into position without exposing our own people. However, if we could knock those out at the top, that would be a different story. We could move against the smaller ones reasonably well."

"I agree," Sergeant Conlan replied. "Capt'n, we tried something on Cape Gloucester and it could work here. We have explosives and plenty of rope. We can work our way up above the entrances and drop satchel charges right down their bloody throats."

Jackson agreed with the sergeant's plan. Conlan and Niles returned to their platoons and quickly briefed their men. They would climb to the top of the ridge, attack the three largest caves first, and then work their way back down one by one. The troops at the base of the cliff would provide covering fire across the ridge, concentrating on any cave opening where they saw movement. Once the men carrying the satchel charges got higher than the mouth of a cave, the defenders would have to show themselves; that was the only way they could attack the Marines above them, who were working their way toward the top of the ridge.

Three Marines volunteered to carry the explosive charges. Quickly tying rope to as many satchels and leaving the comparative safety of the craters behind, the men began their climb. To protect them, riflemen commenced firing, raking the nearby cave openings on the hillside with a fusillade of bullets and rifle grenades. BAR-men concentrated their firepower on fissures near the top of the ridge.

Scurrying up the steep incline, the three soon gained a position above the lower caves. Almost immediately, several Japanese soldiers, armed with rifles, scrambled out from the cave entrances below. Two of them, calmly taking aim at the nearest Marine, killed him.

However, the Japanese soldiers paid a price for their marksmanship; .30-caliber rounds fired by two of Charlie Company's BAR-men cut them down. When hit, four or five soldiers rolled back into the cave entrance; one, however, surviving the BAR assault, began firing on the Marines below. Conlan's men quickly finished him off. His lifeless body rolled down the face of the hillside until entangled in an uprooted tree stump.

With the danger past for the moment, two Marines from Sergeant Niles' platoon rushed from cover. One grabbed the explosive pack from their dead comrade's hand and continued up the hillside. Eventually he caught up to his colleagues just above the lower caves. When the three men came abreast of the top row, more enemy riflemen emerged from below and opened fire on them.

Two more Japanese soldiers paid the ultimate price for this act, but before they died, they killed one man above them and wounded another. The dead Marine was one of the men who rushed from cover to retrieve the TNT satchel dropped by the first man slain on the hillside below.

From his relatively secure crater, Jackson saw the wounded man fall; the other two Marines, however, continued crawling toward the mouth of the nearest cave, dragging the satchel charges behind them. Before reaching their objective, one of the men cried out. He clutched at his face, then lay still. However, the Japanese soldiers responsible for his death were now out in the open; they died quickly. Conlan's BAR men missed few visible targets.

Suddenly, popping out from the mouth of another cave, not twenty feet below the last of Jackson's volunteers, a second enemy soldier fired at the man. Dropping the explosive charge, the Marine grabbed his stomach and pitched forward; he landed below the opening in the earth's crust. He lay there on the hillside, next to the bodies of two enemy soldiers; his body and those of the other volunteers clearly visible to the men of Charlie Company below.

Stunned by these killings, Scott's men lay immobilized. Their company commander's plan failed to accomplish their objective. Several of them began to wonder just who this new company commander was that would send them on such a damn fool venture. One man expressed his thoughts along these lines, only to be overheard by Sergeant Niles. What the young man had yet to learn was that veteran Marine sergeants were quick to react to such negative comments from a troop. His response was automatic.

"You're up next, Mac," he said harshly. "Get off you ass and move out!"

While this exchange was taking place, Jackson noted that no one else voluntarily ventured from his protective cover. *Lord God, help us*, he thought, *we are not staying here. If we do we're dead.*

Before Sergeant Niles' man climbed out of the crater, Jackson made a mad scramble up the ridge. On the way up, he picked up the first satchel charge as he went by the body of the dead private. Continuing to the next man, he bent down to retrieve the second satchel. When he stood upright, he felt a stinging sensation in his backside; water erupted from his canteen. He went down hard, and then heard the roar of a Browning Automatic Rifle. One of Niles' men finished off the enemy soldier who had taken his company commander down.

Getting back on his feet, Scott approached the wounded Marine lying on his back just above the highest cave, his dungarees covered with blood from a shoulder wound. Grabbing a TNT satchel, Scott dropped down beside the injured Marine, his eyes focusing for a moment on the blood smeared across the young man's face where he wiped it away with the back of his hand.

"Show me how to operate this son of a bitch," he said.

The young man merely shook his head. Here he was on the top of a cliff, surrounded by enemy soldiers who were trying to kill them, and his captain did not know how to arm a satchel charge. Scott offered a grim smile at the boy's obvious incredulity.

"Pull that cord and throw it, Captain. That's all you have to do. You've got about six seconds."

Grabbing the loose end of a 50-foot rope, with the other end tied to the charge, he ran to the mouth of the nearest cave. Pulling the arming device, he hurled the satchel straight out from the slope of the hillside. As it fell, he hung on to the end of the long rope; when it snapped taut, the satchel swung down in a graceful arc into the opening below.

The explosion that followed shook the ground where he stood and a small cloud of smoke and debris erupted from the cave. This was followed by a secondary explosion, then a third, each more violent than the first. The mouth of the cave below and the two on either side literally disappeared as the whole hillside collapsed around them. The secondary explosions triggered a rock and debris slide under Jackson and the wounded man's feet, sending them tumbling down the hill.

Holding on to the two remaining satchel charges, the wounded Marine grabbed at Jackson for support. Regaining their balance, the two started up the hillside once more. Reaching the second tier of caves, the young Marine handed another satchel to Scott. Now lying precariously against the steep hillside, Jackson worked his way down until he was within a few feet of the top of the cave. Once in position, he pulled the arming device, then rolled onto his back, violently flinging the charge into the entrance below before scrambling back up the hillside. This time, the secondary explosions were much less violent than the earlier ones, still a plume of black smoke and debris erupted from the cave entrance.

On a roll, he grabbed the third satchel and dashed across the hillside to another opening. As he positioned himself above this miniature fortress, a bullet struck him in the leg, knocking him down. Stunned, he lay there for a moment and then began to look around to see what it was that toppled him. Behind him, the Marine private, with his good arm, propping his M1 rifle across the top of a tree stump, taking careful aim, killed the man who had fired on his captain.

Dazed, Scott sat erect, handing the satchel charge off to the wounded man.

"You'll have to do it, kid," he said, grimacing with pain.

"Okay, Captain."

"Tell me when you're ready."

"Now!" yelled the private.

Jackson pulled the arming cord; the young man stood up, and with his good arm heaved the satchel toward the cave. As the rope tightened, the charge fell once again the length of the line, then into the cave below.

Suddenly there were Japanese soldiers everywhere. In near panic, they came running out, unmindful of the danger from below. Racing to get away before the explosion, they ran headlong into a withering barrage of fire from the men at the base of the cliff.

This was the company's first opportunity to meet the enemy face to face. The Marines took full advantage. It quickly became a turkey shoot. None of the enemy soldiers survived. The whole hillside appeared to be moving, the bodies of more than a score of Japanese soldiers, felled by Marine-gunfire, rolled or slid down the steep incline.

While counting off the seconds until the satchel would explode, the two Marines watched the carnage unfolding below. They were proud of their handiwork. Unfortunately, they failed to see an enemy soldier concealed at the mouth of the cave; the man shot Scott's wounded comrade. Moments later, a secondary blast shook the hillside; the enemy soldier was lost to view in the resulting explosion. With the destruction of this cavern and the annihilation of the occupants, Sergeants Niles and Conlan ordered their men to attack the remaining caves.

Niles calling out, "Harris, Armstrong, Tallman, get your squads ready; Harris, on the left, Armstrong, take the three center caves. Tallman, take the ones on the right. Move out now!" he yelled. The three squads moved quickly; firing rifle grenades into the hillside fortifications, while flamethrower teams moved against the smaller openings in the earth's crust. Secondary explosions soon occurred within the recesses of the escarpment below. Enemy soldiers, some on fire, came running out, escaping the fury of Sergeant Niles' men, only to be cut down by Conlan's people.

Following these attacks, secondary explosions occurred in two of the larger caves; then quite suddenly, the entire hillside shook from a massive eruption within. When it ended, the area reeked with the sickening stench of cordite and burning flesh. A cloud of dust and smoke lay across the ridge. There were bodies everywhere; twenty-two of them were members of Charlie Company.

Watching the progress of Jackson's men through field glasses, General McAffee and Colonel Pugh were encouraged by what took place. Still, there was a ways to go before the company reached the crest of the ridge.

When communications was unable to raise Jackson by radio, General McAffee said, "You'd better give 'em some air support. India Company ain't moving and it looks like Charlie's lost a lot of his people."

After the last explosion, Sergeant Niles reacted quickly. Crawling up the hillside, he called out to the men below.

"Get a corpsman up here, right away."

Scott was sitting up, holding his young colleague in his lap; he was dead, with a gaping hole in the back of his head. Blood and brain tissue, seeping out between Jackson's fingers, ran down the front of his dungarees.

"He's dead, Captain, let me have him," Niles entreated, troubled by this grisly scene.

"No, Sergeant, I've got to know his name. Who is he?"

"Beach, sir, Private David Beach."

"Where's he from?" Jackson asked, the question so often asked by Marine officers of their subordinates, yet so pointless under the circumstances.

"I don't know, Captain. Let me have him," Sergeant Niles pleaded, taking the boy and gently easing his lifeless body to the ground beside his company commander.

"I'm responsible for his death, Sergeant," he responded, obviously shaken by the death of this young man.

"No, sir, you're not responsible," Niles replied, stoically. "Beach was doing what Marines are expected to do... He did a good job."

"I was actually enjoying killing those people. I asked him to throw the last satchel; he did, but it was all unnecessary. I could have thrown it, but I wanted him to get the same thrill I experienced. He was just a kid. If I had thrown that charge he'd still be alive."

"Leave it alone, Captain," Sergeant Niles responded, dispassionately. "We've got a long war ahead of us, just thank God you're still alive."

When the corpsmen arrived, they forced Jackson to lie flat on the ground, as blood from an open wound in his right leg seeped through his dungarees.

"Patch me up, Navy," he said to the corpsman. "We've got a way to go before it gets dark."

"You ain't going anyplace, Captain, but home," Sergeant Niles responded firmly.

"Niles, listen to me," Scott replied, his voice cold and hard. "If we don't get those people off this damn hillside before dark, we'll all go home, but it'll be in a box. Do you understand?" he demanded, yet not wanting an answer. "Now get your people together and get ready to move up to the crest. When they get there, they will need to gather whatever they can for cover. In this coral, they won't be able to dig in. You and Conlan know what you have to do. Now get at it.

"How many people we got left?" he asked, abruptly changing the subject.

"We haven't counted 'em, but it looks like about two hundred, two twenty-five, maybe a few more. We'll get a count."

"Where's our radio man?"

"He's dead, Captain."

"And the radio?"

"It's gone too, sir, the kid got hit hard with a grenade. It killed him, destroyed the radio, and wounded two third squad members."

"What about your radioman?" he asked, turning to Sergeant Conlan.

"Neither one of ours is working, Capt'n. The men got bounced around, the radios did not survive."

"Then get a runner off to Battalion, tell them what we need. Have the man pick up as many radio packs as he can carry.

"Come on, Navy," he growled at the corpsman who was tying a bandage tightly around his leg. "Get me patched up. We've got to keep moving, or we'll be dead before this day's over."

Chapter 11

With his wound bandaged, Scott handed his carbine off to one of Sergeant Conlan's men standing nearby.

"Let me have your M1, Marine; I need a cane to climb this damn hillside," he said, as he began his arduous trek toward the top of the ridge. He had taken but a few steps, when he heard, and then saw the aircraft overhead; it looked like a whole squadron of Corsairs and Hellcats. They were moving in tandem toward the ragged promontory above him. One after another, the planes dropped bombs on this small plateau, then raked enemy positions with their .50-caliber machine guns.

Although still over 200 yards from the top, the men of Charlie Company could feel the ground shake as the bombs exploded above. By the time the last plane completed its run, the ridge disappeared behind a dirty gray pall of black smoke and dust. With a light onshore ocean breeze blowing, the billowing clouds of smoke soon began to clear, leaving Jackson's men exposed once more. As the last plane pulled out of its dive and the now familiar twin contrails drifted across the top of the ridge, enemy troops again reappeared from within the earth's crust. Mortar shells and hand grenades soon greeted the Marines below.

The Japanese soldiers continued to raise havoc with Scott's company until naval and Marine aircraft once again brought their guns into play. This gave Jackson's Company an opportunity to move further up the hillside. However, without communications to Battalion, Scott and the two NCOs knew the risk from "friendly fire" increased immeasurably.

As the last of the naval aircraft cleared the ridge, Jackson called out to his men, "Fix bayonets and move on up to the top." Yet, before his men got underway, the defenders above began again to lob hand grenades over the edge of the cliff. They were deadly accurate at this close range. On the rock-hard coral, the death-dealing missiles often bounced into the air about the time they exploded. Flying shrapnel and shards of rock took their toll, yet the Company continued on its way; reaching the crest before nightfall, with bayonets fixed, they moved quickly out onto the narrow plateau. Blending in with the charred trees and blackened coral, their faces and dungarees now covered with sweat and grime, they were a formidable-looking group of warriors

Moving tireless onward, in a near-frenzied pursuit of their foe, these young men were too much for the Japanese. Enemy soldiers ran for cover into what remained of the jungle's scarred and burnt vegetation. They had no taste for the bayonets, nor the rapid fire of the BAR, M1 rifles, or submachine guns carried by the Americans. The battle for Ridge 120 was soon over, at least for today. There was still an hour of daylight left.

Looking over their conquest, Scott realized the Marine Corps paid a heavy price for this small strip of real estate. Only 120 feet above sea level, at its highest point, the height from which it got its name, the ridge extended northward for no more than 200 yards. Immediately to the west rose a series of higher, irregular ridges, ridges that could pose a threat to his men if they failed to secure their position and find cover before nightfall. Limping over to what remained of a tree, Jackson sat on the ground leaning against the stump. Exhausted, with excruciating pain in his leg, and blood seeping through the bandage, he called to one of the corpsmen.

"I need something to kill the pain," he commented quietly.

"What you need, sir, is to get the hell out of here!" the man responded harshly as he worked on Jackson's leg, seemingly oblivious to his patient's rank. "You open that wound and you'll be in trouble."

Scott laughed at the corpsman's comment, his response brutal. "What the hell do you think we're in now? Just fix me up for tonight, Navy," he ordered. "Maybe we'll all get out of here tomorrow."

The young medic cleaned the wound and replaced the bandage, then handed the officer a small handful of pills. "Take two of these, Captain, and drink some of that water. I'll check this again before dark."

"Okay, but before you go, Navy, get a hold of Conlan and Niles for me."

Waiting for the two sergeants to report, Scott began to study his map, comparing it to what he saw before him. Pockmarked with bomb and shell craters and downed trees, it was hard to comprehend that this small bit of coral had already cost the lives of more than three dozen Marines from his company. Nor did the map represent the true size, or topography of this jagged piece of rock. The plateau he stood on could not be much larger than two football fields.

"How'ya doing, Capt'n?" Sergeant Conlan asked as the two NCOs approached him. "You don't look so good," he added, seriously.

"Huh, you don't look so damn good yourself, Sergeant." Jackson laughed bitterly. "Looks like you need a rest, Sergeant, but right now we've got work to do. This damn map is worthless," he said, folding it and placing it back into his pocket. Then, taking a bayonet, he began to scratch the outline of the plateau onto a blackened coral rock. "Let's set up a series of protective firing points on the north and west ends of the plateau, here, here and there," he added, picking at the coral with the point of the bayonet.

"Start building our main defensive position, like this," he stated, drawing a half circle with the bayonet into the rock with a mark at the center. "We'll set up three machine gun positions across here. Take advantage of the craters and the rocks, and those downed trees. If those people get past us, you know what will happen to our men on the beach."

"Our guys know that, Captain," Donald Niles responded gravely. "But that won't happen; our guys will hold."

"I'd like to believe that, Sergeant, but if we don't get ammunition, we won't stop 'em with a bayonet."

The two sergeants, looking at each other, did not respond; however, both nodded in agreement—unless supplies arrived before morning, what their captain said would happen.

Before dark, the troops moved a mountain of debris, forming a makeshift barricade across the middle of the plateau. They set up a temporary command post on a raised area near the center of the barrier. Broken concrete, tree trunks, and stumps were plentiful; the men quickly rolled or stacked them high enough for an enclosed bunker. With a covering of coconut logs and rocks, it could provide a temporary sanctuary in the event the Japanese overran them.

With this underway, Scott sent a second runner off to Battalion for ammunition and water. Sergeant Niles selected a young corporal from Tennessee, who, when asked how fast he could run, replied he could make it to the battalion CP in less than a half hour.

"Tell them, Corporal," Jackson ordered, his manner and voice clearly indicating the seriousness of their position, "that if we are to survive another day we need ammunition and water, and we need it before daybreak. If you can't get to the battalion CP, try India Company; have 'em pass it on to Battalion."

Sprinting across the pockmarked terrain of this small strip of land, the corporal drew rifle fire from three snipers. Conlan's men quickly silenced two of them, but one found his mark as the runner reached the edge of the ridge; the boy tumbled to the ground, lying there, not moving. Watching him through binoculars, Scott quietly moaned, "Oh God, not another one."

Sergeant Niles, standing nearby, hearing his captain's comment, responded, "I have a second man ready to go, sir."

"No, hold off, he's still alive... He's moving."

With his comrades watching, each dreading the thought that one of them would have to take his place, as quick as the boy from Tennessee went down, he was back up, running once more. Within seconds, he made it to the edge of the plateau and was soon out of sight to both his own people and the hidden rifleman.

Later, with dusk settling over the island, it was time to take stock of Charlie Company's assets. Private Jenkins, the runner sent out earlier, was unable to make it to Battalion. Yet before returning to the plateau, he managed to pick up two radio packs from I Company. With their communication problems solved for the moment, Scott turned his attention to defending his perimeter. For now, his men appeared to be reasonably secure within their makeshift fortification. With two-hour watches for each man, the company settled in for the night.

Of the 300 men of Charlie Company who embarked from the LSTs earlier that morning, 204 remained unscathed. In Marine Corps terminology, "Effectives," the term used to identify men available for duty. Many of the company's casualties occurred during the landing operations. Some succumbed to artillery or mortar fire, others died when they tried to rescue a wounded comrade struggling in the shallow water. However, since Jackson assumed command of the company, more than three dozen good men died. The thought of this weighed heavily upon his shoulders. Nevertheless, he realized this was not the time to be thinking about the dead; he tried to keep focused on the company's present condition. He knew they had to hold on to this plateau, for if they failed, more would die, and those on the beaches below would be in jeopardy.

Just before darkness engulfed the island, he caught a glimpse of more than a score of men hurrying toward his position. Relief was on the way. As they approached the bunker, he could see they were carrying stretchers, radios, and large backpacks. Each of the escort members was heavily armed. The boy from Tennessee was leading the column; the right sleeve of his dungaree jacket, torn away, revealed a blood-soaked bandage.

"I think I've got what you need, Captain!" he exclaimed, obviously proud that he accomplished his mission. "We've got ammunition, food, and water; quite a bit of everything, really." The boy sounded excited.

More than a score of men from Marine Aviation ground support units accompanied the escort party; they came to help evacuate Charlie Company's wounded. With the airstrip still in enemy hands, they would have no planes to service today. The men worked all day at unloading ships and then offered to carry supplies to frontline troops at night. These and hundreds of others, all across the island, in the same circumstances, volunteered to evacuate the wounded. A few, however, never having the opportunity to experience combat firsthand, chose this as a way to test their mettle against the Japanese and possibly take home a souvenir or two. Notwithstanding that, when the relief party came under fire from enemy gunmen hidden in the high caves, some of these would-be soldiers soon realized their mistake—this was not a game.

Sergeant Conlan organized the evacuation of the injured men; if they could get them down to the beach by morning, they would soon be on their way to one of the hospital ships lying offshore. Donald Niles directed the distribution of food, water, and ammunition brought in by the volunteers.

With the wounded en route down off the plateau, Sergeant Conlan's men placed the bodies of twenty-two of their colleagues in a neat row, covering each with a poncho. Soon, these men would join their comrades who perished on the hillside below. Near the water's edge, as nightfall approached, nearly 300 of their fellow Marines lay in a makeshift morgue, awaiting burial. Before the island was secure, the bloated bodies of 200 or more who never made it ashore would wash up on the beach.

This tidy, long row of dead was too much for their company commander. He glanced only briefly at this grisly scene. He knew he could not function logically if he were to continue to blame himself for the deaths of all these young men. Right now, he needed to concentrate on getting the remainder of the company safely through the night.

Shortly after sunset, Japanese soldiers attempted to infiltrate positions on the north end of the ridge, only to retreat in disarray, driven off in a hail of rifle and machine gun fire. However, at

Jackson's direction, his two NCOs ordered their troops to conserve their ammunition and grenades. If the Japanese counterattack came at dawn, as expected, they would need it.

Sergeant Niles initiated a program which, he assured everyone, would discourage the Japanese from penetrating their lines in the dark. At twenty- or thirty-minute intervals, Niles would throw a rock down the north slope of the hill, then periodically a grenade. Although it undoubtedly conserved their grenades, Jackson was not so sure it did more than keep his people awake. *Maybe*, he thought, *that is the sergeant's intent.* For even though exhausted and needing rest, Niles reminded his company commander that from his experience, if the men fell asleep, some would die this night.

Several times, Scott found himself dozing off, his tired and battered body needing rest. Yet, the periodic explosion of a hand grenade or distant small arms fire made sleep impossible. Twice during the night, violent confrontations, along with intermittent gunfire, erupted from the three forward outposts at the northern end of the perimeter. Blood-chilling screams of cursing, dying men accompanied the clamor.

At zero four hundred hours, with the two sergeants reporting in, Scott took them aside. "Stay alert," he said quietly. "They're apt to hit us hard at daylight, but we should be able to hold. Pass the word on to your people. We will fall back to the CP if necessary, but this is as far as we go. If overrun, whichever one of us is still standing, he must call for an air strike on the bunker. You both know what will happen to our people down below if the Nips retake this ridge. We have the only high ground on the island; tell your people we're staying here."

For a moment, neither man responded, merely nodding in agreement, knowing what they must do. Then Sergeant Conlan quietly exclaimed, his face grim in the near darkness of the bunker, "Those bastards ain't gonna drive us off this ridge, Capt'n. We ran 'em off yesterday and we'll do it again." Although not responding to Conlan's prophesy, Jackson was not so sure the company could survive another day without assistance.

With daylight approaching, they discovered that enemy infiltrators killed two men in the forward outposts and wounded three others; however, the Japanese paid a higher price for their nighttime incursion. During the mêlée, Marines killed more than a score of intruders; nevertheless, the bodies of so many enemy soldiers lying nearby gave stark testimony to the determination of the Japanese Army to drive the Americans from atop this ridge. Still, for the Japanese, the death of so many of their men had to be a reminder that they faced a tenacious enemy, an enemy of professional soldiers that would extract a terrible toll upon their comrades should they continue in their efforts to retake this ridge.

Unexpectedly, when daylight arrived, the counter attack by the Japanese never materialized. It appeared that after being driven from this plateau the day before, the Japanese commander needed more time to marshal his forces against this American juggernaut which drove his people off the plateau. Jackson figured this would give him the time and the opportunity to both fortify his makeshift position and concentrate their efforts on a dozen or more snipers holed up high above them in the adjoining ridge. However, what he had not counted on was a scathing rebuke from Colonel Pugh.

"What the hell is holding you up, Captain?" the colonel demanded over the radio. "I want you to get those bastards that got away from you yesterday."

"My people need a rest, Colonel," Scott replied forthrightly.

"I'll tell you when to rest," the man growled. "You can rest when you're dead. Now get your search teams out into the jungle and probe the west side of the ridge. If you don't kill those people, they'll come back and kill you tomorrow."

Stunned by Pugh's scathing invective, Scott merely responded quietly, his mouth grim, "Yes, sir," then handed the telephone receiver off to his radioman. "Have the sergeants come in, Corporal," he ordered.

With the sergeants gathered around, he ordered them to send out a number of patrols, to begin immediately and continue on into the night; there would be no respite for his men. "Find 'em and kill 'em," he said, his voice not much more than a whisper. "But if you get one alive, bring him back for interrogation."

As expected, Sergeant Conlan was the first to protest. "This is a lot of horse manure, Captain; I see our good Colonel Pugh's name all over this order. My people are dead on their feet; what the hell is wrong with that man?"

"Ease off, Sergeant," Scott replied gruffly. "I told you before, you signed on for four more years and you take the bad with the good. Tonight will be rough enough on our people without you complaining about it; so knock it off."

"I know, Captain, but just as long as you know where I'm coming from; this ain't right," Conlan responded quietly.

"I agree with Sergeant Conlan, Captain," Sergeant Niles said, entering the conversation. "We've seen how Pugh operated on the Canal, and dead Marines don't mean a helluva lot to him. He wants that almighty star on his shoulder; but we'll do what we're ordered to do, Captain. You don't have to worry about us."

"I'm not worried about that, Sergeant. I know you'll do what's right and you'll look after you people, but let's get it done," Scott replied, wearily. "Four different probes, to the north, northwest, northeast and east from our front line; rotate the men, quarter to half-mile out and back and report."

The last team to probe deep within the enemy lines returned just before sunrise. During the night, all four squads ran into enemy infiltrators, killing several Japanese soldiers. It appeared that for all of Colonel Pugh's apparent bellicose unconcern for the safety of his men, his decision to probe the nearby jungle during the nighttime paid off. Each team reported that they caught the Japanese off guard, as if, after dark, the enemy commander did not expect to encounter Marines beyond their own lines.

Based upon the information gathered by the nighttime thrust into enemy territory, Jackson directed that probing attacks were to continue, in platoon strength into the forward outposts of the enemy. Although successful, with each foray into enemy country his men returned to the plateau fewer in number. It quickly became obvious to him, regardless of the direction he received from his commanding officer, he could not survive by trading man for man with the Japanese; were he to continue to do so, the end result could be disastrous.

On their fourth night on the plateau, contrary to Colonel Pugh's orders, and acquiescing to Sergeant Conlan and Niles' suggestions, he held his men in place. No nighttime patrols ventured into enemy territory. Jackson was tired and it was obvious his men had reached the stage of near exhaustion. They needed rest.

Before dark, he posted two observers in an ideal position to direct fire upon enemy targets from the ships at sea. As dawn broke, he joined the two men for a moment; it soon became obvious why Colonel Pugh needed Charlie Company on the top of this hill. From their vantage point, the observers could see the entire island laid out before them. With daylight approaching, an exquisite massive carpet of green jungle began to unfold below. Except where torn apart by the Navy's big guns, bombs, and napalm, which turned some of it into an ugly black and gray tangle of broken buildings, uprooted trees and burning implements of war, it was a spectacular sight, a lush green carpet of vegetation.

Jackson returned to the bunker and Sergeant Niles joined the two lookouts. With the sun now breaking above the horizon, Niles began using his binoculars to scan the jungle area immediately below their position. Focusing his view along the western edge of the airstrip, he spotted ten or twelve small Japanese tanks, accompanied by infantry moving toward the Marines dug in along the beach. He alerted Battalion. Yet this was not the only enemy force he found. Looking down on the northeastern shoreline from his vantage point, he spotted eight large barges near a small cove, partially concealed along the jungle's edge. They had not been there the night before.

"Holy Christ!" he exclaimed, startling the two men sitting beside him as he focused his binoculars on the barges and the dense growth of jungle vegetation nearby. "There must be a thousand men down there." He watched as scores of enemy troops, scurrying back and forth between the barges and the tree line, unloaded weapons and supplies.

"Quick, one of you move out; bring the captain over here on the double." As the Marine rushed off toward the bunker, Niles tried to get an estimate of the strength of this new enemy threat. Although nearly a half mile away, he figured each barge was large enough to carry at least 100 troops, or more. That could mean an additional force of 800-1000 enemy infantrymen could have come ashore during the night.

"What've you got, Sergeant?" Jackson asked as he arrived at the observation point.

"Japanese barges, sir, along the beach, below us," he said, pointing. "I count eight, for sure and there may be even two more in that small cove there, beyond the first group. It looks like they are capable of carrying up to one hundred or so… I counted over sixty men off loading equipment. The bastards came in last night. That's one helluva bunch of people and you know who they're coming after."

Taking the binoculars, Jackson studied the concentration of enemy troops below.

"You're right, Sergeant; but it looks like they have moved into the jungle. Aviation can takeout those barges, but they won't be able to find the troops. Come on, we've got work to do." Turning to the two observers, he said, "Keep your eyes on those people down there. If you see any sign of them moving out in force, let me know."

Rushing back to the bunker in the center of the plateau, he called for Sergeant Conlan. When Rick Conlan arrived, he said to both men, "We're not going to stop a battalion with two hundred men. Quick, move the dead into the bunker. Set 'em up so they'll be visible from out here, put a rifle in their hands."

Stunned by the order, Conlan and Niles merely stared at their company commander. Sergeant Conlan, not believing what he heard, was the first to respond. "You want us to do what, Captain?" he exclaimed, flashing a glance of incredulity at

Sergeant Niles. Neither he nor Niles could figure out what their captain was getting at.

"Do what I said, Sergeant," Jackson snapped. "Get your men at this, we ain't got much time. We'll set up a decoy; you'd damn well better pray that it works."

Chapter 12

Moving the bodies of their dead comrades was a loathsome task for all; notwithstanding that, the onset of rigor mortis worked to their advantage. The natural stiffening of the body allowed the men to position the dead upright, visible to anyone approaching from either side of the bunker. With the job completed, nearly a dozen corpses were now propped up near a makeshift gunport, where some part of their body, uniform, or weapon was visible to anyone approaching the bunker from the outside. The bait was in place, the trap set.

"I want six volunteers," Jackson called out to the group of Marines gathered around waiting for further directions. "You'll stay with me in the bunker; the rest of you will withdraw with Sergeant Conlan and Sergeant Niles. There is no way we can hold off a battalion-strength attack, but if we can lure those people to the bunker, they'll be out in the open, and our pilots will pick them off like ducks in pond. When aviation is through with 'em, we'll mop up what's left."

For a moment, no one volunteered to stay behind with their captain, until a short, young man with soot smeared across his face stepped forward, hesitated, and then asked, "What chance do we have, Captain?"

"Fair, that's the best I can offer, but there is no way we can do it alone. If we don't do this, they'll overrun us. There are not enough of us; they will take this whole damn ridge. If that happens, they will kill our people on the beach. But if we can draw them out into this area," he said, pointing to the large open space around the bunker, "aviation will have a field day."

"I'll stay with you, Captain," the private responded.

"Me too, Captain, I'll stay," another man offered, then others stepped forward until he had his six volunteers.

"Good. Load up with ammunition and water and get set up inside. It will have to look like there are thirty or forty men in there. We want those people to come after us, we're the bait."

Turning to his two sergeants, giving them last-minute instructions, he cautioned each that when they pulled back, their retreat had to appear as if it were a complete rout. He knew that neither one of them liked what he told them they must do; Sergeant Conlan expressed these misgivings.

"This is bullshit, Capt'n. You're gonna get yourself killed. There's got to be a better way."

"There's no easy way, Rick," he replied angrily. Jackson was dog-tired and had little time for debate. Clearly, what he needed was support from his two NCOs, yet he could not help but feel that maybe Sergeant Conlan was right. Turning to Sergeant Niles, he lashed out, "What about you, Sergeant? You don't like it either?"

"No, I don't like it, Captain," Niles responded, shaking his head, shocked by the brutality of Jackson's question and tone of voice. "However, under the circumstances, I don't know what else we can do. We can't match 'em man for man with a bayonet, but if you're correct," he responded through clenched teeth, "with a little help from aviation, we can take 'em out."

"It'll work, Sergeant," Scott reassured him, "just remember you've got to pull back in a hurry. Get your men undercover, and then wait. When they move on the bunker, that's when aviation takes over. I'll advise battalion."

Warned by the two forward observers, Scott returned to the edge of the ridge in time to see a huge gathering of well-armed enemy troops emerging from the jungle at the base of the cliff. Within minutes, they were on the move. This would be no banzai charge by drug-crazed fanatics, which the Marines had heard so much about. These were well-trained professional soldiers in battalion strength. Out in front, clearly visible, three officers led the way; the first rays of sunlight reflecting off their long samurai swords.

When the enemy troops began their attack, Scott's left flank came under a withering barrage of rifle and machine gun fire from the Japanese soldiers hidden within the caves on the higher ridge. Jackson called for another air strike and within minutes, the Corsairs came in low, one after the other, dropping bombs across the ridge above them. Moments later, they returned and began strafing the long expanse on the hillside below. Unfortunately, the warplanes could not continue their attack for long, as the whole plateau soon disappeared under one large rolling cloud of dirty black smoke and dust. Although temporarily protecting the Marines from the eyes of enemy soldiers on the higher ridge, it also provided cover for the enemy force, now moving toward Jackson's forward positions.

Never slowing in their relentless climb, as the smoke and dust began to clear, the Japanese reached the Marines' forward positions. Even with the advantage of height and a clear field of fire in the Marines' favor, the attacking force never wavered. They soon overran the three forward outposts, which took the full brunt of the onslaught. All three quickly succumbed. In this savage hand-to-hand struggle, Japanese soldiers killed the men in the first revetment, and then moved on to the second and then the third in turn. Their attack was quick, violent, and decisive. Regrouping, they next moved toward the center of the Marines' defensive fortifications.

"Pull your people back, pass the word," Scott yelled. Sergeants Niles and Conlan responded quickly, moving their people behind the row of previously placed logs, boulders, and tree stumps. These formed a huge curved barrier halfway across the expanse of the plateau. Jackson knew this would be a do-or-die effort on the part of his men, for there was no escape. There was no place to run, or a reserve force to call upon to come to their rescue.

"Hold your fire," he cried out, as the men took up positions behind the long, curved berm, awaiting the inevitable. "Hold your fire," he repeated as he moved rapidly along the line on dungaree-clad men. "Wait until they make their move, then concentrate on those leading the assault. Stay down, choose your target carefully, then move on to the next one in line."

Sergeants Niles and Conlan quickly picked up on their captain's plan, offering words of encouragement of their own. "Hold your positions," they offered, "make every shot count. We have the advantage; they can't see you, so stay down until we get the order to fire."

Jackson waited; he figured the Japanese would concentrate their assault upon the center of their defensive position. Unexpectedly, the attacking forces fanned out, promptly forming two elongated skirmish lines, and then, seemingly without fear, ran toward the barricade. At 200 yards, Scott gave the order to fire.

From the Marines' .30-caliber machine guns, set in place the previous evening along the curved perimeter, the gun crews, with a clear field of fire across the plateau, raised havoc with those leading the charge. Yet the enemy's seemingly endless funneling of men into the fray continued unabated. The carnage in front of the lead machine gun was such that a mound of enemy dead and wounded began to block the view of the gun crew. During a brief lull, a Marine, leaving his cover, scampered over the dead, pulling bodies away to once again clear their field of fire—he died before getting back behind the revetment.

Quite suddenly, the Japanese commander halted the attack, his men scurrying for cover; yet within minutes, they initiated a two-pronged assault upon the outer ends of Jackson's perimeter. It appeared to be a desperate attempt to overrun the two ends of the defensive line. The tactic worked; no longer subject to the withering fire from the machine guns located near the center of the barricade, they charged the right flank, lobbing grenades over the barricade, breaching the Marines' line.

Signaling the two sergeants to pull their men back, Scott and his six volunteers entered the bunker. Before leaving the field of battle, Conlan's men quickly rolled the coconut logs and coral rocks into place, closing the small opening into the redoubt.

Inside, the bunker smelled of death, reeked of cordite, blood, and human excrement. In the darkened interior, until one of the seven men moved, it was near impossible to tell the living from the dead. The bodies of the dead, at rest forever, now propped up before a gunport, were about to play the leading role in Charlie Company's last-ditch stand against this overwhelming onslaught of enemy soldiers. Their success or failure was sure to identify the winner and loser in this battle for the control of Ridge 120.

With the rest of the company in full retreat, quiet momentarily settled across the plateau, giving Jackson an opportunity to calm the obvious fears of his six volunteers.

"Remember; they can't see you unless they come within a few feet of these gunports, so don't expose yourselves any more than you have to. Pick a target, fire two or three quick rounds, and then move to another opening. Our job is to both look and sound like there are two or three dozen men in here. When aviation begins the attack, get down and stay down. Take whatever cover you can find until it's over. When our men come back, we'll join them and finish these people off."

What followed, sounded like what Scott imagined his grandfather was talking about when he told his grandchildren about the mythical banshee's howl of death. The story always amused Scott's parents, but to the young, impressionable Irish-American children in the Jackson household, they were terrified of the old man's imaginary ghosts.

The cacophonic screams of Japanese soldiers, now sure of victory, seemed to come from all sides of the bunker at the same time. The dreadful resonance of automatic weapons soon followed, ringing out across the plateau. There seemed to be no end to the sound, thunderous and deafening to those sealed inside this dark and forbidding cavern of death. Yet the seven men continued to respond, killing every face that tried to peer into their darkened chamber.

"Grenade!" a man yelled as this instrument of death was hurled through one of the larger openings into the bunker. Within seconds, a Marine grabbed it and flung it back outside, where it exploded; the blast elicited a scream from an enemy soldier.

"Keep firing," Jackson yelled again, repeating his earlier directive, "pick a target, fire two or three rounds, then move to the next opening. Don't give 'em a chance to get close to the bunker, pour it on!"

The roar of gunfire from within the enclosure was deafening. With each explosion of a grenade, landing on or near the bunker, the shockwave reverberated throughout this small enclosure. The stench of gun smoke now masked the odor of the corpses, combining into a sickening sweet smell of death. Yet there was no time to think about it, for each man was fighting for his very existence, knowing that this burial chamber might soon be his final resting place on this earth.

"Grenade!" the cry went out again. This time the warning came from the feather merchant. Jackson, turning his attention away from the enemy, tried to locate the grenade peering through the thick, dirty clouds of gun smoke that permeated the bunker. Smoke and dust obscured everything within sight. He could not find it.

"Get down, Captain!" the Marine yelled. Before Scott could move, the young man charged him, striking him with his shoulder, hurling Jackson to the ground as the deadly device exploded.

The first bomb dropped by a Corsair pilot exploded less than fifty yards from the bunker, hurling Japanese bodies across the battlefield, with rocks and debris showering down on the manmade burrow. The explosion rattled the entire structure. One of the overhead logs holding the coral rocks in place gave way; these came crashing down into the enclosure. The sound of gunfire, accompanied by the roar of low-flying aircraft and screams of the dying, now rang out across the battlefield.

There was no need for Jackson to tell his volunteers to take cover; they quickly pulled small bits of logs, rocks or the corpses of their dead comrades over them, waiting for the next bomb to explode. Fortunately, the next one exploded farther away, as did those that followed. Fifty-caliber machine gun rounds soon began to cut their dance of death across the top of the bunker, splintering the coconut logs and smashing the remaining rocks, which so precariously protected the occupants in this deadly enclosure. For those inside, now engulfed in a shower of flying shards of wood and rock and the billowing black smoke cascading throughout the bunker, it seemed that no one would escape. The air attack continued for thirty minutes, but to the men inside, it seemed like hours before the last of the Corsairs pulled up and away from this sanctuary of death.

"Hello, inside; Capt'n Jackson, are you okay?" The voice was that of Sergeant Conlan.

"We're okay, Rick," Jackson responded. "We're coming out; give us a hand with these logs."

Walking out into the sunlight, the men needed to shade their eyes from the glare of the sunshine on the white coral. Those who came to their rescue merely stared at them in disbelief. The six men, carrying their wounded comrade, with sweat and coral dust covering them from head to toe, looked more like walking dead men. No one except Jackson was recognizable, and he only because of his height; he appeared to tower over the volunteers. With the exception of Private Alex Garl, all escaped serious injury; Private Garl, however, appeared to be near death, with grenade fragments peppered across his torso.

Yet, until he looked around and saw the landscape littered with the bodies of hundreds of Japanese soldiers, Scott was not so sure but that he had made a horrendous miscalculation. He risked his life and the lives of six others, not realizing the horrors these men would experience confined in what could have been their burial chamber. Still, they were alive. Maybe the results justified his actions, but he would leave that concern for another day; right now, there was work to do. With two corpsmen taking charge of the wounded man, he called out to his two sergeants.

"Let's move, gentlemen, while they're still on the run, if these people get away, we'll have to fight 'em another day. Rick, move your men along the western edge of the ridge; Sergeant Niles, deploy your people along the east side. Let's move out."

Jackson picked up his radioman and joined Sergeant Conlan's platoon as they moved across the battlefield. There were dead Japanese soldiers everywhere, yet others surprisingly survived the air attack, but now lay motionless, awaiting death, too badly wounded to raise a hand against their enemy.

However, unseen in this rugged and broken terrain, nearly a score of heavily armed Japanese soldiers lay hidden directly in the path of the advancing column. These men, apparently unscathed, lived through the air strike. As Jackson's troops approached, they rushed forward, bayonets at the ready. When the two adversaries came together, a savage, no-holds-barred hand-to-hand battle again took place on the western edge of the ridge.

As the mêlée continued, a young Japanese soldier, armed with a bayonet, leaping from a coral outcropping, knocked Jackson off his feet. Scott's rifle went flying across the coral. He struggled to pull his .45, but the enemy soldier was too quick, pinning both of the older man's arms to the ground. Fighting to get free, he tried to get at his knife, but in his weakened condition, he was no match for the young soldier. As the man struggled to plunge the bayonet into Jackson's throat, a nearby Marine, out of ammunition, swung his empty M1, like a baseball bat. The rifle butt struck the soldier full in the face, shattering the stock and nearly decapitating the young warrior. When Jackson pushed him aside, the man was already dead.

When it ended, the area, no larger than a two football fields, was littered with the dead and dying. The Japanese, now in full retreat, fled first into a series of shell holes and rock crevices beyond the barricade, and then quickly slipped over the north end of the ridge, from where they came. Near quiet returned to the plateau, only to be broken by the crack of a sniper's rifle. Hidden gunmen continued to fire with deadly accuracy upon Jackson's men, until Sergeant Conlan responded. He concealed a half dozen of his best sharpshooters along the western edge of the ridge.

"Keep out of sight," he said. "Locate your target and return fire only when you have a clear shot." His men soon silenced the enemy snipers. However, it was evident to all that a direct assault by infantry would be necessary to dislodge the Japanese snipers from their concealed positions. The only effective weapon against an enemy buried within the earth's crust appeared to be a TNT satchel charge, rifle grenade or flamethrower.

That, however, was not Captain Jackson's greatest concern. His people needed medical care, ammunition, and potable water. More than a score of men became nauseous from drinking the foul-smelling water in their canteens. By mid afternoon, the temperature climbed to over 100 degrees. Some, with empty canteens, drank the brackish liquid that lay in the bottom of the bomb craters; while others retrieved canteens from the bodies of the enemy dead.

Of the original group of ten corpsmen, only four remained uninjured. Two died in this last skirmish; the others lay among the wounded. Several of the more seriously injured men, if they were to live, needed immediate evacuation. Jackson called Battalion, telling the communications officer he wanted to talk to Colonel Pugh. There was a note of urgency in his voice; unfortunately, the radio operator did not pickup on the gravity of the moment.

"Sorry, Captain," the man responded, "Colonel Pugh is tied up with General McAffee, what can I do for you?"

Jackson's response was blunt and to the point. "Get off your ass, Mac, and get the colonel on the goddamn horn!" he cursed.

After what seemed like hours, Colonel Pugh's voice came over the radio. "What's your problem, Captain?" asked Pugh, his voice ringing with a sense of expected confrontation from this junior officer. This Marine Corps colonel did not expect to be disturbed by a subordinate when in a conference with the commanding general.

"Colonel, I have one hundred and fifty-five men able to fight, a dozen grenades, and 4000 rounds of ammunition. I need stretcher bearers, replacements, ammunition, and water. If the Japanese come at us again in the morning they'll take this dung heap in twenty minutes."

Colonel Pugh, a mustang officer, field commissioned during the Nicaraguan Expedition, was no neophyte. The captain's description of Charlie Company's predicament on the ridge above did not surprise him. However, he knew when it came to assessing the readiness and capabilities of a unit under his command his first requisite was to look at the man in charge. What did he know about his company commander? Pugh was aware his captain lacked combat experience. Yet that was true with most of his officers. They truly were citizen soldiers—soldiers suddenly and inextricably thrown into combat. Unfortunately, that was the nature of warfare. In a similar fashion, the next critical factor was to assess the number of professional and experienced mid-level commanders in charge of the operation. Unfortunately, Charlie Company was found wanting in both areas.

On Guadalcanal, he recalled receiving similar requests for help from frontline platoon and company commanders. He was well aware that in combat, more often than not, even experienced officers often underestimated rather than exaggerated their situation. Fatigue and exhaustion played a role in this. Officers engaged in battle frequently failed to assess correctly the readiness of subordinates, expecting more from men already pushed to the brink. Exhaustion, he knew, could cloud the judgment of even his best commanders. Listening to his captain's voice, Colonel Pugh suspected Jackson might have become a liability. The man and his two NCOs, pushed to the very edge today, could conceivably lose this strategic foothold, which they now held so precariously. Even with the recent successes racked up by Charlie against their foe, he doubted that the captain had the expertise, determination, and ability to hold on to this very valuable piece of ground.

Pugh was not one to second-guess his boss, but he thought, *General McAffee might have made a calculated and costly error in selecting this greenhorn, novice captain to fill the shoes of a professional soldier.* Yet, he readily agreed, Charlie Company had performed exceedingly well these past few days under Jackson's command.

Notwithstanding that, there was good reason for the colonel to be concerned. Captain Jackson and Charlie Company held the only high ground taken by the Americans. He could not risk losing it.

"Our supply people are en route, Captain, along with medical help. They're pinned down right below the ridge, but they should be at your CP within the hour."

"Thank you, sir."

"Is there anything else, Captain?"

"No, sir."

Chapter 13

"I'd like to speak to Lieutenant Brown, please. That's Hal Brown," the caller said.

"May I say who is calling, please?" the feminine voice replied.

"My name is Jackson. Scott Jackson."

"Oh! Lieutenant Jackson, I know you," the woman responded, she was obviously excited. "I'm Helen, you remember? I worked for Chief Mullins when you were here. Oh, I am sorry, it's Captain Jackson, isn't it?" she apologized. "I read all about you in *The Star*. Lieutenant Brown will be glad to hear from you... Just one moment, please."

Jackson could hear the girl in the background as she left him holding on the line at Police Headquarters. In a few moments, Brown picked up the receiver.

"Hello, Scott, how are you?" the man answered and asked, his voice immediately recognizable by his caller. "Where are you?"

"I'm here in town. I'm at my mother's house in the north end, can we get together?"

"You bet." Brown sounded pleased that his friend had called. "The sooner the better, I'll get a hold of a couple of the guys. How about lunch? We'll come get you."

"No, Hal, I have Beth's car. I'll meet you at Jimmy's at noon."

When Lieutenant Brown hung up, he exclaimed quietly, "Well, I'll be damned, our conquering hero is home."

Jackson was the first to arrive at the Mandarin House, the Chinese restaurant in Seattle that he frequented so often before the war. When he walked into the restaurant in his Marine-green greatcoat and garrison cap, all eyes turned toward him. The café was crowded with longshoremen, office workers and railroad men, plus several men and women in military uniforms. Jimmy Woo, the owner and longtime friend, coming from the kitchen, did not recognize the tall man in the green uniform.

"Just one for lunch, sir?" the restaurateur asked.

"No, Jimmy," Scott replied, smiling, "there'll be four or five. We'd like to sit at the cops' table."

Woo, taking a closer look at his customer as the Marine officer removed his cap, yelled, "Scotty, it's you. I thought I recognized you," he said, grabbing Jackson in a huge bear hug. "By golly, it's good to see you. You haven't been in here since the war started, where have you been?" he demanded, with a smile. Then, answering his inquiry, he exclaimed, "Oh, of course, you've been in the South Pacific. I knew that. I read about you in the papers. Come with me; come with me," he repeated, taking the man by the arm and escorting him into the kitchen.

"Susie, look who's here." It was nearly three years since Jackson had seen Jimmy and Susie Woo.

It took several minutes for Scott to break away from the Woo family members and the small crowd in the kitchen that gathered around to welcome him home. He felt good about it, for the Mandarin House was probably the closest thing he had to a home in this city. Except for his mother and sister, Beth, he was closer to the Woo family than anyone else in his hometown. As Jimmy escorted him through the noontime crowd to the cops' table in the restaurant alcove, he felt right at home.

Hal Brown, his friend and former colleague, and two others from the force, Sergeant Carl Olander and Lieutenant Bobby Hart, arrived while Jackson was in the kitchen. The three men were seated at a large round table in an alcove off the main floor of the restaurant. Routinely, Woo reserved the table for police officers who worked the Chinatown beat. The secluded location offered a refuge for the officers from the curious and the police buffs, a temporary escape from the public eye, otherwise denied them because of their uniforms.

It was clear the three men were glad to see him. Exchanging handshakes, each offered a warm and friendly greeting to their former colleague. Not seeing his closest friend and former partner, Jackson asked about Police Detective Oscar Johnson.

"I talked to Oscar," Brown responded, "but he told me he could not attend our get-together. He said he would call you later. However, I don't think he'll call," Brown added, obviously disappointed by their former colleague's refusal to join them.

"Why, what's wrong?"

"His son Mickey was killed on Tarawa."

"Oh my God!" exclaimed Scott, shocked by what he heard. "I'm so sorry, I didn't know that."

"He hasn't gotten over it. Oscar will not go anywhere, and he will not come to see us. He doesn't even come here anymore; you know how he liked this place."

"Yeah, I know. We came here often."

"Woo is upset about it, but there's not a damn thing anyone can do about it."

"I am so sorry to hear about his son," Scott replied, obviously troubled by this news. "I knew the boy tried to enlist right after Pearl Harbor. He was only sixteen then, it's too bad."

Bobby Hart quickly changed the subject; the detective lieutenant worked closely with Scott before the war. Jackson first met Hart in 1932, when Hart investigated a shooting involving Scott and his partner, Homer Petersen, after the two men responded to a burglary call in Chinatown. The burglars killed Petersen and wounded Jackson. The detective, a former Army sergeant, served in the Philippines after the First World War. After completing his three-year hitch, he took his discharge at nearby Fort Lawton and soon joined the force. He, like Jackson, was a tall, lean man, well over six feet, with curly red hair. Although quick to smile, his gaunt appearance belied his age. Twenty years working this "manure pile," as he described his assignment to the

Homicide Squad, had taken its toll. He saw more than his share of death.

"Tell us about yourself, Scott. When did you get home? How are you? We read all about you; are you okay?" he asked, in rapid-fire succession, obviously pleased that his longtime friend returned safely from the South Pacific.

"Slow down, Bobby. Yes, I'm fine," Scott chuckled.

"Yeah, Bobby, knock that crap off," Olander interjected with a bitter laugh. "I need a drink first. This has not been one of my better days. I'm buying by the way, what're you gonna have, Scott?"

"Whatever is available. I'm surprised though, I thought after the war started, the state tightened up on use of liquor in public places."

"They did, but not at the Mandarin," he smiled. "Jimmy gets what he wants. If he can't get it from the state, he buys it off the street."

"In that case you can buy me a double shot of Scotch."

"I'll take the same," Brown replied, lighting a cigarette and offering the pack to Jackson, who declined.

"Don't leave me out, Olander," added Hart, with a grin, winking at his Marine friend. "I can't remember the last time you bought me a drink. I'll take bourbon."

The young Chinese waiter quickly returned with four coffee mugs filled to near overflowing with whiskey. Much to the members of the Restaurant Association's chagrin, the effects of Prohibition were still evident in Scott's hometown. With the repeal of the Eighteenth Amendment in 1933, the state legislature took it upon itself to prohibit the consumption of alcohol in public places. Many routinely ignored the new law, just as they did during Prohibition. The boy also carried a small gift for Jackson.

"This is from Mr. Woo," he said.

Inside the box, Scott found a bottle of Johnnie Walker Red, Scotch.

Hal Brown raised his cup and proposed a toast, "We're glad you're home, safe, Scott. Tell us about your travels, we've read about 'em."

"You're front page news around here, Buddy," Hart chimed in, with a smile. "The *Star* ran a story on you nearly every damn day when you were wounded last fall."

"Oh no," Jackson responded, surprised at what he just heard. "That sounds to me like Lew Burke. Although I understand he turned out to be a damn good war correspondent. I saw him when I was in San Diego. You guys must think I have my own press agent," he grinned.

"No, we know you better than that," Olander replied. "But your picture with the President made the front pages of all three papers. That was quite an honor to have him come to visit you in the hospital."

"He didn't come to see me, Carl," Scott chuckled, "he was in San Diego and just dropped by the hospital, that's all."

"For a reporter, Burke has written some damn good things about you, Scott. That's helped us a lot."

"What do you mean, Carl? How'd it help you guys?" Jackson was curious.

"We've been taking a hell of a beating from the press since you joined up. Mayor McCoy left office shortly after the war started and Chief McDonald retired. The new mayor appointed Bill Kregg as chief. Things have gone downhill ever since." Carl Olander, clearly distressed, continued, "The press doesn't give a rat's ass about our people, and Chief Kregg's part of the problem. It's just nice to have something good said about our people in the service. There have been some good stories written about them."

"Yeah," added Hal Brown, "Joe Moody is flying with a fighter group...P50s or 51s in Europe; he's knocked down ten or fifteen Kraut planes. I think he's a three-time Ace."

Brown was obviously pleased with the exemplary performance of so many former city police officers, who were now in the military. Bobby Hart agreed, he nodded, telling their Marine friend about their former colleagues.

"Jack Bowerman won the Silver Star in North Africa, and Charlie Ross has gotten about as much publicity as you have, Scott."

"Oh! I hadn't heard," Scott replied, surprised at the news about Ross, a former police lieutenant and colleague. "I saw Ross before I left; he enlisted in the air corps, didn't he?"

"Yeah," replied Hart, "he's flying B25s. I guess he is one helluva pilot. There are others," he nodded. "It helps."

"My sister told me a lot of cops joined the military, after I left, but I haven't heard anything about 'em. I knew several guys signed up the day after Pearl Harbor. How many left the force?"

"Nearly two hundred, so far," Olander added.

"Good Lord!" Scott exclaimed, "I had no idea—"

"By the end of forty-two, more than a third of the patrolmen and detectives, and about twenty sergeants enlisted," Olander offered. "Some of the older brass were in the reserves; they got called back. Even your old partner sitting there next to you tried to reenlist," he said, smiling and pointing at Hart. "They told him he was too damn old; I can believe that."

"Screw you, you Norwegian bastard," responded Hart. "I ain't near as old as you are."

Jackson laughed at this friendly exchange. He was pleased; it was nice to be home. Yet when he asked his sister if she knew where several of his old high school friends were, the only thing she could tell him was that Paul Addison, Mark McGinnes and Corky Shay were overseas, someplace. She had talked to Kenji Tanaka's sisters, Jolene and Kim, before the Army picked them up, and she still corresponded with Jolene. The two girls, now at an internment camp in Idaho, had not heard from their parents or brother; the girls assumed the worst. They thought the three of them might have been interned in Japan. Beth said the girls were beside themselves with worry; their attorney tried without success to alleviate their fears. He assured them he would reopen their case in the Federal Court, as soon as the war ended.

"What happened in Japantown?" Scott asked, turning to Hal Brown. "I just drove through there; it looks pretty deserted."

"The Japs are all gone, Scott," Lieutenant Brown responded pensively. "Too bad, but I suppose it had to be. The Tanaka kid was a friend of yours, wasn't he?"

"Yeah, we were together all through school, played ball with him at O'Dea. He was a damn good kid."

"Didn't they get caught overseas when the war started, Scott?" Carl Olander asked, as he poured himself another drink, then passed the bottle on to Bobby Hart. "I remember reading something about that. I knew the old man; I walked the beat up there for a couple of years."

"Yes, but the two girls haven't heard anything from them since their parents left San Francisco."

"Where are the girls, Scott?" Brown inquired.

"They're at that internment camp in Idaho. Beth occasionally hears from Jolene, she's the youngest one."

Jimmy and Susie Woo outdid themselves serving soup, egg rolls, barbecued pork, pea pods and beef with noodles and a pot of hot tea. The excellent service and exquisite cuisine reminded Scott of his first meal here, in 1932. The food was still as delicious as ever. After lunch, the men remained at the Mandarin for nearly three hours, reminiscing, while finishing off Jimmy Woo's bottle of Scotch.

"What about McCoy?" Scott asked, directing his inquiry at Lieutenant Brown. "Why did he leave the mayor's office?"

"When the war started he stepped down. He figured he had better tend to business managing the shipyards that he inherited from his old man. The yards went into full-scale production building destroyers in Seattle, and destroyer escorts, and cargo ships in the four other facilities he owns on Puget Sound."

"What about the police department; with the large number of military people in town, your workload must have escalated a great deal."

"It has," Olander offered, "but the military has helped us a lot. Hell, I'll even go farther than that, if it had not been for the Military Police, I don't know what we would have done. Just look around you. Look at the crowd; it's the middle of the afternoon. Come back tonight at midnight, you won't be able to get in the damn place."

"I'll have to admit I don't remember seeing this many people in here, particularly this time of the day," Jackson replied. "The economy must be pretty damn good."

"It is," Hart answered, "but it's your tax dollar at work, Scott, thanks to the war," he smiled. "There must be a half million military people in the Puget Sound region. Our population has exploded in recent months. In forty-two, over fifty thousand people moved into the city. There are people coming here day and night from all over the damn country. They hope to get work in McCoy's Yards, or at the Boeing plant."

"You probably haven't followed the attack on Dutch Harbor," Brown commented. "The city has become the major staging area for operations in the North Pacific," he said, pausing long enough to light another cigarette. "We've got other problems, though; big problems. Most of our officers are working a second job in one of the war industry plants, and then pull a watch on the department."

"But that won't ever change, Hal. Will it?" Scott asked, knowing from his experience that cops routinely worked two jobs to feed their families.

"Maybe not; but since we got the eight-hour day in forty-three, our guys are now able to work a full shift at a defense plant, then eight hours for us. But the poor damn taxpayer is being screwed. The guys are catching up on their sleep in the patrol cars. That's crazy," he added bitterly. "And you all know it."

"I understand you have a union now, is that right?" their former colleague asked. "Beth mentioned it; she's still working at city hall."

Lieutenant Hart laughed. "Yeah, we did have, for a while. The patrol officers and sergeants formed one and began to pressure the city for more money. Unfortunately, the new mayor pulled the rug out from under 'em. He told the council that the union's demands were unreasonable; the no-good bastard said the cops made enough money 'off the street.'" Hart shook his head. "He claimed the city shouldn't be burdened with a tax increase during wartime. What a bunch of crap!"

Hal Brown, watching his friend's obvious disbelief, again entered the conversation. "The mayor treated the firemen worse, Scott; if you can believe that. In a speech he gave at the Chamber the other day, he said he knew of only two occupations where the participants made their money lying on their back. One of those, he said, were firemen." Scott noted the grim smile that crossed the face of his other two friends.

"What about the rest of our group? What happened to 'em?"

"A lot of them, like you, left the department," Brown replied. "Others, with trade skills, went full-time in one of the defense plants and we lost six or seven guys in the last couple of years."

"Ivan Travis, you may remember him, and a new man that came on after you left."

"Yes, I remember Travis," Scott answered, recalling very well that dark-haired man with the friendly smile. In 1935, Patrolman Ivan Travis shot and killed a pimp in Chinatown, who had stabbed Olander. Scott was the investigating officer on the case.

"Ivan made sergeant a couple of years ago; he and a rookie got themselves killed in a stickup at the Western Union office, three soldiers, with .45s. Our people did not have much of a chance. A thirty-eight ain't much of a match against an automatic."

"That's too bad," Scott added sadly. "He was a good friend, wasn't he?"

"Yes, he was, Scott," Carl Olander responded quietly, obviously troubled by the memory of a good friend, now gone. "He was one of the good guys.

"A nervous homeowner killed Gus Anderson with a shotgun blast. You may remember Gus; he used to work at the Columbia City Precinct. He was chasing a burglar through a guy's back yard, in the middle of the night—the son of a bitch capped one off through a bedroom window. It damn near blew Andy's head off." Olander shook his head, biting his lip, and then continued. "Then just two months ago, a young officer was killed in a shootout with a couple of AWOL soldiers. They stuck up a bar on the waterfront; the kid lived for about a week."

With Olander pausing to light another cigarette, Lieutenant Hart, with a grim look, exclaimed, "Enough of that," he said, and he quickly changed the subject. Discussing a police officer's violent death was never pleasant; when he was a close friend, it was something Hart did not want to hear.

"With all our troubles, Scott, it's still a helluva time to be a cop," he interjected, now with a smile, as he poured himself another drink. "There's every kind of a crime being committed here that you could ever imagine. We even have some new ones on the books. Some of 'em, we'd never heard of before.

"Black marketeering, now that's quite a name for a crime," he scoffed. "Stolen and counterfeit gasoline and food ration stamps are big-ticket items. You'd better come back to work, Scott, before this genie is put back in the bottle," he laughed.

The fact that his friends made light of the increased crime problems they encountered almost daily on the streets of his hometown did not surprise Scott. He knew from experience that cops routinely accepted such challenges; after all, street crime was their bread and butter. However, their foreboding prophecy that political corruption within local government would eventually lead to the downfall of their department forced him to rethink his own future. He wondered if, when the war was over, he would not be better off staying with the military.

As fascinated as he was by this chronology of events, he was saddened by what he heard here today. The murder of so many of his former police colleagues and the death of Detective Johnson's son on Tarawa was a shock. Moreover, to hear once again of the tragic circumstances surrounding members of the Tanaka family troubled him.

He thought both Sergeant Olander and Lieutenant Hart looked drawn and older than their age. Hart's face was lined and he could not help but notice how gray his friend had gotten. Olander had always smoked, but not Hart. Today, however, at lunch the detective lieutenant finished off nearly a dozen cigarettes. With that kind of a habit, Scott thought it doubtful that Hart and Hal

Brown continued to workout at the gymnasium, as they did years ago. He did not ask. However, what was truly disconcerting—Carl Olander was drinking again. The former alcoholic gave it up after a suspension for misconduct in 1939.

Compared to what these three professional police officers faced every day on the streets of this city, Scott's last three years in the military seemed rather uncomplicated. Certainly, their job was more challenging than anything he faced in the Corps. He was fully aware that there was great risk in the military; it could cost him his life. Still, these men in their blue uniforms were pursuing a career where the day-to-day challenges were as formidable as anything he faced in the service. The war years appeared to have taken their toll on the men and women in the police department. Today, when he left the company of his friends, he wondered, *How in the world can I ever come back to this?*

Chapter 14

On 10 January 1945, Jackson checked in at the Naval Hospital in San Diego, his ninety-day recuperative leave was over. Shortly after that, Navy doctors declared him "fit for duty." He still suffered some discomfort in his leg from the bullet wounds received on Peleliu, but overall his physical health was good. He had been home for more than two months, but before he left Seattle, he was back working out in the gymnasium for up to four hours each day. His doctors attributed his remarkable recovery to this daily regimen of physical exercise, exercise that would have taxed even the most accomplished athlete.

On 16 January, he reported for duty to Admiral Wycoff's office at the Naval Air Station.

"Hello, Scott," the admiral greeted him, with a smile. They exchanged handshakes, with the admiral placing his arm around Scott's shoulder in an obvious show of friendship. "It's good to see you again, how are you?"

"Good morning, sir. I'm fine, thank you."

The admiral, now sixty-five years old, seemed much older. His hair was almost white, his shoulders sagged, and facial features drawn. Scott recalled their first meeting in 1935 in Seattle. Remembering those years, he thought at the time the man was the picture-postcard example of what a military man should look like—tall, immaculately groomed, with a commanding presence about him. But not today; today he looked haggard and worn. Three years of war had taken its toll on this naval officer.

The admiral escorted his guest into his office. "Let's have a cup of coffee, and then we'll talk."

Wycoff opened a large thermos, filling a cup with strong black Navy coffee and handing it off to Jackson. Then pouring one for himself, he sat at his desk, motioning for Scott to sit nearby.

"Tell me, Scott," he said, his tone of voice more serious than Scott had expected, his lips pursed, "what's happened since we last spoke?"

"You know of course of General McAffee's intervention and of my assignment to command Charlie Company. That precluded completion of our major task to monitor the effectiveness of the LVTs and the amphibious tanks during the campaign. However, our people recovered all of my film and I understand they even added some very good footage of our heavy equipment when it came ashore."

"I talked to General McAffee," Wycoff responded, shrugging as if Scott's sudden change of duty in the Pacific was of little concern to him at this time. "He, of course, explained the urgency of the moment—I can appreciate the difficulties which both of you must have faced at the time; in a crisis we must allow for these things."

The admiral's response was one of complete understanding of the position that this Marine captain found himself in during the Peleliu operation. However, the admiral's calm acceptance of his subordinate's unplanned combat assignment surprised Scott, for he certainly had failed to accomplish his mission. Yet there was no time to worry about that; the admiral had other plans for his aide.

"Let's talk about your future. For now, I'd like you to remain on my staff as an observer, reporting directly to me; would you mind?"

"No, sir, not at all, I'd like that. Of course, I wanted to go back to Charlie Company, but you know what happened there."

"Yes, I do," the admiral, replied with a grimace, with Scott detecting a note of personal anguish in the man's response.

"There's practically no one left, sir," Scott continued quietly, nearly overwhelmed by his own thoughts. Reflecting on the deaths of the young men from Charlie Company, he suddenly realized he could not remember any of their names. He could see their faces now, but they all looked alike, young, innocent, and unsuspecting. Not one of them imagined that they would die on that horrible, windswept rock in the Western Pacific.

It was evident that Admiral Wycoff understood the pain his protégé was experiencing, for there was no misunderstanding between these two men—the Palau Operation needlessly cost the lives of nearly 1,500 young American men and possibly as many as 10,000 Japanese.

"Yes, I know, Scott, that's too bad," he replied, speaking softly, turning to glance at the huge map of the Pacific hanging on his office wall, then back to his guest.

"I understand your company suffered over eighty percent casualties. We have a lot to answer to for that." He paused, and then left his chair, walking over to the map pointing to the Western Caroline Island group.

"You knew of course Admiral Halsey opposed this operation; unfortunately he was overruled by Admiral Nimitz, General MacArthur, and the Joint Chiefs. But it's no secret, Scott; even Admiral Nimitz eventually had his doubts about the wisdom of our invasion of the Palaus. Yet MacArthur had the President's ear."

Scott did not reply. No response was necessary. They both knew it was not the first military blunder that the top brass made in the Pacific War. Marines were on the losing end of more than one of these botched operations. Peleliu would rank with Tarawa among the most ignominious for the Corps.

Returning to his desk, the admiral said, "Hopefully, Scott, the next operation will be better planned and executed. As you might have guessed, we are staging now. I'd like you to get out to the Mariana Islands right away.

"You'll still be my eyes and ears, but this time I want you to look at the whole picture of military hardware. Everything, from the M1 rifle the Marine takes ashore with him to the largest battle tank. The War Department has received some troublesome reports about the performance of the Sherman tank in Europe; this concerns me." His voice was calm, yet Scott noted a worried look about his boss, something he had not seen before.

"In this logistics business, we not only have to know if the equipment works, but also whether or not the Navy delivered it at the right time and place. I understand there was more than one miscue on Peleliu. General McAffee told me that some of our heavy equipment was offloaded on the wrong beach, and the situation with the drinking water was inexcusable."

"That's true, sir. You may recall in my report, a lot of the amtracs and even some of our amphibious tanks got ashore okay, but not too many got beyond the tank barriers until the dozers came in to cut a path. By that time, more than two hundred of them were damaged or destroyed."

"What else?" Admiral Wycoff asked abruptly. "Can you think of anything we should have handled differently?"

"Well, as you know, the pilots did, in my opinion, a remarkable job. Once the airstrip was operational, our people made excellent headway."

"Yes, they really did. I saw the films."

"Admiral, when you can't get your big guns in place to fire directly into a cave, your people on site have to go after them with whatever resources they have."

"Yes." The man nodded in agreement, but it was clear the admiral's thoughts were elsewhere. "By the way, when you arrive in Guam you'll be reporting to General McAffee," the man responded, changing the subject. "However, before you leave, I want you to spend some time at the Army Desert Training Center Ordinance Depot at CAMAS." (California, Arizona Maneuver Area). "Our friends in the Army are better equipped—they have the latest hardware. They may be able to enlighten us on the problems Patton's people encountered with the M4 in Europe. Was there anything—"

Before the admiral finished asking his next question, his secretary interrupted. "Admiral Halsey is on the telephone, sir. He'd like to speak to you right away."

"Thank you, Alice. I must take that, Scott, please excuse me."

While the admiral was talking on the telephone, Scott walked over to look at the map on the back wall of the man's office. The Pacific islands, where death had come to so many of his fellow Marines, appeared as mere specks of land on this huge map. To date, thousands of young American men and presumably hundreds of thousands of enemy soldiers had been lost in America's attempt to dislodge the Japanese from these island fortifications. He doubted that history would be kind to those military leaders who sent so many young men to their death needlessly, on these godforsaken islands.

When the admiral got off the telephone, he turned to Jackson, "If you'll see my aide, Scott, he'll cut your orders for the Ordinance Depot. You should be on your way by the end of the week. We will get you out to Guam after that. McAffee has insisted that you be assigned to his command." Wycoff smiled.

"I didn't know that, sir."

"That's quite an honor, Scott," he added, smiling again as he walked the junior officer to the door. "Mac won't give up, he's an old-time professional, not easily impressed, but you did a good job. He recognized that."

It was obvious Admiral Wycoff had become fond of his young protégé. He accompanied Scott out into the hallway, shook the Marine captain's hand and, with his other firmly gripping Jackson's shoulder, added warmly, "Good luck, Scott—you be careful out there.

"By the way, pass my congratulations on to McAffee; he has been promoted to Major General. As you well know, he earned it the hard way. I'll see you before you depart, Captain," his farewell clearly reflecting the impersonal nature of military command.

Although his boss low-keyed his assignment to the Desert Training Center, Scott knew Admiral Wycoff well enough to understand that something was amiss. He wondered if the man knew more than he let on about the shortcomings of the Corps' armored units—Scott was anxious to find out.

However, his orders gave him five days before he needed to report to the Ordinance Depot in the Mojave Desert. Quickly checking in at NAS Bachelor Officers' Quarters, he called Sophia Kosterman. Since returning from the South Pacific, her ship was tied up on the quay at the naval base and Sophia was working at the Naval Hospital in San Diego.

"Can you get liberty, Sophia?" he asked. "I'm on leave for the next five days."

"Where are you?"

"I'm at the BOQ at North Island."

"I'll pick you up at the main gate, be there at three o'clock. Bring a bag," she said, her tone of voice somewhat unsettling to Jackson. He shrugged it off, thinking she might just be tired.

Kosterman, driving a 1939 Ford convertible, top down, arrived at the North Island Naval Air Station main gate at fifteen hundred hours. Scott had not seen her in weeks. Looking at her, he was immediately concerned. There was no smile, not even a polite hello. Despite her somber mood, and the obvious grim set of her mouth, she was simply gorgeous. Her stunning beauty completely overwhelmed him. She wore the dark blue naval officer's uniform, her long hair hanging over the collar of her white blouse. Her blue skirt matching her coat, which lay on the seat beside her, its sleeves now decorated with the double gold strips of a lieutenant. The uniform fit her like a glove. The short-sleeved white blouse, open at the neck, accented her deep golden-brown California tan. It appeared that military life had been good to her. She still maintained her fantastic hourglass figure; at five-foot-ten, this young woman was a match for any of the Vargas girls. Images of Vargas' scantily clad young women adorned the walls of almost every military barracks in the country. Larger-than-life-size paintings of these voluptuous beauties also decorated hundreds of aircraft bound for the Pacific war.

"Get in," she said, rather brusquely. "How much time do you have?"

"Like I told you, Sophia, I've got five days. Why, what have you got in mind?" he asked, throwing his overnight bag in the back seat of the convertible.

"I have the use of a friend's home; do you want to spend that time with me?"

"Of course I do. I wouldn't have called if I didn't."

Before pulling away from the main gate she turned directly toward him; it was quite apparent she was upset about something. Jackson did not have a clue as to what it could be.

"When you went home from the hospital, you didn't even say good-bye. You haven't called, or written; I haven't heard a damn word from you for months."

Startled by her sharp reproach, her voice cutting, he had not experienced her temper before.

"That's true," he replied, quietly, taken aback by her scolding. "But, Sophia, when we saw each other last, I didn't think you were very understanding. Sometimes you acted downright callous."

"I had other patients, Scott; I did not have time to pamper you. If I did, you would never have recovered as you should."

"Honey, I understood that, but I thought we were more than just good friends. We certainly like each other and we like to do things together, but you seemed unconcerned."

"That's why you didn't write?" Her response was more a statement of fact than a question. It was obvious she was unhappy with her former patient. He decided to try a different tack; however, it was apparent she was not going to be easily placated.

"Sophia, those weeks in the hospital were kind of rough on me physically and maybe mentally. I know I should have written and I am sorry for not saying good-bye."

"Scott, we've known each other for three years, yet a girl has to think about the future," she responded, sounding somewhat conciliatory. "Are we just going to continue as friends?"

"No. I hope not. We're more than just friends, Sophia," he replied, uneasily, with a pained expression.

"Well, I thought we were, but it seems to me that you're preoccupied with that bloody Marine Corps of yours. It's an obsession with you."

"Come on, Sophia," he pleaded. "I've changed; you mean more to me than the Corps."

"No! I don't think so," she exclaimed, her voice unduly harsh. "You haven't changed; I'll bet you were just like this when you were on the police force. There is more to life than wearing that damn uniform. What about us?"

"That sounds like a proposal, honey, is it?" he asked before he realized his glib response may have sounded as if he were entirely insensitive of her feelings.

"Screw you, Captain Jackson," Sophia replied, her voice bristling. It was obvious she was not pleased with his response. With that, she tramped down hard on the accelerator, not uttering another word. The rear tires of the small convertible squealed on the pavement as they spun out into traffic.

While Sophia drove north on Pacific Coast Highway, Jackson sat watching her. It was clear that there was a determination about her that he had not seen before today. He figured this would probably be the end of their relationship.

"What are you looking at?" she demanded, glancing at her passenger.

"You; I'm just trying to figure you out," he replied, smiling. "We've known each other for a long time, Sophia, but maybe I don't know you at all. I loved you... You knew that."

"Well, you found one heck of a way to show it. Your almighty Corps is apparently more important to you than I am."

He was about to respond, then figured he had better leave it alone. What she said was true. Unquestionably, he was preoccupied with the Marine Corps and the minor role he played thus far in this war. Furthermore, he had not written a single letter to her while home on leave. Nor did he call when he returned to

California. It was not until he received this latest assignment from Admiral Wycoff that he made any effort to contact her.

As they approached the small resort city of La Jolla, Sophia turned off the main highway, entering into a beautiful residential area of large houses and magnificently landscaped yards. Each home exhibited a luxuriant display of pink and red flowering bougainvillea or climbing roses. The area reminded Scott of the Crown Hill District in his hometown. Quite abruptly, Sophia pulled into a driveway of an attractive two-story brick home.

"Here we are," she said.

Jackson was surprised. "What the heck is this?" he asked, obviously taken aback by the grandeur of the house and yard with its inextricably beautiful flower gardens.

"Don't you like it?" she snapped. "I'll take you back to the BOQ if you don't."

"Don't be so damn touchy, Sophia, of course I like it. I'm just surprised, I thought we were gonna be alone."

"We are going to be alone," she responded, chiding her friend. "This belongs to Commander Arnold King, he's a surgeon at the hospital, and he's also my boss. He lets the nurses aboard ship use it when we are in port. Come on," she said impatiently, obviously trying to hold her emotions in check. "Let's go inside." Jackson, grabbing the overnight bags from the backseat of the convertible, followed Sophia into the commander's home.

The house sat on a rise high enough for a view of both the ocean and the city below. There was no backyard as such; a swimming pool and tennis court took up the entire back lot. Eucalyptus trees and rose bushes encircled the yard, giving near complete privacy to those who chose to use the recreation facilities.

Entering the master bedroom, he dropped the two small overnight bags on the large bed, then stepped back to admire their accommodations. Strolling out into the living room, and then browsing through the kitchen, he examined the view of the Pacific Ocean and the city below. It reminded him of his own home, with its magnificent view of Puget Sound. However, as pretty as this city was, he thought it could not hold a candle to Seattle. He returned to the bedroom.

"My God, Sophia, I've never been in such a beautiful place. It beats anything I've ever been in."

"It is nice, isn't it?"

"Yes, but what did you have to do to get it?" he asked, a note of uncertainty in his voice.

Sophia, in the process of unpacking her bag and hanging her clothes stopped suddenly. "I don't think I like what you're implying," she snapped, glaring at her friend. "Maybe we'd better forget this and go back into town."

"Hold it, for Christ's sake, Sophia, I'm not suggesting anything." Then suddenly realizing what his inquiry must have sounded like, he pleaded, "I am so sorry, I didn't mean anything by it. I am just flabbergasted that we'd have access to such a beautiful place as this, that's all."

"Scott, I was raised differently than you. My father's income was not always that great, but we had a nice home. In your travels, you slept in the fields, bunkhouses, boxcars, or on a damn fishing boat or God knows where. I know this is something you are not accustomed to, but it is just a house. A very grand house if you will, but these things are not important to me. I am sure you know that about me by now. For God's sake, I'm only interested in you."

With this last outburst, tears began to roll down her cheeks; she quickly turned away. Jackson, walking around the bed, placed his hands on her shoulders and gently turned her around. He kissed her cheeks, tasting the salt from her tears, and then kissed her full on the mouth. Placing his arms around her slim waist, he held her close, where each could feel the warmth of the other's body. Picking her up gently, he placed her on the bed and lay down beside her, with neither one of them saying a word for more than a minute.

"Scott, let's start over. Okay?" she asked, her voice filled with emotion, her eyes sparkling as she tried unsuccessfully to hold back the tears.

"Okay, honey, I'd like that," he nodded, smiling, wiping her tears away with his thumbs as he held her close.

For the next five days, the two of them never left each other's side. From the bedroom to the swimming pool and tennis court, they took advantage of all the amenities Doctor King's home offered. They were in bed early every evening and made love often throughout the night. Up at dawn, they were soon either in the heated swimming pool, or out on the tennis court. On his last day of liberty, they drove into the city. Sophia made an appointment to have her hair done at a local beauty shop. While waiting, Jackson walked through the small business district, then down to the beach.

Three hours later, the two of them were back at the house overlooking La Jolla. This would be their last night together in Doctor King's home. Jackson was to report the next morning for a flight to the Army Ordinance Depot in the Mojave Desert. Sophia was to return to the hospital that evening. He, along with officers from the Army and a few Allied Forces personnel, would attend a ten-day crash course on the latest military hardware coming off production lines in the US.

After dinner, he fixed the two of them what he called his favorite cocktail, a Brandy Alexander, made with vanilla ice cream and a double shot of Christian Brother's brandy.

"That's a five-hundred-calorie drink, Scott. What are you trying to do to me?" she smiled. "I'm already overweight." He laughed at her reply. "But I needed this," she added quietly, taking a sip. "I didn't tell you, but our ship is pulling out next week. I think we're headed back to Hawaii."

"What are you talking about?" Scott demanded. "You can't do that; why can't you stay on at the hospital?" He was shaken to learn that she was to be sent overseas a second time.

"I suppose I could if I asked, but I will not do that. If you are going away, there is nothing here for me. Besides, the gals I'm with, we make a good team; we've looked after each other ever since we joined the Navy."

Jackson tried to understand, but this alarmed him. He was unwilling to accept the fact that women, particularly this woman, should once more have to face the hazards of the South Pacific. His mood changed abruptly.

"I don't like that, Sophia," he responded, sharply. "Talk to your boss, damn it; you shouldn't have to go back over there."

"Why not? You're going back. Why should a Navy nurse be any different? We knew what we were getting into, just like you did."

"For Christ's sake, Sophia it's not the same. I don't want you to go back," he replied sharply.

"Scott, don't make it any harder than it is," she pleaded. "I knew the risks when I joined the Navy."

Jackson was angry. He turned away, then, quite suddenly, in a voice barely audible, asked, "Sophia, will you marry me?"

"What? What did you say?" Sophia asked somewhat abruptly. Reaching out, she grabbed him by the shoulder and turned him around to face her; she could not believe what she heard.

"You heard me; I asked you if you'd marry me."

"Yes, I know;" she responded, stepping back, "but I just didn't expect you to ask me tonight. You surprised me, and you sounded so angry and depressed. When you ask someone to marry you, it's supposed to be one of the happiest times of your life."

"Ease off, Sophia. You're damn right I'm angry," annoyed by her reply, his response much harsher than intended. "I have reason to be angry. I don't want you to go back overseas and I asked you to marry me, because I think I'm in love with you."

"Well, thanks a lot, Scott Jackson!" she snapped, her blue eyes now flashing. "Apparently it doesn't matter to you that we've known each other for years; we've slept together a dozen times, and now you just think you love me. That's some proposal, at least it's different."

"Cut it out, Sophia. For Christ's sake, I meant what I said. I asked you to marry me; can't you just leave it at that?"

"No damn way, Scott Jackson," she responded rudely.

Before the words cleared her lips, she regretted her response. What she would not admit, however, was the fact that she harbored serious reservations about marrying anyone in the military service. Too many of her colleagues aboard ship lived to rue the day they married. Some, with their husbands for only a day or two, then the occasional letter, that was all there was. Sophia wanted more than that. Now plagued by second thoughts, she did not know what to do. Notwithstanding that, it was too late; her temper had gotten the best of her. *Damn it*, she thought, *I want to marry that man. Why could I have not just kept my big mouth shut?*

That evening, the two lovers slept together, but their voracious appetite for sex was not rekindled this night.

At 5:00 a.m., Nurse Sophia Kosterman dropped her friend off at the main gate of NAS North Island. He kissed her good-bye, then handed her a small package.

"You might take a look at this when you get back to your quarters, Sophia. Let me know what you think of it."

"Good-bye, Scott. Good luck. Write to me, will you," she pleaded, trying desperately to hold her emotions in check.

"Good-bye," he replied, dispassionately. Without further comment, he grabbed his bag out of the backseat of the convertible and abruptly turned, and without looking back walked through the main gate.

Sophia did not wait until she got back to the nurses' quarters; on her way, she pulled into a nearby parking lot of an all-night cafe. In the dim glow from the restaurant's lights, she quickly tore the wrapping paper from the package. Opening the box, she found a note. It read, "I love you, Sophia, if you change your mind, let me know." There was no signature. The larger box also contained a ring box; inside she found a beautiful diamond engagement ring.

"Oh, Sophia Kosterman," she said out loud, "you're such a damn fool."

Chapter 15

Scott's ten-day training sojourn at the Army Ordinance Depot in the desert went by quickly. In the three years since the war began, he found an astonishingly high number of technical improvements in military weaponry, particularly in the firepower now available to tank crews. Unfortunately, most of it was yet to find its way into Marine Corps inventory. Before departing for overseas, he briefed Admiral Wycoff and three members of the admiral's staff, Marine Colonel David English, Navy Lieutenant Commander Theodore "Ted" Porter, and Coast Guard Commodore Peter Elland.

Colonel English expressed skepticism when Scott told them the American forces in the European Theater found the M4 to be inferior in nearly every respect to the German Panzer.

"What you're saying doesn't make any sense to me, Captain," the colonel responded, obviously dubious of Scott's assertion. "The M4 has served the Corps well for the past two years. We've had few complaints from the field."

"That may be true, sir," Scott replied, glancing at their boss, "but our people have not had to face heavy armored units such as the Army encountered in North Africa and Europe."

"That's a lot of bull, Captain," Colonel English lashed out with a sardonic grin. "The Japanese threw everything they could at us in the Solomon Islands, still we prevailed. The M4 has been the mainstay of the Corps' armored units in the Pacific; that tank has served our people well."

Although the colonel was correct, what he left unsaid was that Marine aviation and infantry troops were in the forefront of the Solomon Island victories. His comments also left the intended implication that he was a part of that campaign and proud of it. What he did not say, however, was the fact that the only part he played in the war to date was that of an administrative supply officer. Yet now he was challenging the findings of some of the Army's best combat soldiers.

"I understand where you're coming from, Colonel," Scott responded politely, "but I have to tell you the Army considers the M4 little more than a steel coffin. Its two-and-one-half-inch armor and seventy-five-millimeter canon was no match for the Germans in North Africa with their high-velocity armor-piercing ordinance. And now, the enemy's Tiger tank, equipped with four inches of armor, and eighty-eight-millimeter cannon, is even more formidable than the Panzer."

"Well, the Japanese don't have any Tiger tanks," English responded, looking around the room, as if for support for his contention. "In your report to the admiral on the Palau campaign, you readily admit that our people used the bazooka quite effectively against their armored units. I don't think we'll learn much from the Army."

Lieutenant Commander Porter and Commodore Elland remained quiet during what appeared to be the beginning of an intra-agency squabble. It was obvious Colonel English was not about to accept this junior officer's assessment of the Marine Corps' armored capabilities, nor was he prone to give the Army its due. However, it was not until Scott mentioned that the Third Armored Division lost more than one-quarter of their equipment in their first engagement with the enemy in France, that the two men interjected themselves into this conversation.

"I want to hear more about what you learned in the Desert Training Center, Scott," Ted Porter spoke out, forcefully. "What Colonel English says may be true, but the Army has clearly come up against a more formidable concentration of enemy armored units than the Corps. We can learn from this."

"I agree," responded Pete Elland. "Please continue, Scott," he said, glancing first toward Colonel English and then at Admiral Wycoff. "I want to hear more."

Before responding, Scott took from his briefcase a list of instructors at the Desert Training Center, handing these out to the admiral and his staff. It contained the names of a dozen former members of General George Patton's staff, men who served as tank commanders in both Italy and North Africa. Then turning to Colonel English, he handed him a group of pictures taken during the North African Campaign of damage inflicted upon American armored units in Tunisia. Before continuing, he took time out to refill each man's coffee cup, giving the admiral's staff an opportunity to review the documents.

"As you can see, gentlemen, several of the officers on that list were on the receiving end of German armor in North Africa. They clearly articulated the risks which tank crews can expect should they come up against similar firepower in the Pacific. These are all professional soldiers. They told us that in 1940, the War Department warned Congress that the American tanks were no match for the Germans. That message apparently went unheeded until our armored units suffered these catastrophic losses at the hands of the Germans."

"That's correct, Scott," Admiral Wycoff stated, interjecting himself into this conversation for the first time. "As you recall, I was with the War Department in Washington at that time. It was quite a revelation for the political leadership of the country. However, Congress has since corrected this problem. As you are aware, the more advanced M26 Pershing tank is now rolling off production lines in Detroit. Unfortunately, the European Theater has first claim on these."

"That's what they told us at the Training Center, sir," Scott responded.

"That may be true, today, Captain," Admiral Wycoff replied, "but it's our responsibility to convince the War Department otherwise. Scott, you will continue to be active with our field units, and the rest of you folks will work with me here at home. We must convince the Joint Chiefs of the need for an upgrading of our armored units in the Pacific." Wycoff planned that the terrible carnage inflicted upon Third Army in Europe would not occur when American forces invaded Japan.

With dawn breaking on the eastern horizon, Scott stepped out of the BOQ; there was sufficient light to see three US Army Air Force B24 Consolidated Liberator bombers parked on the nearby tarmac. One of these aircraft was to be his transportation to Guam, or at least for the first leg of that journey. He would arrive at Hickam Army Air Force Base in Hawaii that afternoon. The planes were ready for flight. Flight crews, standing nearby, were enjoying a last-minute cigarette and cup of coffee before takeoff. Naval Aviation Ground Control service personnel soon joined them.

Making his way to Flight Operations, Scott found nearly two dozen men waiting to check in with Naval Air Ground Control for the flight to Hawaii. It soon became obvious why the Army Air Force was involved; one of the passengers was an Army major general. Two noncom aides accompanied him.

An Air Force captain and a Navy chief petty officer with NAS Ground Control checked each man's orders against the flight manifest. When satisfied that all were present, the officer addressed the group.

"Gentlemen, everyone is here, so I'll take a minute to brief you on your trip. First, all of you should get out your flight jackets or greatcoats. It is warm here and it will be warm in Hawaii, but it will be cold when these planes reach their cruising altitude. You will need warm clothing. Also, grab a life jacket and put it on. Do it before you get on the aircraft.

"If you smoke, do it now. You have a long flight ahead, and there will be no smoking during your trip; the planes are loaded to the hilt with cargo and mail. It'll be a tight squeeze."

Leafing through the pages of his manifest, he continued, "As I call your name, the first seven men will report to the farthest B24, the next seven to the middle aircraft and so on. Your flight crew is ready. They will take off as soon as you are onboard. Good luck, gentlemen."

"General Harman," the captain called out, respecting military protocol in his performance of this somewhat dreary task. He would do his best, however, to assure the military that this cargo of human souls would leave on time, even if he could not guarantee that they would arrive safely at their destination.

Jackson, with five other officers and a Marine sergeant, boarded the last aircraft. While waiting to board, he could see that the first of the three airplanes was already moving into a holding area to test the four 1200 HP turbo-supercharged Pratt and Whitney engines. His plane would soon follow. Each aircraft was fully loaded with a crew of ten, four officers and six enlisted men, plus their seven guests. In addition, the bomb bay of each carried more than eight tons of medical supplies and mail.

One after the other, the planes took off to the southeast. Before turning west, Jackson's pilot guided the aircraft over the beaches of the Silver Strand, the long, low peninsula just west of the city of San Diego. It was here that the Navy introduced Scott to the Corps' amphibious operations. Looking down on the beaches and then back over the city, he caught a glimpse of the Grant Hotel.

Settling back in his seat, he thought back to 1942 and to the good times he and Sophia had spent at that hotel. On their days off, it became almost a ritual, dinner and dancing, stretching into early dawn before returning to their barracks. He smiled, there were some advantages to living in a world turned upside down by war. Sophia and he would not have met were it not for this war; he wondered if he would ever see her again.

Slowly the plane began its turn to the west, out over the Pacific. He tried again to locate the hotel, but it was already lost to view. From the starboard side of the aircraft, the long California coastline soon disappeared. He could see the other two planes above and to the right. They looked like two elephantine mammoths, with their enormously large, rounded bellies and stubby wings; he marveled that they could even fly.

Yet as ponderous as these aircraft looked, a member of the crew told him their craft was not only capable of carrying a larger bomb load than the B17, the aircraft's range was greater than the Boeing plane. This was of some comfort; Scott knew there was a long voyage ahead.

Two hours into the flight, while cruising at an altitude of 10,000 feet, the pilot, Captain James Worden, came through the belly of the aircraft to see how his passengers were faring. Although a veteran pilot, Worden was only twenty-six years old. He was a small man, probably no taller than five-eight and slight of build; his small stature helped him navigate his way along the narrow catwalk through the bomb bay, now filled to capacity with mail sacks.

Worden explained, "We can go higher of course, but the lack of oxygen would be a problem, and at the higher altitude, the headwinds are much stronger. As it is, there's at least ten, or even up to twelve hours' flying time ahead of us.

"We have a pretty heavy load," he continued, "but if everything goes according to plan we should arrive at Hickam Field by fifteen hundred hours, Hawaiian time.

"Make yourselves as comfortable as you can. If you need 'em, there are more blankets up front; stretch out on those mail sacks if you'd like. I see you've found the thermos jugs; the crew will bring some sandwiches around in an hour or so."

When the pilot returned to the cockpit, Jackson finished his coffee, then grabbing a blanket tried to get some sleep. Stretching out across several canvas mail sacks, he slept soundly for more than two hours until aroused by a crew member handing out sack lunches. The food, prepared at the officers' mess, included cold meat sandwiches, apples, and cookies, standard Navy fare.

While eating, he studied the faces of the other passengers, they were young—younger than he was, he suspected. Three were Army Air Force fighter pilots, two light colonels, and a captain. They were on their way to Guam, where they would meet up with their aircraft. A cargo ship was to deliver their twin-engine P38s ahead of them.

One man, a naval lieutenant commander, was destined to assume command of a destroyer escort; the ship's captain died in the battle of the Philippine Sea. The commander would join the ship at Pearl Harbor. The seventh passenger, Marine Sergeant John Lone, perched high up on the mail sacks, sat quietly eating his sack lunch.

Lone, a Navajo Indian from Window Rock Arizona, wounded on Tarawa, was returning to the Pacific to rejoin a Marine communications group. He was part of a JASCO communication team. Marine Communications used Navajo Indian "Code Talkers" on Tarawa and in the Palau Islands to thwart any effort by the Japanese to decipher radio/telephone messages. It proved very effective. The Marine Corps took full advantage of the Navajo Indians' communication skills.

Scott remembered meeting several Navajos in 1941 in boot camp and again on Peleliu. He was well aware of just how important these Code Talkers were to the Marine Corps—much more than he, he suspected. All he could offer was his police experience, and the Corps was not using that, even if that were his own doing.

Finishing the last of his sandwich, he was about to pour himself a second cup of coffee when he heard one of the crew members on the starboard side of the aircraft yell. The man, quickly donning his radio headset, pointed out the window of the waist-gunner's hatch. He yelled again, this time into the mouthpiece of his radio.

Jackson could see the other planes, not 500 yards off the starboard wingtip. They were still flying in formation, but smoke was coming from the left inboard engine of the nearest aircraft. As he watched, flames suddenly erupted from under the engine cowling, the smoke turning from a dirty gray to white, then black.

Soon, the stricken plane began to lose altitude. Scott noticed the roar of the engines on his own aircraft drop off as the pilot throttled back to keep abreast of the burning craft. For a moment, the black smoke from the fire diminished and he heard a crew member yell.

"He's hit it with the fire extinguisher, but it ain't doing the job. He's going down."

The two planes were now within 100 yards of each other and perilously close to the water. While the men on Captain Worden's plane watched, the fire spread across the port wing of the stricken aircraft. Suddenly, the left inboard engine vented a large plume of black smoke. Within seconds, the plane hit the water and was lost from view as Captain Worden's aircraft quickly passed beyond the crash site. Glancing upward, Jackson could still see the third aircraft high overhead, continuing on its original course.

The roar of the big engines on their plane refocused his attention on the present emergency; Captain Worden pushed the throttles forward to regain airspeed and altitude. The aircraft appeared to be only inches above the ocean waves. On the intercom, the pilot told the crew they would only have time enough for two passes over the downed plane, everyone on board was to keep a sharp lookout for survivors.

Crew members, quickly moving passengers out of the way, opened the two gun turret hatches on either side of the airplane. A torrent of warm ocean air burst through the openings, scattering blankets, hats and paper cups throughout the interior of the aircraft.

Worden's plane, now climbing, banked sharply to the right, turning back over the site of the downed aircraft. A small amount of debris floated about the crash site, but only the tail section of the stricken craft remained above the waterline. They saw no sign of men in the water.

The pilot continued the turn, the B24 coming full-circle, back onto its original course. Once again, he crossed over the location of the downed airplane; passengers found viewing space on the starboard side. Passing over the location once more, there was no sign now of the downed aircraft.

"There they are," shouted one of the crew members, pointing at the water. "There are two...three."

"There are four," another man yelled as he dropped two smoke flares into the water. "They're in the raft."

Shortly thereafter, with the B24 slowly climbing, the pilot corrected his course for Hawaii. Without comment, crew members closed the two hatches, cutting off the furious force of air and sound of the wind rushing through the airplane.

For a time, Scott found himself studying the faces of the crew members and passengers around him. Their grim expressions reminded him of the men of Charlie Company in the Palaus. Many of the men who survived that first encounter with the Japanese believed that somehow they were to blame for the deaths of those who did not make it. He remembered that no one said anything. The Marines nervously looked at one another and when they made eye contact, quickly turned away. For some inexplicable reason they were still alive, but their friends were all dead. Had he gotten on General Harman's ill-fated aircraft, Scott wondered if he would still be alive.

In a few minutes, Lieutenant Richard Small, the copilot, made his way back to the passengers gathered in the belly of the aircraft. With the plane struggling to regain altitude, the lieutenant needed to shout over the roar of the four engines. "There's nothing more the captain could do," he said, grimly, shaking his head. "Hopefully we have enough fuel on board to make it to Hickam Field. These planes only have a three-thousand-mile range."

Then as if to reassure their passengers, he added, "The Navy has a 'Jeep' carrier and two destroyers on the way to Pearl; they're within a hundred miles of Zeek's aircraft," referring to the pilot of the downed plane, Captain Dan Zeek of Yonkers, New York. "Hopefully they'll locate them. There are still a few hours of daylight."

The passengers had little to say during the remaining hours of their flight. Jackson was sure these men were probably thinking the same thing he was. *There but for the Grace of God… If he or any of the others in the belly of this airplane accompanied General Harman and his two enlisted aides, they, too, may now be dead.* It was a sobering thought; he reflected on his own good fortune.

"Brace yourselves," a crew member shouted. "The captain says we may have a pretty rough landing; we're almost out of fuel."

Looking out the port side of the aircraft, Scott saw Diamond Head, less than a mile or two in the distance. It seemed that it was much larger, but less alluring than when he first viewed it a year ago from the deck of the troopship *Zachary Taylor*. At that time, however, he was so seasick that any bit of land would have been a welcome sight. Within minutes, the plane touched down on the tarmac at Hickam Field. After its roll-out, the pilot cut the two outboard engines and the craft turned onto a taxiway, heading toward the Airport Control Tower.

After checking in with Hickam Field Flight Operations, Scott got a lift to the BOQ. Because Jackson's name was not on any of his lists for Guam, the watch officer told him he would check with Marine Corps Headquarters, Hawaii.

"I will call you, Captain," he said, "as soon as I hear anything. In any case, you should plan to be here at least three days or maybe even longer. We don't have anything scheduled out for Guam before Friday."

Tired and dirty, Scott needed a hot bath. After showering, he lay on his bunk, but could not sleep. When he closed his eyes, he would see the flames from the engine, and the smoke rolling out from under the wing of the stricken Liberator before it ditched in the middle of the Pacific Ocean.

Thinking of all those young men, he muttered quietly, "Oh Lord, what a waste." Getting up, he dressed and headed for the officers' club; it was nearly nineteen hundred hours when he arrived. Entering the building, he was surprised; the officers who traveled with him from San Diego were all here. Captain Worden and Lieutenant Small, sitting near the bar, waved him over to their table.

He made his way across the room toward the two men. Several of those with him on the aircraft that day greeted him as he passed by their table; it was as if he were a long-lost friend, a friend who suddenly and quite inexplicably returned. Yet he did not even know their names. He wondered if this was the model for wartime friendships. Were these men, whom one really did not know, truly friends? Probably not, he thought. After all, he was a cop; outside the force, cops had few friends in real life. Then he smiled at what he was thinking; for there was no more real-life venture than what these men experienced this very day. However, one thing he had in common with these men—they were among the lucky bastards who, by chance alone, did not fly with General Harman today aboard Captain Dan Zeek's aircraft.

Jackson gulped down a double Scotch and quickly ordered another. The two pilots were good company and he soon felt more relaxed. He needed to get his mind off the events of today, yet he knew he would not be able to sleep until he heard from Jim Worden. He wanted to know what had really happened out there over the ocean.

Worden explained, "These three planes were all new, Scott. This should not have happened; the Liberator is an excellent plane. The Ford Motor Company built them for Consolidated Aircraft. Before accepting them into Air Force inventory, our people flight-tested all three of them at Fairfield Air Base in California."

Worden and Zeek both flew B24 aircraft in Europe; after twenty-five missions they returned home on furlough, and then reported in for assignment to the Pacific Theater. In the skies over Europe, their plane was hit several times by enemy gunfire, yet they never lost an aircraft, or a member of their crew.

"You never know though," he said, "when you're flying this far, against some pretty strong headwinds, almost anything can happen. Unfortunately, when it happens over an ocean, there's no place to set it down."

When asked about the chances of anyone surviving, Worden responded, "If the crew made it into a raft, with three Navy ships in the vicinity, the odds are in their favor. One of the naval units could arrive at the crash site before nightfall."

Scott was unconvinced. Still, he kept this skepticism to himself; he wondered if liquor might have prompted this rather optimistic response from the Air Force officer.

"It depends on a lot of things," Worden continued, with a look of concern. "How rough the seas are, did the crew salvage the flares? What kind of shape they're in, physically. No one really knows what is going to happen to you out there on the water. It can be a very lonely place." He paused as if to reflect on his own good fortune. "You realize, Scott, had we stayed out there another five or ten minutes, all of us would be in the drink with 'em."

Changing the subject, the two pilots wanted to know more about their VIP passenger. In a more cheerful tone, Worden commented, "Scott, we don't know anything about you. What do you do in the Marine Corps? Where're you headed?"

"Not sure what my final destination will be," he responded quietly. "My next stop is Guam. I'm supposed to be there by the end of the month. We're due out of here in three days."

Taking a drink from his glass, he added, "What I do is rather uneventful compared to your job; logistics is my specialty. We match the equipment needs of the troops in the field with the task. If the Corps doesn't get their heavy equipment when and where it's needed, or if it doesn't work when it gets there, that's where I come into the picture."

"That doesn't sound too uneventful to me," Warden offered. "It appears that if those things ain't working, your butt's hanging out in the cold."

"Y'know," added Lieutenant Small, grinning, "that sounds like a forward ground observer's job; like someone sends you out on the line to see why a damn tank ain't moving, or something like that. That's too close to the enemy. I want to be in a nice, comfortable airplane, high above those bastards." Both Jackson and Worden laughed at the lieutenant's remarks. It was past midnight when the men made it back to the BOQ; all three were quite drunk.

The next day, after his breakfast of toast and coffee, Jackson began a search for Lieutenant Kosterman. It had been almost a month since she set sail from San Diego. After four telephone calls, he found the hospital ship tied up in the harbor and soon traced Sophia to the Ala Moana Hotel in downtown Honolulu. That afternoon, he met her in the lobby of the hotel; she appeared very pleased to see her friend. Grabbing him by both arms and looking up at him, she exclaimed, "Let me look at you. Oh my, you certainly look better than when I saw you last," then she kissed him full on the mouth.

"It's only been a few weeks, Sophia, I didn't look that bad, did I?"

She laughed. "No. I guess not, you were moody though, you seemed so unhappy."

"I'm sorry for the way I acted, but I didn't want to leave you, and I certainly didn't want you coming back out here. I was really down, but I'm okay now," he smiled. "Let's get out of here."

The two of them left the hotel and walked out onto the beach at Waikiki; it was a warm, typically beautiful afternoon in Hawaii. They were greeted by bright sunlight, and a few brilliant white cumulus clouds, their massive domes churning high overhead in the distance. Both were in uniform, she in a freshly laundered and starched white skirt and blouse, he in his suntans. Arriving at the beach, they removed their shoes and walked in their bare feet in the wet sand.

"You know, Lieutenant, we're both out of uniform," he remarked, with a grin. "The Corps doesn't look too kindly upon officers who don't follow regulations."

Grabbing him by the arm, she laughed, "You and your Marine Corps. I bet you were this way when you were on the police department."

Scott, chuckling softly, responded, "How'd you guess?"

"I can read you like a book, Captain Jackson," she answered, with a smile. "If it's not in your little rule book it can't happen."

"That's not true, Sophia," he protested. "Both services have their traditions and if you wear the uniform you should respect it."

"Oh, I do," she conceded, still smiling, then somewhat suggestively, added, "If you feel so strongly about it though, let's go to my place, where we can take off our uniforms."

"That's a great idea," he grinned, taking her hand and leading her away from the water's edge. "Let's do it."

This young Navy nurse appeared genuinely pleased to be with her friend once more. She held on to him tightly as they strolled along the waterfront. They ate an early dinner in one of the many restaurants that dotted the Waikiki shoreline, and then caught a cab to her apartment, near Diamond Head, where Kosterman shared quarters with two other nurses from the ship.

When in port, the apartment gave the women some respite from the sparse hospital-ship accommodations. It also helped to relieve stress, a common experience in time of war within the nursing profession. Their suite was small but well furnished, with kitchen cabinets stocked with both food and liquor. Of equal importance, it was just a short distance to the beach.

Once settled, Jackson notified Hickam Field Flight Operations, where he would be. Kosterman called and switched workdays with a colleague.

"Catch," she said, tossing him a bathing suit from a bedroom dresser drawer. "Let's go for a swim before it gets dark."

They stayed on the beach until well after the sun disappeared beyond the horizon. Although both spent months in the South Pacific, they were still surprised how quickly it got dark in the tropics once the sun went beyond the curvature of the earth. With the wartime brownout in effect, the walk to Sophia's temporary home was in near total darkness.

Arriving at her apartment, he fixed the two of them drinks— her, rum and coke, and him, his Scotch on the rocks. "Here's to us, Sophia," he offered with a smile, handing Kosterman her drink. She looked pleased, touching her glass to his.

"What happened between us, Scott?" she asked, quite suddenly. "Why didn't you answer my letters?"

"I don't have a reason," he replied, getting up and adding additional ice to his drink. "I suppose I felt sorry for myself. You were in San Diego and I was home; there were many miles between us. It doesn't make any sense, I know, but I really don't have an excuse."

"Yes, you do, Amy was there and I wasn't," she replied quietly, with a pained look on her face.

Without waiting for his reply, she set her drink aside and went into the bedroom, emerging shortly with a large towel, tossing it to him.

"Take your shower; I'll see what we have to eat in the kitchen."

Standing under the hot water, he found himself comparing Sophia Kosterman to Amy Donahue. Both, he thought, were great specimens of American womanhood, attractive, talented, well educated, certainly better educated than he. Then he wondered if he would ever marry. When he asked Kosterman to marry him just a few weeks ago, he was surprised at her response; she apparently was not interested.

"Christ, maybe there's something wrong with me," he muttered, quietly.

What would happen, he wondered, if he proposed again? Would she turn him down once more? From her question just minutes ago, it was obvious she had not forgotten about his former girlfriend. When he was home on leave, he dated Amy Donahue a half dozen times, yet Donahue made it perfectly clear he was not to be included in her future.

Oh damn, he thought, *why should I worry about this now*? While still deep in thought, letting the hot water flow over his body, Sophia suddenly pulled aside the curtain and stepped into the enclosure with him. He was surprised, and pleased, yet somewhat embarrassed. He quickly drew her warm body to his under the flowing hot water.

That evening, as they lay naked between clean white bed sheets, she asked him about Donahue. "Scott, what about Amy?"

Oh Christ, he thought, *she won't leave it alone*. He was sorry that he even mentioned Donahue to her. That was just one more mistake he had made in his dealings with the opposite sex. He knew he should have kept his mouth shut about this former lover.

"I forgot I told you about her," he lied. "No, that's history, Sophia," he answered quietly. "I took her out a couple of times when I was home. But that's over."

"Did you love her?" she probed, fully aware he was trying to avoid the subject.

"Oh, I don't know," he responded cautiously. "I guess I did. Years ago I'd asked her to marry me; she turned me down."

"My God, Scott Jackson, you guess!" she exclaimed, flashing an unpleasant glance at her friend. "What do you mean, you guess? Knowing you as I do, you probably said that to her. In San Diego, you treated me the same way, no wonder she refused your proposal."

"Hey, let's drop it, Am…" he said, catching himself before Amy Donahue's name escaped his lips. However, it was too late.

"You bastard!" she said in an angry tone, suddenly pushing herself out from his embrace. "You don't even know who the hell you're sleeping with."

"Drop it, Sophia," he responded, annoyed by her persistence. "You brought the subject up, for Christ's sake, leave it alone."

"Why should I?" she demanded, her eyes flashing. "You're sleeping with me. I think I have a right to know where we stand. Are you telling me it's over between you and Donahue?"

"Sophia," he replied, now nearly exasperated with her, "I asked the girl to marry me; she turned me down. I don't need to be hit on the head with a rifle butt; I got the message. Of course it's over."

"You men are all alike. You are in the middle of a damn war and you ask some girl to marry you, or you 'kind of asked.' You really don't know anything about the opposite sex, do you?"

"Oh, yes, I do," he protested.

"No, you don't know a damn thing about women!" she exclaimed, flashing an angry glance at her friend once again. "You haven't the slightest idea how a woman feels about such things."

"Oh, I think I do," he replied, annoyed by her continuing probing into his former love life, and now this sudden outburst.

"Scott, no woman is going to accept a halfhearted proposal of marriage, particularly from some guy who's on his way to a battlefield. If you were dumb enough to join the good old Marine Corps, you're probably dumb enough to get yourself killed."

He did not respond verbally to this unexpected outburst of emotion; he merely shook his head, with a slight grimace crossing his face. He knew the startling implications of her outburst; in this war, the life expectancy of a Marine infantry officer could be very short.

Kosterman, stunned by her own words, placed her hand over her mouth, and then added quickly, "Oh my God, Scott, I shouldn't have said that."

"Leave it alone, Sophia," he said, his arm encircling her waist, pulling her close.

Before they went to sleep that night, they agreed, there would be no further discussion between them about the war, or the effect it may or may not have upon their love life.

Chapter 16

The following morning, Sophia and Scott walked the two miles to the small shopping district along Waikiki Boulevard. Like the day before, the morning was cool, but by noon, the temperature reached nearly 80 degrees. They enjoyed each other's company, with Sophia laughing at her friend's insouciant Irish humor. He regaled her with stories about him and his high school classmates. Their escapades, all carried out while under the watchful eye of the Christian Brothers at O'Dea High, amused her.

Sophia admitted she had no idea that young men could get away with such devilment while attending a Church-managed high school. When he told her about what he now called the "rope trick," which deftly removed the back bumper of Bishop O'Dea's automobile, she was in stitches.

"I don't believe that, Scott," she laughed. "Where I come from, your whole gang would have been expelled."

He grinned, but did not respond, he was watching her closely and could not help but compare her to Amy Donahue. The two women in his life were a lot alike, but as children, they had little in common. Joe Donahue figured the only reason his daughter entered the military service was that she felt she needed some recognition. At least something where there was a greater challenge in life than that which her father's money always provided.

Sophia, on the other hand, grew up poor, in a home wracked by violent outbursts, frequently triggered by an often unemployed, alcoholic father. She fought to get through high school and eventually won a scholarship at the University of Pennsylvania, where she studied nursing. In school, she worked as a waitress in a series of restaurants and bars, but still graduated near the top of her class. When she graduated, she chose the Navy Nurse Corps for both pay and security.

Not motivated initially by the need to help in the war effort, once she witnessed the havoc created on the battlefields, with its aftermath of broken bodies, there was no greater advocate for the Navy Nurse Corps. Jackson appreciated just how fortunate he was to have this very captivating young woman as a friend.

Shortly after the two returned to Sophia's apartment, Scott was to learn his stopover in Honolulu would last longer than expected. When he called Hickam Flight Operations, the duty officer told him he was to report to Lieutenant Commander Moore's office at CinCPac.

Lieutenant Commander Moore was one of Admiral John Wycoff's junior naval logistics officers. His job was to ensure that before the fleet sailed the Navy loaded out appropriate military ordinance and supplies for the Marines. In Jackson's short naval career, this did not always happen. He had met Tyler once before. They were on the same ship in 1944 en route to the Island of Pavuvu in the South Pacific. Tyler Moore remained onboard and continued on to the Naval Supply Depot on the nearby Island of Banika. Scott remembered the man well, as did most officers aboard the USS *Taylor*.

Moore, the son of the Democratic senior senator from the State of Maine, the Honorable Tyler Claude Moore, was a know-it-all aboard ship. He also made sure that every officer knew just who his father was, and of the "important role" his family played in the American war effort. Senator Moore, a staunch supporter of the Democratic Party, backed Franklin Delano Roosevelt during all four of FDR's campaigns for the presidency. When the war started, he called in his marker at the War Department. The younger Moore, appointed to the rank of lieutenant, was within months elevated to the rank of lieutenant commander. That was quite an accomplishment for this young man, particularly after one of the top Ivy League universities saw fit to boot him out for failure to meet their academic standards.

However, the Navy brass did not need a lot of convincing to understand that it would be in their best interest to take care of Senator Moore's son. Junior, with some fanfare, took the oath of a naval officer in his father's office at the nation's capital. Shortly after that, he arrived at Headquarters, Twelfth US Naval District in San Francisco; he was to be one of the many naval logistics officers stationed at the huge Port Hueneme Naval Supply Depot in Southern California.

One of his first duty assignments was to assure the Navy that the Marines had plenty of fresh water once they got ashore on an enemy held island. That should not have been too difficult a task for most anyone in his position.

Yes. Scott wanted to see that no-good son of a bitch who filled 55-gallon gasoline drums with drinking water and sent them ashore with the troops on Peleliu. In the oppressive 100-degree heat of the island, as the steel barrels warmed, the putrid mix of gasoline and water sickened hundreds of men. Yes indeed, this Marine wanted to meet Lieutenant Commander Tyler Moore once again.

After checking in at Security, an armed guard escorted him to Commander Moore's office. He found the man buried in paper in a back room at CinCPac. For some reason, Scott remembered Moore as being older than when he first met the man en route to Guadalcanal. Now however, looking at the naval officer, his first thought was, *The guy is just a damn kid.* He was probably no more than twenty-four or twenty-five years old.

Yet, to Jackson it seemed that nearly every officer, Marine or Navy, with few exceptions, was younger than he was. He would soon be thirty-three years old. Where could the time have gone, he wondered. Upon seeing Scott, Moore sprang to his feet and rushed to meet his guest before he could enter his office.

"Captain Jackson, come in, come in, please," he said, with a note of trepidation in his voice; the two men quickly exchanging handshakes.

"I'm very glad to see you, Captain, but before you say anything, I apologize. I'm the guy that sent those gasoline drums over to your people to be used for drinking water. It was my responsibility to make sure they were not contaminated. I didn't do my job." The man held up his hands, as if to admit his culpability in the debacle that sickened hundreds of Marines. "There's no excuse," he added, "nor could there be for what I did. I am truly sorry."

Surprised as he was by Moore's unasked-for acknowledgment that he was the one responsible for a major supply blunder, the naval officer's next statement startled Scott.

"If my father was not a United States Senator, I'm sure I would have faced a court-martial long ago. Nevertheless, he is, and all I can do is express my regret for the damage I inflicted upon your people. That's all I can say. CinCPac has made sure that it will not happen again. I am buried here for the duration of the war. Now come on in, please, and let's talk."

Jackson's feelings toward this naval supply officer had not waned over the past several months. Yet the man whom he could have killed six months ago appeared to be genuinely remorseful and contrite over the role he played in the drinking water debacle. Yet, he thought of his own shortcomings on that island; he held himself responsible for the heavy loss of life in Charlie Company. Were he to have left the business of killing to the professionals, he believed many of the men he commanded on that Godforsaken, rat-and-land-crab-infested atoll in the Western Pacific would still be alive.

While the two men were talking, an older man walked into Moore's office. He was a tall gaunt individual, with shirt sleeves rolled to his elbows, showing thin, almost emaciated arms, their yellowish tan exhibiting the telltale signs of malaria or something worse. He wore no insignia of rank on his faded khaki shirt, which hung loosely on his bone-thin skeletal body, yet with the black shoes and web belt it was obvious he was a naval officer. With a pencil, wedged alongside his ear, held in place by his glasses, Scott thought he looked more like schoolteacher than a naval officer.

Walking directly over to Scott and holding out his hand, he greeted the Marine officer.

"This must be Captain Jackson, I've heard much about you," the man smiled, his voice warm and friendly.

"Captain Jackson," Moore quickly interjected, "this is my boss, Captain Cinkovich."

"How do you do, sir? I'm pleased to meet you."

"And I, you, Scott," the captain responded, holding on to his guest's hand, while he looked the Marine officer over. "I've heard and read much about you; it's an honor to meet you. General McAffee and Colonel Pugh were through here a few months ago. They told us about the problems you folks encountered in the Palaus. The general said he was glad to have soldiers like you and your people serving with him."

"That's quite a tribute coming from the general, sir."

"Yes, it is, he's from the Old Corps, you know. He is not one to extol the accomplishments of junior officers. You ran into some problems on your way over too, is that correct?"

"It wasn't our crew, sir, but yes, a B24 went down about five hundred miles out from Pearl."

"I understand that. We picked up four; they're still searching for the others." Then, shaking his head, added, "I'm afraid it doesn't look good..."

"That's too bad sir," Scott was surprised, "but this is the first that I've heard that some of them were rescued. That's good news."

"Yes, it is. Anyway, let's get on with the business at hand, come on down to my office and we'll talk."

The three men walked through a long corridor past the open doors of a series of offices occupied by members of all four branches of the military. They soon entered a large room, which appeared to have been a gymnasium at one time; it was the

CinCPac War Room. Standing in front of a map on the wall, Scott recognized the gray-haired man holding a metal pointer in his hand. Even the most novice military officer in the Pacific knew of Admiral Chester W. Nimitz and that he was commander in chief of the Central Pacific Theater of Operations (CinCPac). Nimitz, informally dressed in Navy khaki, appeared to be explaining something of interest to a group of officers nearby.

There were representatives in the room from every allied nation involved in the Pacific Theater of Operations. Jackson saw men in uniform from the UK, Canada, Australia, New Zealand, and even India. All seemed intent on what the admiral was saying. Others stood or sat at an array of desks scattered about the room, some cluttered with books, maps, or poster-sized pictures of military bases and airports.

The men closest to Admiral Nimitz appeared to be involved in some type of single-minded, yet chaotic search for a solution to a problem. Scott did not expect to become privy to their objective; yet he could not help but notice that the large map on the wall of the Bonin Islands held their attention. He wondered if the outcome of the battle for Iwo Jima would affect his assignment. The world's press was busily reporting that US forces landing on the island had run into fierce opposition from the Japanese defenders.

Leaving the large room behind, the three men walked down another hallway to Captain Cinkovich's office. From across the hall, the captain's secretary quickly joined them, carrying a large pot of hot coffee. She poured a cup for her boss, who handed it off to Jackson. Pouring the second cup, she handed it to Moore and finally one for Cinkovich, then quietly left the office, closing the door behind her.

"Gentlemen, please take a seat," Cinkovich offered. "Captain, we've studied your report. Our errors in judgment in the Palau campaign in both tactics and logistical support, which you identified so aptly, will not reoccur. You can be sure of that." Cinkovich's tone of voice was grim. He paused, taking a sip of coffee, then, without looking at Commander Moore—the man responsible for one of the most egregious supply blunders in the

Palau campaign—continued, "Never again shall we jeopardize a military campaign because our delivery system has gone awry; but that's behind us.

"You saw what was happening in there," with a wave of his hand toward the War Room, "and I'm sure you've seen the headlines in the newspapers. The Fourth and Fifth Divisions went ashore on Iwo Jima on 19 February; they have run into some tough opposition. Some of your people are up there, aren't they?" he asked, pointing to the map of the Western Pacific hanging behind his desk.

"That's my understanding, Captain. I believe some of the men were transferred to the Fourth, they're part of that."

"Good, they'll do a good job. In any case, General Smith has assured us we will secure the Island in a few days." Cinkovich sounded optimistic. "The Third Division has also been committed," he added. "That should provide the necessary punch to close out that campaign.

"Nevertheless, that doesn't get you to Guam, does it?" he added, opening a desk drawer, removing an envelope with Jackson's name on it. "Well, things have changed since you left stateside, the schedule for Operation Iceberg has been moved back a full month.

"You don't know what I'm talking about, do you, Captain?"

"No, sir, I don't," Scott replied, puzzled by Cinkovich's remarks.

"You will soon enough. We are going to fly you to Guam and then on to Iwo Jima as soon as possible. We will let you know when. You will join up with Admiral Spruance's Fifth Fleet. That is all I can tell you for now. But you'll be with the First and the Sixth Marine Division, I'm sure you'll see many of your people there.

"You're a lucky man, Captain," he continued, now speaking softly, his voice friendly. "You lived through a terrible ordeal, but now you're going to have the opportunity to be involved in the greatest onslaught of military power ever assembled in this hemisphere. We're going to take the war home to the Japanese."

"I am glad to hear that, sir," Scott answered, nodding his head in agreement. "It's time."

"It's payback time, Scott...big time," Cinkovich replied grimly, his voice cold. "We are quite optimistic about this; our forces are going to strike the Japanese where it hurts. With the Mariana and Bonin Islands in our hands, the 29s can hit every city in Japan. With naval support, our ground forces will take the Japanese homeland island by island.

"It won't be easy; I'm sure you can testify to that. Nevertheless, our people will do it. I would love to go with you, Scott; you will see history in the making. It will not be just another island invasion though. Historians will compare this action in the Pacific to Eisenhower's Great Crusade in Europe."

Cinkovich went on to explain to Moore and Jackson what the expected ordinance needs would be for Operation Iceberg. The size of the proposed strike force against Japan's home islands would be monumental. Admiral Wycoff's directives to his logistics people called for hundreds of LSTs, tanks, amtracs, landing craft and artillery pieces. Troops would number in the hundreds of thousands. When Cinkovich finished, he paused, studying these two junior officers, then asked, "Do either of you have any questions?"

"No, sir," replied Jackson, "I understand. I'll work closely with Commander Moore on this. But you're certainly right, Captain, this will be a tough job."

"I'm sure you're up to it, Scott," Captain Cinkovich replied, handing Jackson the envelope taken from his desk. "These were your original orders, I have amended them; they'll cover you here in the islands. Commander Moore will let you know when your plane will leave. You'll probably have a week; make the best of it while you can. Good luck and good-bye." The man rose from his desk to shake Jackson's hand

"Scott, let me add my personal congratulations, you did one hell of a job for us. But," he paused, adding quietly, his face grim, "this campaign will be one of our most difficult. You be careful out there; we want you back in one piece," the admonition appeared to be offered in complete sincerity by this ailing Navy captain. Scott could not help but note that the captain's farewell message was nearly identical to that offered, just days ago in San Diego, by Admiral Wycoff.

Jackson was to learn later from Tyler Moore that the captain knew of what he spoke. Wounded in action, the man lost a cruiser with over 300 men in the Battle of the Coral Sea. Obviously, he was not well. Still, he stayed on in Hawaii, doing what he could to make it easier for men like Jackson and others, who would soon carry the war home to the Japanese.

Commander Moore walked his visitor through CinCPac security, then on to the main gate, where Scott would catch the Navy shuttle for the return trip to Honolulu. When the two shook hands, the Navy officer handed him an envelope.

"Take this, Scott, it's the key to my folks' winter cabin on Maui, the address is inside; it's a nice place with a good beach. Nearby there is an old fishing village that dates back to the eighteenth century. You'll like it."

"I can't do that, Tyler," he protested. "I have an obligation here."

"Look, I can get you out of here on the seven o'clock morning mail plane. Maybe I'm not able to carry water for the Marines, but I really do a helluva job with the mail," he grinned.

"Yes, I know, Tyler, but she's an old friend; I promised her we'd spend some time together."

"Take her with you; don't turn me down on this, please. This is the only way I know how to make amends. I'll get a message to you when your orders are cut."

"Well, I'll talk to her. We'll see..."

"By the way, I hope you're an early riser. Molokini Crater is a little island just two thousand yards off our beach front; the Navy uses it as a practice bombing range, they start early." Both men laughed at this last remark, with Scott recalling an incident that occurred aboard ship on his way to Guadalcanal. He was asleep on the deck of the troopship, when unannounced an antiaircraft gun crew fired a salvo at a towed target. Bounced into the air off the steel deck, he was not hurt, but the noise of the blast affected Scott's hearing for several days. Before boarding the bus for his return to the city Captain Jackson stopped off at the base chaplain's office.

Sophia had returned from the beach just moments before Scott rang the doorbell. When she opened the front door, he handed her a bouquet of flowers.

"What's this, Scott?" she smiled. "You've never brought me flowers before."

"Tomorrow is our anniversary, Sophia; we met almost three years ago, to the day."

She giggled, "What kind of an anniversary is almost three years?"

"It's a very important anniversary for us. I want you to marry me today."

"Scott, cut it out. Don't tease," she pleaded.

"I'm not teasing, Sophia," he replied, solemnly, grabbing both her arms before she had a chance to set the bouquet down. "I'm serious. I want you to marry me right now."

"Oh, Scott, you know I'll marry you," she responded, dropping the flowers and kissing him passionately. "But we couldn't get married today even if we tried. You talk about the Corps rules, traditions, and all those things. I would have to get permission from my superiors; I bet you will too. You know how the Navy feels about wartime marriages."

"Sophia, those rules were put in place so parents would be assured the Navy was looking out after their sons and daughters. We are not children. After all, we're much older than most of these kids out here; we're supposed to be adults."

"Just the same, it's a Navy reg. You know it and we can't ignore it."

"The heck we can't," he retorted, tersely.

"Well, I can't, and I won't. And incidentally" she added, with a grin, "Captain Jackson, I'm not that old. Don't make me any older than I look." Jackson smiled at her response.

"Do we obey only the regulations we want to and dance around the others? I don't think we can do that," she said. "You personify the professional Marine, are you going to throw all that away?" She was serious.

"Yes, if you'll marry me," he replied, clearly impatient with the way this conversation was going. "Sophia, I've got a week, ten days at most, and then I'm off to God knows where. I talked to Father Morris today at CinCPac; he said he could marry us this week."

"Oh, Scott yes, I want to marry you." She picked up the flowers and tossed them onto a nearby table, then threw herself into his embrace.

"If Father Morris thinks it can be done, let's do it; but I've got so many things that I have to do first." Sophia quickly rattled off a list of tasks she needed to accomplish before their "big day."

"I want a church wedding. I want a white wedding dress, with a long veil, and I want two of my friends as bridesmaids. My best friend will be maid of honor. And, Mr. Jackson, I want you in one of those fancy red and blue Marine uniforms, with all your buddies present, with their long swords."

Not prepared for this, Jackson shook his head in disbelief. "Whoa, hold on just a damn minute, Sophia. Come down to earth," he responded, shocked by the litany of tasks Kosterman outlined. "You're talking stateside talk, honey. We are in the middle of a damn war zone. This is the real world for us. I've got a key to a cabin on the beach at Maui, we can be there tomorrow; we'll have five, maybe six days before I have to leave."

"Oh, Scott, don't you think I know it's the real world, I hoped we could escape from it for just one day. I see those kids going home blind, or without legs or arms and so many not going home at all."

"I know, honey, but you've got to hang on. This war has engulfed the whole world, but this is our chance to salvage some time just for ourselves."

"Damn this war!" she cursed, tears beginning to form, her dark blue eyes glistening.

"Come on, Sophia, don't do that; forget about this madness for a while," he said, wiping away her tears.

"I can't. Don't blame me if I sound like I am living in a dreamworld. I wish to God I was. I keep thinking that you may be one of those kids, if you stay in that damn uniform."

"For Christ's sake, Sophia, cut it out," he pleaded, shaking his head. "We can't change the way things are. We live with what we have, and right now, all we have is a few days. Let's not waste it."

"Oh, Scott, why does it have to be that way?" she cried. "You're right of course," she agreed, reluctantly. "I'll put my dreams aside for another day. Let's go see Father John."

"I want to stop downtown first," he replied, "I found some wedding rings you might like. We'll take a look, okay?"

"Okay," Sophia smiled, and then walking across the room, she removed a small box from a desk drawer, handing it to Jackson.

"Remember this?"

"I should," he responded, grinning as he opened the box; taking out the ring he gave to her in San Diego, he slipped it onto her finger.

Two hours later, Sophia, in her freshly ironed whites and he in a clean set of suntans, were picking out matching wedding bands at a small jewelry store near Waikiki Beach. Upon entering the store, they noticed the sign in the window, it proclaimed that the owner was an American citizen; he was a man in his sixties, obviously of Hawaiian and Japanese ancestry.

Late that afternoon, the two of them were sitting in Captain John Morris's Chapel office at Naval Base Oahu. The couple was happy with their decision to proceed immediately with their wedding plans.

The priest appeared pleased that Jackson and Sophia selected to be married in the Church. When Scott introduced Sophia to the man, he smiled, taking her hand and leading the two of them into his office.

"You probably don't know this, Lieutenant Kosterman, but I first met your fiancé aboard ship; we were on the USS *Zachary*

Taylor en route to Guadalcanal. That seems like such a long time ago."

"It was eons ago, Father John," Sophia replied, smiling. Then glancing at her fiancé, she continued, "I was there; however, Scott didn't know I was there and I did not know he was there. The Navy was of the opinion that the Island of Pavuvu was too dangerous for us nurses; they wouldn't let us go ashore."

"You know, Sophia, Pavuvu was not a very nice place to visit," Jackson responded, defending the Navy's decision.

"I grant you that, Scott," she shot back, "but it wasn't the Japanese; the Navy brass believed us women might corrupt some of their young men."

Smiling, Scott replied, "I don't think I'll respond to that."

Changing the subject, the chaplain interceded, "You don't know this, Sophia, your fiancé doesn't either; on Peleliu, I administered the Last Rites of the Church to your future husband. Few of us believed at the time that he'd make it home; but I'm very pleased that he did."

"As you can see, Father John," she smiled, grabbing hold of Jackson's arm, "I am also very pleased that he did."

"Unfortunately, I can't marry the two of you today."

"Why not?" asked Scott, somewhat surprised. "When I talked to you earlier, you said you would be glad to officiate. What is wrong with today, or tomorrow, if you can work us into your schedule? It shouldn't take long."

"When we talked about this, Scott, I did not suspect this was an urgent matter. You said you had a few days, I never thought it would be this soon."

Sophia reached out and put her hand on her fiancé's shoulder, casting a worrisome glance, first at her future husband, then back toward the priest.

"Don't be shocked, Sophia," the chaplain continued, immediately sensing her trepidation. "You two can avoid the Navy's regulation requiring your CO's permission, unfortunately I can't."

"Yes, sir, I know that. I mentioned that to Scott."

"You can also go to one of the chapels on Waikiki and be married in an hour. A lot of our people become impatient and go there, but I don't want you to do that; let me take care of the details."

"Okay, Scott?" she pleaded, looking at her fiancé.

"Okay. If that's the way it has to be," Jackson agreed, reluctantly.

"I know your boss, Sophia. It will just be a matter of a phone call. And, Scott, I'll talk to Captain Cinkovich tomorrow—let me look at my calendar."

With daylight beginning to fade, the priest walked over to the door and switched on an overhead light. The single bulb cast an eerie glow throughout the sparse interior of the chaplain's office. It was not until then that Scott realized the man's office was also his living quarters. In one corner was a single steel bed with its accompanying footlocker; nearby stood a small washstand. The man's dress uniform, along with two khaki shirts and a pair of dungarees, were hanging in an open wall closet. The Spartan life of a clergyman was not something that this Marine captain ever wanted to emulate. Austere living quarters on a United States military base was normal for officers and enlisted men alike. Yet for some reason he did not expect it to be so apparent in the base chaplain's office.

Returning to his desk, the priest said, "Well, let's see, today is Monday, why not schedule the wedding for Saturday morning. Okay?" he did not wait for their reply. "Right after the nine o'clock Mass would be a good time. What do you think about that?"

Neither of his guests answered, but looked at each other, with Sophia smiling and nodding; Scott finally nodded in agreement, mouthing the word "Okay."

"We'll have flower girls from some of the parishioners' families and, Sophia, you'll be able to have your friends included. I assume all of the bridesmaids of course will be in their uniforms. I am afraid you will not find a wedding dress on this island on such short notice, but it will be a grand wedding. You will never regret doing it this way, I promise. Now, you two get out of here and enjoy this lovely evening. I'll see you Saturday morning at ten sharp."

The decision to delay their wedding was contrary to Scott's wishes, but as Sophia was delighted, he accepted the priest's suggestion. She would have her church wedding, with nearly all the trappings of a formal ceremony.

On Tuesday morning, the engaged couple caught the seven o'clock mail plane out of Hickam Field for Maui. Friday afternoon, they would catch the plane's return flight to Honolulu.

The weather was clear and warm, as the aircraft lifted off, it circled out over the shoreline, where they could see from Battle Ship Row all the way to Diamond Head. As they passed over Ford Island, the blackened superstructure of the Arizona with its hundreds of entombed Navy and Marine Corps personnel was a grizzly reminder of the horrors of this war. It was a sobering sight for Jackson and his fiancée, on this, one of the happiest days of their lives.

Chapter 17

To call Tyler Moore's home on Maui a cabin was quite a misrepresentation of reality. It was a marvelously decorated single-story building of brick and black lava stone, with all the amenities for guests or family. It sat back from the beach about 100 yards, with a small swimming pool in the front yard. A smaller house, located on the back of the property, served as caretaker's quarters. A well-manicured lawn surrounded the buildings; there were dozens of tropical plants near the house, many in bloom this warm February day.

The Japanese-American caretaker, living on the property with his wife, met Sophia and Scott when they arrived. The couple had served Senator Moore and his family for more than twenty years.

Yoshio and Alice Yamaguchi were born on Maui, the children of Japanese immigrants. Their parents migrated to the islands at the turn of the century to work in the sugar and banana plantations. Among the nearly 200,000 Japanese Americans living in the Hawaiian Islands today, Yosh and Alice Yamaguchi were not unlike many of their neighbors. They worked hard, raised one son, and attended the nearby Buddhist Temple. When the Japanese attacked Pearl Harbor, the boy was nineteen years old, a second-year student at the University of Hawaii. Shortly after the attack, he enlisted in the US Army.

In the nearby fishing village of Kihei, there was a small grocery store. However, as Lieutenant Commander Moore informed Scott, the Yamaguchis made sure that Jackson and his fiancée would have no need to travel there for provisions. The liquor cabinet was full; the kitchen cabinets and refrigerator were well stocked with food. Senator Moore and his wife had not been to the islands since the war began, but their son was a frequent visitor to his parents' winter home on Maui.

Tyler Moore Junior may have been an incompetent military supply tactician, but he surely knew how to take care of his guests—money had its advantages. Jackson and Sophia spent that first afternoon on the island lying in the sun on the warm beach. The temperature stayed in the mid eighties; to cool their bodies, periodically they waded into the surf, swimming for a few minutes, then returning to their blankets on shore.

Lying there that first afternoon, the couple could see in the distance an aircraft carrier, with its destroyer escorts heading toward Maui. It soon became apparent that flight operations were underway, for the carrier, now less than ten miles distant, was maneuvering slowly, keeping its bow into the wind. From this distance, aircraft lifting off the ship's deck looked no larger than a flock of birds.

Within a few minutes, the planes began closing on their target on Molokini Atoll. Scott quickly identified the latest version of the Navy's fighter bomber hardware. He was fascinated watching the planes as the pilots turned to make their pass over the bombing range. It was a dramatic sight. The exercise reminded him of the naval and Marine aviators' attacks on entrenched Japanese positions on Peleliu. As on that island in the Palaus, each time an aircraft pulled out of a steep dive from their mock run on the atoll, they left behind the unmistakable double contrail, seen so often during the Palau campaign. These wisps of moisture glistened in the bright sunlight and then disappeared as quickly as they formed. However, on Peleliu, when a pilot pulled up to avoid the ridges occupied by enemy soldiers, the double contrails curved skyward only feet above Charlie Company's positions. More than

200 of Scott's men now lay buried below that promontory which by now was labeled *Bloody Nose Ridge*.

Turning his attention back to Sophia, he grinned. "According to Tyler, he said if we hear explosions in the morning, don't be surprised. Apparently, the Navy gives the Islanders twenty-four hours' warning before they use live explosives. It cuts down on the false air raid alarms."

"That's all right, just as long as they don't wake us before ten o'clock," she smiled.

"You got to be kidding, honey. The Navy's never let anyone sleep in until ten o'clock."

"You mean ten hundred hours. Where could you have gotten this ten o'clock business?" she mimicked him playfully. "You're supposed to be so GI. You may look like a military man, but you are just another civilian at heart. Just like me."

"We'll all be civilians soon, Sophia, this war's damn near over," he replied confidently.

"That's not what I hear. I think we will invade China and Japan next. It'll just go on and on forever."

"Maybe Japan," he shrugged, "but not China. I don't think anyone wants to get into a shooting war on the Asian mainland, although our guys are in Burma now."

"Well, how'll they get the Japanese out of China? They must have a whole Army there?"

"Honey, when we start bombing Tokyo, like we've done in Berlin, that will be the end of this war."

"That hasn't happened yet," she replied. She was not as confident as he that the war in the Pacific would end so soon. "A few more bombing raids aren't going to make them quit."

"No. You may be right, Sophia. However, the Japanese home islands are within range of our airfields on Guam, and Iwo is one step closer. When I was in Seattle last year, there were dozens of B29s all over the place; the Japanese will pay a heavy price if they continue the war much longer."

Changing the subject, Sophia asked, "Scott, what do you know about Operation Iceberg?"

"Where the devil did you hear that?" he asked. He was surprised that she knew the code name for the upcoming assault upon the Japanese home islands. In his meeting with Captain Cinkovich earlier in the week, the captain mentioned that code word.

"We were briefed last week in Pearl. They are loading our ship now. We have a completely new group of stateside RNs arriving next week. Something big is in the works, but you've heard that term, haven't you?"

"Yeah, Sophia, I've heard it, I'm involved. Next week I am supposed to go to Iwo. One of my jobs will be to help gather the ordinance necessary to carry out the operation."

"Oh, Scott, this damnable war," she again protested bitterly. "Let's not talk about it anymore, okay?"

Sophia's last remark, accompanied by a pained look about her, startled him. She appeared apprehensive, or even frightened about the prospects of another invasion.

He tried to reassure her. "Look, honey, it's almost over," he responded. Taking her face in the palms of his hands, he kissed her. "We should be home within just a few weeks; hang on, okay?"

"Okay."

Although quietly acquiescing to his plea, even offering a faint smile, it was clear Sophia was frightened. He wondered if she was worried about him, or could it be something else? Surely, she would not be this worried about their upcoming wedding; he thought it must be the war. He made a mental note, if the problem continued after they got home he would talk to Father Roberts. Joe Roberts was good at unraveling the mysteries of the female mind.

That evening, they walked into the nearby village of Kihei, visiting the few small shops that were still open, but most of the stores had closed for the day. The periodic blackouts did not help the evening business. Although the huge training camp used by the Fourth Marine Division was located in the hills, just above the village, most of the troops had since moved on to the Mariana Islands.

When the two of them returned to Tyler Moore's home, Scott fixed drinks carrying the glasses out onto the lanai. There, they watched as the sun disappeared beyond the western horizon. When it went down below the curvature of the dark and forbidding ocean, Sophia shuddered and quickly moved closer to her lover.

They were in bed early that evening; the night was warm and they slept with only a single sheet covering their naked bodies. Both slept throughout the night, until suddenly wakened by the roar of an aircraft overhead, followed by a loud explosion. Rushing out onto the lanai, they saw a group of Navy aircraft circling high over the Molokini Crater.

Jackson identified one of the planes to Sophia; it was the latest version of the Grumman Hellcat. It was making a "run" on the island. This was one of the Navy's newest fighter bomber aircraft, just off the assembly line. After the plane dropped its bombs, smoke spiraled skyward over the western side of the island. In the light breeze that swept the channel between the two islands, the billowing black cloud of smoke slowly moved toward them.

When the second bomber began its run, Sophia returned to the bedroom. After watching two more planes drop their bombs on target, Scott reentered the house. To his surprise, he found Sophia curled up on the bed with a pillow covering her head. Pulling it aside, he was taken aback by her appearance, she was crying.

"Sophia, what's wrong?" he asked, sitting on the bed beside her.

"I hate those machines," she cried out. "I'm sorry but I have nothing but loathing for anyone who flies them, Japanese or American."

Startled by her vehement response, he protested, not fully comprehending the anxiety, or fear, now showing in the face of this young nurse.

"Why, Sophia?" he asked, trying to comfort her, then explaining, "They're part of what we are. We are in the military to win this war. If we don't bomb the Japanese, it may cost us thousands of lives and we could still lose this war."

"I know that," she said, wiping away her tears on the bed sheet. "You men see them as a tool to win the war, but I see the other side of it. I help patch up the kids on the receiving end of those dreadful machines. I hate what they stand for."

"Honey," he responded softly, "we agreed last night not to talk about the war while we were here. Let's drop the subject." Then, taking her hand he said, "Come on, jump in the shower, I'll get breakfast."

Sophia, wiping her tears with the back of her hand, further smudging the streaks of mascara that edged across her cheeks, retired to the bathroom. At ten hundred hours, the Navy bombing exercise ended; within the hour, the two returned to the beach.

Lying on a blanket with his arms around her, he could not believe just how beautiful this young girl was. She lay across his body with both elbows resting on his bare chest. Deliberately moving her head slowly back and forth, her long dark brown hair, glistening in the sunlight, drifted seductively across her lover's face. Except for the top of her snow-white breasts, which peeked above the skintight one-piece bathing suit, her body from head to toe, was the color of burnished bronze. She suddenly kissed him, first on the nose, then passionately full on the mouth, their bodies now tenderly locked together as one, in an erogenous embrace.

"If you do that again, Sophia," he said, smiling, "we'll have to go back to the house."

She laughed, and rolled onto the blanket. "Come on," she yelled, as she ran into the surf, "jump in and cool yourself off."

For the next hour, the two of them swam and played in the surf, returning to their blanket on the beach only when both were nearly exhausted. Here they talked about what they would do after the war, where they would live, and how many children they would have. He said five. She laughed at that and consented to two at most, a boy and a girl. She was unyielding—no more than two, she insisted.

He would return to the police department of course, and she would take an RN's job somewhere in the city, close to their new home. She was curious about his house. He described it to her and told her he got the money to buy it from working two jobs and by doing favors for politicians and businessmen.

Her response surprised him.

"We, of course, won't live there, we can't live in a home purchased with tainted money. Besides, with two incomes we'll be able to buy *our own* home," she said, emphasizing "our own."

"Sophia," he protested, troubled by her comment, "why are you calling it tainted money? I didn't steal it."

"Of course you didn't, and I didn't mean to imply that you did, but people that give public employees money want something in return. You even said that yourself."

"Well, that's human nature. It's standard practice; cops accept gifts, and even food from the people they protect. I never strong-armed anyone. The man that walked the beat before me accepted money as part of his expected income; the man that followed me continues to collect it today."

"Why couldn't they live on their salary?" she asked.

Surprised by her apparent naïveté, he patiently tried to explain. "During the Depression, Sophia, policemen went for weeks without a paycheck. What we got from some kindhearted citizen was the only thing we had to live on. You could not change that system, honey, even if you wanted to. It will continue. It may not be right, but that's the way it is."

"You're rationalizing," she protested.

"No, not at all; it's an accepted fact of life in every big city in the country."

"It doesn't have to be that way, Scott. In the early years of this century and even before that, nurses experienced the same problems."

"That's different."

"No, it's not different," she replied, with some annoyance. "Many women left the nursing profession because of low wages; that forced people to rethink what our profession was all about and what we brought to the health industry. When that happened, our income went up and the nursing service became more professional."

"Come on, that ain't gonna happen in law enforcement, at least not in our lifetime."

"Why not? Certainly if a bunch of women could do it, policemen should be able to accomplish the same thing."

"You make it sound so easy, Sophia. It is not that simple. In most of the large metropolitan areas of our country it is part of the political structure, it's not going to change."

"It could." She was dead serious, now pointing her finger at him. "You said your friends on the police department were all straight arrows, as you put it. That kind can change the whole world. Given the chance, they'll do it—you just watch 'em."

"Okay, honey. If you say so, I'm convinced," he mocked, jokingly.

"No, you are not even listening to me. You've turned me off. Men are so predictable. You don't think a woman should express an opinion about worldly things like labor issues, or politics, or even military strategy. Do you?"

Annoyed by his patronizing reply, her sharply worded retort was not lost on her friend.

"Okay, Sophia," he said, holding up his hands in surrender, resigned to the fact that he could not win this argument. "How the heck did we get on this subject anyway?" he asked. "You know we're talking about something that's not too damn important to us right now. Let's talk about you and me."

"Fair enough," she answered with a smile. "Anyway, you lost this argument, so let's put it aside, and talk about our wedding. Who is going to be your best man? I'll bet you didn't even think about that, did you?"

He laughed at her contention that she won this, their first-ever argument, but figured he had better leave it alone.

"Sophia, what do I need a best man for? I'm the best man."

"No, we are going to do this right. When we go in, I'll call Betty Hanson; she'll be my maid of honor. The rest of the girls from the ship will be there too, but you'll have to have someone."

"Well…let me think about it. Maybe Tyler would be best man, we'll see."

The following morning, Jackson left Sophia sleeping; by 6:00 a.m., he was exercising on the beach. He jogged for more than five miles, then swam for nearly an hour. When he heard the first of the Navy hellcats again making their bombing run on Molokini Atoll, he headed for Tyler Moore's house.

Entering the master bedroom, he again found Sophia curled up under a sheet with a pillow over her head. Pulling the pillow aside, he could see she was crying. He sat on the edge of the bed, holding her close, her tears absorbed by his sweatshirt.

"Sophia, what's wrong?"

"Oh, Scott I don't like this place," she sobbed. "Those god-awful machines scare me to death, let's get out of here."

"We've only got two more days, honey," he replied calmly, trying to comfort her. "But if it will make you feel better we'll go to the other side of the island; we'll find a quiet place."

"No! We won't do that!" she suddenly exclaimed, pushing herself out of his embrace and wiping away the tears with her hands. "Tomorrow we'll just get up early and go to the other side of the island for breakfast; by the time we get back it will be all over."

Jackson did not reply; he was surprised, however, for a moment ago, she was clearly distressed, and now, suddenly, she seemed to be in complete control of her emotions.

"You must think I'm such a crybaby. Here we have this beautiful home to stay in, and I want to leave it. It's just those bombs, they scare me to death."

Her tear-stained face, with streaks of mascara crisscrossing her cheeks, again troubled him. He knew she had seen more than her share of pain and suffering as a Navy nurse, maybe too much. In any case, before the bombing began tomorrow, he would make sure they were on the far side of the island. He thought there should be plenty of hotel accommodations, now that the men of the Fourth Division had left the island. There, they would not have to listen to the explosions that had upset her so badly these past two days.

That afternoon, Sophia appeared to have completely forgotten the bombing exercise, and her response to it. She was again in a bathing suit; it was black, skintight, clearly exposing her incredibly beautiful figure. She ran across the beach and dived into the surf, then swimming with powerful, seemingly effortless strokes she caught a wave and rode it in toward the shoreline. She had no trouble in the surf staying abreast of her partner, although, as Jackson admitted, he was one of the world's most inept swimmers. In fact, he told her, he just barely passed the swimming test at Quantico. Sophia thought that was funny, a Marine officer and former fisherman who could not swim.

"How in the world did you ever get into Officer Candidate School?"

"Well, it certainly wasn't because of my swimming competence, but..." he grinned, "I was a damn good cop." They both laughed at that. Running back up the beach to their blankets, they lay for over an hour, their bodies entangled together, drying in the warm sun.

"Captain, Lieutenant Kosterman," they heard over the sound of the surf, someone calling their name, and then again, "Captain Jackson."

Getting to their feet, they saw Yoshio Yamaguchi coming toward them from the direction of the Moore residence.

"Over here," Scott waved to the caretaker. "What is it, Yosh?"

"It's Commander Tyler, sir. He wants you to call him right away, he says it's urgent."

"Okay, Yosh, thank you for coming to get us. We'll be right up."

Watching Senator Moore's property custodian and gardener return to the house, Sophia said, "I don't like the sound of that. What do you suppose Commander Moore wants?"

"Don't worry about it, Sophia. He's probably just calling to find out if we have enough food, or if I found the booze cabinet. It can't be very serious; we still have three days leave."

Sophia showered while Jackson placed a long-distance call to Oahu—Moore had not left a number. Scott figured the man would be in his little, paper-filled office at CinCPac, but when he called, all circuits were tied up. He would try later. Quickly slipping out of his swimming trunks, he stepped into the shower with Sophia.

"I figured that if you could interrupt my shower, I could do the same," he said.

She turned around, draping both her arms around his neck, holding him tight against her nude body. "What did our friend Mr. Moore want?"

"Like I said, he just wanted to know if I found the good booze," he smiled.

"No, Scott, I can tell when you're teasing. Don't do that," she said forcefully, shaking her head.

"You're right, I didn't get through; the circuits are all busy. We'll try him again after we get out of the shower, if I have any strength left." He grinned, slipping his arms around her in a tight embrace. "Right now I have other things on my mind. Okay?"

"Okay," she said. "I know what you've got on your mind, but let's go in on the bed." He quickly turned off the shower, then, without drying off, picked Kosterman up and carried her to bed.

"This is Captain Jackson returning Lieutenant Commander Tyler Moore's call from CinCPac. Yes, I'll hold."

While he waited to have his call put through, he was standing in the doorway of the bedroom, watching Sophia, his body wrapped in a towel at the waist. She was nearly naked and standing just outside the bathroom door drying her hair. He marveled at the curves of her unclad body; *God, she is beautiful*, he thought. When she finished, she grabbed a light pink blouse in one hand and one of her white uniform blouses in the other; smiling, she held them up.

"Which one, Captain?" she asked, without smiling.

"The pink one, of course," he replied.

Sophia walked into the closet as Tyler Moore came on the line. "Is that you, Scott?"

"Yeah, Tyler, what've you got?"

"I have your orders here; you're to fly out of Hickam tonight. General McAffee wants you to join him and Colonel Pugh on Guam tomorrow. You're to oversee the recovery and embarkation of some of the heavy equipment the Marines are using on Iwo."

"Damn it to hell, Tyler, not tonight! We were going to be married Saturday."

"I know that, Scott; I am sorry." He sounded sincere. "The *Push* Captain Cinkovich was talking about is on; you're part of it. You will have to catch the mail plane out of Maui this evening. You have three hours. They will be expecting you. I talked to Father John, he feels bad about it. Lieutenant Kosterman's group has also been ordered to report, can I tell her boss that you've given her the word?"

"Yeah, I'll tell her."

"We've picked up your gear at the BOQ; I'll take it over to Flight Operations at Hickam. You will not have time to go after it; you leave at twenty-two hundred hours. I picked up your mail also; I'll leave it there with the duty officer.

"By the way, you've been promoted; you're going to be General McAffee's new liaison officer with the Sixth Division. The general will pin your oak leafs whenever you catch up with him. Be on that plane tonight. Good luck, Scott. I wish I could go with you." He was gone before Jackson could reply.

Holding on to the telephone, he stood in the doorway of the bedroom, staring at the floor, not moving. After a few moments, he glanced up and saw Sophia in the doorway of the walk-in closet, dressed in her Navy uniform. She had heard his conversation with Commander Moore.

Looking at her, grim faced, he nodded. "You knew?"

"Yes."

"When?"

"When Mr. Yamaguchi came to the beach," she answered. "Damn the Navy!" she exclaimed bitterly. Then, striking out ferociously, she attacked those she believed responsible for the predicament in which they now found themselves. "Damn the Marine Corps! Damn this war! What's more, you can damn your priest and me too, Scott Jackson! This could have been our honeymoon, except for me. I let that chaplain talk us into putting it off. I wanted that big wedding. How much time do we have?"

"Not much, Sophia. We have to be at the airport in three hours."

"What about when we get to Pearl?"

"Not much time there either, Sophia," he repeated.

"Damn you, Scott Jackson!" she cried out, trying desperately to hold back the tears. "Tell me; I want t'know."

"You have to report to your ship, right away, I leave Hickam Field at twenty-two hundred hours. Apparently my plane will have a stopover in Guam."

"Oh, Scott," she sobbed, "that ain't fair." Now in tears, Sophia turned and threw herself face down on the bed.

Jackson made no effort to comfort her. He turned and left the bedroom and went directly to the liquor cabinet. Selecting a bottle of the Senator's Scotch, he poured himself a large drink and gulped it down. With nothing more than the towel still wrapped around his waist, he poured another, then walked out onto the lanai and sat, looking out at the ocean.

He was surprised at how he felt about this latest turn of events in his life. Here he was, in his thirties, with an opportunity to marry a beautiful young girl, one who loved him, and one he loved, so completely. Yet when the chance came earlier this week, they did not get married. He knew that was a mistake.

Watching the surf pounding the rocks beyond the secluded beach, he thought of those hundreds of young men who died on Peleliu. Most were never given the chance to marry; and would never know the joy of loving a woman, or of having children of their own. Many of them never even finished high school. Some of them were company commanders like he was, or platoon lieutenants. More than half the line officers from the First, Third and Fifth Regiments died in the butchery that raged on that island for more than three months. Yet he survived. *Why?* he wondered.

Watching the seagulls soaring high above the surf, he took a drink, then lay back on the lounge. He was thinking about Sophia and his relationship with her. It would be nice, he thought, if they could just go home and start living some type of a normal life. He was tired of this damn war. For more than four years, the Empire of Japan had controlled his every move. "God, I'll be glad when this thing is over," he muttered, quietly, wondering what was to come next.

Hearing a noise behind him, he turned around. Sophia, coming out onto the lanai, now wrapped in a towel, took his hand in hers. "Come with me," she said softly, and led him back into the house.

Chapter 18

Lieutenant Seth McNeilly, the US Army Air Force duty officer at Hickam Field Flight Operations, met Scott when he checked in. The soldier handed him a sealed envelope addressed to *Major Scott Jackson, USMCR*.

"Hello, Captain," the man offered with a friendly smile.

"Good afternoon, Lieutenant," Scott responded. "What have you got for me?"

"This was delivered earlier today; a CinCPac messenger dropped it off. It looks like you've gotten yourself a promotion; congratulations, or you forgot to put your oak leaves on this morning." He was still smiling. "But it must be for you; we don't see too many Marine officers on this base. CinCPac ordered VIP treatment for you, such as it is. We're ready when you are."

In the envelope, Scott found a copy of his orders dated nine hundred hours 23 February 1945.

Major Scott Allan Jackson, USMCR #161566, shall report to Major General Howard D. McAffee, Headquarters Sixth Marine Division, Agana, Guam. Transportation via United States Army Air Forces, Hickam Field, Oahu twenty-two hundred hours this date.

By order Admiral Chester W. Nimitz, CinCPac. Signed: Captain Robert L. Cinkovich, Ex. USN.

Scott handed a copy of the order to the Air Force officer and McNeilly compared it to his passenger manifest.

"There's a flight of 29s due out at twenty-two hundred hours for Guam and we have you on our list, Major. Commander Moore dropped your gear off this afternoon. Your weapon is in the CO's desk; just a moment, I'll get it. There's also some mail."

While waiting, Scott walked over to the large second-floor window of the Flight Operations office with its all-encompassing view of the airfield. He tried to envision what must have occurred here on December 7, 1941; whatever damage the Japanese inflicted upon the facility was no longer visible and military operations today appeared unhampered.

Army Air Force personnel seemed to be everywhere and planes were taking off or landing every few minutes. There was no sign of bombed-out buildings, or other devastation caused by the Japanese raid. Civilian contractors were busily fulfilling their construction commitments to the Air Force. New buildings were going up along the perimeter of the airport and a new control tower was under construction. Paradoxically, many of the construction workers were obviously of Japanese/Hawaiian ancestry; Scott wondered how this squared with what happened in his hometown. While these workmen, with their olive skin and almond-shaped eyes, had access to this huge military facility, the Japanese kids at home, including Kenji Tanaka's sisters, were all locked up. In 1941, the fear was the Tanaka family and their relatives might give aid and comfort to the enemy. It was difficult for Scott to understand the reasoning behind such a decision, which wreaked havoc on the lives of his lifelong friends; while here in the islands the country gave these Hawaiians of mixed Japanese ancestry carte blanche entree onto one of the most critical military installations in the Pacific.

Yet, there was little time to think about that as the duty officer dropped his holster, gun belt, and automatic on the counter.

"Air Operations is waiting, Major. You're due out within the hour."

Nearly fifty USAAF officers awaited instructions in the Operation's Ready Room. Twelve others, from the four military services, listed as passengers, along with two Royal Australian Air Force pilots, were standing by.

Upon entering the crowded room, Scott handed a copy of his orders to a Flight Operations master sergeant. The man checked his name off a list attached to a clipboard, and then introduced him to his pilot, Captain Donald Mays. From San Francisco, Mays was thirty-three years old, and like Scott, he enlisted in 1941, shortly after the attack on Pearl Harbor. The two men exchanged handshakes.

"Nice to meet you, Major; we're waiting for my boss, General Mitchell Adamson. We call him 'Mick.' He'll assume command of Fifth Air Force operating out of the Mariana Islands. All our guys are former B17 Flying Fortress crew members. We just completed flight training on the B29. Honolulu is just a stopover on our way to the Western Pacific. Our final destination is North Field, Guam."

Before boarding the aircraft, Jackson took time to open and read his mail. He received three letters—one from his mother, another from his sister Beth, the third was an overdue light bill, dated July 7, 1943. Apparently, his renter had not paid a long overdue electric bill; he smiled and dropped it into a wastebasket.

The letters from his mother and sister were both short, which was unusual, for his family tried their best to keep him up to date on what was happening at home. However, today they reported the same news; his friend Captain George "Corky" Shay, with General George Patton's Third Army, was killed in action in France. Beth added that Jolene Tanaka wrote and told her that they had still not heard from Kenji; and their attorney had not contacted them since their incarceration. They were worried.

Once on board the aircraft, Scott wrapped himself in a blanket, closed his eyes, and lay back in his seat. He tried to picture Shay and Peewee Tanaka; what did they look like? All he could remember about Shay was that overweight, happy-go-lucky kid who took great pride in duping the local streetcar conductors into a free ride to school for him and his friends. It was years since he had seen or heard from the man. The last letter he received from this former high school friend came in 1940. Corky wrote after a particularly vicious attack by the local press upon members of the police force. Scott, targeted, along with others in the investigations bureau, received the brunt of the criticism. Another one of several unsolved criminal cases gave the media the opportunity to vilify once again the men and women who wore the blue uniform.

Shay's note at that time had been short. *Scott, don't let the bastards get you down,* he wrote. It was signed, *Your friend, Corky.*

He reread his sister and mother's short letters, and then wondered, with Shay's death, how many more members of the O'Dea High School, class of '28, would die before this war ended. With a grimace, and a shake of his head, he quietly muttered, "So long, Corky."

Then thinking about Kenji Tanaka, he wondered what could have happened to his Japanese friend; no one had heard a word from him or about him since the war started.

The flight from Oahu to Guam was uneventful; it was a beautiful night over the Western Pacific. With a full moon, a glimmer of light rippled across the whitecaps on the ocean below. Trailing contrails from the B29s, stretching out behind the bombers, sparkled only briefly in the moonlight before fading from view in the frigid tropospheric air.

Comfortably wrapped in the blanket, he slept throughout most of the nearly ten-hour flight. When he awoke, the sun was shining. He closed his eyes again and lay back in his seat thinking about his friends. He promised himself that when he got to Guam he would write a letter to Shay's widow. Two of his other friends from high school, Paul Addison and Mark McGinnes, were aboard ship, somewhere here in the Pacific; he assumed they probably already knew about Shay.

Thinking about those other two persons from his hometown, who were so very close to him for such a long time, he wondered if he would ever see or hear from Amy Donahue, or Kenji Tanaka again. He figured Kenji might make it home after the war, yet there was no telling where he might be now. Amy was another story.

He first met Amy when they were in high school; their relationship went far beyond friendship. They were, he believed, true lovers in every sense of the word. Yet for her, marriage to him apparently was out of the question. Why? Surely a missed dinner with her family would not justify the breakup of their engagement. Yet he had no answer, but now he believed it would be best if he could put her out of his mind forever. Try as he might, he knew he would never be able to do that.

In the three years since he first met Sophia Kosterman they were together for only a few days at any given time. Was it unfair of him, he wondered, to propose marriage so soon after breaking up with Donahue? Probably not, but he had been truthful with Kosterman. Sophia knew who his first love was and how it turned out. Yet she was willing to marry him. Unfortunately, Operation Iceberg put their wedding plans on hold, for now; for that, he blamed himself. He knew he should never have listened to John Morris.

It was past nine o'clock when the Air Force squadron arrived over Guam. Circling over the island in preparation for landing at North Field, he could see the huge airbase below. The long red dirt runways with their temporary interconnecting network of steel mats contrasted sharply with the surrounding jungle. There appeared to be over 100 B29 bombers already on the field; six or eight were lined up in preparation for takeoff, with more already moving out onto the dirt taxiways. Whirlwinds of red dust from their prop wash outlined others emerging from revetments on either side of the airstrip. Upon landing, the men from Captain May's plane had a ringside view of these huge bombers moving into position for takeoff. Scott and the others stood transfixed by this massive movement of aircraft, not turning away until the last plane was in the air and well out over the ocean.

Shortly before noon, he made his way to General McAffee's headquarters, located near the small village of Agana. The town, a former Spanish military fort and naval base, was also the capital of the Mariana Island group. Headquarters, Sixth Marine Division, operated out of a half dozen large tents set up nearby. Along the shoreline and on the hillsides above, as far as the eye could see was a vast array of military tents and thousands of dungaree-clad Marines.

Near the village, men were loading a whole series of LSTs and smaller craft lined up like a row of dominos along the beach. Others serviced a collection of M4 Sherman tanks, half-track personnel carriers, and amtracs. Scott was encouraged by the sight of several of the latest-model amphibious craft within the group, all heavily armored. These miniature warships were superior in nearly every respect to the earlier models used on Tarawa and Peleliu.

Upon arrival, he introduced himself to General McAffee's chief of staff, Lieutenant Colonel Eli Webber, handing the man a copy of his orders.

"Oh," Webber said, "you're Jackson, good…good," he repeated enthusiastically, "you're just in time. The general will be going to lunch in a few minutes; he will want you to join him. We all do, that is, he likes his staff to accompany him whenever he eats lunch with the troops. And if you don't know him, that's damn near every day."

Webber guided Jackson into the back recesses of one of the large tents, where McAffee was in conference with members of his immediate staff. Upon seeing his new arrival, the general greeted him with a smile and handshake.

"It's good to see you again, Scott. You look much better than when we saw each other last. By the way, I have something for you, Eli, where'd we put those oak leaves?"

"Right here, General," the colonel responded, handing General McAffee a set of miniature bronze oak leaves.

"Gentlemen," he announced proudly, "gather around while I pin these on our newest Marine Corps major; this is Major Scott Jackson. Major, this is my staff; you'll get a chance to work with these folks over the next few days as we get this operation underway. First, however, let's get to your promotion. Well done, Major Jackson," he said, shaking Scott's hand. "You earned these the hard way." With that, he pinned the brass oak leaves on the collar of Scott's dungaree jacket.

"Thank you, sir," Scott replied quietly.

"All right, gentlemen," McAffee said, "let's join the Marine Corps' newest Division for lunch. Major Jackson, please come with us."

The general led the way out of the headquarters tent into the hot sun; it was a half mile to the enlisted men's mess. They walked along a dirt road toward a group of tents that housed the mess kitchen for members of Sixth Division's Twenty-Second Marines. Walking briskly along the roadway, small puffs of red dust kicked up around them; within minutes, Jackson's boots took on the reddish hue of those of his colleagues.

Nearby troops with their BAR and M1 rifles began to stack weapons in preparation for the noontime meal. Each group, hailing the general as he passed by, always asked the same question: "Where're we going, General?"

His answer never varied: with a smile and a wave of his hand, he replied, "Tokyo, boys, that's our next stop."

When the group arrived at the mess tent, they found more than a 1,000 enlisted men standing in six different food queues. General McAffee and his staff split up into groups of two or three and joined the long lines.

In his dungarees, except for the gray hair, the man blended right in with the enlisted men. His relationship with this crowd of young men fascinated the Corps' newest major. He not only appeared to care for the well-being of his troops, he made sure that he and his staff did their best to keep up morale. To that end, when in the field with the troops, every member of his command knew what their boss expected of them. An officer endured the same hardship, ate the same rations, slept in a tent or on the ground, or in whatever was available for his men. Under those circumstances, rank had no privileges in General McAffee's command.

Scott joined Colonel Mike Gibson, the Division's intelligence officer, and Major Pete Bradley, for a lunch of hamburger, boiled potatoes, canned peaches, and coffee. He thought it was a good meal, certainly better than canned rations, the typical meal for troops in a combat zone. The three men sat with a group of NCOs, all of whom tried, without success, to get Colonel Gibson to enlighten them as to the Division's next stop.

"I don't know where we're going, gentlemen," he replied straightforwardly. "Even if I did, I couldn't tell you. You'll just have to wait until you go aboard ship."

"Don't be too anxious, guys," Pete Bradley responded, interjecting himself into the conversation. "You know it won't be as nice as it is here." He laughed.

Although his intent may have been to relieve the obvious anxiety these men exhibited here today; in watching their expressions Scott was concerned that Bradley's words might have had just the opposite effect. Two of the men nodded in agreement and smiled; while another, a tall, gangly master sergeant, with a touch of gray in his hair, grimaced and looked away, trying to conceal his displeasure with the officer's glib response.

When they finished eating, the staff returned to the general's temporary headquarters, where Colonel Robert Pugh met them. Jackson had not forgotten his former battalion commander from Peleliu, then a lieutenant colonel. Pugh appeared genuinely glad to see him. Reaching out to shake Jackson's hand, he was smiling.

"Hello, Scott," he said, "congratulations on your promotion, I hope you are well."

"Yes, sir, Colonel, I am. Thank you. It's good to see you again. I never did get the chance to thank you for your recommendation on my behalf to General McAffee and to the Commandant's Office. You were overly generous."

"No, Scott," he responded solemnly, "you earned the right to be recognized by the Congress. Besides, those people needed to know firsthand what happened to our men on that godforsaken island."

On Peleliu, Scott was wary of this man's sincerity. Later, however, he learned that the commendation extolling the last-ditch efforts of the men from Charlie Company on Bloody Nose Ridge was initiated by his colonel. General McAffee concurred in Pugh's recommendations to the Commandant's Office.

"Bob, please come join us," McAffee said to Colonel Pugh. The group retired to a corner of the large tent.

"Major Jackson," McAffee began, "you're new to our command, so I'll just briefly touch on what we've got here."

McAffee explained that the First, Second and Sixth Divisions would join forces and be designated Third Amphibious Corps. They would become part of the Tenth Army, under the command of Marine Lieutenant General Roy Geiger. This would be the first time in the long tradition of the Corps that a Marine general was to command an American Army in the field.

Tenth Army would carry out Operation Iceberg against the Japanese home islands. For security reasons, the exact location was to remain top secret until the troops were aboard ship. General McAffee was in charge of Sixth Division, General Anderson the First Division, and General Lloyd Sampson the Second. Jackson, assigned as liaison officer, would report directly to McAffee. His duties were to coordinate the ordinance needs of all three divisions within Third Corps.

"This must be a comprehensive and coordinated effort," the general said. "Our liaison personnel must assure the soldier and Marine in the field that they will receive proper support.

"Most of you know that did not happen on Guadalcanal, nor on Tarawa, and more recently on Peleliu. Please understand me, gentlemen," he said, his voice firm, his meaning unmistakably clear, "that shall not happen again."

For more than three hours, General McAffee and his staff discussed the aspects of the combined operation they were about to undertake. When it was over, Third Corps commanders briefed Jackson on the expected logistical support needed. They identified the number of people requiring ship-to-shore transport and available amphibious troop and heavy equipment carriers needed to carry out Operation Iceberg. It was obvious that for such an enormous force it would be necessary to field a minimum of 800 ships and/or amphibious craft. They would also need to double the inventory of tanks and armored personnel carriers in Sixth Division. Fortunately, most of the required vehicles were available in the Mariana Island group and Third Corps would pickup additional amphibious craft when the Bonin Islands campaign ended.

Along the shoreline, Captain Robert Cinkovich's personnel were overseeing loading operations. Scott recognized one of the men; it was Coast Guard Commodore Peter Elland. His staff of naval and Marine specialists was well aware of the naval supply blunders that had jeopardized the Palau Island campaign. Potable water, loaded aboard trucks in five-gallon cans or in 600-gallon water trailers, towed behind armored vehicles, would take care of the invading force's emergency water needs. After completing this intense scrutiny and inspection of the available military ordinance on the island, Scott reported his findings to General McAffee.

That evening, he visited the Naval Air Amphibious Base below the city of Agana, where he met Lieutenant Commander George Henderson. Henderson, a PBY pilot, was to fly Scott and his newly acquired liaison team of ordinance officers from Guam to Iwo Jima. They were to leave the next day. Lieutenants Joe Churchill and Thomas Bean, and Platoon Sergeant Andrew Schneider, all Guadalcanal veterans, were now members of the Liaison Group.

Before turning in for the night, Scott joined the PBY pilot and other members of the squadron for a beer at the officers' mess. When Henderson learned that Jackson was from Washington, he asked Scott if he knew Paul Addison, or Mark McGinnes.

"Yeah, I know 'em both," Scott replied. "I went through high school with those guys. How do you happen to know them?"

"I was in flight school with them at Corpus Christi."

"Y'know anything about where they might be now?" Scott asked. "I think Addison was flying a scout plane off one of the cruisers and heard McGinnes was on the *Franklin*."

"Addison's dead," the man replied, quietly. "He was shot down on the nineteenth; it happened just hours before our ground troops went ashore on Iwo."

Stunned by the news that another high school friend was gone, he sat quietly shaking his head. Now, he and Mark McGinnes, and presumably Kinji Tanaka were the only Gladiators still alive from O'Dea's class of '28. However, there was no telling what may have happened to Kenji; after three years of war, it was quite possible that he too was dead. Scott would miss the tall, skinny kid he played basketball with; he had not seen Addison since meeting him and McGinnes at the Naval Recruiting Office in 1941. He and Peewee attended the man's wedding in 1937 and he knew Paul's wife and two children still lived in their hometown.

"What about McGinnes?" Scott asked gloomily. "Is he still flying?"

"Yes, he's still on the *Franklin*, as far as I know. I ran across him about a month ago at the Ulithi Naval Base."

The next day, at fourteen hundred hours, a PBY naval observation plane carrying the Marine major, his two lieutenants and Platoon Sergeant Schneider circled high above Iwo Jima. As they approached, a shroud of black smoke drifted across the island into the near cloudless sky; it came from literally dozens of burning tanks, trucks, and amtracs and merged with billowing clouds of smoke from exploding ordinance casting a dirty-gray pall of smoke across the entire island.

Marine infantry and armored units were on the move all across the landscape. The ground forces were driving the Japanese defenders toward the northern reaches of the island. Operating offshore, dozens of LVTs left their short, wide wake as they transported troops and supplies to and from ships anchored nearby.

Iwo Jima's fine black volcanic sand stood in stark contrast to the red clay of Guam, or, for that matter, the brilliant white coral on the Island of Peleliu. Dirty gray volcanic dust swirled around the tracked vehicles and lay in thick waves throughout the interior of the armored units. It covered the crews in a layer of grit mixed with sweat, and with each breath, the volcanic dust, drawn into their lungs, began to take its toll.

Nor were the huge Continental or twin Cadillac V-8 engines on the amphibious vehicles spared. Within days of the initial beach assault, several tracked vehicles, their air filters clogged, ground to a halt. Some of the crews tried to run the machines without the filter, only to have the vehicle become completely inoperable. Had they been short of amphibious craft, the results could have jeopardized the safe and efficient movement of troops across the island.

Most tank crews escaped this problem. With spare parts and maintenance equipment readily at hand, their primary enemy was not the microscopic volcanic ash; Japanese artillery and explosive carrying infantry continued to be the nemesis of Marine tanks in this war.

Upon landing, Scott reported to Fifth Marine Division's makeshift headquarters on the island's southeastern shoreline. Handing a copy of his orders to Colonel Paul Thompson, Division Chief of Staff, the man filled him in on the status of the Iwo operation.

"Before you arrived, Scott," Colonel Thompson explained, "we hit the mountain with an intense artillery barrage and followed up with an infantry attack to take Mount Suribachi. Now the Japanese are on the run. Still our forces continue to meet severe resistance. Notwithstanding that, we estimate we will secure the island within a week, two at most."

Unfortunately, Thompson would be mistaken; his prediction, like General Smith's, was premature. A week later, Scott watched from the slops of Mount Suribachi as a column of diehard Japanese soldiers launched a suicidal banzai attack upon the Marines. They moved rapidly, in broad daylight, across the northern plains of the Island. Armed with machine guns, grenades and satchel charges, they left a path of destruction and death in their wake. Still, the assault proved futile for the enemy. Marines, in battalion strength, counterattacked, nearly annihilating the enemy force. Few of the Japanese soldiers survived the American onslaught.

Although not secured until 20 March, Fifth Division Command on Iwo Jima authorized the transfer to Third Corps inventory of thirty fully loaded LSTs held in reserve for the Bonin Island campaign. Operation Iceberg ordinance requirements had been met.

Before leaving Iwo Jima, Jackson observed a dimension of modern warfare first introduced by the Japanese at Guadalcanal and again during the Philippine campaign. He watched as kamikaze planes attacked American warships lying off the coast of this small atoll. The destructive violence of the kamikaze was not lost upon this Marine major and his staff. Before the battle for Iwo Jima was over, thousands of US naval personnel and Japanese warriors alike would become victims of this schizophrenic form of warfare.

Chapter 19

On 24 March, Operation Iceberg got underway. A huge armada of over 1,400 Allied ships took up positions off the coast of Okinawa. This was the largest landmass in the Ryukyus chain of islands in the South China Sea. As Captain Cinkovich had predicted, the American military was bringing the war home to the Japanese. At eight hundred hours, the greatest concentration of naval weaponry in the history of warfare began unleashing a massive bombardment on the cities and coastal defenses of the island. The heavy fusillade, accompanied by air attacks, continued without letup for seven days.

On D-day (or, as it was called for this operation, "L-day"), Tenth Army launched the invasion; more than 250,000 men were involved. It was Sunday, 1 April 1945. Before the day was over, 60,000 troops from the Army, Navy and Marine Corps would scramble ashore on this island fortress. Fortunately, unlike the Palau Islands operation, most of the fleet's smaller ships were able to deliver their heavy equipment directly onto the beach along with their human cargo.

Coming ashore in a half-track, driven by Marine Corporal Peter Ireland, Major Jackson and his liaison group came heavily armed. In addition to the turret-mounted .50-caliber machine gun, Lieutenants Churchill and Bean carried Browning Automatic Rifles, Jackson a Thompson submachine gun, and all five men carried sidearms. Sergeant Andrew Schneider would ride "shotgun" with the machine gun. The armored unit carried grenades, TNT explosives and more than 10,000 rounds of ammunition.

Jackson knew that speed and firepower were essential to his task. He would be traveling great distances between commands. Not forgetting an earlier encounter with the Japanese, they towed a water tank trailer behind the half-track. His squad needed to be self-sufficient. This was a formidable-looking group of young men.

The American forces came ashore virtually unopposed, and even as the Sixth Division moved inland, the Marines met little organized resistance. Landing near the Oruku peninsula, Jackson's group followed the armored units of the Division as it began moving north along the western slope of the island. First Division troops, accompanying XXIV Army Corps, turned south to engage Japan's Thirty-Second Army. Under the command of General Mitsuru Ushijima, the Thirty-Second occupied the southern third of the island.

At first, it appeared General Ushijima was willing to concede to the US this island bastion in the Ryukyus. However, it did not take long for Scott and his aides to be convinced otherwise. Before the day was over, they watched as a seemingly endless mass of Japanese aircraft appeared overhead. The aircraft came in low, heading directly toward US and Allied ships of the Fifth Fleet lying offshore. Admiral Marc Mitscher's Task Force Fifty-Eight, in the west, and Admiral Richmond Turner's Task Force Fifty-One, at the southern end of the island, bore the brunt of these attacks.

When their armored unit stopped on a small hilltop, Sergeant Schneider yelled out, "Holy Christ, look at those guys!" pointing to the group of low-flying Japanese aircraft. Bypassing the armored force on the ground, they began their run on an American warship on the horizon. "They'll sink the whole damn Navy."

Dirty-gray clouds of smoke and fire soon erupted from two burning aircraft as they spiraled into the sea. Yet clouds of black smoke rolled across the horizon as one or more enemy planes found their way onto the deck of an American warship.

"It looks bad, Major," responded Lieutenant Churchill. "They got one over here, too," he said, pointing to the west, where another ship was afire, "Looks like a tin can or cruiser. My God, they're everywhere! They've hit two more."

"Shut it down, Corporal," Scott said to his driver, "we'll watch for a while." Exiting their armored unit, the five men stood alongside the vehicle watching this horrific scene unfold before them. The kamikaze pilots' attack upon the naval ships had an unsettling effect upon the men. They expressed feelings of helplessness. Scott too was worried, for Sophia Kosterman was out there somewhere. The large Red Cross painted on either side of a hospital ship gave no assurance that it would escape the ravages of a kamikaze assault.

"Those guys are nuts!" Lieutenant Bean exclaimed, walking out from the others, as if to get a closer look at the carnage before them. "Major, this isn't war; these bastards are intentionally blowing themselves up. It's insanity." Returning to where the others were standing, he looked stricken. "What can we do, Major?" Jackson had no answer for him.

"Climb aboard, gentlemen," he said, trying desperately to hide his fear for the safety of his fiancée. "We have our own war ahead of us."

Although he did not consider himself a religious man, when he saw an enemy plane in the distance slam into an American ship, he prayed it was not a hospital ship.

Before the week was over, members of the First Marine Division ran into major opposition in the southern reaches of the island. In the north, however, Scott and his staff, accompanying Sixth Division, had yet to meet any organized resistance. They moved relentlessly northward in two enormous columns, one on either side of this narrow eighty-mile-long island.

Riding in the half-track, driven by Corporal Ireland, Jackson and his aides, Lieutenants Churchill and Bean, followed close behind the lead tanks. Sergeant Schneider, a veteran of both Guadalcanal and Tarawa, with the ever-present cigar in his mouth, helmet, cocked to one side, standing, gripping the mount on the .50-caliber machine gun, was, by all appearances, the master of this armored craft.

In the incessant heavy rains that engulfed the island, mud and slush thrown up by the tracks frequently obscured this fast-moving unit. At times, Schneider was the only one visible within the armored car, he with his poncho trailing in the wind and a wet cigar clamped firmly between clenched teeth. On 4 April, lead elements of the Division encountered increasing enemy opposition and began taking casualties. As daylight broke, enemy forces unleashed a barrage of small arms and mortar fire on the forward units. In spite of that, as the column rolled to a stop, the tank crews quickly silenced the enemy guns.

"It looks like our friends have finally got their act together," Scott said to his men as the lead tanks came under attack.

That night, after servicing the vehicle and their weapons, with Corporal Ireland taking the first watch, Scott and his two lieutenants and Sergeant Schneider discussed the past week's events.

"We're making good progress, Major; what do you think?" Lieutenant Churchill asked, a note of optimism in his voice. "From what we were told, I figured we'd be hit hard by now. These guys this morning just kind of melted away."

"So far, so good, Joe," Jackson replied, biting his lip, his face grim. "Earlier this year, I predicted the war would be over within a few months; now I'm not so sure. After what we saw off the coast this past week, these people are sinking our ships faster than we can build 'em. That's bad news for all of us."

"That's true, Major; but where are their ground troops? They can't win this war just using air power alone. We haven't met any resistance to speak of and we've damn near covered the whole island."

"They're here, Joe," responded Lieutenant Bean. "They just haven't come out of their holes. On Peleliu, we believed that way for a time, until they came out of the jungle, then they hit us with everything they had. These people have been fighting for more than ten years; they know all the tricks of the trade. I just hope Command remembers that."

"I hate to admit it, Tom, but I think you're right," Jackson responded quietly. "Although I have to ask myself why; why are they retreating without putting up a fight, unless they plan to draw us into a trap, or separate us from XXIV Corps? They've had the opportunity to engage us on ground, where they held the advantage. They could have a surprise for us, possibly an incursion of soldiers from Honshu, or Kyushu... I just don't know."

"I hope you're wrong, Major," replied Lieutenant Bean, shaking his head.

The next day, as they pressed on, they quickly overran several Japanese strongpoints, outdistancing their infantry support. Enemy resistance continued to be lighter than expected, allowing the armored units to keep moving forward at an unprecedented rate. The Marines moved so quickly, artillery and aviation units were not always clear as to the exact location of the Division's forward units.

Reaching the Mobotu peninsula on the western edge of the island, Second Battalion split off from the main column with Jackson's squad following close behind.

When the armored units slowed to explore the deep brush, Scott placed his hand on his driver's shoulder, "Hold it here, Pete," he said. "Let the tanks probe this area; we don't want to get too far in."

His warning came too late—quite suddenly they found themselves surrounded; the entire column came under heavy machine gun and mortar fire. Enemy troops, concealed in the tall underbrush, remained hidden as the lead elements of the battalion moved through their position. When the armored units rolled over their foxholes, soldiers scurried out, disabling three tanks with satchel charges. With the first explosions, hundreds of Japanese infantry attacked the column from all sides.

Caught out in the open, Jackson and his men found themselves surrounded. Pushing his driver out, he yelled, "Get down!" Lieutenants Churchill and Bean moved quickly, firing their weapons as they rolled out of the vehicle. Taking aim at the enemy soldiers as they closed in, the five men unleashed a weathering barrage of automatic weapons fire. Still, more than a dozen Japanese made it to within yards of the armored car. The men quickly found themselves in the middle of a firestorm. Emptying their weapons, they rapidly reloaded and continued firing into the advancing group of heavily armed troops. Fortunately, the Japanese appeared more intent on silencing Schneider's gun than going after the four men partially concealed behind the armored unit.

One soldier, scrambling up onto the half-track, made a lunge for the sergeant with his bayonet. Lieutenant Churchill, rolling out from under the vehicle, fired a quick burst, killing the man before he got to Schneider's position. Another soldier, hurling himself at the lieutenant, who was still on his back, was cut down by Jackson with a long burst of gunfire from his submachine gun.

Quite suddenly, as ground troops caught up with the armored units, there were Marines everywhere. Enemy soldiers, scattering like leaves in the wind, ran for cover with Second Battalion troops pursuing them into the heavy underbrush.

Lieutenant Churchill was unhurt and Scott called out to Sergeant Schneider. "Andy, are you okay?"

"I'm okay, Major, just a scratch," he said, as blood from an arm wound ran down the side of the vehicle. "But you'd better take a look at Ireland," he added.

Walking around the armored vehicle, Jackson found Corporal Peter Ireland dead. Nearby lay the bodies of two Japanese soldiers.

"I'll take care of him, Major," Lieutenant Bean offered, finding it difficult to control his emotions. "He was a good kid; he was close to some guys in Second Battalion. I'll talk to their CO and the chaplain."

Bean covered the young man's body with his poncho, then, taking a spare M1 rifle from the armored unit, attached a bayonet. "Damn it to hell," he uttered, shaking his head, as he thrust the blade into the ground. Without comment, Jackson picked up Ireland's helmet and placed it on the butt end of the weapon.

In the rout that followed, Second Battalion pushed the remaining enemy forces to the ocean shore. With the sea to their back, several Japanese soldiers took their own lives. The Navy's small boat crews pulled others from the water as they tried desperately to swim to nearby islands. Those who continued to fire upon the advancing column died a violent death.

Within the week, Marines from the Second Battalion completely cleared the peninsula, but casualties were higher than first anticipated. Left behind, the remains of nearly 100 Marines kept the regiment's burial detail busy. With the battle over, Major Jackson once again undertook his most difficult task of this war; he wrote a short note of condolence to Corporal Ireland's parents. It would be the first of many such letters he would write before the Okinawa campaign ended.

Lieutenant Churchill took over as driver of the half-track, with Sergeant Dominic Polchlopecski replacing Sergeant Schneider on the .50-caliber machine gun. At the Regimental Aid Station, medics told Jackson that Schneider would be off the line for at least three months.

"Don't believe that, Major," Schneider responded with a grin; he was not eager to sit out the end of the war in a military hospital. "I'll be back in a week."

"Take it easy, Andy," Scott replied, as he said good-bye to his sergeant. "This war ain't gonna be over in three months, so there'll be plenty to do when you come back."

Polchlopecski, a three-stripper buck sergeant from Oxnard, California, was also a veteran of Guadalcanal. In boot camp, finding his name difficult to pronounce, and nearly impossible to spell, he had been tagged early on by his sergeant with the nickname "California." He seemed to relish the sobriquet, particularly after his drill instructor threatened him for blooding the nose of one or more fellow "boots" for calling him the "Polack." He told his DI he was not Polish. He claimed to be the only "true" American in the Marine Corps—part Spanish, Irish, Italian, and Polish. With his black hair and dark complexion, the name "California" fit him well.

Moving on after the Mobotu Peninsula engagement, Jackson's group continued to stay close to the lead elements. Here they could quickly assess the Division's ordinance needs, ordering heavy transport in to retrieve, or to replace damaged armored units as needed.

Within three weeks of the Mobotu peninsula engagement, the entire north end of the island was swept clear of enemy troops. Marines literally pushed the northern contingents of the Japanese Army into the ocean. Many enemy soldiers died in futile attempts to swim to a number of small atolls lying offshore.

With fighting in the area ending, the Division regrouped, resupplied and repaired their vehicles. A contingent of reinforcements was soon to arrive; they would need training. On 20 April, approximately 800 replacements disembarked from LSTs on the west coast of the island. What Scott saw, as he watched the troops come ashore, worried him. Most of the replacements were young and inexperienced. The second lieutenants seemed to be in their mid-twenties, enlisted men younger.

Lieutenant Churchill commented wryly, "They look like a bunch of damn kids, Major. Do you suppose we were ever that young?"

"That's what they are, Joe; they were in boot camp just weeks ago and most of the officers came directly from OCS. Fortunately, the NCOs are experienced people. They have been through this before."

With the arrival of these additional troops, McAffee brought the officers together for a briefing on the present situation of Sixth Division.

Standing before the assembled group, he said, "We have little time, gentlemen, to integrate and train our new men. I expect we will soon embark for either Kyushu or Honshu Island. So let's get them assigned and equipped; they need the opportunity to work with their sergeants and unit commanders before we move on."

Working as General McAffee's liaison officer, Scott found himself in a unique position. He realized just how fortunate he was. His duties brought him into daily contact with company, battalion, and regimental commanders. This gave him the opportunity to learn the Art of Warfare from some of the nation's most able military commanders. However, the overuse of this expression by the military bothered him. Warfare, as he experienced it, was not an art in any sense of the word. It was a brutal event. It was a contest, where young American soldiers tried to kill as many young Japanese soldiers as they could, before they, too, were killed. Still, the men he now served with were truly masters of their craft; they were veterans of Guadalcanal, Tarawa, Peleliu and the Marshall, or Mariana Islands' campaigns. Jackson figured that he was very fortunate to be with this group of young professional warriors.

On 24 April, General McAffee assembled his command staff to assess the Division's readiness. He was concerned; in their drive north, a large number of amtracs and tanks were lost to accidents, many of which were only indirectly related to combat. Entering the headquarters tent, where his staff gathered, McAffee greeted the staff without fanfare.

"Good morning, gentlemen. I asked Major Jackson to compile data on our armored losses since 1 April. Tell us what you found, Major," he said, calling on Jackson to report his findings.

"General, gentlemen." Jackson knew there was no time for amenities and took only a few minutes to brief the general's staff. "Since coming ashore on Okinawa, we have lost nearly eight percent of our amtracs and a half dozen tanks; these units suffered severe damage. The corrosive effects of salt water caused some problems; however, mortar, artillery, and/or mines accounted for most of the damage. We lost five tanks and seventeen amtracs through direct contact with explosive charges, either a mine or

Japanese infantry and four to artillery fire. Two of the tanks and nine amtracs were repairable and are now back on line. Ordinance has cannibalized parts from the rest of them as necessary.

"Yet, as you are aware, our armored units achieved remarkable results. Frequently, both the M4 and particularly the latest-model LVT have performed at a level above that expected by the design engineers. Few obstacles have deterred the men who operate these units.

"Nevertheless," he added, shaking his head, "with the armored units, fourteen men were injured and two killed in accidents. Most of these were operator error accidents; as a rule, the younger operators have a correspondingly higher rate of injury.

"We lost six men in truck-related incidents, with eighteen injured. Two of these struck mines, but one-third of them were due to carelessness on the part of the driver. Even so, your men have done an excellent job; but here again, further training and closer supervision by the NCOs should reduce our casualties due to operator error."

When Jackson's presentation ended, General McAffee closed the meeting with a stern admonition. "You know what you have to do, gentlemen. Let's get it done. I don't want any more letters going home to these young men's families telling parents that they lost a son in an accident on this godforsaken island. It's bad enough when that happens in combat; let's put a stop to it now."

No one misunderstood the seriousness with which the general viewed this problem.

Two planeloads of III Corps mail caught up with the Sixth Division on 28 April. Jackson received a letter from his mother, two from his sister, Beth, and one from Sophia Kosterman. Sophia's letter, dated 25 March 1945, was short—she was at sea. Most of her comments related to their personal misfortune, she apologized for spoiling their wedding plans in Hawaii.

We'll correct that when we get home, she wrote, *I can't wait.* Jackson knew home meant Hawaii.

Walking back to his tent, he said a silent prayer. He was thinking of Sophia and the continuing kamikaze attacks upon the ships in the South China Sea. He was aware the Navy was taking a severe shellacking from those "crazy kamikaze bastards," as his men called them. Yet, he reasoned, they probably would not attack a hospital ship. Logically, a battleship, aircraft carrier, or heavy cruiser would be the more sought-after prize by a Japanese warrior doomed to commit hara-kiri for his emperor. Yet, he knew that in the heat of battle, logic quickly became the first victim in any violent struggle.

Entering his tent, he sat on the edge of his cot and began to write. He had written Sophia three times since leaving Hawaii. However, it was obvious from her correspondence the only letter she received from him was the one he mailed before departing Guam. That was nearly two months ago.

On 2 May, General McAffee called an emergency staff meeting of battalion and regimental commanders. Tenth Army was in trouble on the southern end of the island. After coming up against enemy defenses on the Shuri Line, General Hodge's XXIV Corps had made little progress since the invasion. In their attempt to dislodge Japanese forces from entrenched positions, the First Marine Division and Army 62nd Infantry Division personnel suffered heavy casualties. With four weeks of heavy fighting behind them, they had advanced less than ten miles.

Major Jackson's next destination would not be Kyushu, nor Honshu, as anticipated, or anywhere else on the Japanese mainland. In the south, with XXIV Corps facing fierce resistance, General Hodge ordered Sixth Division to respond immediately. By mid morning, Scott's group, again accompanying the lead tanks, with their half-track now carrying nearly a dozen infantrymen, headed south. Except for the rain and mud, this fast-moving column of armored units reminded Scott of Major Bob Evanston's training group at Camp Pendleton—that seemed like such a long time ago.

By the end of the day, more than two-thirds of Sixth Division's personnel and equipment were retracing their route of only one month earlier. Five days later, Scott's small liaison unit moved into position with the lead elements of the column as they relieved 62nd Infantry. The Marines quickly came under intensive fire from their well-entrenched foe; no more than 500 yards separated the two forces.

War correspondents described the fighting that followed as a horrifying experience for the Americans. On their first day on the line, as light began to appear in the eastern horizon, the men on the western end of the front came under a weathering barrage of interlocking machine gun and artillery fire. Their adversary's favorite targets were Marine armored units and the officer corps. An infantry attack soon followed, Japanese soldiers came at the Americans in waves, across a front less than two miles wide.

Line units called upon the ships of the Fifth Fleet, lying off the southwestern shores in the East China Sea, for support. The Navy was quick to respond. Devastating air strikes with bombs, rockets, and napalm soon followed.

When these were over, hundreds of Japanese soldiers, both dead and wounded, were visible on the narrow plain that separated the two forces. However, when the aircraft attacked, most of the enemy soldiers simply darted back into the caves below the ridges on either side of this heavily fortified hillside. As in previous encounters with the Japanese, enemy soldiers simply disappeared into the bowels of the earth.

Jackson's people were overwhelmed with ordinance requests. Accompanied by escort personnel, Scott's Liaison Group joined the Ordinance Recovery Group and at night attempted to recover damaged mechanized units. Few of these endeavors succeeded. The recovery and repair units suffered severe losses of both officers and support personnel.

It quickly became evident that neither naval bombardment, nor use of air support would dislodge the Japanese from the Shuri Line fortifications. As on Tarawa and Peleliu, it would be up to the infantry to neutralize this well-entrenched enemy.

On 11 May, General McAffee ordered a frontal assault with infantry troops from the Twenty-Second Regiment. Second Tank Battalion was to provide armored support. With the first rays of sunlight beginning to appear over the eastern horizon, Marines began moving out across the narrow plain toward the high ground held by the Japanese. This was a small hill, no higher than 60 or 70 feet, 300 yards across and a half-mile deep.

Almost immediately, the regiment came under intense machine gun and artillery fire. Japanese heavy weapons near the top of the ridge unleashed a withering barrage down upon the advancing American units. Accompanying enfilading fire from mortars and heavy machine guns located on either side of the plateau began to take a heavy toll of both armored units and Marine infantry. Although some men made it to the base of the hill, enemy troops forced them to withdraw before dark.

The regiment pressed the attack again the following morning. This time more than 100 men made it to the top of the hill, but they could not hold the position. On the fourth, and again on their fifth day on the line, Marines continued to mount attacks against the Japanese defenders. Their results were indistinguishable from the preceding days, except the casualty toll increased tenfold.

During this short period, the regiment mounted eleven different attacks upon the "goddamn hill," as the survivors so appropriately dubbed this small bit of land, now pockmarked by bombs and artillery gunfire. Each attack failed. Over 100 armored units littered the battlefield, with smoke billowing skyward from many of the burning hulks.

Enemy mines and foot soldiers carrying lethal charges, emulating the role of their airborne kamikaze colleagues, were almost as effective as Japanese artillery. Their objective was to destroy the armored units and annihilate their enemy. When properly placed, the satchel charge carried by infantry personnel was deadly. Even with a top-priority order issued directly by General McAffee, Jackson and his staff faced a severe challenge trying to find armored units sufficient to meet the regiment's needs.

Ground around the base, side, and top of the hill became a cesspool of dead and mangled bodies. Their blood turned the earth's crust into a dirty-brown hue and there was no way to escape the stench that emanated from this mélange of unburied corpses. Many of the wounded, on both sides of this devastating conflict, failed to make it back to their lines; they lay in the open, their cries soon to be stilled by death. When a corpsman or comrade sought to rescue a wounded colleague, they, too, often paid the ultimate price.

The war was over for the dead; however, if an injured Marine made it back to his own lines, he was quickly evacuated to one of the hospital ships lying offshore, but the killing continued. The battlefield took on the macabre appearance of a monstrous slaughterhouse. Before every rise, outcropping of rock, pillbox, or burnt-out tank or amtrac lay scores of dead Marines and Japanese soldiers. Soldiers from these two giant armies were now engaged in one of the most fierce hand-to-hand struggles ever witnessed in the history of modern warfare.

With the enemy's resolve to resist to the death, it became perfectly clear that there was no respite in sight for Sixth Division. It was also clear that if battle losses continued at this staggering level, Sixth Division may soon exist in name-only. At times, Division Command had no idea who was actually in charge of each platoon, company, or battalion on the line. With the violence continuing, Twenty-Second Regiment's platoon commanders suffered 100% casualties.

Company and battalion commanders fared little better; snipers killed the First and Third Battalion commanders after only two days on the line. Moving between command posts, it quickly became obvious why the officer corps suffered such a high mortality rate. The Japanese targeted anyone exhibiting the appearance of command, forcing officers to remove any sign of authority from their uniforms. For his own survival, as Scott moved between Company and Battalion Command Posts, he entered, or left the comparative safety of the CP at a dead run.

Chapter 20

On 16 May, Jackson was ordered to report to General McAffee at Division Headquarters. When Scott arrived, he was surprised by McAffee's appearance. The man seemed to be exhausted; he was gaunt and pale and it appeared that he had not shaved in more than a week. Wearing a pair of soiled dungarees, he looked more like the men Scott left behind on the line than a ranking officer assigned to a headquarters unit with his own orderly. This was most unusual for this spit-and-shine Old Corps officer.

"Hello, Scott," the general offered quietly, his mouth grim as the two men shook hands. "I need you to take over the Twenty-Second. I know I don't have to tell you but we're in trouble here. As you're well aware, we are facing a critical stage in this campaign. If the Nips continue their attacks on our naval vessels, our troops may very well lose air support. If that happens, the outcome of this campaign may be placed in jeopardy."

McAffee was clearly concerned about the naval losses and for his men, yet he made no mention of what happened to the former regimental commander, Colonel Tommy Nicholson. The Twenty-second Regiment had lost their second CO to sniper fire in as many weeks. And most everyone in a command position within the Division knew that Nicholson and McAffee were not only longtime colleagues, but close personal friends. Under the circumstances, Jackson thought, it was no wonder his boss appeared haggard and worn. The death of Nicholson and so many other young men had taken its toll on this ageing warrior.

Sniper attacks upon the officer corps continued unabated and pressure from above to destroy General Ushijima's ability to wage war never eased. To date, Sixth Division lost nearly 4,000 of its officers and men, yet Admiral Nimitz was unyielding in his resolve for a quick end to this campaign. The reason, although not clearly understood at the time by many of the troops, was that the Japanese kamikazes were wreaking havoc on the American Fifth Fleet offshore.

Scott responded, sympathetically, yet with a note of optimism in his voice, "You're tired, General; but you know our people better than I do. We'll come through this on top, no matter what happens."

Scott's encouraging words were meant to assuage his commanding officer's obvious discouragement and to lighten his burden of command. Yet, he could not help but wonder how many more good men would die before the brutality and violence of this encounter with the Japanese Army ended.

"Yes, I know, Scott. Forgive me; I am tired, I guess I lost sight of our objective for a moment. But you are right," he added, now confidently nodding his head, "we will end this on our terms, not on General Ushijima's. We will destroy his Army; there is no doubt about that."

21 May was a particularly hard day for Jackson. The night before, Second Battalion had moved 200 inexperienced replacements into the line. Just a few months earlier, they were at home attending high school.

Before the inevitable morning attack, commanders tried to team each man up with an experienced combat infantryman, but there were too few old-timers left. Consequently, as dawn broke over the Western Pacific, company commanders were guiding a band of seventeen-, eighteen-, and nineteen-year-old green recruits across what now was a no-man's-land. Few of them made it to their objective. Those who did retreated before nightfall. They left their dead behind, along with several wounded among the hundreds of dead Marines and Japanese soldiers killed there during the past month.

That night, when regimental officers gathered to assess the day's losses and plan for the next day's attack, Scott found a thoroughly disillusioned group of men. During the preceding ten days, some of these very same field commanders had lost more than half of their troops. Delta Company, Third Platoon, now operated with nine men, its top NCO a corporal with less than two years' experience.

The mounting casualties exacted a toll upon the morale of both the officers and their troops. Several of the officers now believed that Nimitz's military strategy was a disaster in the making. Captain Todd Bidwell, commander of Alpha Company, a three-year veteran of the Pacific battles, never known to be critical of his superiors, suddenly unleashed a scathing attack upon the Navy hierarchy. It was he and his men who led the assault upon the Japanese line today.

"This is bullshit, Major," he said, his voice, cold and bitter, reverberating ominously within the confines of the darkened command post. "I have lost a third of my men since we came here. I say we put this thing on hold until Command gets their act together."

"They've completely forsaken us, Scott," Captain Christopher Brown, of F Company, growled. "For what? For their precious Navy, I agree with Todd. Tell McAffee we want to sit this next one out, at least through tomorrow. I need time to get my guys squared away."

It was not only Todd Bidwell and Chris Brown, however, who felt that way. Others believed Nimitz had abandoned the ground troops in favor of his revered Navy. Some of them, caught up in this maelstrom of violence, believed nobody gave a damn, they were just Marines and they were expendable, ships of the line were not.

281

The officers were in an ugly mood, embittered, dispirited and with unrestrained rage and fury they spoke out. Three other captains, all experienced combat veterans, quite vociferously criticized their naval commanders' decisions on the conduct of this war. Neither Admiral Nimitz nor General McAffee escaped their wrath. Jackson had never before heard Marine officers question the judgment or integrity of their military commanders in such harsh tones. However, tonight was different. Nevertheless, he needed to convince them that the regiment must not only continue to put pressure on enemy lines; they had to dislodge the Japanese from these positions. Should they fail to do so, the consequences would be felt across the entire island. They would place Sixth Division personnel in jeopardy, and the results could be catastrophic for men of the First Division on the other end of the Shuri Line.

He knew the first thing he needed to do was to try to restore his staff's confidence in the Navy hierarchy. Yet, that would be only half the battle. He also had to rekindle in his commanders their faith in their own ability as Marine officers, to breathe new life into their troops. However, from what he heard this evening in this darkened command post, unless he could persuade his command staff of that responsibility, men would die tomorrow needlessly.

He began quietly by complimenting each of the company commanders personally and informally, using only their first names.

"Your people did fine today, Todd," he said to the commander of Alpha Company. "I know you lost some men and that's unfortunate, but they more than held their own against the Japanese." Captain Bidwell merely grimaced and shook his head; he was not convinced.

Turning to Captain Brown, he offered, "Chris, your leadership of F Company these last few days has been phenomenal. Just look at what your people have accomplished. Under your command, the kill ratio of your company is more than twenty to one. It may not seem that way, but your people are helping to end this bloody mess. At some point in time, the Japanese leadership is going to have to say, 'Enough!' and it will end."

Scott was doubtful that his encouraging words were accomplishing the desired effect. Still, he knew he must try to convince these good men that what they were doing was critical to the success of this invasion. Turning to the rest of the command staff, in a somber mood, he pressed on quietly.

"I know it is tough to lose these young guys; however, if we don't do our job to the best of our ability, we will lose a heck of a lot more of them. Unless we do what we came here to do, this war will not go away. All I can ask is that you do your best; that's all General McAffee asks of any of us. If we do our part, we can end this madness. If we are not successful," he added quietly, "the Japs will stall Tenth Army in its tracks and we may jeopardize the entire operation."

With the officers gathered in the darkened bunker to plan for the next morning's attack, a possible solution suddenly arose. It was an approach not yet attempted. Lieutenant Dan Nelson made the suggestion; he was quite straightforward about it.

"Let's go around that damn hill, Major!" he exclaimed, his voice cold and brutal; he was unable to conceal his frustration. "We can't lose any more men than we've already lost. Counting the walking wounded, I've only got sixty-three men left in my company."

Nelson, a farm kid from North Carolina, sounded weary and tired. He had assumed command of Bravo Company Second Battalion yesterday. His captain suffered multiple wounds that morning, leading an attack across ground taken, and lost, too many times to count.

"What would you have us do, Dan?" Jackson asked.

"I would try to outflank these bastards. We're gonna get hit hard, Major, no matter which way you take us," Nelson responded. "Maybe we just let them think we're going to attack, and then we break off and try to suck 'em in. If, after the initial attack, we pull back and maybe get them to follow… I don't know, Major, it was just a thought. We sure as hell ain't getting anywhere now."

"Let's kick this around, gentlemen," Jackson responded. "What if, as Lieutenant Nelson has suggested, we sent two companies, with tank and artillery support, out at dawn? We would start out as if to bypass the hill completely. It would be a ruse, but it may work, especially since they'll have to move from the security of their stronghold to follow us. Once there is a clear commitment from them to head us off, our reserves could hit 'em hard on their left flank. If we caught them out in the open they would be vulnerable to both artillery and attack from carrier aircraft. What d'you think, gentlemen?"

"Try it," one man replied. "Anything would be better than what we have accomplished thus far."

"I agree," responded Captain Ethan Thomas, the commanding officer of G Company. "It could backfire on us, if we're not careful, but if we watch closely what they do, and we don't tip our hand, it may just work."

"Are the rest of you in agreement?" Jackson asked. In the darkened bunker, each man quietly responded affirmatively.

Scott called Division, explaining his plan, requesting approval. General McAffee's reply, delivered within the hour by Colonel Webber, was not unexpected.

"Major, the general said, 'If you think the plan will work, do it, but you must hold back your reserves.' When you give us the go-ahead, the Twenty-fourth's Third Battalion will attack the Nips' left flank. We'll start shelling them at dawn and let aviation drop napalm in front of your people; good luck." Then, his voice tinged with weariness, he added quietly, "Major, you're to stay the hell off the Line. The general said he could not spare another regimental commander. That's not a request, Scott, that's a damn order."

Despite encountering a firestorm of enemy machine gun and rifle fire, Nelson's plan worked. By noon, his company, with armored support advanced quickly, driving the enemy from the plain between the hill and the surrounding ridge. To ward off Nelson's attack, the Japanese moved several hundred defenders from defensive positions on the left flank to support their soldiers facing Second Battalion. The Twenty-fourth's Third Battalion moved swiftly into the gap. They caught the defenders out in the open; the result was a complete rout. Unfortunately, Nelson did not live to see it happen. Japanese machine gun fire cut him down as he led his men through a gap on the enemy's right flank. But before the day was over, the bodies of nearly 500 Japanese soldiers lay scattered around the base of this mound of earth, now christened unofficially by the press as "Sugar-Loaf Hill."

The men of the Twenty-Second Regiment paid a horrible price for this small bit of turf in the Western Pacific. However, the taking of the "goddamn hill," as the troops still called it, gave some respite for Sixth Division personnel. The attack triggered an across-the-board withdrawal by the Japanese from their fortified positions.

With the Japanese in near full retreat, General McAffee brought his commanders together for a conference. Much to the consternation of the general, Colonel Mike Gibson arrived in time to deliver a long-drawn-out report on Intelligence personnel's assessment of the location and strength of the remaining Japanese forces on the island. McAffee was tired, as were his commanders; yet Gibson had a reputation for professionalism, rarely granted to staff by line officers; thus the general allowed the man to continue. In civilian life, Gibson was a lawyer by trade. Speaking in a soft, monotone voice, he presented a clear and precise, if somewhat tedious assessment of what could lie ahead for the Americans.

"Gentlemen, before the invasion, we estimated that there were close to one hundred thousand Japanese soldiers billeted on the island. That number came from preinvasion intelligence, aerial photographs, visible traffic, shipping, and radio traffic. We have learned since the invasion, from Korean laborers and several Japanese soldiers, that your men have captured, that their strength was closer to one hundred and twenty-five thousand troops, along with a large contingent of naval personnel. As you might have expected, not all of their soldiers are willing to commit hara-kiri for their emperor, and some of these guys are only too willing to talk.

"We also know that they are short of food and medical supplies. Most of their communications are down and several members of General Ushijima's command staff are dead. From our perspective, the downside of all this is that they have an abundant supply of weaponry. We believe, and your people have found out the hard way, there are heavy weapons and ammunition caches in nearly every cave. Our enemy has had more than twenty-five years to build their defenses and as you have learned, they are a formidable force. They will fight to the bloody end, and most of them will not surrender."

After pausing for a drink of water and to light a cigarette, Gibson continued. Scott thought that if this were a courtroom setting, instead of battle zone, his humorless, monotonic utterances would have been enough to put even the most wide-awake juror asleep. However, when the colonel began to reveal what his men learned from the Japanese prisoners, he captured the attention of the entire staff.

"We have approximately two hundred prisoners; nineteen are officers of various ranks. Some have been severely wounded."

"What's the highest-ranking officer you have, Colonel?" McAffee inquired.

"One colonel, sir, and a couple of captains; one of the captains can speak excellent English. He said he was educated in the States."

"Is he talking?"

"No, sir, but we think the colonel will. He appears to be quite proud that he was a member of General Ushijima's personal staff."

When Gibson finished his briefing, General McAffee ended the meeting with a note of caution, followed by a harshly worded edict. In this, he exhibited a firmness of purpose his staff had never seen before.

"We've taken a lot territory on this island and inflicted some severe penalties upon General Ushijima's forces, yet we have a long way to go. As you heard here today, we have destroyed most of his tanks; in spite of that, he can still hit us hard. His people are holed up all across the front and he has plenty of fire left in his belly. We can slug it out, cautiously seizing one defensive position after another, or hit him hard, all across the front. I choose to hit him hard.

"Our casualties have been high; however, if we are overly cautious and take a slow, methodical approach to destroying this enemy, he will kill us. Therefore, we will attack him all across the front and hit him with everything we have. We will keep on hitting him until he quits or until he is dead. You will prepare for an attack at first light. We'll hit him in the morning, in the afternoon, and when he thinks we have let up for the evening, you will hit again after dark. The only option we shall give him is to run or surrender."

During General McAffee's bluntly worded exhortations to his troop commanders, more than one officer exchanged a nervous glance with his fellow field commanders. They knew what to expect from such tactics; their men would quickly overrun the enemy's strongholds, or die trying. However, no one here believed this would be an easy victory.

When the meeting broke up, Colonel Gibson called out to Scott. "Hold up a minute, Scott," he said, apparently anxious to talk.

"Sure, Mike, what've you got?"

"I want you to look at one of the prisoners. He's a captain of engineers. Third Battalion picked him up yesterday; he was wounded. He's over in sick bay, the MPs are holding him there for now."

"Is this the guy you said was educated in the States?"

"Yes. He mentioned Washington, but nothing else. I figured you might be able to get something out of him."

Colonel Gibson's driver drove the two men to the Regimental Aid Station. Entering the compound, Gibson and two corpsmen were present when Scott confronted the wounded Japanese officer.

"They tell me you speak English, Captain. Is that correct?"

The soldier appeared to have been on the receiving end of a flamethrower or napalm attack. Blood-stained bandages covered his chest, arms and the lower part of his face. He appeared surprised by the question, his eyes flashing first to Jackson, then on to Colonel Gibson and back to Scott. When he responded, a thin smile crossed his lips.

"Yes, I do, Major," he responded in near perfect English.

"Where did you learn English, Captain?"

"The same place you did, Major," the man responded, speaking softly, enigmatically.

"Where was that?"

"In the States."

"I understand that, Captain, but tell me about it. When did you go there; where did you go to school?"

Looking at Jackson, then to Colonel Gibson and the two corpsmen standing nearby, the man turned away. He did not respond to the question.

"That's about all we got out of him, Scott," Colonel Gibson said. "We'll leave you alone with him for a while, okay?" Gibson said as he and the two corpsmen left the tent. When they were gone, Scott tried once again to elicit a further response from the badly wounded man.

"Where did you go to school, Captain?" he asked a second time.

The soldier turned back toward Scott and tried to sit up, with Jackson gently restraining him.

"Don't get up, Captain; you are badly burned."

"Yes, I know, Scotty," the man replied straightforwardly, his response startling Jackson. "I thought that was you when you first talked to me, but I wasn't sure. I didn't want to say anything in front of your colleagues."

"My God!" exclaimed Jackson. "Is that you, Peewee?"

"Yes, it's me, Scotty—it's been a long time."

"What are you doing here? What happened to you? Where are your parents?" Jackson asked, in his excitement at learning just who this soldier was, not waiting for Kenji Tanaka's reply.

"Yes, it's me, Scotty, but it's been a long time since anyone has called me by that name," he laughed quietly.

It was near dark when Jackson finally walked out of the tent; the two former high school friends had talked for more than two hours. Colonel Gibson was waiting. Scott told him the full story. When he finished, Gibson, always the intelligence professional, asked, "What did he tell you about General Ushijima's forces, anything, Scott?"

"Nothing, Mike, he wouldn't talk about that. He told me the Japanese Army drafted him when he and his parents were caught overseas when the war started. He is a trained civil engineer and claims he has built roads, bridges, and military fortifications from Burma to Malaya and as far south as Singapore. He said when our forces moved into the Mariana Islands he was brought out to Okinawa to shore up the island's defensive positions."

"Then he obviously knows the schematics of the island fortifications; he has to know where the big guns are and the entire network of underground structures."

"Undoubtedly he does, Mike, but he won't tell me. He is a resentful young man, bewildered in some respects, and torn between his loyalty to the US and to Japan. His father died before he could return to the States and his mother is a virtual prisoner in a country that she knows very little about. She never took out her citizenship papers in the US, consequently our immigration people held up her reentry."

"He's an American, right, Scott?" Gibson inquired.

"As American as you and I, Mike. I think under the circumstances we should at least let his family in the US know he is alive."

"You may feel that way, Scott," Gibson replied, shaking his head, "but you must realize that won't pass muster in the intelligence community. Our people will hold that over his head to see if they can get some worthwhile info out of him. Theoretically, they have some pretty good leverage over him; you know he could be considered a traitor."

"I suppose you're right," Scott replied, shaking his head, "but that's your decision. When the war began, Kenji had the option, military service for the Emperor, or prison for both him and his parents. That's not much of a choice. If he talks to us, he will be considered a traitor by the Japanese. If he does not, the outcome will, I am sure, be the same," Scott exclaimed quietly. "He won't be able to go home. Either way, he's a dead man."

In the days that followed, Scott's regiment continued its drive south, meeting only light resistance along the East China Sea coast. In the west, however, First Marine Division troops still faced a well-entrenched, unyielding, and implacable foe, yet even they moved relentlessly on, pushing the Japanese before them toward the southern tip of the island.

On 27 May, Scott's men seized the capital city of Naha. A week later, the regiment made an amphibious landing behind enemy lines on the Oruku Peninsula. It soon became evident that the end was near for General Mitsuru Ushijima's Thirty-Second Army on the Island of Okinawa. However, the men of the Twenty-Second Regiment were exhausted, physically and mentally. Fatigue set in and many succumbed to the erroneous conclusion that the battle for this island fortress was over. They had done their part, now it was up to someone else to end this terrible nightmare. Unfortunately, it was far from over, and there was no one else, no magic wand would be waved. Tenth Army would suffer more than 2,000 additional casualties before it ended. Over 700 of these men came from the ranks of Sixth Division.

One night, with heavy clouds obscuring the moon, Japanese infantrymen carrying high explosives slipped undetected into Second Battalion frontline positions. They killed twenty-two Marines and wounded more than thirty. A week later, in the early morning hours as Jackson slept on a cushion taken from a nearby truck and jerry-rigged into a bed, a Japanese soldier threw a satchel charge into the Regimental Command Post. The blast killed three members of Scott's staff who were sleeping nearby. The force of the explosion threw Jackson into the air, hurling him against the side of an amtrac parked near the CP as machine gun and small arms fire erupted all along the line.

After the explosion, dazed from the violent destruction around him, Scott lay still for a few moments. He could not comprehend what was happening. When he tried to get up, another explosion felled him. When he awoke, it was daylight; the sun was just cresting on the eastern horizon. Lying on the ground near the remains of the shattered command post, he saw that he was not alone. While a Navy corpsman was busily bandaging his forearm, the scene that greeted him was one of complete devastation. The CP was an unrecognizable heap of debris. The night before, he had moved two armored units into place to provide cover for him and his staff; one of them was now a burnt-out hulk, lying on its side.

At the entrance to the command post, there were a half dozen bodies lying in a row, covered with ponchos. Nearby lay the bodies of several Japanese soldiers, many bearing the obvious signs of death from high explosives. The tenacity of the Japanese foot soldier was not a myth, as evidenced by the surrealistic picture of death and destruction presented at this bloody site.

When the corpsman finished his task, Major Jackson, against the wishes of the man, got up and walked over to his own people. He knew he was lucky. Except for a minor wound in his left arm and a ringing sensation in his ears, he was in surprisingly good shape. He found Lieutenant Joe Churchill, critically injured, his head wrapped in bandages. Nearby, two corpsmen worked feverously on Sergeant Dominic "California" Polchlopecski, trying to stop the flow of blood from multiple wounds to his upper body.

"He's a bleeder, Major," one of the corpsmen responded quietly, glancing up at Jackson. "If we can stop it, he's got a chance." Scott did not respond, he knew the two young men would do their best, he had seen their work before. Nevertheless, he could not help feeling responsible for the sergeant's injury. When he had assumed command of the regiment, he took Churchill and "California" with him, realizing now that they would have been better off had they stayed with the liaison group.

"Hello, Scott. You're back with us; we thought for a while you might not make it." It was Major Albert Swartz; he had assumed command of the Liaison Group when Jackson moved on to Regiment. Swartz, a career officer with the Corps, previously commanded both amphibious and tank units in the Solomon Islands. Jackson respected the man as a military professional with an exceptional understanding and knowledge of the strength and weaknesses of the Corps' armored capabilities.

"Hello, Al. Yeah, I'm okay. How bad did we get hit?"

"It's pretty bad, Scott. This was much more than just an assault upon your regiment's CP. It was an organized attack up and down the line. Those people were resolved to die for their Emperor and they clearly intended to take as many Marines with them as possible. They hit us all across the front. Your men took the brunt of the assault, but they held their ground."

"How many did we lose?" Scott asked quietly.

"We don't know, yet; somewhere around fifty. We have counted thirty-three dead so far, with ten or twelve still unaccounted for. About one hundred of your men are wounded; company commanders are still gathering the data for me. You were out for about three hours. I talked to Colonel Webber; he said that you are to report in to McAffee as soon as you can."

"Thanks, Al. It looks like this was a wake-up call for the entire Division. It's clear the Japanese intend to resist as long as any of them are alive. Did Webber say what the general had in mind?"

"No, but he's called for a meeting tomorrow with the field commanders. I have a driver lined up for you. "

"Any word about additional armored units or replacements?"

"Yeah, Captain Williams has been busy lining up additional personnel and he said there's a convoy of trucks and tanks that should arrive tomorrow."

Chapter 21

It was nearly twelve o'clock when Scott arrived at Division Headquarters. General McAffee and his staff, now located in a bombed out building in the island's capital city were less than ten miles from the front. Colonel Webber was there to greet him.

"Are you okay, Scott?" Webber asked, closely examining Jackson's torn and blood-stained dungarees and haggard appearance.

"I'm fine, Colonel, a little shook up, that's all. My arm will be a problem for a while, but if I could get a change of clothing I'll be set for..."

Weber cut him off abruptly. "I don't think so. We will get you some clothes, but I think General McAffee has other plans for you. Father Morris is over from the First Division. He is with the general now; he wants to talk to you too. I don't know what that's all about."

General McAffee's makeshift office was in a tent-like structure that his staff raised inside a large, now roofless building. Greeting Jackson as he got out of the Jeep, the general's first concern was as always the welfare of his men. This wounded officer was no exception. Placing his hand on his subordinate's shoulder, with a worried look, he examined, and then asked about Scott's injury.

"Are you okay, Scott?"

"Yes, I am, sir, thank you," Scott replied, and then added gloomily, "Our perimeter was breached last night. I lost a lot of my people."

"Yes, I've been told that; I am so sorry."

"Captain Williams has been very helpful, General; he's already lined up our replacements, so we should be ready to go in the morning."

"We'll worry about that later, Scott. Come in, Father Morris wants to talk to you."

Except for the small cross on his faded dungarees, John Morris, the ranking Catholic chaplain with the First Marine Division, was indistinguishable from any other middle-aged Marine officer. Jackson had not seen the man since he and Sophia Kosterman visited his office in Hawaii. He stopped suddenly, hesitant to enter the tent, terrified by what he may find inside. He guessed the chaplain's trip to McAffee's command might have something to do with Sophia Kosterman. He did not have to wait long before he heard the dreadful news.

"Hello, Scott," the priest said, pausing, a look of concern crossing his bearded face; he was obviously surprised by the ragged and bloodied appearance of this Marine officer. Jackson did not respond.

"I'm afraid I have bad news for you, Major; Lieutenant Kosterman is dead. She died in April at her duty station on board a hospital ship. A kamikaze plane struck the ship, killing Sophia and several other nurses."

Stunned by the chaplain's announcement, Jackson grew faint; this accumulation of disastrous events was too much for him. Just hours ago, dozens of his people had been killed or wounded by the Japanese, now his fiancée was gone. With his arms flailing the air, his face pale and drawn, Morris and General McAffee grabbed him, setting him down on a nearby ammunition box. The general, seeing the anguish the man was experiencing, called for a corpsman, but Jackson, his voice laced with anger, quite suddenly stood up, lashing out. "How and when, Priest?" he demanded angrily.

Morris, unperturbed by the major's demeanor and harsh response, simply answered, "I received a letter from Lieutenant Kosterman's mother; when the Navy notified the family of Sophia's death, Mrs. Kosterman wrote, asking that I let you know. Sophia told her parents about your wedding plans; unfortunately, the Navy notifies only the next of kin in these cases. She died on the tenth of April."

"My God, man!" Scott snarled, shaking his head. "Why the hell wasn't I told?"

Unperturbed by the major's brutally worded query, the chaplain continued calmly. "I spoke with a member of Admiral Turner's staff; he told me a kamikaze aircraft struck the hospital ship while it was in the East China Sea. The explosion killed twenty-seven naval personnel, including eight nurses. Lieutenant Kosterman was in surgery when the plane hit. No one survived in that compartment."

"You're the son of a bitch who said we should wait," Scott replied, his voice laced with bitterness as he fought back tears.

"I am truly sorry, Scott," the chaplain offered solicitously.

"If it wasn't for you we'd have been married," Jackson moaned, his eyes wild, his body shaking uncontrollably. He could not breathe; he needed to get out of there. He headed toward the tent entryway.

"Hold on, Scott," McAffee intervening, addressed his regimental commander. Shaken by what he just witnessed, the general chose his words carefully, speaking to his junior officer sternly.

"Scott, you and I have seen a lot of death on this bloody island, and I'm truly sorry about Lieutenant Kosterman. Unfortunately, before this battle is over, more men and women will die. It's up to you, and me, to see that their lives are not wasted."

Jackson stood mute, his anguish turning to sorrow, his body tremors slowly beginning to wane.

"I realize that's of little comfort to you; what has happened here is tragic. But in this struggle we can't forget our responsibilities to the living," McAffee continued, calmly. "We have a long way to go before this war is over." He paused, and then added quite forcefully, "I can't afford to have an officer of my command disabled by grief."

"I'm all right, sir," Jackson replied, trying desperately to control the torment raging within him.

"No!" McAffee responded sharply, then quietly added, "You're not all right. Right now, I want you to take stock of yourself. My orderly will take you to my tent; you stay there tonight. Get yourself cleaned up and get some rest, we will talk about this tomorrow. You'll find a bottle of Scotch there, use it."

"I don't want to be relieved, General," he blurted out.

"No one said anything about relieving you. I said we would talk about this tomorrow. Now get out of here."

The general's orderly and a corpsman accompanied Jackson to McAffee's tent, where Scott bathed in a small tin basin and the corpsman cleaned and bandaged his wounds. When the Navy man finished, General McAffee's orderly handed him a clean set of dungarees, underclothes and a bottle of Scotch. Jackson dressed, and then, sitting on the cot in the general's tent, he took a long drink from the bottle.

When he awoke, he was not sure where he was. He lay on the cot watching dust molecules floating in the bright rays of sunlight that came through the open flap of the tent. Lying there, listening to the rumble of the big guns in the distance, he suddenly remembered what Sophia Kosterman said about this "damn war," as she called it. "It'll just go on and on forever."

Turning over on the cot, the pain in his left arm quickly reminded him where he was. He could hear voices outside, accompanied by the sound of a motor running nearby. Sitting up on the edge of the cot, he immediately felt the aftereffects of the general's liquor—he had a hangover. Glancing at his watch, he could not believe it, it was nearly noon. It was almost twenty-four hours since he came off the line.

Walking out into the bright sunlight, it reminded him of home; it was like a warm summer day in the Northwest. In surveying the surrounding terrain, however, it clearly was not home. In the city of Naha, not a building remained intact. The town simply had disappeared. To ease Tenth Army's logistical needs, engineers were busily bulldozing the bombed-out structures into enormous mounds of rubble. A vast array of tanks, trucks, amtracs, and armored personnel carriers were on the move along the main roadway leading into the city. Walking around the tent, he encountered Marine Captain Hugh O'Keefe, an aide to General McAffee.

"Good morning, Colonel."

"I'm Major Jackson, Captain."

"Yes, sir," the man replied, with a quizzical look. "I'm sorry, sir. I was under the impression you were the Twenty-Second regimental commander."

"That, I am, Captain," he replied quietly.

Nearby, watching the massive movement of troops and equipment, were several members of General McAffee's immediate staff. Upon hearing their captain's greetings, they turned to look at the man with the bandaged forearm and ten-day growth of beard.

"The general would like you to join him and his staff after lunch; he's over at Division," O'Keefe offered politely.

"Fair enough, Captain. Give me a few minutes."

"The head's around back; after you've shaved and cleaned up, I'll run you over there. There is food and hot coffee out front; we also have some mail for you. I'll chase it down."

As he was about to shave, Scott was startled by what he saw in the tin mirror hanging above the washbasin. His face, thin and drawn, his beard, with its flecks of gray, made him look older than his thirty-three years. Yet, except for his aching muscles and a dull throbbing pain in his arm, he felt surprisingly refreshed. Twenty hours of uninterrupted sleep had its own recuperative effect on an ageing body.

A short time later, Captain O'Keefe returned, handing two letters to Jackson. One of these was from his mother, the other from Lieutenant Sophia Kosterman. He stared at Sophia's letter, not opening it; he knew what she would say. She would write about their future, their planned wedding, and words of love, words meant only for his eyes. He would not share it with others; this was something to be read in private. Tucking the letter into his jacket, he would read it when the opportunity for privacy presented itself.

Opening the letter from his mother, he was stunned; she enclosed a newspaper clipping from *The Daily Star*. It was a small headline: LOCAL NAVAL OFFICER MARK MCGINNES, KILLED IN BATTLE. The paper reported that the Navy officer was killed in action in the Western Pacific. He left behind a wife and five children. Jackson stood frozen in place, an audible groan escaping his clenched teeth. When Captain O'Keefe came to check on him, he found Scott sitting on an empty ammunition box holding his head in his hands, tears in his eyes.

Arriving at Division Headquarters shortly after three o'clock, Scott found the chief of staff briefing more than a score of recently arrived replacements. The group included two majors, five captains and fourteen lieutenants, all seated in a makeshift conference room, with ammunition boxes for chairs.

Many of the ranking officers were veterans of one or more of the Pacific Islands' campaigns, but the lieutenants were recent OCS graduates. Rather than be drafted into the Army, they joined the Marine Corps; they were about to experience combat for the first time. General McAffee greeted Jackson with a firm handshake and hand on his shoulder; he said nothing about the previous day's conversation. When the chief of staff completed his briefing, McAffee addressed the group.

"Gentlemen, hopefully this island engagement will be over this week. Unfortunately, First Division is still encountering considerable resistance." Then, shaking his head, he added, "It looks like we're going to have to push these people right into the damn ocean.

"Tomorrow at daybreak we'll begin the final phase of this operation. If they will surrender, we of course will accept them. However, some of them are using the white flag to their advantage, so caution your people. We have lost troops because of this duplicity; enemy soldiers are also using civilians as shields, so be careful. The entire Division will move out at daybreak. God willing, this will be over soon."

As Scott walked out of the tent, McAffee stopped him, shook his hand again, and handed him two miniature silver eagles. "Take these, Scott, God knows you've earned 'em." Then without any mention of the preceding day's events, General McAffee simply said, "Good luck, Colonel." Jackson, looking at the two silver eagles, simply nodded his head and slipped the two small pieces of metal into his pocket. He turned, and without comment, walked away. Both men knew nothing more was required; the life expectancy of battalion and regimental commanders, since coming up against General Ushijima's troops on the Shuri Line, was measured in days, not weeks.

Returning to the regiment, Captain Charlie Williams briefed Scott on the status of his personnel.

"The nighttime infiltration cost us nearly three hundred casualties, Scott. Sixty-three men are dead; others have suffered various injuries from shock to severe trauma. Most of them are en route to a hospital ship by now. However, even with our recent replacements, regimental strength is still down over forty percent."

"That's not very good news is it, Captain?"

"No, I'm sorry, Colonel, but General McAffee's assessment of our immediate future looks pretty good."

"Yes, I'll agree with you on that. All of us will be glad to get off this damn island." Captain Williams did not respond.

When the sun came up the next morning over the Western Pacific, in this final drive to the sea, Scott climbed aboard the lead tank. In front of them, he could see hundreds of Japanese soldiers interspersed with Okinawa civilians and Korean laborers. All were fleeing this massive onslaught of American troops. With some enemy troops using civilians as shields, they opened fire upon the advancing Marines. Caught in between the two armies, the toll of dead and injured civilians mounted to catastrophic proportions. Bodies of men, women, and children littered the battlefield.

The exploits of Navy medics overshadowed the combatants this day. Corpsmen faced a brutal dilemma: there was not enough time to tend to the injured civilians, and hundreds of others were near death from starvation. Medical care came too late for most of the children, they were so emaciated, and sickly medics could do little for them.

Soon, there was no place for the Japanese to run. Before the end of the second day, the regiment moved within a half mile of the southern tip of the island. Tank crews, who had seen hundreds of their own die at the hands of the Japanese soldiers, now stood in open turrets watching this massive movement of humanity. They wanted a firsthand look at this maelstrom as it unfolded before them. When the enemy troops reached the cliffs high above the beach, hundreds of soldiers and civilians alike jumped to their death below. With the tide at its low ebb, the broken bodies of men, women, and children began to stack up on the rock-encrusted shoreline 500 feet below. Death was preferable to surrender to the Americans.

It was obvious to Colonel Jackson that at this moment in history a drama of cataclysmic proportion was in the making. He was witnessing the death throes of this Japanese island's entire population. As Captain Cinkovich predicted, the Americans brought the war home to those who started it.

To end the carnage occurring below the high cliffs, the Navy moved patrol boats close into the beach. Japanese-speaking GIs, using loudspeakers, tried to convince enemy troops and civilians alike to surrender. Some tried, only to be shot by Japanese officers standing nearby; for a moment, Marines stood watching in disbelief. Since coming ashore in April, the Americans developed a grudging respect for their enemy, an enemy who, despite horrific odds, waged a formidable defense of their homeland. Now, however, that same enemy was killing unarmed civilians and their own comrades.

Jackson held up the column in order to give the Navy more time to convince those trapped between the sea and his troops that if they surrendered, they would have nothing to fear. Few heeded the plea of the GIs.

Scores of diehard enemy soldiers still concealed in the caves and rock crevasses above the nearby beaches continued firing, their bullets ricocheting off the lead tanks and amtracs in the column. In the evening twilight, a group of enemy soldiers carrying white flags approached Second Battalion's forward positions. Several of them carried concealed explosive charges, with a few approaching near enough to inflict casualties upon the now wary Marines.

The next morning, as dawn broke over the Eastern Pacific, General McAffee assembled the Headquarters staff and regimental commanders for a briefing.

"I hope that today we will see the end of the battle for this island," he said, his voice a mixture of weariness and elation. "Lord knows our people need to get away from here. They've been truly tested by the Japanese and have prevailed—all of you have, but let's be careful now. I want you to move cautiously and with your armored units out front, where our enemy can see what awaits him if he continues this fight. God willing, this will be the last day of this battle."

Returning to the Regimental Command Post, Jackson's briefed his staff, advising them of General McAffee's' directions.

"We will keep closing the loop we initiated yesterday and try to encircle the remaining enemy soldiers. We'll probably run across a lot more civilians than we've seen to date. Do what you can for them, but continue to tighten the ring around the Japanese soldiers; some may surrender. Coordinate your advance and move forward methodically, but carefully. We don't want to lose any of our people because of carelessness. Put your armored units out front; I want some of these diehard bastards to see what is going to happen to them if they continue to fire on us."

As the Marines began to move forward, they encountered sporadic machine gun and mortar assaults. Within the hour, it became apparent that the Americans would have to kill nearly every enemy soldier capable of shouldering a weapon. Before the day was over, Division Command ordered an all-out assault to dislodge the Japanese from within the caves along the hillside above the island's beaches.

Scott moved Second Battalion along the beach while the Third pushed across the ridge above. When in place, men from the Third Battalion began making their way down the face of the cliffs. Sporadic small arms and machine gun fire soon greeted them; it came from within a half dozen cave entrances; some of Scott's men dived for cover; others, undeterred by this latest assault, responded quickly. Flamethrowers and rifle grenades soon silenced the hidden gunmen.

Scott, standing in the lead tank, with his upper torso exposed, shot a Japanese soldier who suddenly dashed out toward the armored vehicle from a dense growth of brush.

"Look out, Colonel," an accompanying Marine called out as another Japanese soldier, rising up from a stand of tall grass, hurled a satchel charge at Jackson's tank. It exploded harmlessly nearby as the young rifleman's bullets cut him down. Unseen by the passing column, three other enemy soldiers lay concealed under a pile of debris and rock. As the lead tanks moved closer, they rushed out at the last minute, carrying explosive charges, but before they could reach the column, alert crews in another tank killed all three men.

Jackson marveled at the calm, matter-of-fact way his men responded to these repeated assaults upon their ranks. Most of his troops were kids who were in boot camp just weeks ago, now they performed as professional soldiers. To him this was an awe-inspiring episode in the history of the American military. This Army of young soldiers and Marines defeated one of the most experienced and capable armies in the world.

In the Far East, Japan's Thirty-second Army Group overran the Chinese in Manchuria and defeated the British and French Armies in Southeast Asia. Yet, in less than eighty days, the Americans destroyed this elite Imperial Force. The reason, Scott believed, was more than just the fact that the Japanese faced a mammoth array of allied air and sea power; he was convinced his Marines were better soldiers than the Japanese. Still, he had to admit that in the last four years he and his troops learned a great deal about the *art of warfare* from these Japanese warriors.

At last, upon reaching the edge of the cliff, he could not believe what he saw. A vast array of dead, injured, or starving civilians lay before him; it was almost incomprehensible. Witnessing the horror and brutality of this war, along with the death of Sophia and all those men who died under his command, made him realize he could never be a career soldier. He would return to civilian life when this was over.

On this last day of the battle for Okinawa, after deploying his troops along the shoreline and above the beaches, he climbed down off the lead tank to get a closer look at the carnage below. Looking down from the edge, he could see scores of uniformed Japanese soldiers intermingling with the civilians, many of whom were dressed in their traditional white robes.

A stream of soldiers continued to enter the ocean in unsuccessful attempts to escape. Others tried to commit suicide by swimming out to sea; most of these efforts failed. Naval personnel quickly pulled many of them out of the water. Some soldiers simply sat on the beach, cowering below the Americans standing on the cliffs above.

Sickened by what he witnessed, Scott turned away and walked back toward the tank. Suddenly, two Japanese soldiers darted toward him from a small outcropping of rock. One carried a light machine gun, the other, a satchel of explosives.

When he turned to meet his attackers, two bullets fired at close range hit him. The man with the deadly explosive package rolled under the front of the tank. The satchel exploded, killing the soldier and wounding two Marines standing alongside the armored vehicle. The crew in a nearby tank opened fire, killing Scott's assailant.

The war was over for Colonel Scott Jackson. One bullet from the Japanese soldier's gun hit him in the left hip; the other struck him squarely in the abdomen. Corpsmen were on the scene within minutes, they worked feverishly to save their commander's life.

Scott knew his wounds were serious, for he could not move, yet he thought it strange that he felt no pain. Although gunfire continued to erupt around him, he was entirely at ease. He was amazed at this lack of concern for his own well-being. His thoughts turned to Sophia Kosterman. He wondered what life would have offered if the two of them had lived through the war. Still, he had no regrets, he was sure he would soon join her, wherever she was.

Chapter 22

On 2 July 1945, the Okinawa campaign was officially over and the island declared "Secure." By that time, Colonel Jackson was on his way to Hawaii. This was the second time in his military career that he came home as a patient aboard a hospital ship. He lost a great deal of blood, but he was still alive when he reached the Regimental Aid Station on Okinawa. Surgeons had removed one bullet from his leg, the other passing through his lower abdomen. The prognosis for his recuperation remained in doubt for some time. However, by the end of the month, he appeared to be on the road to recovery. Yet after his arrival in Hawaii, his doctors became concerned for his mental health.

Day after day, he lay in his hospital bed, speaking to no one and refusing to eat. With his mental condition deteriorating, the medical staff decided to send him stateside. He traveled to California aboard one of the Navy's air medical evacuation ambulance transports. When he entered the US Naval Hospital at San Diego, there was little hope for his recovery. Although placed in the care of one of the Navy's finest nurses, Navy Lieutenant Commander Carrie O'Neil, the head nurse in the Naval Hospital Intensive Care Unit, his health continued to deteriorate.

O'Neil, a wartime widow, tried to spend an hour or two each day with her new charge. There was some improvement in Jackson's condition since arriving in the ICU, but his prognosis for full recovery was not promising.

One night, as she was leaving the ICU, she met Lieutenant Joe Churchill in the hallway heading toward the facility. By now, the lieutenant was well on his way to recovery and on occasion even engaged in horseplay by racing up and down the hallways in the middle of the night with other patients in their wheelchairs.

"How's he doing, Commander?" Churchill asked, with a grin, knowing that patients were not to be out of their room at that time of night.

"Joe, what the devil are you doing out here? You want to get me in trouble?" she asked with feigned anger. She was fully aware that many of her patients routinely ignored hospital rules, particularly when they became physically able to get out on their own. It was always a good sign; they were well on their way to recovery and would soon be going home.

"Nah, you won't get in trouble, Carrie," he laughed. "After all, you made up the damn rules; I just wanted to look in on him. How's he doing?"

"Not good, Joe; he's not responding to treatment. The doctors are not hopeful for his recovery."

"Well hell, you don't have to be a doctor to tell you what's wrong with him; a blind man could tell you that. You'd've thought by now the shrinks would've figured it out."

"Suppose, while I wheel you back to your room, you tell me what the problem is, Doctor Joe Churchill, and I'll pass it onto the shrinks, as you call them," she responded with a smile.

"It was a woman, Carrie; it's always a woman, didn't you know that? His fiancée was killed on the hospital ship *Mercy*. Didn't anybody tell them that?" he replied sardonically.

"No, Joe, no one told us that; suppose you tell me about it."

Before returning the lieutenant to his ward, the two of them stopped at the cafeteria for coffee. Here, Churchill told O'Neil of Scott and Sophia Kosterman's planned wedding and of her death off the coast of Okinawa. It was nearly two o'clock in the morning when the two of them finished talking; by that time, Carrie O'Neil had developed in her mind a rehabilitative plan of her own for her patient. She knew what she had to do.

Physically, Scott appeared to be making progress, his mental outlook was quite another matter. During his first month in the hospital, he spoke to no one. His mood was ugly and he refused all attempts by the medical staff to communicate with him. Navy doctors became impatient; they considered moving him to the psychiatric ward. Commander O'Neil opposed Jackson's transfer; in a heated exchange with Scott's doctors, she obtained permission to take complete charge of their unmanageable patient.

"We have people here, Commander, who want to get well, and go home," Doctor Larry Ryan, chief of Rehabilitative Services said. "I don't have time to waste on someone who's not willing to help himself. And neither do you," he added, disapprovingly.

"A few days, Doctor, please. That's all I ask."

"Okay, O'Neil, but keep me advised."

With that, Carrie O'Neil took it upon herself to see that her patient recovered, not only from his physical injuries, but also from the obvious trauma of losing the woman he loved. It was not long before she got Jackson out of bed and into a wheelchair. Each evening, she took him through the beautiful gardens which surrounded the medical facility; then before returning to the ward, she stopped at the small chapel in the hospital. At first, he showed little interest in his surroundings, never uttering a word to his nurse. One evening, she took him out to a band concert on the hospital grounds; ICU Nurse Nan Olson, a longtime friend of O'Neil, accompanied the two of them to the performance.

Jackson, lethargic, with no interest in the music, or in O'Neil's friend, sat between the two women as they visited back and forth during the performance. Shortly before the band quit playing for the evening, Olson casually commented, "Your husband would've liked this band, Carrie, if only he were alive to hear it."

O'Neil responded, nodding her head in agreement, "Oh, he'd be out there marching. He loved this kind of music."

Quite suddenly, her patient glanced at Olson, and then at O'Neil. For the first time since arriving at the naval hospital, he gave some indication that he was aware of his immediate surroundings and of the conversation between these two women. O'Neil was surprised.

"Scott, you understand," she said, with a smile. "You know what's going on, I'm so glad." He made no reply.

Later that evening, while O'Neil was checking the chart at the foot of his bed, her patient blurted out, "Commander, I am sorry about your husband. I didn't know..."

"Of course you didn't, Scott," she responded, calmly, as she made a notation on the hospital record. "You have your problems, and I have mine. Maybe we could work them out together. My husband died in Europe. Lieutenant Churchill told me all about Sophia. I am so sorry she is gone, but so is my husband. We cannot change that. We will never forget them, and we will always remember the joy that they brought into our lives, but life must go on. However, the good Lord only gave us so much time on this earth, and, Scott, you've wasted quite a bit of that precious gift." Jackson did not reply.

On 15 September, Lieutenant Commander Carrie O'Neil received an unexpected visitor in her office; it was Sergeant Dominic "California" Polchlopecski; California had spent the last several weeks at the naval hospital in San Francisco. Upon his release, he was to return to Camp Pendleton, where he would receive his discharge from the Corps. En route, he undertook a mission for Chaplain John Morris. The sergeant was to deliver a letter found by Father Morris at the Regimental Aid Station on Okinawa; it was from Sophia Kosterman, addressed to "Major" Jackson.

When medics cut off Jackson's dungaree jacket in their frantic efforts to save the man's life, they found the letter, unopened in a jacket pocket. Morris asked Sergeant Polchlopecski to deliver it on his way home. Apparently, because of Jackson's feelings toward the chaplain, the man believed a personal visit by him might only exacerbate Scott's deteriorating mental condition.

O'Neil escorted the sergeant into Scott's room. He was shocked at Jackson's frail, gaunt, and emaciated appearance, and disappointed. The patient ignored his greeting, staring first at Carrie O'Neil, then at Sergeant Polchlopecski without a hint of recognition. California stayed in the room only a few minutes; before he left he placed Sophia's letter in Jackson's listless hands.

That evening, Carrie O'Neil made a point of checking on her patient every few minutes, but it was after midnight before Scott opened Sophia's letter. When she checked him in the morning, there was no sign of the letter. Later, when clearing the nightstand, she noticed the edge of the soiled envelope protruding out from one of the hospital library books. When the orderly served breakfast, Scott ate two pieces of toast and drank his coffee. O'Neil seemed pleased.

Over the next several days, there was a marked improvement in the patient's mental and physical health. As time passed, the nurse and her patient became close friends. It was not long until they were seen together in the evening, he, at first, still in the wheelchair, then on crutches. Jackson found this remarkable woman easy to talk to, eventually telling her of his love for Sophia, of their time together and of her death off the Coast of Okinawa.

"I am envious of you and yes, even somewhat envious of Sophia," she said one evening as the two of them talked together in the ward.

"Why would you say that, Commander?" Scott asked, somewhat incredulous with her reference to Sophia Kosterman.

"You and Sophia had three years, Scott. You were not always together, but you knew each other, and from what I've heard, they must have been wonderful years."

"Yes, you're right; looking back on that time, I wish we had it all to do over again."

"I knew my husband only a few months before we were married, Scott. He left for overseas right after our wedding and never came home," she replied, her voice tinged with bitterness. "He was with the Third Army in Europe."

"I guess that's the tragedy of our times, isn't it?" Scott responded gloomily. "Sophia called it 'this damn war.' She thought it would never end."

"Well, it's over, thank God," O'Neil responded quietly, her eyes closed for a moment, almost as if lost in prayer. Then quite suddenly, smiling and looking directly at her patient, she changed the subject. "With Christmas just around the corner, Scott, it's a time to be thankful to our Maker. I understand your mother and sister are to be here tomorrow."

"Yes, a friend of mine is bringing them down; he was a reporter, turned war correspondent; he and I have been friends for years."

"That's great, Scott," she smiled. "The brass has invited us to a Christmas Eve party at the Grant Hotel. You can celebrate with him and your family." When O'Neil mentioned the name of the hotel, it brought back a flood of memories; Sophia Kosterman would not be forgotten.

"You'll be there, Carrie?" Scott asked. There was a note of uneasiness in his voice, almost as if after all these months he only now realized he would soon leave the safe haven provided for him by O'Neil and the people at the Naval Hospital.

"Yes, Scott," she smiled, for she had seen this reaction before when former friends and relatives came to visit a seriously wounded patient. Most worried that some member of their family may be disappointed, or even shocked by their loved one's physical condition. It was not always comforting to see the look on a visiting family member's face when the patient was missing an arm, or leg, or suffered from a disfiguring injury. "I'll be there; but you'll be going home. You will soon be on your own, Scott, and you will do just fine."

Jackson doubted that he could ever return to his old job on the police force. Being confined to a hospital wheelchair was not to your advantage when it came to passing a police physical examination. He had never expressed this fear to anyone, but he also had misgivings in his ability to be a successful member of society in any field of endeavor other than law enforcement.

On the morning of 24 December, Jackson's mother and sister, Beth, accompanied by his friend Lewis Burke, arrived at the hospital. After the war, Burke had returned to his job as a reporter with the *Seattle Star*. Commander O'Neil met Scott's visitors in the hospital lobby and escorted them to the wounded man's room.

Christmas Eve in San Diego turned out to be a delightful time for the recovering Marine and his family and friends. This evening was special; it was the family's first get-together in more than two years. Earlier that day, Scott had received the news he had been expecting from his doctors; they would release him in January. The Veterans' Hospital in his hometown could provide whatever outpatient care he would require after that. Mrs. Jackson was pleased; with the war over, this mother would have both of her children safe at home for the first time in many years.

Carrie O'Neil and Burke made plans for the five of them to attend the Naval Hospital's Christmas Eve party in the ballroom at the Grant Hotel. Commanders from the Navy and Marine Corps military bases in the area hosted the party. When the group finished eating, the women joined an entourage of out-of-state guests to meet their hosts. The absence of the three women gave the two men time to catch up on their travels. The reporter had not seen his friend since 1944, when Scott was here in this same hospital ward recovering from wounds received in the battle for the Palau Islands. Lew Burke was pleased the two would be able to renew their friendship.

"I understand you were with the fleet off Okinawa for a time, Lew, am I correct?" Scott asked.

"Yes, for a while. I was with Admiral Mitscher's Fifth Fleet in the East China Sea. We were close enough to see the *Franklin* when it was targeted by the kamikaze. It suffered such extensive damage none of us figured it would remain afloat. That's where your friend McGinnes got killed, wasn't it?"

"Yes, I understand a kamikaze pilot took him out in the air. The bastard saw to it that Kenji Tanaka and I became the last survivors of O'Dea High School's young Gladiators, class of twenty-eight," he laughed bitterly.

"I'd forgot about that," Burke smiled. "You guys were good friends, weren't you? What did Intelligence ever do with Tanaka?"

311

"Mike Gibson came by the hospital a few days ago; he told me he talked to you on Okinawa."

"Yes, he did. I got two or three good stories from him."

"I understand he told you about my relationship with Kenji."

"Yes. He said Tanaka would not talk to anyone but you. That would make a helluva human interest story, Scott, why not tell it?"

"That may be so; but what about his family, Lew? His sisters have been locked up since the war started and his mother is still in Japan. How would a story like that affect them?" he asked, studying his friend. "There is so much hostility toward the Japanese; I don't think this is the right time. When I get home, I'll talk to the girls; if they want to pursue it, I'll call you."

"Fair enough; I'll look forward to that."

"If they agree, we'll contact the law firm that handled their parents' immigration case; hopefully we can get Peewee and his mother back home."

"By the way, whatever happened to him?"

"I don't know, Lew. I understand Intelligence turned him over to the Army and they shipped him out to a POW camp. Gibson figured he should be back in Japan by now."

Lew Burke covered the Marine Corps' clashes with General Ushijima's Army on the Shuri Line. Before the Okinawa campaign was over, he interviewed General McAffee about Jackson's role in the battle for Sugar-Loaf Hill. The story received national recognition.

"I suppose you made me out as a damn hero again?" Scott complained, referring to Burke's dispatches to his former newspaper, which extolled the exploits of this hometown hero during the Palau campaign.

"Indeed I did," Burke countered with a smile, raising his glass in a mock salute. "But I wrote it the way it happened."

Then, as if reflecting on the battle, the smile disappeared, replaced by a grim expression, betraying his true feelings. "Sure. I mentioned you, but the story was not about you. It was about all those young warriors that won't be coming home this Christmas."

"I understand, Lew," Scott responded, somewhat embarrassed by his contentious response. "I am sorry."

"Don't be, I know where you're coming from. Navy censors took care of much of my stuff though. The Navy didn't clear it for publication until the war was over. By then it was old news."

"How come? I heard the War Department gave you people carte blanche treatment."

"No way," Burke responded, shaking his head as if to emphasize the fact that war correspondents were bound by the Navy's censorship rules, as much, if not more so than the military's own people.

"Kamikazes hit over three hundred American ships off Okinawa, Scotty," Burke continued. "Thirty were blown out of the water." Then he added grimly, "The crazy bastards, your people called 'em that, remember; they truly were. They killed thousands of our people. Actually, we suffered more than 50,000 casualties in the Okinawa campaign—over 12,000 of our people died there. That wasn't something the Navy brass wanted to release at the time; you of all people should know that."

"We lost a lot of people, Lew, I knew that," Scott replied quietly. "But I would never have guessed there were that many." Reflecting back on those men and women who died before their time was something that he had tried to put out of his mind.

"In the Pacific Theater, Scott, the death toll on Okinawa was second only to the number killed in the Philippine campaign, but the Shuri Line operation was more costly than any single battle during the war."

This surprised Jackson. "I didn't know that," he responded. "I thought all the big battles were in Europe."

"No, the Navy did everything they could to reduce the carnage the Japanese were inflicting upon your people. But they were taking a helluva shellacking at sea."

"Yeah, I guessed that. We witnessed some of it—those crazy bastards never let up."

"The Nips damn near destroyed an entire task force, Scott. When that happened, the War Department began to hold up our dispatches. I suppose it served its purpose at the time, but I never really believed it did much good."

"How come?" Scott inquired.

"The battles were usually over by the time a dispatch or letter got out of a combat area; so we couldn't do any damage."

"You're right, I suppose," Scott replied. "However, there are some things that should not become pubic knowledge at the time. It's appropriate, I think, to conceal information about casualties, troop movements, and weaponry."

"That's true," Burke acknowledged.

"You can't always rely upon your own people either, Lew. Some of our guys tried to pass classified information on to their families; they didn't use common sense."

When the women returned to the table, Beth was excited, her eyes flashing. "Scott!" she exclaimed. "I got to meet two generals and an admiral. I asked the admiral if he knew my big brother, he said he did not; how come, Scotty?"

Her brother was amused. "Marine colonels are not very high on the Navy's list of priorities, Beth. They have their own problems."

"Well, he should have known about you," she said. She was offended; it bothered her that not one of the base commanders knew her big brother.

"I told him he should come to our table and meet you. They should see what Lew wrote about you, they'd know who you were then."

After casting a knowing glance at Burke, Scott responded with a smile. "Beth, Lew told some really, really big fish stories before the war; he hasn't changed." They all laughed at his comment.

When the music began, Carrie O'Neil took her patient's hand and led him out onto the dance floor. "Come on, Marine, let's dance. We've never been on a dance floor together."

Adept on the dance floor as in a hospital ward, she gracefully guided her patient across the large ballroom. It was obvious to those watching that these two enjoyed each other's company. For her part, O'Neil was surprised; Jackson had little trouble keeping up with her as the musicians played a medley of old waltzes. Scott thought he could not have asked for a better evening. His friends and family were present, and an attractive woman of whom he had become very fond was in his arms. They held each other close and stayed out on the floor, returning to their table only when the band took a break.

On 30 January 1946, released by his doctors at the Naval Hospital, Jackson received an honorable discharge from the Marine Corps. Before checking out, he made his rounds, saying good-bye to Lieutenant Joe Churchill and others in the ward. Churchill faced several more weeks of rehabilitative therapy before he would be going home to Texas.

Scott's last stop was at Lieutenant Commander Carrie O'Neil's office, he would miss this kind woman. She could easily have claimed credit for her patient's remarkable recovery. He was sure she would not do that; she was truly a professional nurse in every sense of the word. Her patients came first; he knew she had already taken two more critically injured Marines under her wing.

Jackson said good-bye and offered his hand. She took it and then grabbed him by the arm. "You're not getting away that easy. I'm going to see you off, Scott Jackson." O'Neil was smiling.

Arm in arm, the two walked slowly down the long hallway toward the hospital lobby. Several patients and nurses, aware of O'Neil and Jackson's close relationship, offered best wishes to her departing friend. One of the nurses called out, "Don't let him go, Commander, he'd make a great catch," the woman laughed.

O'Neil, feigning a pained expression, responded quietly, "Oh, that girl."

Upon reaching the lobby, he offered his hand once again; her reaction, in front of a small group of nurses, surprised and pleased him.

"I told you, Scott, you're not going to get away that easy." She threw her arms around him, forcefully kissing him on the mouth. "So long, Marine," she said as tears came to her eyes. "You write to me. I want to know what happens to you on the streets of that big city of yours."

Later that day, Scott and fifteen other naval hospital patients, all from the Pacific Northwest, boarded a US Marine Corps C46 transport at the nearby Miramar Naval Air Station, destination Sand Point NAS, in Washington. Upon arrival in Seattle, he was surprised; his former girlfriend Amy Donahue, accompanied by his sister, Beth, was there to meet him. The two women took him to his mother's home.

Over the next several weeks, Jackson participated in rehabilitative exercises at Veterans Administration Hospital, with Amy Donahue driving him to and from the hospital twice a week. After these early morning workouts, the couple would stop for breakfast at a favorite restaurant, one they visited often before the war.

One day, while at the hospital John McCoy, the former mayor of the city, dropped by to see him. When Scott was a young police officer, he served for a while as a member of the mayor's security detail. McCoy followed Jackson's military career by reading Lewis Burke's articles in *The Daily Star*, where Burke extolled the local man's exploits in the South Pacific.

"Hello, Scott," the man said. "It's nice to have you home again." He smiled as the two men exchanged handshakes.

"Hello, Your Honor," he offered with a grin, respectful of his former boss' position in the political world, where most of his constituents held the man in high regard. "Thank you for coming; and thank you for looking in on my mother while I was away."

"Is she well, Scott?"

"Yes, sir, she's fine. I'll be with her until I go back to work later this year."

"Are you going back to work for the city?" he asked.

"I plan to, sir."

"Are you going to be well enough? If not, you might think about coming to work for me. I can find a place for you; you just say the word."

"Thanks, Mayor. No, I'll be fine. I should be able to pass the medical in a month or two."

"If you have a problem, let me know. Okay?"

Jackson knew the man's offer was genuine, yet he had to suppress a smile. When he was a young police officer, he learned just how powerful this millionaire businessman and former mayor was in this city. He knew if he truly needed McCoy's help, the mayor would be there. The man held an enormous amount of political influence in their hometown.

Before leaving, the mayor presented Jackson with a membership in Sharp's Gymnasium, now called the Northwest Athletic Club. Scott would soon begin an arduous exercise routine at the popular sports center.

This former police lieutenant, now more determined than ever to get his job back, was the first to arrive at the gymnasium each morning. He knew his wounds might prevent him from passing the department's rigorous medical/physical screening examination. Each day, he ran two to four miles before working out in the weight room, followed by a stint in the swimming pool. In spite of this strenuous exercise, he tired easily and his recovery was slow.

He had been home nearly two months when Donahue suggested at breakfast that he might like to attend a Saturday night dance at one of their old haunts. "I'd love to," he replied. Yet, quite unexpectedly, images of Sophia Kosterman immediately came to mind. Then he remembered what Commander Carrie O'Neil had said about the dead; he would not forget her. However, his nurse was right; it was time.

After that first evening out with Donahue, the two became nearly inseparable companions. By the end of May, Scott's health improved to the point that his doctor predicted that with continued care and exercise, he would meet the police department's physical standards and be able to return to work.

On June 25, 1946, he reported for his medical examination at City Hospital. The examining physician identified some lingering weakness in his injured left leg, yet he scrawled across the bottom of his report, *This candidate meets the minimum medical/physical standards for duty in the police, or fire services of the city.*

Handing a copy of the report to the former Marine, the doctor extended his hand. "Welcome back to city service, Mr. Jackson," he said, smiling.

On the evening of July 4, Jackson and Amy Donahue attended the annual Independence Day celebration at Seward Park on Lake Washington. She fixed a small picnic basket of fruit, sandwiches, and cold chicken. When they finished eating, they sat quietly on the lakeshore listening to a band concert while watching a pyrotechnics display over the water.

It was a warm evening and thousands of young and old alike came to the park and beaches around the lakeshore for this annual event. Families and friends played games in between the intermittent light show overhead. Others lay on the warm ground, listening to the music and watching the fireworks display. It was a huge crowd and they appeared to be enjoying the performance. Donahue, with her head resting on her friend's shoulder, was unusually quiet.

"What's wrong, Amy?" he asked, troubled by her silence.

"Nothing," she replied, her self-imposed stillness suddenly giving way to a poignant response. "I was watching all these children and thinking about our friends and their families. Do you miss that, Scott?" she asked, her face now upturned next to his.

"Do I miss it?" he asked, reflectively, thinking about his family. "Heck, I don't know. I never had a family to speak of, other than my sister Beth. Jimmy Woo, down at the Mandarin House, and his children are more family to me than anything I have ever known. Why? Why do you ask?"

"Because I still love you, Scott Jackson," she replied, her voice soft and charged with emotion, "and I want you to be the father of my children."

"Whoa! Wait just a damn minute," he replied gruffly, taking her arms and gently pushing her away. "I don't think I heard you correctly. You've got a short memory, young lady, have you forgotten? Before the war, I asked you to marry me, remember?"

"I remember," she replied softly, a note of sadness in her voice. "But that was a long, long time ago, Scott, and the war is over."

Jackson, now smiling, with his arms encircling Amy's waist, shifted his body so he could look directly at her. With her lips parted, just inches from his, he could feel the warmth of her breath on his face. With tears beginning to flow, her eyes mirrored the dazzling array of fireworks overhead. Immediately filled with a burning desire, he wanted to claim this woman before she slipped away again. Placing both his hands on her face, he tenderly wiped away the tears with his thumbs, and then kissed her.

"Amy," he responded anxiously, "there's a DC-3 flight out of here every morning at seven o'clock. It stops at Portland, then goes on to Reno. We could be there by noon, grab a JP, and be married before you know it. Are you game?"

"I love you, Scott Jackson," she said, throwing her arms around his neck, holding him tightly. "We've wasted so much time. Shouldn't we take someone with us? We'll need a witness, won't we?"

"Heck no," he grinned, "we'll find a cop down there who'll act as a witness. All we'll need is a license and a ring. You don't have one, do you?" he asked coyly. She smiled in reply.

*

Other books by this author:

Cops, Crooks & Politicians, published 1994

<u>Fiction</u>
Renaissance Cop, published 2006

Printed in the United States
74254LV00003B/118-213